Francis M. Crawford

Pietro Ghisleri

Francis M. Crawford

Pietro Ghisleri

ISBN/EAN: 9783337406387

Printed in Europe, USA, Canada, Australia, Japan

Cover: Foto ©Andreas Hilbeck / pixelio.de

More available books at **www.hansebooks.com**

PIETRO GHISLERI

PIETRO GHISLERI,

BY

F. MARION CRAWFORD

AUTHOR OF "SARACINESCA," "THE THREE FATES," ETC.

New York
THE MACMILLAN COMPANY
LONDON: MACMILLAN & CO., Ltd.
1899

All rights reserved

Twentieth Thousand

Norwood Press:
J. S. Cushing & Co. — Berwick & Smith.
Boston, Mass., U.S.A.

PIETRO GHISLERI.

CHAPTER I.

THE relation of two step-sisters is unusual. When the Honourable Mrs. Carlyon came to Rome twenty years ago, a young widow and the mother of a little girl named Laura, she did not foresee the complications which her second marriage was to produce. She was a good woman in her way, and if she had guessed what it would mean to be the step-mother of Adele Braccio she might have hesitated before marrying Camillo of that name, commonly known as the Prince of Gerano. For the Prince had also been married before, and his first wife had left him this one child, Adele, who was only a year and a half older than little Laura Carlyon. No children were born to the Gerano couple, and the two girls were brought up together as though they were sisters. The Prince and Princess were deeply attached to each other and to them both, so that for many years Casa Gerano was justly looked upon as a model household.

Mrs. Carlyon was very poor when she came to Rome. Her husband had been a careless, good-humoured, and rather reckless younger son, and when he broke his neck in coming down the Gross Glockner he left his widow about as much as men of his stamp generally leave to their families; to wit, a fearful and wonderful confusion of unpaid debts and a considerable number of promises to pay money, signed by persons whose promises were not of much consequence, even when clearly set down on

paper.   It seems to be a peculiarity of poor and good-
natured men that they will lend whatever money they
have to impecunious friends in distress rather than use
it for the paying of the just debts they owe their tailors.

Gerano was rich.   It does not by any means follow
that Mrs. Carlyon married him for his money, though
she could not have married him without it.   She fell in
love with him.   He, on his part, having made a marriage
of interest when he took his first wife, and having led
by no means a very peaceful existence with the deceased
Princess, considered that he had earned the right to
please himself, and accordingly did so.   Moreover, Mrs.
Carlyon was a Catholic, which singularly facilitated matters in the eyes of Gerano's numerous relations.   Jack
Carlyon had been of the Church of England; and though
anything but a practising believer, if he believed in anything at all, he had nevertheless absolutely insisted that
his daughter should be brought up in his own creed.   On
this one point he had displayed all the tenacity he possessed, and the supply then seemed to be exhausted so
far as other matters were concerned.   His wife was a
very conscientious woman, altogether superior to him in
character, and she continued to respect his wishes, even
after his death.   Laura, she said, should choose for herself when she was old enough.   In the meantime she
should go to the English Church.   The consequence was
that the little girl had an English nurse and afterwards
an English governess, while Adele was taken care of and
taught by Catholics.   Under these circumstances, and as
the step-sisters were not related by blood or even by race,
it is not strange that they should have grown up to be as
different as possible, while living under the same roof
and calling the same persons father and mother.

The question of religion alone could certainly not have
brought about the events here to be chronicled, and it
may be as well to say at once that this history is not in
the least concerned with matters of faith, creed, or dogma,
which are better left to those good men whose business

it is to understand them. The main and striking points of contrast were these. Adele was barely more than pretty. Laura was all but beautiful. Adele was a great heiress, and Laura had nothing or next to nothing to expect at her mother's death. Adele was quick-witted, lively, given to exaggeration in her talk, and not very scrupulous as to questions of fact. Laura was slow to decide, but tenacious of her decisions, and, on the whole, very truthful.

In appearance, so far as generalities were concerned, the contrast between the two girls was less marked. Both were of the dark type, but Laura's complexion was paler than Adele's and her hair was blacker, as well as thicker and more glossy. Laura's eyes were large, very deep set, and dark. There was something strange in their look, something quite unusual, and which might almost be called holy, if that were not too strong a word to use in connexion with a woman of the world. Spicca, the melancholy duellist, who was still alive at that time, used to say that no one could possibly be as good as Laura Carlyon looked; a remark which showed that he was acquainted with the sayings of a great English wit, and was not above making use of them. Probably some part of the effect produced by Laura's eyes was due to the evenly perfect whiteness of her skin and the straight black brows which divided them from the broad low forehead. For her hair grew low, and she wore it in a simple fashion without that abundance of little curls which even then were considered almost essential to woman's beauty. Her pallor, too, was quite natural, for she had a good constitution and had rarely even had a headache. In figure she was well proportioned, of average height and rather strongly made, with large, firm, well-shaped hands. On the whole, a graceful girl, but not in that way remarkable among others of her own age. In her face, and altogether in her presence, the chief attraction lay in the look of her eyes, which made one forget to notice the well-chiselled nose, — a little short perhaps, — the really beautiful mouth, and the perfect teeth. The chin, too, was broad and firm — too firm, some might have said, for one so young. Considering all these facts together, most people agreed that Laura was not far from being a great beauty.

Adele was somewhat shorter than her step-sister, and more inclined to be stout. Her black eyes were set nearer together, and her eyebrows almost met, while her lustre-less hair curled naturally in a profusion of tiny ringlets upon her forehead. The small fine nose reminded one of a ferret, and the white teeth looked sharp and pointed when the somewhat thin lips parted and showed them; but she was undoubtedly pretty, and something more than pretty. Her face had colour and animation, she carried her small head well, and her gestures were grace-ful and easy. She was fluent, too, in conversation and ready at all times with a quick answer. Any one could see, in spite of her plump figure, that she was of a very nervous constitution, restless, unsettled, and easily moved, capable of considerable determination when really affected. She never understood Laura, nor did Laura really understand her.

In the natural course of events, social and domestic, it became necessary to choose a husband for Adele so soon as she made her first appearance in society. At that time Laura was not yet seventeen. Gerano had already looked about him and had made up his mind. He was a little dark-eyed man, grey, thin and nervous, but gifted with an unusually agreeable manner, a pleasant tone of voice, a frank glance, and an extremely upright character — a man much liked in the world and a good deal respected.

He had determined that if possible his daughter should marry Don Francesco Savelli, a worthy young person, his father's eldest son, heir to a good estate and a still better name, and altogether a most desirable husband from all points of view. Gerano met with no serious difficulty in bringing about what he wished, and in due time Don Francesco was affianced to Donna Adele, and was privileged to visit at the Palazzo Braccio almost as often as he pleased. He thus saw Laura Carlyon often, and he very naturally fell in love with her. He had no particular inclination to marry Donna Adele, but obeyed his father blindly, as a matter of course, just as Adele obeyed Gerano. That was a part of the old Roman system. Laura, however, did not fall in love with Francesco. She was perhaps too young yet, or it is quite possible that Francesco was too dull and uninteresting a personage in her eyes. But Adele saw these things, and was very angry when she was quite sure that her future husband would have greatly preferred to marry her step-sister. She may be pardoned for having been jealous, for the situation was hardly bearable.

Francesco did not, indeed, make love to Laura. Even had he been rash enough for that, he was in reality too much a gentleman at heart to have done such a thing. He knew very well that he was to marry Adele, whether he cared for her or not, and he behaved with great propriety and with not a little philosophy. The virtue of resignation had been carefully developed in him from his childhood, and Francesco's parents now reaped their reward: he would not have thought of opposing them by word or deed.

But he could not hide what he felt. Like many good young men, he was sensitive, and if he alternately blushed and turned pale when Laura spoke to him, it was not his fault. His father and mother could assuredly not expect him to control the circulation of his blood when it chose to rise above the line of his collar, or seemed to sink to the level of his boots. Adele was, however, at first very angry, and then very jealous, and at last hated her step-sister with all her heart, as young women can hate under circumstances of great provocation.

Meanwhile, Laura remained calmly unconscious of all that was happening. Francesco Savelli's outward and worldly advantages did not appeal to her in the least. The fact that he was fair had no interest for her any

more than the fact that the old Prince of Gerano was
dark. She talked to the young man a little, when the
conversation was general, just as she talked to every one
else, when she had anything to say, because she was not
naturally shy. But she never attempted to manufacture
remarks when nothing came to her lips, because she was
not yet called upon to do so. Nor was her silence by
any means golden, so far as Savelli was concerned.
When she was not speaking to him, she took no notice of
him. His hair might be as yellow as mustard and his
eyes as blue as periwinkles, as his admirers said; she did
not care. If possible, Adele hated her even more for
caring so little.

In due time Francesco Savelli married Adele Braccio
and took her to live under his father's roof. After the
great event peace descended once more upon the household for a time, and Laura Carlyon saw much less of her
adorer. Not, indeed, that there had been any open conflict between the step-sisters, nor even a declaration of
war. Laura had attributed Adele's coldness to her
excitement about the marriage, natural enough under the
circumstances, and had not been hurt by it, while Adele
had carefully kept her jealousy to herself; but when the
two met afterwards, Laura felt that she was immeasurably
far removed from anything like intimacy or real friendship with the bride, and she was surprised that Francesco
should pay so much attention to herself.

The young couple came to the Palazzo Braccio at regular intervals, and at all these family gatherings Savelli
spent his time in making conversation for Laura. He
was a very worthy young man, as has been said, and his
talents were not of the highest order, but he did his best,
and succeeded at least in making Laura think him passably agreeable. She was willing to hear him talk, and
Adele noted the fact. When she drove home from her
father's house with her husband, he was generally ab-
stracted and gave random answers to her questions or
observations. At the end of a year it was clear that he

still loved Laura in a hopeless, helpless, sentimental fashion of his own, and Adele hated her more than ever. A second year and a third went by, and Laura had been some time in society; still the situation remained un·changed. The world said that the young Savelli were a very happy couple, but it always looked at Laura Carlyon with an odd expression, as though it knew something strange about her; something not quite right, which it was willing to tolerate for the sake of the amusement to be got by watching her. The world is the generic appellation of all those who go down to the sea of society in long gowns or white ties, and live and move and have their being therein. Other people do not count, even when they are quite bad, although they may have very big names and a great deal of money. The world, therefore, wagged its head and said that Laura Carlyon was in love with her brother-in-law, or, to be quite accurate, with her step-brother-in-law, because she was dark and his hair was so exceedingly yellow. The world also went on to say that Donna Adele behaved very kindly about it, and that it was so good of Francesco Savelli to talk to Laura just as if there were nothing wrong; for, it added, if he were to avoid her, there would certainly be gossip before long. No one who does not live in society need attempt to follow this sequence of ideas. As usual, too, nobody took the least trouble to find out the origin of the story, but everybody was quite sure of having heard it at first hand from the one person who knew.

The Princess of Gerano took her daughter everywhere. She had conscientiously done her duty towards Adele, and was sincerely fond of her besides; but she loved Laura almost as much as the good mother in the story-book loves her only child when the latter has done something particularly disgraceful. She was at first annoyed and then made seriously anxious by the young girl's total failure in society, from the social point of view. Laura was beautiful, good, and accomplished. Ugly, spiteful, and stupid girls succeeded better than she, though some of them had no better prospect of a dowry. The good lady sought in vain the cause of the trouble, but failed to find it out. Had she been born in Rome, she would doubtless have had many kind friends to help her in the solution of the difficulty. But though she bore a Roman name, and had adopted Roman customs and had led a Roman life for nearly twenty years, she was tacitly looked upon as a foreigner, and her daughter was treated in the same way, though she, at least, spoke the language as her own. Moreover, the girl was not a Catholic, and that was an additional disadvantage where matrimony was concerned. It became evident to the Princess that she was not likely to find a husband for her daughter — certainly not such a husband as she had dreamed that Laura might love, and who was to love her and make her happy.

It must not be supposed that Gerano himself would have been indifferent if he had known the real facts of the case. But he did not. Like many elderly Romans, he hardly ever went into society and took very little interest in its doings. He was very much concerned with the administration of his fortune, and for his own daughter's welfare in her new surroundings. He spent a good deal of time at his club, and was often in the country, even in the height of the season. He supposed that no one asked for Laura's hand because she was dowerless, and he was sincerely sorry for it; but it did not enter his mind to provide her with a suitable portion out of his abundance. He was too conscientious for that. What he had inherited from his father must go down intact to his child and to her children, — a son had already been born to the young Savelli, — and to divide the property, or to take from it anything like a fortune for Laura, would be little short of actual robbery in the eyes of a Braccio.

Laura herself was perhaps less disturbed by the coldness she encountered than her mother was for her sake. She had a certain contempt for young girls of her age and younger, whose sole idea was to be married as soon as possible and with the greatest advantage to themselves. She was not very vain and did not expect great admiration on the one hand, nor any particular dislike on the other. Her character, too, was one that must develop slowly, if it were ever to attain its mature growth. She doubtless had moments of annoyance and even of depression; for few young girls, and certainly no women, are wholly unconscious of neglect in society. But although she was naturally inclined to melancholy, as her eyes clearly showed, she was not by nature morbid, and assuredly not more than usually imaginative.

The result of all this was, that she bore herself with considerable dignity in the world, was generally believed to be older than she was, and was to be seen more often dancing or talking with the foreigners at parties than with the Romans.

"Who is that, Ghisleri?" asked Lord Herbert Arden of his old friend, one evening early in the season, as he caught sight of Laura for the first time.

"An English Roman girl," answered the Italian. "The daughter of the Princess of Gerano by her first marriage — Miss Carlyon."

Lord Herbert had not been in Rome for three or four years, and was, moreover, by no means acquainted with all Roman society.

"Will you introduce me?" he asked, looking up at Ghisleri.

Ghisleri led him across the room, introduced him and left the two together, he being at that time very particularly engaged in another quarter.

The contrast between the two men was very strong. Lord Herbert Arden was almost, if not quite, a cripple, the victim in his infancy of a serving-woman's carelessness. The nurse had let him fall, had concealed the accident as long as she could, and the boy had grown up misshapen and feeble. In despite of this, however, he was eminently a man at whom every one looked twice.

No one who had seen him could ever forget the extreme
nobility and delicacy of his pale face. Each feature
completed and gave dignity to the next — the broad,
highly modelled forehead, the prominent brow, the
hollows at the temples, the clear, steady brown eyes,
the aquiline nose and sensitive nostrils, the calm, straight
mouth, and the firm, clearly cut chin — all were in harmony. And yet in all the crowd that thronged the
great drawing-rooms there was hardly a man with whom
the young Englishman would not have exchanged face
and figure, if only he might stand at the height of other
men, straight and square, and be free forever from the
halting gait which made life in the world so hard for
him. He was very human, and made no great pretence
of resignation, nor indeed of any other virtue.

Pietro Ghisleri was a very different personage except,
perhaps, in point of humanity. He had seen and enjoyed
much, if he had suffered much also, and his face bore the
traces of past pleasure and of past pain, though he was
not more than two-and-thirty years of age. It was a
strong face, too, and not without signs of superior intelligence and resolution. The keen blue eyes had that
trick of fixing themselves in conversation, which belongs
to combative temperaments. At other times they were
sad in expression, and often wore a weary look. Ghisleri's complexion might almost have been called weather-
beaten; for frequent and long exposure to sun and
weather had permanently changed its original colouring,
which had been decidedly fair. To adopt the simple
style of his passport, he might be described as six feet
high, eyes blue, hair and moustache brown, nose large,
mouth normal, chin prominent, face somewhat bony, —
particular sign, a scar on the left temple. Like his old
friend Lord Herbert, he was one of the dozen men who
always attract attention in a crowded room. But of all
those who looked at him, having known him long, very
few understood his character in the least, and all would
have been very much surprised if they could have

guessed his thoughts, especially on that particular evening when he introduced Arden to Miss Carlyon. As for the rest, he was alone in the world, his own master, the last of a Tuscan family that had refused to bear a title when titles meant something and had not seen any reason for changing its mind in the course of three or four centuries. He had a small fortune, sufficient for his wants, and a castle somewhere, considerably the worse for war and wear.

"I cannot dance, you see," said Arden, seating himself beside Laura, "and I am afraid that I am not very brilliant in conversation. Are you a very good-natured person?"

Laura turned her sad eyes upon her new acquaintance, and immediately felt a thrill of sympathy for him, and of interest in his remarkable face.

"No one ever told me," she answered. "Do you think you could find out? I should like to know."

"What form of sin do you most affect?" asked Arden, with a smile. "Do you more often do the things you ought not to do, or do you leave undone the things which you ought to do?"

"Oh, I leave the good things undone, of course!" answered Laura. "I suppose everybody does, as a rule."

"You are decidedly good-natured, particularly so in making that last remark. I am less afraid of you than I was when I sat down."

The young girl looked at him again. His conversation was so far not like that of the Englishmen she had known hitherto.

"Were you afraid of me?" she asked, beginning to smile.

"A little, I confess."

"Why? And if you were, why did you make Signor Ghisleri introduce you to me?"

"Because nobody likes to own to being afraid. Besides, Ghisleri is a very old friend of mine, and I can trust him not to lead me into danger."

"Have you known him long?" asked Laura. "I have often wondered what he is really like. I mean his character, you know, and what he thinks about."

"He thinks a great deal. He is one of the most complicated characters I ever knew, and I am not at all sure that I understand him yet, though we have known each other ten years. He is a good friend and a rather indifferent enemy, I should say. His chief apparent peculiarity is that he hates gossip. You will not find it easy to get from him a disagreeable remark about any one. Yet he is not good-natured."

"Perhaps he is afraid to say what he thinks," suggested the young girl.

"I doubt that," answered Arden, with a smile. "He has not a particularly angelic reputation, I believe, but I never heard any one say that he was timid."

"As you pretend to be," added Laura. "Do you know? You have not answered my question. Why were you afraid of me, if you really were?"

Lord Herbert answered one question by another, and the conversation continued pleasantly enough. It was a relief to him to find a young and beautiful girl of his own nationality in surroundings with which neither he nor she were really in sympathy. In the course of half an hour they both felt as though they had known one another a long time. The admiration Arden had felt for Laura at first sight had considerably increased, and she on her side had half forgotten that he was a cripple. Indeed, when he was seated, his deformities were far less noticeable than when he stood or painfully moved about from place to place.

The two talked of a variety of subjects, but, with the exception of the few words spoken about Ghisleri, there was no more reference to personalities for a long time.

"I am keeping you away from the dancing," Arden said at last, as he realised that the room was almost empty and that he had been absorbing the beautiful Miss Carlyon's attention longer than might be pleasant to her.

"Not at all," answered Laura. "I do not dance much."

"Why not? Do you not like dancing?" He asked the question in a tone of surprise.

"On the contrary. But I am not taken out very often — perhaps because they think me a foreigner. It is natural enough."

"Very unnatural, it seems to me. Besides, I believe you are exaggerating, so as not to make me feel uncomfortable. It is of no use, you know; I am not at all sensitive. Shall we go into the ball-room?"

"No; I would rather not, just yet."

"Shall I go and get Ghisleri to take you back?" inquired Arden, with a little smile.

. "Why?"

"Because I might make you look ridiculous," answered the cripple, quietly.

He watched her, and saw a quick, pained look pass over her face. It was at that particular moment that he began to love her, as he afterwards remembered. She turned her eyes upon him as she answered after a moment's hesitation.

"Lord Herbert, will you please never say anything like that to me again?"

"Certainly not, if it offends you."

"It does not offend me. I do not mean that."

"What, then? Please tell me. I am not at all sensitive."

"It pains me. I do not like to fancy that any one can think such things of me, much less . . ." she stopped short and looked down, slowly opening and shutting her fan.

"Much less?"

Laura hesitated for some seconds, as though choosing her words with more than ordinary care.

"Much less one whom it might pain to think them," she said at last.

The smile that had been on Arden's face faded away

in the silence that followed, and his lips moved a little as though he felt some kind of emotion, while his large thin hands closed tightly upon his withered knee.

"Have I said too much?" she asked, suddenly breaking the long pause.

"Or not quite enough, perhaps," he answered in a low voice.

Again they were both silent, and they both wondered inwardly that in less than an hour's acquaintance they should have reached something like a crisis. At last Laura rose slowly and deliberately, intending to give her companion time to get to his feet.

"Will you give me your arm?" she said when he stood beside her. "I want to introduce you to my mother."

Arden bent his head and held up his right arm for her hand. He was considerably shorter than she. Then they walked away together, she erect and easy in her girlish gait, he weak-kneed and awkward, seeming to unjoint half his body at every painful step, helping himself along at her side with the stick he held in his free hand — a strangely assorted couple, the world said, as they went by.

"My mother's name is Gerano, Princess of Gerano," said Laura, by way of explanation, as they came within sight of her.

"And is your father — I mean, is Prince Gerano — living?" asked Arden. He had almost forgotten her name and her nationality in the interest he felt in herself.

"Yes; but he rarely goes into society. I am very fond of him," she added, scarcely knowing why. "Mother," she said, as they came up to the Princess, "Lord Herbert Arden."

The Princess smiled and held out her hand. At that moment Pietro Ghisleri came up. He had not been seen since he had left Laura and Arden together. By a coincidence, doubtless, the Contessa dell' Armi had disappeared at about the same time: she had probably gone home, as she was not seen again in the ball-room that evening. But the world in its omniscience knew that there was a certain boudoir beyond the supper-room, where couples who did not care to dance were left in comparative peace for a long time. The world could have told with precision the position of the small sofa on which Ghisleri and the lovely Contessa invariably spent an hour when they met in that particular house.

"Will you give me a turn, Miss Carlyon?" asked Ghisleri, as Arden began to talk with the Princess.

"Yes." Laura was really fond of a certain amount of dancing when a good partner presented himself.

"What do you think of my friend?" inquired Pietro, as they moved away together.

"I like him very much. He interests me."

"Then you ought to be grateful to me for bringing him to you."

"Do you expect gratitude in a ball-room?" Laura laughed a little, more in pleasant anticipation of the waltz than at what she said.

"A little more than in the average asylum for the aged and infirm, which most people call home," returned Ghisleri, carelessly.

"You have no home. How can you talk about it in that way?"

"For the sake of talking; shall we dance instead?"

A moment later they were in the thick of the crowd.

"There are too many people; please take me back," said Laura, after one turn.

"Will you come and talk in the conservatory?" asked Ghisleri as they reached the door.

"No; I would rather not."

"You were talking a long time with Arden. I saw you come out of the drawing-room together. Why will you not sit five minutes with me?"

"Lord Herbert is different," said Laura, quietly. "He is an Englishman, and I am English."

"Oh! is that the reason?"

He led her back and left her with her mother. Arden was still there.

CHAPTER II.

In spite of his own declarations to the contrary, Lord
Herbert Arden was a very sensitive man. When he
said he was not, he was perhaps trying to deceive himself, but the attempt was at best only partially successful. Few men in his circumstances can escape the daily
sting that lies in comparing their unfortunate outward
personality with the average symmetry of the human
race. Women seem to feel deformity less than men, or perhaps one only thinks so because they bear it more bravely;
it is hard to say. If Darwin is right, men are far more
vain of their appearance than women; and there are
many who believe that a woman's passive courage is
greater than a man's. Be that as it may, the particular
sufferer who made Laura Carlyon's acquaintance at the
ball was in reality as sensitive a man in almost all respects
as could be met with anywhere in ordinary life. When
he discovered that he was seriously in love with Laura
Carlyon, his existence changed suddenly, and for the
worse, so far as his comfort was concerned.

He reviewed the situation as calmly as he could, when
a fortnight or more had passed and he had seen her a
dozen times at her step-father's house and in the world.
One main fact was now quite clear to him. She was not
what is called popular in society; she had not even any
intimate friends. As for his own chances, he did not like
to think of them. Though only the younger brother of a
peer of high rank, he was entitled to expect a large fortune from an uncle on his mother's side, who had never
made any secret of his intentions in regard to his property, and who, being over eighty years of age, could not
be expected to live much longer in the ordinary course of
nature. At present his modest portion was quite sufficient for himself, but he doubted whether it would suffice for his needs if he married. That, however, was of

minor importance. The great fortune was safe and he was an exceedingly good match from a financial point of view. Miss Carlyon was poor, as he knew from Ghisleri, and Ghisleri had very probably told her that Arden was rich, or would be before long. He refused to believe that Laura, of her own free will, might marry him for his money; but it was intolerable to think that her mother and step-father might try to force her into the match from considerations of interest. He was not just to the Princess of Gerano, but he knew her very slightly as yet and had no means of forming a positive opinion.

In the meantime he had been introduced to Donna Adele Savelli, who had received him with the greatest warmth, protesting her love for the English people and everything English, and especially for her step-mother and step-sister. He had also renewed his acquaintance with young Savelli, whom he had known slightly during a former visit to Rome, and who now, he thought, met him rather coldly. He attributed Adele's gushing manner to a desire to bring about a marriage, and he did not attempt to account for Don Francesco's stiffness; but he liked neither the one manifestation nor the other, for both wounded him in different degrees.

Above all other difficulties, the one which was most natural to his delicately organised nature was of a purely disinterested kind. He feared lest Laura, who evidently felt both pity and sympathy for him, should take the two together for genuine love and sacrifice herself in a life which would by and by become unbearable to her. He could not but see that at every meeting she grew more interested in his conversation, until when he was present, she scarcely paid any attention to any one else. Such a friendship, if it could have been a real friendship, might have made Arden happy so long as it lasted; but on his side, at least, nothing of the kind was possible. He knew that he was hopelessly in love, and to pretend the contrary to himself was real pain. He guessed with wonderful keenness the direction Laura's heart was taking, and he was appalled by the vision of the misery which must spread over her young life if, after she had married him, she should be roused to the great truth that pity and love are not the same, though they be so near akin as to be sometimes mistaken one for the other.

His weak health suffered and he grew more and more restless. It would have been a satisfaction to speak out a hundredth part of what he felt to Ghisleri. But he was little given to making confidences, and Ghisleri was, or seemed to be, the last man to invite them. They met constantly, however, and talked upon all sorts of topics.

One day Ghisleri came to breakfast with Arden in his rooms at the hotel, looking more weather-beaten than usual, for he was losing the tan from his last expedition in the south, and there were deep black shadows under his eyes. Moreover, he was in an abominably bad humour. with everything and with everybody except his friend. Arden knew that he never gambled, and he also knew the man well enough to guess at the true cause of the disturbance. There was something serious the matter.

They sat down to breakfast and began to talk of politics and the weather, as old friends do when they are aware that there is something wrong. Ghisleri spoke English perfectly, with an almost imperceptible accent, as many Italians do nowadays.

"Come along with me, Arden," he said at last, as though losing patience with everything all at once. "Let us go to Paris or Timbuctoo. This place is not fit to live in."

"What is the matter with it?" asked Arden, in a tone of amusement.

"The matter with it? It is dull, to begin with. Secondly, it is a perfect witches' caldron of scandal. Thirdly, we are all as bad as we can be. There are three points at least."

"My dear fellow, I do not see them in the same light. Take some more hock."

"Oh, you — you are amusing yourself! Thank you — I will — half a glass. Of course you like Rome — you always did — you foreigners always will. You amuse yourselves — that is it."

"I see you dancing every night as though you liked it," observed Arden.

"No doubt!"

Ghisleri suddenly grew thoughtful and a distant look came into his eyes, while the shadows seemed to deepen under them, till they were almost black. He had eaten hardly anything, and now, regardless of the fact that the meal was not half over, he lit a cigarette and leaned back in his chair as though he had finished.

"You are not looking well, Arden," he said at last. "You must take care of yourself. Take my advice. We will go somewhere together for a couple of months."

"There is nothing I should like better, but not just at present. I will stay in Rome until the weather is a little warmer."

Arden was not in the least conscious that his expression changed as he thought of the reason which kept him in the city and which might keep him long. But Ghisleri, who had been watching for that particular hesitation of manner and for that almost imperceptible darkening of the eyes, knew exactly what both meant.

"Oh, very well," he answered indifferently. "We can go later. People always invent absurd stories if one goes away in the middle of the season without any apparent object."

The remark was a little less than general, and Arden was at once confirmed in his suspicion that something unpleasant had happened in Ghisleri's life, most probably in connection with the Contessa dell' Armi. His friend was in such a savage humour that he might almost become communicative. Arden was a very keen-sighted man, and not without tact, and he thought the opportunity a good one for approaching a subject which had long been in his mind. But he had been in earnest when he had told Laura that he knew Ghisleri's character to be what he called complicated, and he was aware that Pietro's intelligence was even more penetrating than his own. He was therefore very cautious.

"You say that Rome is such a great place for gossip," he began, in answer to Ghisleri's last observation. "I suppose you know it by experience, but I cannot say that we strangers hear much of it."

"Perhaps not," admitted Ghisleri, rather absently.

"No, we do not hear much scandal. For instance, I go rather often to the Gerano's. I do not remember to have heard there a single spiteful story, except, perhaps," — Arden stopped cautiously.

"Precisely," said Pietro, "the exceptions are rare in that house. But then, the Prince is generally away, and both the Princess and her daughter are English, and especially nice people."

Arden helped himself to something that chanced to be near him, and glanced at his companion's rather impenetrable face. He knew that at the present moment the latter was perfectly sincere in what he said, but he knew also that Ghisleri spoke of most people in very much the same tone. It was something which Arden could never quite understand.

"Do you think," he began presently, "that the fact of their being English has anything to do with Miss Carlyon's unpopularity here?"

"My dear fellow, how should I know?" asked Ghisleri, with something almost like a laugh.

"You do know, of course. I wish you would tell me. As an Englishman, the mother interests me."

"From the point of view of our international relations, I see, collecting information for an article in the Nineteenth Century, or else your brother is going to speak on the subject in the Lords. What do you think about the matter yourself? If I can put you right, I will."

"What an extraordinary man you are!" exclaimed Arden. "You always insist upon answering one question by another."

"It gives one time to think," retorted Ghisleri. "These cigarettes are distinctly bad; give me one of yours, please. I never can understand why the government monopoly here should exist, and if it does why they should not give us Russian —"

"My dear Ghisleri," said Arden, interrupting him, "we were talking about the Princess Gerano."

"Were we? Oh, yes, and Miss Carlyon, too, I remember. Do you like them?"

"Very much; and I think every one should. That is the reason why I am surprised that Miss Carlyon should not receive much more attention than she does. I fancy it is because she is English. Do you think I am right?"

"No," said Ghisleri, slowly, at last answering the direct question, "I do not think you are."

"Then what in the world is the reason? The fact is clear enough. She knows it herself."

"Probably some absurd bit of gossip. Who cares? I am sorry for her, though."

"How can there be any scandal about a young girl of her age?" asked Arden, incredulously.

"In this place you can start a story about a baby a year old," answered Ghisleri. "It will be remembered, repeated, and properly adorned, and will ultimately ruin the innocent woman when she is grown up. Nobody seems to care for chronology here — anachronism is so much more convenient."

"Why are you so absurdly reticent with me, Ghisleri?" asked Arden, with some impatience. "You talk as though we had not known each other ten years."

"On the contrary," answered Pietro, "if we were acquaintances of yesterday, I would not talk at all. That is just the difference. As it is, and because we are rather good friends, I tell you what I believe to be the truth. I believe — well, I will allow that I know, that there is a story about Miss Carlyon, which is commonly credited, and which is a down-right lie. I will not tell you what it is. It does not, strictly speaking, affect her reputation, but it has made her unpopular — since you have used that word. Ask any of the gossips, if you care enough — I am not going to repeat such nonsense. It never does any good to repeat other peoples' lies."

Arden was silent, and his long white fingers played uneasily upon the edge of the table. It had been a hard matter to extract the information, but such as it was he knew that it was absolutely reliable. When Ghisleri spoke at all about such things, he spoke the truth, and when he said that he would positively say no more, his decision was always final. Arden had discovered that in the early days of their acquaintance. Perhaps Pietro went to absurd lengths in this direction, and there were people who called it affectation and made him out to be an even worse man than he was, but his friend knew that it was genuine in its way. He was all the more disturbed by what he had heard, and it was a long time before he spoke again.

Ghisleri smoked in silence and drank three cups of coffee while Arden was drinking one. He looked at that time like a man who was living upon his nerves, so to say, instead of upon proper nourishment.

An hour later the two men went out together, Arden taking Pietro with him in his carriage. The air was bright and keen and the afternoon sunlight was already turning yellow with the gold of the coming evening. The carriage was momentarily blocked at the corner of the Pincio near the entrance, by one that was turning out of the enclosure opposite the band stand. It chanced to be the Princess of Gerano's landau, and she and her daughter were seated in it, closely wrapped in their furs. It was Arden's victoria that had to pull up to let the Princess drive across, and by a coincidence the Savelli couple were in the one which hers would have to follow in the descending line after crossing the road.

Francesco Savelli bowed, smiled, and waved his hat, evidently to Laura rather than to her mother. With a rather forced smile Adele slowly bent her head. Arden bowed at the same moment, and looked from one carriage to the other. Ghisleri followed his example, and there was the very faintest expression of amusement on his face, which Arden of course could not see. A number of men on foot lined the side of the road close to the carriage.

"People always come back to their first loves!" said a low voice at Arden's elbow.

He turned quickly and saw several men watching the Savelli across his victoria. He knew none of them, and it was impossible to guess which had spoken. Ghisleri, being on the right side, as Arden's guest, could not have heard the words. Having just noticed the rather striking contrast between Francesco Savelli's demonstrative greeting and his wife's almost indifferent nod, it naturally struck the Englishman that the remark he had overheard might refer to the person he was himself watching at that moment. Donna Adele Savelli's expression might very well be taken for one of jealousy, but her husband's behaviour was assuredly too marked for anything more than friendship. Arden coupled the words with the facts and concluded that he had discovered the story of which Ghisleri had spoken. Francesco Savelli was said to be in love with Laura Carlyon. That was evidently the gossip; but he had seen Laura's face, too, and it was quite plain that she was wholly indifferent. On the whole, though the tale reflected little credit on Savelli, it was not at all clear why it should make Laura unpopular, unless people said that she encouraged the man, which they probably did, thought Lord Herbert Arden, who was a man of the world.

The more he considered the matter the more convinced he became that he was right, and the conviction was on the whole a relief. He had been uneasy for some time, and Ghisleri's guarded words had not satisfied him; chance, however, had done what Ghisleri would not do, and the mystery was solved. The Princess of Gerano was at home that evening, and Arden of course went to the palace early, and was the last to leave.

Three times between half-past ten and half-past two o'clock Laura and he installed themselves side by side at some distance from the drawing-room, and each time their conversation lasted over half an hour. It was not a set ball, but one of the regular weekly informal dances of which there are so many in Rome during the season. The first interruption of Arden's talk appeared in the shape of Don Francesco Savelli, who asked Laura for a turn. Oddly enough she glanced at Lord Herbert's face before accepting, and the action sent a strange thrill to his heart. He struggled to his feet as she rose to go away with Savelli, and then sank back again and remained some time where he was, absently watching the people who passed. His face was very pale and weary now that the excitement of conversation had subsided, and he felt that if he was not positively ill, he was losing the little strength he had with every day that passed. Late hours, heated rooms, and strong emotions were not the best tonics for his feeble physical organisation, and he knew it. At last he made an effort, got up, and moved about in the crowd, exchanging a few words now and then with a passing acquaintance, but too preoccupied and perhaps too tired to talk long with indifferent people. He nodded as Ghisleri passed him with the Contessa dell' Armi on his arm, and he thought there was a bad light in his friend's eyes, though Pietro was looking better than in the afternoon. The two had evidently been dancing together, for the Contessa's white neck heaved a little, as though she were still out of breath. She was a short, slight woman of exquisite figure, very fair, with deep violet eyes and small classic features, almost hard in their regularity; evidently wilful and dominant in character. Arden watched the pair as they went on in search of a vacant sofa just big enough for two.

They had scarcely sat down and he could see that Ghisleri was beginning to talk, when Anastase Gouache appeared and stood still before them. To Arden's surprise the Contessa welcomed him with a bright smile and pointed to a chair at her side of the sofa. Anastase Gouache was a celebrated painter who had married a Roman lady of high birth, and was a very agreeable man, but Arden had not expected that he would be invited so readily to interrupt so promising a conversation. Ghisleri's face expressed nothing. He appeared to join in the talk for a few minutes and then rose and left the Contessa with Gouache. She looked after him, and Arden thought she grew a shade paler and frowned. A faint smile appeared on the Englishman's face and was gone again in an instant as Ghisleri came near him, returning again to the ball-room. Ghisleri had glanced at him as he passed and had seen that he was not talking to a lady.

"May I have the next dance, Miss Carlyon?" asked Pietro, when he found Laura in a corner with Francesco Savelli. "Thanks," he said, as she nodded graciously, and he passed on.

"Will you give me the dance after the next?" he inquired a few minutes later, coming up with Donna Adele, who was moving away on young Frangipani's arm.

"Certainly, caro Ghisleri," she answered, with alacrity, "as many as you please."

"You are very good," he said, with a slight bow, and withdrew to a window near Laura to wait until the waltz began. He could see Arden through the open door from the place where he stood.

When the dance was over he led Laura out and took one turn through the rooms, making a few commonplace remarks on the way. Coming back, he stopped as though by accident close to Lord Herbert.

"I am afraid you will think me very rude if I ask you to let me leave you," he said. "I am engaged for the next dance — it is a quadrille — and I must find a vis-à-vis."

Arden of course heard and presented himself immediately in Ghisleri's place. Laura was quite ready to go back with him to the sofa in the corner, and they resumed their conversation almost at the point at which it had been interrupted by Francesco Savelli. Neither of them ever knew that Ghisleri had brought them together again by a little social skill, just beyond what most people possess. Arden looked after him, half believing that he had only given Laura an excuse for leaving her in order to return to the Contessa dell' Armi, who was now surrounded by half a dozen men, beginning with old Spicca, who, as has been said, was still alive in those days, and ending with the little Vicomte de Bompierre, a young French attaché with a pleasant voice, a bright smile, and an incipient black moustache. But to Arden's surprise Ghisleri took quite a different direction, and began to speak to one man after another, evidently trying to secure a vis-à-vis for the square dance.

"You must not let me bore you, or rather you must not bore yourself with me," said Arden to Laura, after a short pause in the conversation. "You are altogether much too good to me."

"You never bore me," answered the young girl. "You are one of the few people who do not."

Arden smiled a little sadly.

"I am glad to be one of the 'few people,'" he said, "even if I am the last."

"You are too modest." She tried to laugh, but the effort was not very successful.

"No, I am not. I have much more vanity than you would suppose, or think possible, considering how little I have to be vain of."

"Opinions may differ about that," answered Laura, looking into his eyes. "You have much that many men might envy, and probably do."

"What, for instance?"

Laura hesitated, and then smiled, without effort this time.

"You are very good looking," she said after a moment.

"No one has ever told me that before," he answered. A very slight flush rose in his pale face.

"It is not of much importance, either. Would you like me to enumerate your good qualities?"

"Of all things!"

"You are honest and kind, and you are very clever, I think, though I am not clever enough to be sure. You have no right to be unhappy, and you would not be if you were not so sensitive about — about not being so strong and big as some men are. What difference does it make?"

"You will almost tempt me to think that it makes none, if you talk in that way," said Arden.

"Do you mean to say that you would really and truly change places with any one? With Signor Ghisleri, for instance?"

"Indeed I would, with him, and very gladly. I would rather be Ghisleri than any man I know."

"I cannot understand that," answered Laura, thoughtfully. "If I were a man, I would much rather be like you. Besides, they say Signor Ghisleri has been dreadfully wild, and is anything but angelic now. You used that very word about him the first evening we met; do you remember?"

"Of course I do; but what has that to do with it? Must I necessarily choose a saint for my friend, and pick out one to exchange places with me if it were possible? A woman saint may be lovable, too lovable perhaps, but a man saint about town is like a fish out of water. But you are right about Ghisleri, up to a certain point, only you do not understand him. He is an exceedingly righteous sinner, but a sinner he is."

"What do you mean by a righteous sinner?" asked Laura, gravely.

"Do not bring me down to definitions. I have not at all a logical mind. I mean Ghisleri — that is all I can say. I would much rather talk about you."

"No, I object to that. Tell me, since you wish so much to be Signor Ghisleri, what do you think you would feel if you were?"

"What he feels — everything that a man can feel!" answered Arden, with a sudden change of tone. "To be straight and strong and a match for other men. Half the happiness of life lies there."

His voice shook a little, and Laura felt that the tears were almost in her eyes as she looked earnestly into his.

" You see what I am," he continued, more and more bitterly, "I am a cripple. There is no denying it — why should I even try to hide it a little? Nature, or Heaven, or what you please to call it, has been good enough to make concealment impossible. If I am not quite a hunchback, I am very near it, and I can hardly walk even with a stick. And look at yourself, straight and graceful and beautiful — well, you pity me, at least. Why should I make a fool of myself? It is the first time I ever spoke like this to any one."

"You are quite wrong," answered Laura, in a tone of conviction. "I do not pity you — indeed I do not think you are the least to be pitied. I see it quite differently. It hardly ever strikes me that you are not just the same as other people, and when it does — I do not know — I mean to say that when it does, it makes no painful impression upon me. You see I am quite frank."

While she was speaking the colour rose in two bright spots on Arden's pale cheeks, and his bright eyes softened with a look of wonderful happiness.

" Are you quite in earnest, Miss Carlyon? " he asked, in a low voice.

" Quite, quite in earnest. Please believe me when I say that it would hurt me dreadfully if I thought you doubted it."

"Hurt you? Why?"

She turned her deep, sad eyes to him, and looked at him without speaking. He was on the point of telling her that he loved her — then he saw how beautiful she was, and he felt his withered knee under his hand, and he was ashamed to speak. It was a cruel moment, and his nerves were already overstrained by perpetual emotion, as well as tired from late hours and lack of sleep. He hesitated a moment. Then bent his head and covered his eyes with his hand. Laura said nothing for several moments, but seeing that he did not move, she touched his sleeve.

"Dear Lord Herbert, do not be so unhappy," she said softly. "You really have no right to be, you know."

"No right?" He looked up suddenly. "If you knew, you would not say that."

"I should always say it. As long as you have friends — friends who love you, and would do anything for you, why should you make yourself so miserable?"

"I want more than a friend — even than friendship."

"What?"

"I want love."

Again she gazed into his eyes and paused. Her face was very white — whiter than his. Then she spoke.

"Are you so sure you have not got that love?" she asked. Her own voice trembled now.

Arden started and a look of something almost like fear came into his face. He could hardly speak.

"Love?" he repeated, and he felt he could say nothing more.

"Yes, I mean it." So she chose her fate.

She thought there was a touch of the divine in poor Arden's expression as he heard the words. Then his face grew pale, the light faded from his eyes, and his head sank on his breast. Laura did not at first realise what had happened. She felt so strongly herself, that nothing in his manner would have surprised her. She heard nothing of the hum of the voices in the room, or if she did, she heard the harmony of a happy hymn, and the great branches of candles were the tapers upon an altar in some sacred place.

Still Arden did not move. Laura bent down and looked at his face.

"Lord Herbert!" She called him softly. "Herbert, what is the matter?"

No answer came. She looked round wildly for help. At that moment the dance was just over and Ghisleri passed near her with Donna Adele on his arm. Laura rose and overtook him swiftly, touching his arm in her excitement.

"Lord Herbert has fainted — for heaven's sake, help him!" she cried, in a low voice.

Pietro Ghisleri glanced at the sofa.

"Excuse me," he said hastily to Donna Adele, and left her standing in the middle of the room. He bent down and felt Arden's forehead and hands.

"Yes, he has fainted," he said to Laura. "Show me the way to a quiet place."

Thereupon he took his unconscious friend in his arms and followed Laura quickly through the surging crowd that already filled the room, escaping in haste from the heat as soon as the dance was over in the ball-room beyond.

For a few seconds one of those total silences fell upon the party which always follow an accident. Then, as Ghisleri disappeared with his burden, every one began to talk at once, speculating upon the nature of Lord Herbert Arden's indisposition. Heart disease — epilepsy — nervous prostration — most things were suggested.

"Probably too much champagne," laughed Donna Adele in the ear of the lady nearest to her.

CHAPTER III.

It is perhaps useless to attempt to trace and recapitulate the causes which had led Laura Carlyon to the state of mind in which she had found courage to tell Arden that she loved him. There might be harder moments in store for her, but this had been the hardest she had known hitherto. Nothing short of a real and great love, she believed, could have carried her through it, and she had been conscious for some days that if the opportunity came she meant to do what she had done. In other words, she had been quite sure that Arden loved her and that she loved him. This being granted, it was in accordance with her character to take the initiative. With far less sympathy than she felt in all her thoughts, she would have understood that a man of his instincts would never speak of his love to her unless almost directly bidden to do so. Laura was slow to make up her mind, sure of her decision when reached, and determined to act upon it without consulting any one. Many people said later that she had sacrificed herself for Lord Herbert's expected fortune, or for his position. A few said that she was a very good woman and that, finding herself neglected, she had decided to devote her life to the happiness of a very unhappy man for whom she felt a sincere friendship. That was at least the more charitable view. But neither was at all the right one. She honestly and really believed that she loved the man: she saw beyond a doubt that he loved her, and she took the shortest and most direct way of ending all doubts on the subject. On that same night when Arden had quite recovered and had gone home with Ghisleri, she spoke to her mother and told her exactly what had happened.

The Princess of Gerano opened her quiet brown eyes very wide when she heard the news. She was handsome still at five and forty, a little stout, perhaps, but well proportioned. Her light brown hair was turning grey at the temples, but there were few lines in her smooth, calm face, and her complexion was still almost youthful, though with little colouring. She looked what she was, a woman of the world, very far from worldly, not conscious of half the evil that went on around her, and much given to inward contemplation of a religious kind when not actively engaged in social duty. She had seen Laura's growing appreciation of Arden and had noticed the frequency of the latter's visits to the house. But she had herself learned to like him very much during the last month, and it never suggested itself to her that he could wish to marry Laura nor that Laura could care for him, considering that he was undeniably a cripple. It was no wonder that she was surprised.

"Dear child," she said, "I do not know what to say. Of course I have found out what a really good man he is, though he is so fond of that wild Ghisleri — they are always together. I have a great admiration for Lord Herbert. As far as position goes, there is nothing better, and I suppose he is rich enough to support you, though I do not know. You see, darling, you have nothing but the little I can give you. But never mind that — there is only that one other thing — I wish he were not —"

She checked herself, far too delicate to hurt her daughter by too direct a reference to Arden's physical shortcomings. But Laura, strange to say, was not sensitive on that point.

"I know, mother," she said, "he is deformed. It is of no use denying it, as he says himself. But if I do not mind that — if I do not think of it at all when I am with him, why should any one else care? After all, if I marry him, it is to please myself, and not the people who will ask us to dinner."

The young girl laughed happily as she thought of the new life before her, and of how she would make everything easy for poor Arden, and make him quite forget that he could hardly walk. Her mother looked at her with quiet wonder.

"Think well before you act, dear," she said. "Marriage is a very serious thing. There is no drawing back afterwards, and if you were to be at all unkind after you are married —"

"O mother, how can you think that of me?"

"No — at least, you would never mean it. You are too good for that. But it would break the poor man's heart. He is very sensitive, it is not every man who faints when he finds out that a young girl loves him — fortunately, not every man," she added with a smile.

"If every one loved as we do, the world would be much

happier," said Laura, kissing her mother. "Do not be afraid, I will not break his heart."

"God grant you may not break your own, dear!" The Princess spoke in a lower voice, and turned away her face to hide the tears that stood in her eyes.

"Mine, mother!" Laura bent over her as she sat in her dressing-chair. "What is it?" she asked anxiously, as she saw that her mother's cheek was wet.

"You are very dear to me, child," murmured the Princess, drawing the young head down to her breast, and kissing the thick black hair.

So the matter was settled, and Laura had her way. It is not easy to say how most mothers would have behaved under the circumstances. There are worldly ones enough who would have received the news far more gladly than the Princess of Gerano did; and there are doubtless many who would refuse a cripple for a son-in-law on any condition whatever. Laura's mother did what she thought right, which is more than most of us can say of our actions.

The Prince was almost as much surprised as his wife when he learned the news, but he was convinced that he had nothing to say in the matter. Laura was quite free to do as she pleased, and, moreover, it was a good thing that she should marry a man of her own faith, and ultimately live among her own people, since nothing could make either a Catholic or a Roman of her. But he was not altogether pleased with her choice. He had an Italian's exaggerated horror of deformity, and though he liked Lord Herbert, he could never quite overcome his repulsion for his outward defects. There was nothing to be done, however, and on the whole the marriage had much in its favour in his eyes.

The engagement was accordingly announced with due formality, and the wedding day was fixed for the Saturday after Easter, which fell early in that year. Not until the day before the Princess told the news to every one did Arden communicate it to Ghisleri. He had perfect confidence in his friend's discretion, but having said that he

would not speak of the engagement to any one until the
Princess wished it, he kept his word to the letter.   He
asked Pietro to drive with him, far out upon the campagna.   When they had passed the last houses and were
in the open country he spoke.

"I am going to marry Miss Carlyon," he said simply,
but he glanced at Ghisleri's face to see the look of surprise he expected.

"Since you announce it, my dear friend, I congratulate
you with all my heart," answered Pietro.   "Of course I
knew it some time ago."

"You knew it?"   Arden was very much astonished.

"It was not very hard to guess.   You loved each other,
you went constantly to the house and you spent your
evenings with her in other people's houses, there was no
reason why you should not marry — accordingly, I took
it for granted that you would be married.   You see that
I was right.   I am delighted.   Ask me to the wedding."

Arden laughed.

"I thought you would never enter one of our churches!"
he exclaimed.

"I did not know that I had such a reputation for devout
obedience to general rules," answered Ghisleri.

"As for your reputation, my dear fellow, it is not that
of a saint.   But I once saw you saying your prayers."

"I dare say," replied Pietro, indifferently.   "I sometimes do, but not generally in the Corso, nor on the Pincio.
How long ago was that?   Do you happen to remember?"

"Six or seven years, I fancy — oh, yes!   It was in that
little church in Dieppe, just before you went off on that
long cruise — you remember it, too, I fancy."

"I suppose I thought I was going to be drowned, and
was seized with a passing ague of premature repentance,"
said Ghisleri, lighting a cigarette.

"What a queer fellow you are!" observed Arden, striking a light in his turn.   "I was talking with Miss Carlyon about you some time ago, and I told her you were a
sinner, but a righteous one."

"A shade worse than others, perhaps, because I know a little better what I am doing," answered Ghisleri, with a sneer, evidently intended for himself.

He was looking at the tomb of Cecilia Metella, as it rose in sight above the horses' heads at the turn of the road, and he thought of what had happened to him there years ago, and of the consequences. Arden knew nothing of the associations the ruin had for his friend, and laughed again. He was in a very happy humour on that day, as he was for many days afterwards.

"I can never quite make you out," he said. "Are you good, bad, or a humbug? You cannot be both good and bad at once, you know."

"No. But one may be often bad, and sometimes do decently good deeds," observed Ghisleri, with a dry laugh. "Let us talk of your marriage instead of speculating on my salvation, or more probable perdition, if there really is such a thing. When is the wedding day?"

Arden was full of plans for the future, and they drove far out, talking of all that was before the young couple.

On the following day the news was announced to the city and the world. The world held up its hands in wonder, and its tongue wagged for a whole week and a few days more. Laura Carlyon was to marry a penniless cripple of the most dissipated habits. How shocking! Of course every one knew that Lord Herbert had not fainted at all on that night at the Palazzo Braccio, but had succumbed, in the natural course of events, to the effects of the champagne he had taken at dinner. That was now quite certain. And the whole world was well aware that his father had cut him off with a pittance on account of his evil ways, and that his brother had twice paid his gambling debts to save the family name from disgrace. Englishmen as a race, and English cripples in particular, were given to drink and high play. The man had actually been the worse for wine when talking to Laura Carlyon in her mother's house, and Ghisleri had been obliged to carry him out for decency's sake before anything worse happened. Scandalous! It was a wonder that Ghisleri, who, after all, was a gentleman, could associate with such a fellow. After all, nobody ever liked Laura Carlyon since she had first appeared in society, soon after dear Donna Adele's marriage. It was as well that she should go to England and live with her tipsy cripple. She was good-looking, as some people admitted. She might win the heart of her brother-in-law and induce him to pay her husband's debts a third time. They were said to be enormous.

The men were, on the whole, more charitable. Conscious of their own shortcomings, they did not blame Lord Herbert very severely for taking a little too much "extra dry." They did, however, abuse him somewhat roundly at the club, for having gone to the Gerano party at all when he should have known that he was not steady. Of the facts themselves they had not the slightest doubt. Unfortunately for one of them who happened to be declaiming on the subject, but who was really by no means a bad fellow, he did not notice that Ghisleri had entered the room before he had finished his speech. When he had quite done, Ghisleri came forward.

"Arden is my old friend," he said quietly. "He never drinks. He has a disease of the heart and he fainted from the heat. The doctor and I took him home together. I hope that none of you will take up this disgusting story, which was started by the women. And I hope Pietrasanta, there, will do me the honour to believe what I say, and to tell you that he was mistaken."

Ghisleri was not a pleasant person to quarrel with, and moreover had the reputation of being truthful. His story, too, was quite as probable as the other, to say the least of it. Don Gianbattista Pietrasanta glanced quickly from one to the other of the men who were seated around him as though to ask their advice in the matter. Several of them nodded almost imperceptibly, as though counselling him to do as Ghisleri requested. There was nothing at all aggressive in the latter's manner, either, as he quietly lit a cigarette while waiting for the other's answer. Suddenly a deep voice was heard from another corner of the room. The Marchese di San Giacinto, giant in body and fortune, had been reading the paper with the utmost indifference during all the previous conversation. All at once he spoke, deliberately and to the point.

"It is no business of mine," he said, "as I do not know Lord Herbert Arden except by sight. But I was at the dance the other night, and half an hour before the occurrence you are discussing, Lord Herbert was standing beside me, talking of the Egyptian difficulty with the French ambassador. I have often seen men drunk. Lord Herbert Arden was, in my opinion, perfectly sober."

Having delivered himself of this statement, San Giacinto put his very black cigar between his teeth again and took up the evening paper he had been reading.

In the face of such men as Ghisleri and the Marchese, it would have been the merest folly to continue any opposition. Moreover, Pietrasanta was neither stupid nor bad, and he was not a coward.

"I do not know Lord Herbert Arden myself," he said without affectation. "What I said I got on hearsay, and the whole story is evidently a fabrication which we ought to deny. For the rest, Ghisleri, if you are not quite satisfied —" He stopped and looked at Pietro.

"My dear fellow," said the latter, "what more could I have to say about the affair? You all seemed to be in the dark, and I wanted to clear the matter up for the sake of my old friend. That is all. I am very much obliged to you."

After this incident there was less talk at the clubs, and in a few days the subject dropped. But the world said, as usual, that all the men were afraid of Ghisleri, who was a duellist, and of San Giacinto, who was a giant, and who had taken the trouble to learn to fence when he first came to Rome, and that they had basely eaten their words. Men were such cowards, said the world.

Lord Herbert and Laura lived in blissful ignorance of

what was said about them. The preparations for the wedding were already begun, and Laura's modest trousseau was almost all ordered. She and Arden had discussed their future, and having realised that they must live in a very economical fashion for the present and so long as it pleased Heaven to preserve Arden's maternal uncle among the living, they decided that the wedding should be as quiet and unostentatious as possible. The old Prince, however, though far too conscientious to have settled a penny of his inherited fortune upon Laura, even if she had chosen to marry a pauper, was not ungenerous in other ways, and considered himself at liberty to offer the pair some very magnificent silver, which he was able to pay for out of his private economies. As for Donna Adele, she presented them with a couple of handsome wine-coolers — doubtless in delicate allusion to the fictitious story about the champagne Lord Herbert was supposed to have taken. The implied insult, if there was any, was not at all noticed by those who had never heard the tale, however, and Adele had to bide her time for the present.

Meanwhile the season tore along at a break-neck pace, and Lent was fast approaching. Everybody saw and danced with almost everybody else every night, and some of them supped afterwards and gambled till midday, and were surprised to find that their nerves were shaky, and their livers slightly eccentric, and their eyes anything but limpid. But they all knew that the quiet time was coming, the Lent wherein no man can dance, nor woman either, and they amused themselves with a contempt for human life which would have amounted to heroism if displayed in a good cause. "They" of course means the gay set of that particular year. As the Princess of Gerano gave regular informal dances, and two balls at the end of Carnival, she and her daughter were considered to belong more or less to the company of the chief merry-makers. The Savelli couple were in it, also, as a matter of course. Gouache was in it when he pleased, a dozen or fifteen young members of the diplomatic corps, old Spicca, who

always went everywhere, the Contessa dell' Armi, whose
husband was in parliament and rarely went into society,
Ghisleri and twenty or thirty others, men and women who
were young or thought themselves so.

About three weeks before Ash Wednesday, Anastase
Gouache, the perennially young, had a brilliant inspira-
tion. His studio was in an historical palace, and consisted of three halls which might have passed for churches
in any other country, so far as their size was concerned.
He determined to give a Shrove Tuesday supper to the
gay set, with a tableau, and a long final waltz afterwards,
by way of interring the mangled remains of the season,
as he expressed it. The supper should be at the usual
dinner hour instead of at one o'clock, because the gay set
was not altogether as scarlet as it was painted, and did
not, as a whole, care to dance into the morning of Ash
Wednesday. The tableau should represent Carnival
meeting Lent. The Contessa dell' Armi should be in it,
and Ghisleri, and Donna Adele, and possibly San Giacinto
might be induced to appear as a mask. His enormous
stature would be very imposing. The Contessa, with her
classic features and violet eyes, would make an admirable
nun, and there would be no difficulty in getting together
a train of revellers. Ghisleri, lean, straight, and tall,
would do for a Satanic being of some kind, and could head
the Carnival procession. The whole thing would not last
five minutes and the dancing should begin at once.

"Could you not say something, my friend?" asked
Gouache, as he talked the matter over with Ghisleri.

"I could, if you could find something for me to say,"
answered the latter. "But of what use would it be?"

"The density of the public," replied the great painter,
"is, to use the jargon of science, as cotton wool multiplied
into cast iron. You either sink into it and make no noise
at all, or you knock your head against and cannot get
through it. You have never sent a picture to the Salon
without naming it, or you would understand exactly what
I mean. They took a picture I once painted, as an altar

piece, for a scene from the Decameron, I believe — but that was when 1 was young and had illusions. On the whole, you had better find something to say, and say it — verse, if possible. They say you have a knack at verses."

"Carnival meeting Lent," said Ghisleri, thoughtfully. Then he laughed. "I will try — though I am no poet. I will trust a little to my acting to help my lame feet."

Ghisleri laughed again, as though an amusing idea had struck him. That night he went home early, and as very often happened, in a bad humour with himself and with most things. He was a very unhappy man, who felt himself to be always the centre of a conflict between opposing passions, and he had long been in the habit of throwing into a rough, impersonal shape, the thoughts that crossed his mind about himself and others, when he was alone at night. Being, as he very truly said, no poet, he quickly tore up such odds and ends of halting rhyme or stumbling prose, either as soon as they were written, or the next morning. Whatever the form of these productions might be, the ideas they expressed were rarely feeble and were indeed sometimes so strong that they might have even shocked some unusually sensitive person in the gay set.

Being, as has been said, in a bad humour on that particular evening, he naturally had something to say to himself on paper, and as he took his pencil he thought of Gouache's suggestion.   In a couple of hours he had got what he wanted and went to sleep.   The great artist liked the verses when Ghisleri read them to him on the following day, the Contessa consented to act the part of the nun, and the affair was settled.

It was a great success.   Gouache's wife, Donna Faustina, had entered into her husband's plans with all her heart. She was of the Montevarchi family, sister to the Marchesa di San Giacinto, the latter's husband being a Saracinesca, as every Italian knows. Gouache did things in a princely fashion, and sixty people, including all the gay set and a few others, sat down to the dinner which Anastase was pleased to call a supper. Every one was very gay. Almost every one was in some fancy dress or mask, there was no order of precedence, and all were placed where they would have the best chance of amusing themselves. The halls of the studio, with their magnificent tapestries and almost priceless objects of art, were wonderful to see in the bright light. Many of the costumes were really superb and all were brilliant. No one knew what was to take place after supper, but every one was sure there was to be dancing, and all were aware that it was the last dance before Easter, and that the best dancers in Rome were all present.

One of the halls had been hastily fitted up as a theatre, with a little stage, a row of footlights, and a background representing a dark wall, with a deep archway in the middle, like the door of a church. When every one was seated, a deep, clear voice spoke out a little prologue from behind the scenes, and the figures, as they were described, moved out from opposite sides of the stage to meet and group themselves before the painted doorway. Let prologue and verse speak for themselves.

"It was nearly midnight — the midnight that ends Shrove Tuesday and begins Ash Wednesday, dividing Carnival from Lent. I left the tables, where all the world of Rome was feasting, and pretending that the feast was the last of the year. The brilliant light flashed upon silver and gold, dyed itself in amber and purple wine, ran riot amongst jewels, and blazed upon many a fair face and snowy neck. The clocks were all stopped, lest some tinkling bell should warn men and women that the day of laughter was over, and that the hour of tears had struck. But I, broken-hearted, sick in soul and weary of the two months' struggle with evil fate, turned away from them and left them to all they loved, and to all that I could never love again.

"I passed through the deserted ball-room, and my heart sank as I thought of what was over and done. The polished floor was strewn with withered blossoms, with

torn and crumpled favours from the dance, with shreds
of gauze and lace; many chairs were overturned; the light
streamed down like day upon a great desolation; the
heated air was faint with the sad odour of dead flowers.
There was the corner where we sat, she and I, to-night,
last week, a week before that — where we shall never sit
again, for neither of us would.   I shivered as I went out
into the night.

"Through the dark streets I went, not knowing and
not caring whither, nor hearing the tinkling mandolines
and changing songs of the revellers who passed me on
their homeward way."

At this point a mandoline was really heard in the very
faintest tones from behind the scenes, playing scarcely
above a whisper, as it were, the famous "Tout pour
l'amour" waltz of Waldteuffel.

"Suddenly," the voice resumed, above the delicate
notes of the instrument, "the bells rang out and I knew
that my last Carnival was dead."   Here deep-toned bells
struck twelve, while the mandoline still continued.
"Then, all at once, I was aware of two figures in the
gloom, advancing towards the door of a church in front
of me.   The one was a woman, a nun in white robe and
black hood, whose saintly violet eyes seemed to shine
in the darkness.   The other was a monk."

The Contessa dell' Armi came slowly forward, her pale,
clear face lifted and thrown into strong relief by the black
head-dress, grasping a heavy rosary in her folded hands.
Behind her came San Giacinto, recognisable only by his
colossal stature, his face hidden in the shadow of a black
cowl.   Both were admirable, and a murmur of satisfaction ran through the room.

"As they reached the door," continued the reader, "a
wild train of maskers broke into the street."

Ghisleri entered from the opposite side, arrayed somewhat in the manner of Mephistopheles, a mandoline slung
over his shoulder, on which he was playing.   Donna
Adele and a dozen others followed him closely, in every

variety of brilliant Carnival dress, dancing forward with tambourines and castanets, their eyes bright, their steps cadenced to the rhythm of the waltz tune which now broke out loud and clear — fair young women with flushed cheeks, all life, and motion, and laughter; and young men following them closely, laughing, and talking, and singing, all dancing in and out with changing steps. Then all at once the music died away to a whisper; the nun and the monk stood back as though in horror against the church door, while the revellers grouped themselves together in varied poses around them, Ghisleri the central figure in the midst, bowing with a diabolical smile before the white-robed nun.

"In front of all," said the voice again, "stood one whose face I shall never forget, for it was like my own. The features were mine, but upon them were reflected all the sins of my life, and all the evil I have done. I thought the other revellers did not see him."

Again the music swelled and rose, and the train of dancers passed on with song and laughter, and disappeared on the opposite side of the stage. Ghisleri alone stood still before the saint-like figure of the Contessa dell' Armi, bowing low and holding out to her a tall red glass.

"He who was like me stayed behind," continued the reader, "and the light from his glass seemed to shine upon the saintly woman's face, and she drew back as though from contamination, to the monk's side for protection. I knew her face when I saw it — the face I have known too long, too well. Then he who was like me spoke to her, and the voice was my own, but as I would have had it when I have been worst."

As the reader ceased Ghisleri began to speak. His voice was strong, but capable of considerable softness and passionate expression, and he did his best to render his own irregular verses both intelligible and moving to his hearers, in which effort he was much helped by the dress he wore and by the gestures he made use of.

"So we meet at the last!   You the saint, I the time-proved sin-
     ner;
You the young, I the old; I the world-worn, you the beginner;
At the end of the season here, with a glass of wine
To discuss the salvation and — well — the mine and thine
Of all the souls we have met this year, and dealt with,
Of those you have tried to make feel, and those I've felt with:
Though, after all, dear Saint, had we met in heaven
Before you got saintship, or I the infernal leaven
That works so hot to kill the old angel in me —
If you had seen the world then, as I was able to see
Before Sergeant-Major Michael gave me that fall, —
Not a right fall, mind you, taking the facts in all, —
We might have been on the same side both.   But now
It is yours to cry over lost souls, as it's mine to show them how
They may stumble and tumble into the infernal slough.
So here we are.   Now tell me — your honour true —
What do you think of our season?   Which wins?   I?   You?
Ha, ha, ha!   Sweet friend, you can hardly doubt
The result of this two months' hard-fought wrestling bout.
I have won.   You have lost the game.   I drive a trade
Which I invented — perhaps — but you have made.
Without your heaven, friend Saint, what would be my hell?
Without your goodness, could I hope to do well
With the poor little peddler's pack of original sin
They handed me down, when they turned me out to begin
My devil's trade with souls.   But now I ask
Why for eternal penance they gave me so light a task?
You have not condescended from heaven to taste our carnival
     feast,
But if you had tasted it, you would admit at least
That the meats were passably sweet, and might allure
The nicest of angels, whose tastes are wholly pure.
Old friend — I hate you!   I hate your saintly face,
Your holy eyes, your vague celestial grace!
You are too cold for me, whose soul must smelt
In fires whose fury you have never felt.
But come, unbend a little.   Let us chatter
Of what we like best, of what our pride may flatter, —
Salvation and damnation — there's the theme —
Your trade and mine — what I am, and what you seem.
Come, count the souls we have played for, you and I,
The broken hearts you have lost on a careless jog of the die,
Hearts that were broken in ire, by one short, sharp fault of the
     head,

Souls lifted on pinions of fire, to sink on wings of lead.
We have gambled, and I have won, while you have steadily lost,
I laughing, you weeping your senseless saintly tears each time you
  tossed.
So now — give it up ! Dry your eyes ; your heaven's a dream !
Sell your saintship for what it is worth, and come over — the
  Devil's supreme !
Make Judas Iscariot envy the sweets of our sin —
Poor Judas, who ended himself where I could have wished to
  begin !
A chosen complexion — hell's fruit would not have been wasted
Had he lived to eat his fill at the feast he barely tasted.
Ah, my friend, you are horribly good ! Oh ! I know you of old ;
I know all your virtues, your graces, your beauties ; I know they
  are cold !
But I know that far down in the depths of your crystalline soul
There's a spot the archangel physician might not pronounce whole.
There's a hell in your heaven ; there's a heaven in my hell. There
  we meet.
What's perdition to you is salvation to me. Ah, the delicate sweet
Of mad meetings, of broken confessions, of nights unblest !
Oh, the shadowy horror of hate that haunts love's steps without
  rest,
The desire to be dead — to see dead both the beings one hates,
One's self and the other, twin victims of opposite fates !
How I hate you ! You thing beyond Satan's supremest tempta-
  tion,
You creature of light for whom God has ordained no damnation,
You escape me, the being whose searing hand lovingly lingers
On the neck of each sinner to brand him with five red-hot fingers !
You escape me — you dare scoff at me — and I, poor old preten-
  der,
Must sue for your beautiful soul with temptation more tender
Than a man can find for a woman, when night in her moonlit glory
Silvers a word to a poem, makes a poem of a commonplace story !
So I sue here at your feet for your soul and the gold of your heart,
To break my own if I lose you — Lose you ? No — do not start.
You angel — you bitter-sweet creature of heaven, I love you and
  hate you !
For I know what you are, and I know that my sin cannot mate
  you.
I know you are better than I — by the blessing of God ! —
And I hate what is better than I by the blessing of God ! ·
What right has the Being Magnificent, reigning supreme,
To wield the huge might that is his, in a measure extreme ?

What right has God got of his strength to make you all good,
And me bad from the first and weighed down in my sin's leaden
    hood ?
What right have you to be pure, my angel, when I am foul ?
What right have you to the light, while I, like an owl,
Must blink in hell's darkness and count my sins by the bead —
While you can get all you pray for, the wine and the mead
Of a heavenly blessing, showered upon you straight —
Because you chance to stand on the consecrate side of the gate?
Ah! Give me a little nature, give me a human truth!
Give me a heart that feels — and falls, as a heart should — without
    ruth!
Give me a woman who loves and a man who loves again,
Give me the instant's joy that ends in an age of pain,
Give me the one dear touch that I love — and that you fear —
And I will give my empire for the Kingdom you hold dear!
I will cease from tempting and torturing, I will let the poor sinner
    go,
I will turn my blind eyes heavenward and forget this world below,
I will change from lying to truth, and be forever true —
If you will only love me — and give the Devil his due! "

It had been previously arranged that at the last words
the nun should thrust back his Satanic majesty and take
refuge in the church. But it turned out otherwise. As
he drew near the conclusion, Ghisleri crept stealthily up
to the Contessa's side, and threw all the persuasion he
possessed into his voice. But it was most probably the
Contessa's love of surprising the world which led her to
do the contrary of what was expected. At the last line
of his speech, she made one wild gesture of despair, and
threw herself backward upon Ghisleri's ready arm. For
one moment he looked down into her white upturned face,
and his own grew pale as his gleaming eyes met hers.
With characteristic presence of mind, San Giacinto, the
monk, bent his head, and stalked away in holy horror as
the curtain fell.

CHAPTER IV.

As the curtain went down, a burst of applause rang through the room. The poetry, if it could be called poetry, had assuredly not been of a high order, and as for the sentiments it expressed, a good number of the audience were more than usually shocked. But the whole thing had been effective, unexpected, and striking, especially the ending, over which the world smacked its lips.

"I do not like it at all," said Laura Carlyon to Arden, as they left the seats where they had sat together through the little performance.

"They looked very well," he answered thoughtfully. "As for what he said, it was Ghisleri. That is the man's character. He will talk in that way while he does not believe a word he says, or only one out of ten."

"Then I do not like his character, nor him," returned the young lady, frankly. "But I should not say it to you, dear, because he is your best friend. He shows you all the good there is in him, I suppose, and he shows us all the bad."

"No one ever said a truer thing of him," said Arden, limping along by her side. "But I admire the man's careless strength in what he does."

"It is easy to use strong language," replied Laura, quietly. "It is quite another thing to be strong. I believe he is weak, morally speaking. But then, how should I know? One only guesses at such things, after all."

"Yes, it is all guess-work. But I think I understand him better to-night than before."

A moment later the sound of dance music came from the most distant and the largest of the rooms. Ghisleri and the Contessa dell' Armi were already there. She was so slight of figure, that she draped her nun's dress

over her gown, and had only to drop it to be herself again.
They took a first turn together, and Ghisleri talked softly
all the time as he danced.

"Shockingly delightful — the whole thing!" exclaimed
Donna Adele, watching them. "How well they acted it!
They must have rehearsed very often."

"Quite often enough, I have no doubt," said the Marchesa di San Giacinto, with a laugh.

An hour or two passed away and Laura Carlyon found
herself walking about with Ghisleri after dancing with
him. He was a very magnificent personage in his scarlet,
black and gold costume, and Laura herself looked far
more saintly in her evening gown than the Contessa dell'
Armi had looked in the dress of a nun. The two made a
fine contrast, and some one said so, unfortunately within
hearing of both Adele Savelli and Maddalena dell'
Armi. The latter turned her cold face quickly and
looked at Laura and Ghisleri, but her expression did
not change.

"What a very uncertain person that dear Ghisleri is!"
observed Donna Adele to Pietrasanta, as she noticed the
Contessa's movement. She spoke just so loud that the
latter could hear her, then turned away with her companion and walked in the opposite direction.

Meanwhile Ghisleri and Laura were together. The
young girl felt an odd sensation as her hand lay on his
arm, as though she were doing something wrong. She
did not understand his life, nor him, being far too young
and innocent of life's darker thoughts and deeds. She
had said that she disliked him, because that seemed best
to express what she felt — a certain vague wish not to
be too near him, a certain timidity when he was within
hearing which she did not feel at other times.

"You did not mean any of those things you said, did
you, Signor Ghisleri?" she asked, scarcely knowing why
she put the question.

"I meant them all, and much more of the same kind,"
answered Pietro, with a hard laugh.

"I am sorry — I would rather not believe it."

"Why?"

"Because it is not right to think such things, nor even to say them in a play."

Ghisleri looked at her in some surprise. Laura felt a sort of impulse of conscience to say what she thought.

"Ah! you are horribly good!" laughed Ghisleri, quoting his own verse.

Laura felt uncomfortable as she met his glance. He really looked very Satanic just then, as his eyebrows went up and the deep lines deepened between his eyes and on his forehead.

"Either one believes or one does not," she said. "If one does — " She hesitated.

"If one does, does it follow that because God is good to you, He has been good to me also, Miss Carlyon?"

His expression changed, and his voice was grave and almost sad. Laura sighed almost inaudibly, but said nothing.

"Will you have anything?" he asked indifferently, after the short pause. "A cup of tea?"

"Thanks, no. I think I will go to my mother."

Ghisleri took her to the Princess's side and left her.

"You seemed to be having a very interesting conversation with Miss Carlyon just now," said the Contessa dell' Armi as he sat down beside her a quarter of an hour later. "What were you talking about?"

"Sin," answered Ghisleri, laconically.

"With a young girl!" exclaimed the Contessa. "But then — English — "

"You need not raise your eyebrows, nor talk in that tone, my dear lady," replied Ghisleri. "Miss Carlyon is quite beyond sarcasms of that sort. Since you are curious, she was telling me that it was sinful to say the things you were good enough to listen to in the tableau, even in a play."

"Ah? And you will be persuaded, I dare say. What beautiful eyes she has. It is a pity she is so clumsy and

E

heavily made.   Really, has she got you to promise that
you will never say any of those things again — after the
way I ended the piece for you?"

"No.   I have not promised to be good yet.   As for
your ending of the performance, I confess I was surprised."

"You did not show it."

"It would hardly have been in keeping with my part,
would it?   But I can show you that I am grateful at
least."

"For what?" asked the Contessa, raising her eyebrows
again.   "Do you think I meant anything by it?"

"Certainly not," replied Ghisleri, with the utmost
calmness.   "I suppose your instinct told you that it would
be more novel and effective if the Saint yielded than if
she played the old-fashioned scene of crushing the devil
under her foot."

"Would you have let yourself be crushed?"

"By you — yes."   Ghisleri spoke slowly and looked
steadily into her eyes.

The Contessa's face softened a little, and she paused
before she answered him.

"I wish I knew — I wish I were sure whether I really
have any influence over you," she said softly, and then
sighed and looked away.

It was very late when the party broke up, though all
had professed the most positive intention of going home
when the clock struck twelve.   The Princess of Gerano
offered Arden a seat in her carriage, and Pietro Ghisleri
went away alone.   As he passed through the deserted
dining-room, and through the hall where he had sat so
long with the Contessa, he could not help glancing at the
corner where they had talked, and he thought involuntarily of the prologue to the tableau.   His face was set
rather sternly, but he smiled, too, as he went by.

"It is not my last Carnival yet," he said to himself,
as he drew on a great driving-coat which covered his costume completely.   Then he went out.

It is very hard to say whether he was a sentimental man or not. Men who write second-rate verses when they are alone, generally are; but, on the other hand, those who knew him would not have allowed that he possessed a grain of what is commonly called sentimentality. The word probably means a sort of vague desire to experience rather fictitious emotions, with the intention of believing oneself to be passionate by nature, and in that sense the weakness could not justly be attributed to Ghisleri. But on this particular night he did a thing which many people would undoubtedly have called sentimental. He turned aside from the highway when he left the great palace in which Gouache lived, and he allowed himself to wander aimlessly on through the older part of the city, until he stopped opposite to the door of a church which stood in a broad street near the end of the last byway he had traversed. The night was dark and gloomy and the stillness was only broken now and then by a distant snatch of song, a burst of laughter, or the careless twang of a guitar, just as Ghisleri had described it. Indeed it was by no means the first time that he had walked home in the small hours of Ash Wednesday morning, after a night of gaiety and emotion.

It chanced that the church upon which he had accidentally come was the one known as the Church of Prayer and Death. It stands in the Via Giulia, behind the Palazzo Farnese. He realised the fact at once, and it seemed like a bad omen. He stood still a long time, looking at the gloomy door with steady eyes.

"Just such a place as this," he said, in a low tone. "Just such a church as that, just such a man as I am. Is this the comedy and was this evening the reality? Or is it the other way?"

He called up before his eyes the scene in which he had acted, and his imagination obeyed him readily enough. He could fancy how the monk and the nun would look, and the train of revellers, and their movements and gestures. But the nun's face was not that of the Contessa. Another shone out vividly in its place.

"Just God!" ejaculated the lonely man. "Am I so bad as that? Not to care after so much?"

He turned upon his heel as though to escape the vision, and walked quickly away, hating himself. But he was mistaken. He cared — as he expressed it — far more than he dreamed of, more deeply, perhaps, in his own self-contradictory, irregular fashion than the woman of whom he was thinking.

People talked for some time of the Shrove Tuesday feast at Gouache's studio. Then they fell to talking about other things. Lent passed in the usual way, and there was not much change in the lives of the persons most concerned in this history. Ghisleri saw much less of Arden than formerly, of course, as the latter was wholly absorbed by his passion for his future wife. As for the world, it was as much occupied with dinner parties, musical evenings, and private theatricals as it had formerly been with dancing. The time sped quickly. The past season had left behind it an enormous Corpus Scandalorum Romanorum which made conversation both easy and delightful. How many of the unpleasant stories concerning Lord Herbert Arden, Laura Carlyon, Pietro Ghisleri, and Maddalena dell' Armi could have been distinctly traced to Adele Savelli, it is not easy to say. As a matter of fact, very few persons excepting Ghisleri himself took any trouble to trace them at all. To the average worldly taste it is as unpleasant to follow up the origin of a delightfully savoury lie, as it is to think, while eating, of the true history of a beefsteak, from the meadow to the table by way of the slaughter-house and the cook's fingers.

Holy week came, and the muffled bells and the silence in houses at other times full and noisy, and the general air of depression which results, most probably, from a certain amount of genuine repentance and devotion which is felt in a place where by no means all are bad at heart, and many are sincerely good. The gay set felt uncomfortable, and a certain number experienced for the first

time the most distinct aversion to confessing their misdeeds, as they ought to do at least once a year. As far
as they were concerned, Ghisleri's verses expressed more
truth than they had expected to find in them. Ghisleri
himself was rarely troubled by any return of the qualm
which had seized him before the door of the Church of
Prayer and Death, and never again in the same degree.
If he did not go on his way rejoicing, he at all events proceeded without remorse, and was wicked enough and selfish enough to congratulate himself upon the fact.

Arden and Laura were perfectly happy. They, at
least, had little cause to reproach themselves with any
evil done in the world since they had met, and Arden had
assuredly better reason for congratulating himself. It
would indeed have been hard to find a happier man than
he, and his happiness was perfectly legitimate and well
founded. Whether it would prove durable was another
matter, not so easy of decision. But the facts of the
present were strong enough to crush all apprehension for
the future. It was not strange that it should be so.

He could not be said to have led a lonely life. His
family were deeply attached to him, and from earliest
boyhood everything had been done to alleviate the moral
suffering inevitable in his case, and to make his material
existence as bearable as possible, in spite of his terrible
infirmities. But for the unvarying sympathy of many
loving hearts, and the unrelaxing care of those who were
sincerely devoted to him, Arden could hardly have hoped
to attain to manhood at all, much less to the healthy moral
growth which made him very unlike most men in his condition, or the comparative health of body whereby he was
able to enjoy without danger much of what came in his
way. He was in reality a much more social and sociable
man than his friend Ghisleri, though he did not possess
the same elements of success in society. He was, indeed,
sensitive, as has been said, in spite of his denial of the
fact, but he was not bitter about his great misfortune.
Hitherto only one very painful thought had been con-

nected with his deformity, beyond the constant sense of
physical inferiority to other men.   He had felt, and not
without reason, that he must renounce the love of woman
and the hope of wedded happiness, as being utterly beyond
the bounds of all human possibility.   And now, as though
Heaven meant to compensate him to the full for the
suffering inflicted and patiently borne, he had won, almost
without an effort, the devoted love of the first woman for
whom he had seriously cared.   It was almost too good.

Love had taken him, and had clothed him in a new
humanity, as it seemed to him, straightening the feeble
limbs, strengthening the poor ill-matched shoulders,
broadening and deepening the sunken chest that never
held breath enough before wherewith to speak out full
words of passionate happiness.   Love had dawned upon
the dusk of his dark morning as the dawn of day upon a
leaden sea, scattering unearthly blossoms in the path of
the royal sun, breathing the sweet breeze of living joy
upon the flat waters of unprofitable discontent.

To those who watch the changing world with its manifold scenes and its innumerable actors, whose merest farce
is ever and only the prologue to the tragedy which awaits
all, there is nothing more wonderful, nothing more beautiful, nothing more touching — perhaps few things more
sacred — than the awakening of a noble heart at love's
first magic touch.   The greater miracle of spring is done
before our eyes each year, the sun shines and the grass
grows, it rains and all things are refreshed, and the dead
seed's heart breaks with the joy of coming life, bursts and
shoots up to meet the warmth of the sunshine and be kissed
by the west wind.   But we do not see, or seeing, care for
none of these things in the same measure in which we
care for ourselves — and perhaps for others.   We turn
from the budding flower wearily enough at last, and we
own that though it speak to us and touch us, its language
is all but strange and its meaning wholly a mystery.
Nature tells us little except by association with hearts
that have beaten for ours, and then sometimes she tells

us all. But the heart itself is the thing, the reality, the seat of all our thoughts and the stay of all our being. Selfishly we see what it does in ourselves, and in others we may see it and watch it without thought of self. It is asleep to-day, lethargic, heavy, dull, scarce moving in the breast that holds it. To-morrow it is awake, leaping, breaking, splendidly alive, the very source of action, the leader in life's fight, the conqueror of the whole opposing world, bursting to-day the chains of which only yesterday it could not lift a link, overthrowing now, with a touch, the barriers which once seemed so impenetrable and so strong, scorning the deathlike inaction of the past, tossing the mountains of impossibility before it as a child tosses pebbles by the sea. The miracle is done, and love has done it, as only love really can.

But it must be the right sort of love and the heart it touches must be neither common nor unclean in the broad, true sense — such a heart, say, as Herbert Arden's, and such love as he felt for Laura, then and afterwards.

"My life began on the evening when I first met you, dear," he said, as they sat by the open window on Easter Day, looking down at the flowers on the terrace behind the Palazzo Braccio.

"You cannot make me believe that you loved me at first sight!" Laura laughed happily.

"Why not?" he asked gravely. "No woman ever spoke to me as you did then, and I felt it. Is it strange? But it hurt me, too, at first, and I used to suffer during that first month."

"Let that be the first and the last pain you ever have by me," answered the young girl. "I know you suffered, though I cannot even now tell why. Can you?"

"Easily enough," said Arden, resting his chin upon his folded hands as they lay upon the white marble sill of the window, scarcely less white than they. The attitude was habitual to him when he was in that place. He could not rest his elbow on the slab as Laura could, for he was too short as he sat in his chair.

"Easily?" she asked. "Then tell me."

"Very easily. You can understand it too. When I knew that I loved you, I knew — I believed, at least, that another suffering had been found for me, as though I had not enough already. Of course, I was hopeless. How could I tell, how could any one guess that you — you of all women — with your beauty, your youth, your splendid woman's heart — could ever care for me? Oh, my darling — dear, dearest — is there no other word? If I could only tell you half!"

"If you could tell me all, you would only have told half, love," said Laura. "There is mine to tell, too — and it is not a little." She bent down to him and softly kissed the beautiful pale forehead.

The bright flush came to Arden's cheek and died away again in the happy silence that followed. But he raised his head, and his two hands took one of hers and gently covered it.

"You must always be the same to me," he said, almost under his breath. "You have given me this new life — do not take it from me again — the old would be impossible now, not to be lived."

"It need never be lived, it never shall be, if I live myself," answered Laura. "If only I could make you sure of that, I should be really happy. But you do not really doubt it, Herbert, do you?"

"No, dear, to doubt you would be to doubt everything — though it is hard to believe that it can all be so good, and last."

"It does not seem hard to me. Perhaps a woman believes everything more easily than a man does. She needs to believe more, I suppose, and so she finds it easy."

"No woman ever needed to believe as much as I," answered Arden, thoughtfully. He still held her hand, and passed one of his own lightly over it, just pressing it now and then, as though to make sure that it was real. "Except yourself, dear one," he added a moment later, with a sharp, short breath, as though something hurt him.

Laura was quick to understand him, and to feel all that he felt. She heard the little sigh and looked into his face and saw the expression of something like pain there. She laid her free hand upon his shoulder and gazed into his soft brown eyes.

"Herbert dear," she said, "I know what you are thinking about. I was put into the world to make you forget those things, and, God willing, I will. You shall forget them as completely as I do, or if you remember them they shall be dear to you, in a way, as they are to me.".

A wonderful look of loving gratitude was in his face, and he pressed her fingers closely in his.

"Tell me one thing, Laura — only this once and I will not speak of it again. When you touch me — when you lay your hand on my shoulder — when you kiss my forehead — tell me quite truly, dear, do you not feel anything like — like a sort of horror, a kind of repulsion, as if you were touching something — well — unpleasant to touch?"

Poor Arden really did not know how much he was loved. Laura's deep eyes opened wide for an instant, as he spoke, then almost closed again, and her lips quivered. Then suddenly without warning the bright tears welled up and overflowed. She hid her face in her hands and sobbed bitterly.

"Oh, Herbert," she cried, "that you should think it of me, when I love you as though my heart would break!"

With a movement that would have cost him a painful effort at any other time, Arden rose and clasped her to him and tried to soothe her, caressing her thick black hair, and kissing her forehead tenderly, with a sort of passionate reverence that was his own, and speaking such words as came to his lips in the deep emotion of the moment.

"Forgive me, darling, how could I hurt you? Laura — sweetheart Laura — beloved — do not cry — I know it now — I shall never think of it again. No, dear, no — there, say you have forgiven me!"

"Forgiven you, dear — what is there to forgive?" She looked up with streaming eyes.

"Everything, love — those tears of yours, first of all —"

She dried her eyes and made him sit down again before she spoke, looking out of the window at the flowers.

"It is not your fault," she said at last. "I have not shown you how I love yet — that is all. But I will, soon."

"You have shown it already, dear — far more than you know."

The world might have been surprised could it have seen the two together — the tipsy cripple, as it called Arden, and the girl who loved Francesco Savelli, as it unhesitatingly denominated Laura. It would have been a little surprised at first, and then, on mature reflection, it would have said that it was all a comedy, and that both acted it very well. Was it not natural that Arden should want a pretty wife and that Laura should take any husband that presented himself, since she could get no better? And in that case why should not each act a comedy to gain the other's hand? The world did that sort of thing every day, and what the world did Arden and Laura could very well afford to do; and after all, it was not of the slightest importance, since they were both going away, so why should one talk about them? The answer to that last question is so very hard to find that it may be left to those who put it. Donna Adele seemed satisfied, and that was the principal consideration for the present.

"My poor sister!" she exclaimed to Ghisleri one day.

"Step-sister," observed Pietro, correcting her.

"Oh, we were always quite like real sisters," answered Adele. "Of course, my dear Ghisleri, I know what a splendid man Lord Herbert is, in everything but his unfortunate deformity. Any one can see that in his face, and besides, you would not have chosen him for your friend if he were not immensely superior to other men."

Ghisleri puffed at his cigarette, looked at her, laughed, and puffed again.

"But that one thing," continued Adele, "I cannot understand how she can overlook it, can you? I assure you if my father had told me to marry Lord Herbert, I should have done something quite desperate. I think I should almost have refused. I would almost rather have had to marry you."

"Really?" Pietro showed some amusement. "Do you think you could have loved me in the end?" he inquired as though he were asking for information of the most commonplace kind.

"Loved you?" Adele laughed rather unnaturally. "It would have been something definite, at all events," she added. "Either love or hate."

"And you do not believe that your step-sister can ever love or hate Arden? There is more in him than you imagine."

"I dare say, but not of the kind I should like. Besides, they say that though he never drinks quite too much, he is sometimes very excited and behaves and talks very strangely."

"They say that, do they? Who are 'they'?" Ghisleri's eyes suddenly grew hard, and his jaw seemed to become extremely square.

"They? Oh, many people, of course. The world says so. Do not be so dreadfully angry. What difference can it make to you? I never said that he drank too much."

"If you should hear people talking about him in that way," said Ghisleri, quietly, "you might say that the story is not true, since there is really no truth in it at all. Arden is almost like an invalid. He drinks a glass of hock at breakfast and a glass or two of claret at dinner. I rarely see him touch champagne, and he never takes liqueurs. As for his being excited and behaving strangely, that is a pure fabrication. He is the quietest man I know."

"It is really of no use to be so impressive," answered Adele. "It makes me uncomfortable."

"That is almost as disagreeable a thing as to meet a looking-glass when one comes home at seven in the morning," observed Pietro. "Let us not talk about it."

Donna Adele had gone as near as she dared to saying

something unpleasant about Lord Herbert Arden, and Ghisleri had checked her with a wholesome shock. In his experience he had generally found that his words carried weight with them, for some reason which he did not even attempt to explain. If the truth were known, it would appear that Adele was at that time much inclined to like Ghisleri, and was willing to sacrifice even the pleasure of saying a sharp thing rather than offend him. The short conversation here reported took place in her boudoir late in the afternoon, and when Ghisleri went away his place was soon taken by the Marchesa di San Giacinto — a lady of sufficiently good heart, but of too ready tongue, with coal-black, sparkling eyes, and a dark complexion relieved by a bright and healthy colour — rather a contrast to the rest of the Montevarchi tribe.

"Pietro Ghisleri has been here," observed Adele, in the course of conversation.

"To meet Maddalena, I suppose," laughed the Marchesa, not meaning any harm.

"No. They did it once, and I told Pietro that I would not have that sort of thing in my house," said Adele, with dignity.

As a matter of fact, she had not dared to say a word to Ghisleri on the subject, but he and the Contessa had decided that Adele's drawing-room was not a safe place for meeting, and it was quite true that they had carefully avoided finding themselves there together ever since. But Adele was well aware that Flavia San Giacinto and Ghisleri were by no means intimate, and were not likely to exchange confidences; and though the Marchesa was ready enough at repeating harmless tales in the world, she was reticent with her husband, whom she really loved, and whose good opinion she valued.

"Was he amusing?" asked Flavia. "He sometimes is."

"He was not to-day, but the conversation was. You know how intimate he is with Laura's little lord?"

"Of course! What did he say?"

"And you remember the story about the champagne at the Gerano ball, when he carried Arden out of the room and put him to bed?"

"Perfectly," answered the Marchesa, with a smile.

"Yes. Well, I pressed him very hard to-day, to find out what the little man's habits really are. You see he is to be of the family, and we must really find out. My dear, it is quite dreadful! He says positively that Arden never touches liqueurs, but when I drove him to it, he had to admit that he drinks all sorts of wines — Rhine wine, claret, burgundy, champagne — everything! It is no wonder that it goes to his head, poor little fellow. But I am sorry for Laura."

"After all," said Flavia, "one cannot blame him much, if he tries to be a little gay. He must suffer terribly."

"Oh, no, one cannot blame him," assented Adele.

Flavia San Giacinto was somewhat amused, knowing, as she did, that Adele had herself originated the tale about Lord Herbert. And late that evening the temptation to repeat what she had heard became too strong for her. She told it all in the strictest confidence to her dearest friend, Donna Maria Boccapaduli. But Donna Maria was a little absent-minded at the moment, her eldest boy having got a cold which threatened to turn into whooping cough, and her husband having written to her from the country, asking her to come down the next day and give her advice about some necessary repairs in the castle.

On the following afternoon — it was still during Lent — she met the Contessa dell' Armi on the steps of a church after hearing a sermon. The Contessa was very pale and looked as though she had been crying.

"Only think, my dear," began Donna Maria. "It is quite true that Lord Herbert drinks. Adele knows all about it."

"Does she?" asked the Contessa, indifferently enough. "How did she find it out?"

"Ghisleri told her ever so many stories about it yesterday afternoon — in the strictest confidence, you know."

"Indeed! I did not think that Signor Ghisleri was the sort of man who gossiped about his friends. Goodbye, dear. I shall see more of you when Lent is over."

Thereupon the Contessa got into the carriage with rather an odd expression on her face. As she drove away alone, she bit her lip, and looked as though she were trying to keep back certain tears that rose in her eyes.

CHAPTER V.

On the Saturday succeeding Easter, Lord Herbert Arden and Laura Carlyon were married. The ceremony was conducted, as they both desired, very quietly and unostentatiously, as was becoming for a young couple who must live economically. Few persons were asked to be present at the wedding service, and among them was Pietro Ghisleri. He had seen English weddings before, but he looked on with some curiosity and with rather mixed feelings of satisfaction and regret. He thought of his own life as he stood there, and for one moment he sincerely wished that he were only awaiting his turn to be dealt with as Arden was, to be taken by the hand, joined to the woman he loved, and turned out upon the world a well-behaved, proper, married man. The next moment he smiled faintly and rather bitterly. Marriage had not been instituted for men like him, thought Ghisleri. If it had been, it would hardly have been so successful an institution as it has proved itself. As for the young couple, he wished them well. Arden was almost the only man for whom he felt any attachment, and he had the most sincere admiration for Laura.

Without feeling anything in the least resembling affection for the lovely English girl, he was conscious that he thought of her very often. Her eyes, which he called holy, and saintly, and sweet, and dark in his rough rhymed

impressions of the day, haunted him by night, like the
eyes of a sad angel following him in his unblest wanderings through life. Of love for her, he felt not the slightest thrill. His pulse never quickened when she came,
nor was he at all depressed by her departure. If he had
cared for her in the very least, it must have caused him
some little pain to see her married to another before his
eyes. Instead, the only passing regret he felt, was that he
could not himself stand in some such position as Arden,
but by another woman's side. To that other he gave all,
as he honestly believed, which he had to give. It was
long, too, since the very possibility of loving a young girl
had crossed his mind, and since his early youth there had
not been anything approaching to the reality of such a
love in his life. And yet he knew that he was in some degree under Laura's influence, and in a way in which he
was assuredly not under that of the Contessa dell' Armi.
The consciousness of this fact annoyed him. There was
a good deal of a certain sort of loyalty in his nature, bad
as he believed himself to be, and bad as many honest and
good people who read this history will undoubtedly say
that he was. If such badness could be justified or even
excused, it would not be hard to find some reasonable excuses for him, and after all he was probably not worse
than a hundred others to be found in the society of every
great city. He thought he was worse, sometimes, as he
had told Arden, because he himself also thought that he
was more fully aware than most men of what he was doing and of the consequences of his deeds. It is most
likely, considering his character, that at that time Laura
Carlyon represented to him a species of ideal such as he
could admire with all his heart at a distance, and so
nearly coinciding with his own as to be very often in his
thoughts in the place of the one he had so long ago contracted for himself. All this sounds very complicated,
while the facts in the case were broadly plain. He
appreciated Laura in the highest degree, and did not love
her at all. He was sincerely glad that his best if not

his only intimate friend should marry her, and when he bid them good-bye he did not feel the smallest twinge of regret except as at a temporary parting from two persons whom he liked.

"You must come and stop with us this summer," said Arden, looking up at him with flushed and happy face. "You know how glad my brother always is to see you. Besides, you are an old friend of my wife's, if any further reasons are necessary. She wants you to come too."

"Of course I do," said Laura, promptly, as she held out her hand.

Strange to say, she had felt far less of that unpleasant, half-timid, half-pained dislike for Ghisleri, since she had grown used to the idea of being Herbert Arden's wife.

And now that her name was really changed, and she was forever bound to her husband, she felt it not at all. It was strange, considering the circumstances, that she should have the certainty that Arden could and would protect her, come what might. The poor little shrunken frame certainly did not suggest the manly strength to shield a woman in danger, which every woman loves to feel. The thin, white hand would have been but a bundle of threads in Ghisleri's strong grip. And yet Laura Arden, as she now was to be called, knew that she would trust her husband to take her part and win against a stronger and a worse man than Ghisleri, should she ever be in need; and, what is more, Ghisleri saw that she did, and his admiration rose still higher. There must be something magnificent in a woman who could so wholly forget such outward frailness and deformity in the man she loved, as to forget also that sometimes in life a man's hand may need that same common brute strength, just to match it against another's, for a woman's dear sake. Such love as that, thought Pietro, must be supremely noble, unselfish, and lasting. Being founded upon no outward illusion, there was no reason why anything should undermine it, nor why the foundation itself should ever crumble away.

That was his view, and, on the whole, it was not an unjust one. For the facts were true. If, when they drove away to the station, Herbert Arden had suddenly, by magic, been clothed in the colossal frame and iron strength of San Giacinto himself, Laura would have felt no safer nor more perfectly shielded and guarded from earthly harm than she really did while she was pulling up the window lest her husband should catch cold even in the mild April air, and lovingly arranging the heavy silk scarf about his neck.

They went southward by common consent, as indeed they did everything. They would go to England later in the year, in June perhaps, when it was warmer. In the meanwhile Arden's brother had offered them his yacht, and they could cruise for a month in the Mediterranean, almost choosing their own climate day by day, and wholly independent of all the manifold annoyances, inconveniences, and positive sufferings which beset the path of young married couples who have not yachts at their disposal. What both most desired was to be alone together, to have enough of each other at last, free from the tiresome daily little crowd of social spectators, and this they could nowhere accomplish so pleasantly and completely as in the luxuriously fitted vessel lent them by Arden's brother. The latter had not seen fit to come to the wedding, but Arden had in no way taken it amiss, though the world had found plenty to say on the subject, and not by any means to Arden's credit. The said brother was a decidedly eccentric person of enormous wealth, who hated anything at all resembling publicity or public ceremony, and was, moreover, a very bad correspondent.

"I am very glad to hear of your engagement, my dear old brother," he wrote. "They say Miss Carlyon is good and beautiful. I have no doubt she is, though I do not at this moment recollect knowing any woman who was both. I have sent the yacht to Naples for you, if you care for a cruise. Keep her as long as you like, and telegraph if you want her sent anywhere else — Nice, for instance, or Venice. Ask your wife to wear the pearls by way of making acquaintance at second hand. They are what I could find. I send a man with them, as they might get lost. Now good-bye, dear boy, enjoy yourself and come to us as soon as you can. Yours ever, HARRY.

"P.S. As it is often such a bore to draw money in those funny Italian towns, I enclose a few circular notes which may be useful. Bess and the children are all well and send love and lots of congratulations. I suppose you have written to Uncle Herbert."

The few circular notes thus casually alluded to amounted to two thousand pounds, and it would be unsafe to speculate on the value of the pearls which the messenger brought on his person and delivered safely into Arden's hands. "Harry" was not over-lavish, except where his brother was concerned, and always inwardly regretted that Herbert needed so little and insisted upon living within his modest income. To "give things to Herbert" was one of the few real pleasures he extracted from his great fortune. On the present occasion Arden was glad to accept the money, for he had the very most vague notions of the expense of married life, and had anticipated real economy during his honeymoon, which, of course, could not be quite as pleasant to Laura as having plenty of money to spend. That last little difficulty being removed, he felt that he could give himself up light-hearted to the idyl of perfect love which Laura had brought into his existence.

And forthwith the idyl began, delicate, gentle, lovely as love's life can be where soul and heart are in harmony, heart to soul, while purity teaches innocence what it is to be man and wife.

The harmony was real. Laura and her husband had much in common, intellectually and morally. Not, indeed, that she made any pretence to superior intelligence or extended culture. Even had she possessed very remarkable capabilities, the surroundings in which she had been brought up had not been of a nature to develop them beyond the average. But she was not especially gifted, except perhaps in having a good memory and a somewhat unusually sound judgment in most matters. Yet she was not without taste, and such as she had was not only both healthy and refined, but coincided to an extraordinary degree with Arden's own. Both liked the same authors, the same general kind of art, the same things in nature, and very generally the same people. Both were perhaps at that time somewhat morbidly inclined to a sort of semi-transcendentalism, Arden by nature and circumstances, and Laura by attraction. It must not be supposed that they went to any lengths in that direction. They did not speculate on spiritual marriage, nor did they agree with that famous philosopher who at the last was sure that the earth was turning into a bun and the sea into lemonade in order that man might eat, drink, and be happy without effort. They did not pursue improbable theories nor offer subtle perfumes before the altar of impossibility. But they felt a certain almost unnatural indifference to the concrete world, and lived in a world of ideas, thoughts, and affections which were quite their own. It was impossible to predict whether such an existence would last, or whether it would ultimately change into one more evidently stable, if also less removed from earth. For the present, at least, both were indescribably happy.

The question how far it is possible for one of two loving beings to forget and grow unconscious of very great physical defect in the other is in itself interesting as showing how far, in a well-organised nature, the immaterial can get the better of grosser things. To explain what Laura felt would be to explain the deepest impulses of humanity, and those may attempt it who feel themselves equal to the task and are attracted by it. The fact, as such, is undeniable. On the whole, too, it may be said that there is no great reason why a very refined intelligence should not overlook material considerations as completely as in the majority of cases the more coarsely planned consciousness forgets the existence of intellectual and moral deformity.

Such extreme refinement may not be durable. There is a refinement of nature, inborn, delicate, and sensitive, and there is a refinement which depends for its existence upon youth and innocence. Laura possessed all the latter, and something of the former as well. She would have been shocked and deeply wounded had she been told that she had married Herbert Arden out of pity, and yet pity had undeniably given the first impulse to her love.

The circumstances, too, were favourable for its growth. Neither had felt much regret in leaving Rome. Apart from her affection for her mother, Laura had never found much that was congenial in the city in which she had been brought up as though it had been her birthplace. As for Arden himself, he was too much accustomed to travelling from place to place to prefer one city to another in any great degree. So the two were alone together and desired nothing beyond what they had, which, perhaps, is the ideal condition for lovers. To most people, however, the honeymoon is a terrible trial — probably because most young couples are not very desperately in love with each other. They wander aimlessly about in all directions, a sort of joint sacrifice, perpetually tortured and daily offered up on the altar of the diabolical courier, crushed beneath the ubiquitous Juggernaut hotel-keeper, bound continually in new and arid places to be torn by the vulture guide, and ultimately sent home more or less penniless, quite temperless, and perhaps permanently disgusted with one another and with married life. And yet the absurd farce is kept up, in ninety and nine cases out of a hundred, because custom sanctions it — as though the sanction of custom were necessary when two people wish to be harmlessly happy in their own way.

But with the Ardens it was quite different. They were quite beyond the regions of the guide, the courier, and the hotel-keeper, and they loved each other so much that neither ever irritated the other, a condition of exist-

ence probably closely resembling that of the saints in
paradise.

Nothing could exceed Laura's watchfulness and care
where Arden's health was concerned, and, fortunately
for her, he was not one of those men who resent being
constantly taken care of.   Indeed, poor man, he needed
all she gave him in that way, for the winter season with
its unusual gaiety and the necessary exposure to a certain amount of night air in all weathers, had severely
tried his constitution.   But now the sea and the southern
sun strengthened him, and sometimes there was even
something like healthy colour in his face.   Happiness,
too, is said to be a good medicine, better perhaps than
any in the world, and Arden had his share of it, and a
most abundant share.   Never, he said to himself, had a
man been so blessed as he, nor at a time when he so little
expected blessings, having made up his mind that all he
could hope for had already been given him in this world.
He almost forgot that he was a cripple, as he sat in his
deep cane chair by Laura's side, looking from her to the
dancing light on the water, and from the blue water to
her dark eyes again.   He seemed to go every day through
a round of beauty, from one delicious vision to another,
returning between each to that one of all others which
he loved best, and knew to be all his own.   And those
same eyes of Laura's grew less sad than they had been in
the beginning.   The sunlight got into them, as into dark
jewels, and made stars of light about their central depths.
The soft wind blew on her clear white cheek and lent her
natural, healthy pallor a warmth it had not before.   Her
very step grew more elastic, and the firm, well-shaped
hands seemed more than ever strong.   Almost beautiful
before, there were moments when she was quite beautiful
indeed, as innocent girlhood changed to pure womanhood
in the sweet southern air.

Laura read aloud a great deal in the intervals of conversation, and the days passed almost too quickly.   The
vessel was a large steam-yacht, of the modern type, com-

fortable in the extreme, and capable of accommodating
a large party — for two persons it was almost palatial.
Whatever the weather, cool or hot, rainy or dry, rough
or fair, there was always a place where they could install
themselves in the morning or the afternoon, and talk and
read to their hearts' content. They had no fixed plan
either in their wanderings, but went where their fancy
took them, to Palermo, to Messina, to Syracuse. They
sat together in the vast ruined theatre above magic Taor-
mina, and gazed on the sunlit sea and Etna's snowy crest.
They went to Malta, they drove, side by side, through
the lovely gardens of Corfu. They ran in fair weather
up to the lagoons of Venice, and wandered in a gondola
through the wide canals and narrow water lanes of the most
beautiful city in the world. Then down the long Adri-
atic again, past Zara and Xanthe, round Matapan to the
Piræus — then, when they had had their fill of Athens,
away by one long run to Sicily again, to Algiers next,
and then to Barcelona and the Spanish coast, homeward
bound at last, towards England. For the weather was
growing warm now, and Laura noticed that she saw less
often in Arden's face the colour she had watched with
such pleasure during the first weeks. There was no cause
for anxiety, she thought, but it was possible that he
needed always an even temperature, neither cold nor hot,
and it was time to reach England, before the July sun
had scorched the southern land.

And throughout all this quiet time the song of happiness was ever in their ears. The world they cared so
little for, and which had taken the trouble to say such
disagreeable things about them, was left infinitely far
behind in their new life. From time to time letters
reached Laura from Rome, and Arden had one from Ghisleri, containing little detailed news, but full of angry
threats at a kind of general undefined enemy, which might
be humanity taken all together, or might be some one
particular person whom the writer had in his mind. Pietro
generally wrote in that way. Rarely, indeed, did he mention people by name, and then only when he had some-

thing to say to their credit. It was a part of what Arden called his absurd reticence, and which, absurd or not, was certainly exaggerated. Possibly Ghisleri had, at some time in his youth, experienced the extremely unpleasant consequences of being indiscreet, and had promised himself not to succumb to that form of weakness again. At all events, he found that though Arden sometimes laughed at him, he never got into trouble through being discreet, and other people were not disposed to be merry at his expense. It was a long time since he had quarrelled with any one, and, having turned peaceable, the world promptly accused him of cynicism and indifference, an accusation which did not annoy him at all. Indeed, it was rather convenient than otherwise, that people should think of him as they did, since the result was that less was expected of him than of most people.

Laura's mother wrote loving letters, full of simple household news, and of solicitude for her daughter and Arden, asking many questions as to their plans for the future, and continually expressing the hope that they would spend the coming winter in Rome.

"What do you think of it?" Laura asked one day, as they sat together on deck in the sunshine.

"That is one of those things which you must decide, dear," answered Arden. "Of course I suppose I ought to spend the winter in the south as usual. I do not believe I could stand England in December and January. There are lots of delightful southern places where we could stay a few months, besides Rome — but then, in Rome you will have your mother. That makes a great difference."

"You are first now, love," said Laura. "You come before my mother — much as I love her."

"Darling — how good you are!" He took her hand and kissed it softly.

"Not half as good as I ought to be. But there are two things to be considered, dear. There is the climate, as you say, and then there is a social question we have never talked about — it seems so far away now. In the first place, does Rome really suit you? Are you always well there, as you were last winter?"

"Oh, yes. I have always been perfectly well in Rome, and I like the place immensely, besides."

"And you have your friend, Signor Ghisleri, too. That is another point. On the other hand, I do not think either of us would ever wish to stay a whole winter with my mother and step-father. We must live somewhere by ourselves, and we shall have to live very quietly."

"The more quietly the better. Is that the social question, darling?"

"No," answered Laura, "but it is connected with it. There is something I never spoke of. Did it ever strike you, when you first knew me, that somehow I was not so much liked as other girls in society? Do not think I ask the question out of any sort of vanity. I want to know what your impression was. Tell me quite frankly, will you?"

"Of course I will. It did strike me — I never knew whether you were aware of it. I even tried to find out the reason of it, and to some extent I believe I did."

"Did you?" asked Laura, with sudden interest. "I wish I knew — I have so often thought about it all."

Arden laughed, leaning back in his chair and looking at her face.

"It is the most absurd story I ever heard," he said. "I ought not even to say I heard it, for I guessed it from little things that happened. People think that your step-sister's husband, Savelli, is in love with you, and I suppose they imagine that you have something to do with it — encouraged him, and that sort of thing. I am quite sure that Donna Adele — am I to call her Adele now? — is jealous, for I have witnessed the manifestation with my own eyes. It is all too utterly ridiculous, but as you are quite English you were at a disadvantage, and were not as popular as you ought to have been."

He laughed again, and this time Laura joined in his laughter.

"Is that it?" she cried. "Poor Francesco! To think
of any one suspecting that he could be in love with me,
when he is so perfectly happy with his wife! And he is
always so nice, and talks to me more than any one.
Whenever I am stranded at a party, he comes and takes
care of me."

"That is probably the origin of the gossip," observed
Arden, still smiling. "But I do not think we shall
have any nonsense of that sort now. Do you think your
mother understood it all?"

"No — and I believe she was far less conscious that
there was anything wrong, than I was. Poor Francesco!
I cannot help laughing."

Laura was sincerely amused by the tale, as she well
might be, and as Pietro Ghisleri would have been, had
he heard it. The story Arden had put together out of
the evidence he had was, as a matter of fact, the very
converse of the one actually circulated.

"I do not see," said he, "why this bit of fantastic
gossip need be taken into consideration, when we are
talking of our winter in Rome. What difference can it
possibly make?"

"For you, dear — and a little for me, too. Neither
of us would care to go back to a society where there was
anything to make us disliked. As you say, there are
plenty of other places, and as for my mother, she could
come and see us, and stop a little while, and I am sure
she would if we asked her."

"Do you mean to say, Laura, that you seriously believe
our position would not be everything it ought to be?"
asked Arden, in some surprise.

"Oh, no; it would be all right, of course. Only we
might not be exactly the centre of the gay set."

"Which neither of us care to be in the least."

"Not in the least. We are our own set, you and I —
are we not?"

Laura thought of what Arden had told her for a long
time afterwards, and tried to explain to herself by his

theory all the infinitesimal details which had formerly shown her that she was not a universal favourite. But the story did not cover all the ground. Of one thing, however, she became almost certain — Adele was her enemy, for some reason or other, and was a person to beware of, should Laura and her husband return to Rome. It had taken her long to form this conviction, but being once formed it promised to be durable, as her convictions generally were.

It was with sincere regret that the couple left the yacht at last. They had grown to look upon it almost as a permanent home, and to wish that it might be so altogether. Nevertheless Laura could not but see that Arden's health improved again as they reached a cooler climate and travelled northward towards his brother's home. The season was not yet over in London, but "Harry" did not like London much, and did not like the season there at all. What the Marchioness thought about it no one knows to this day, but she appeared to resign herself with a good grace to the life her husband chose to lead. The latter welcomed his brother and Laura in his own fashion, with an odd mixture of cordiality and stiffness, the latter only superficial, the former thoroughly genuine and heartfelt, as Arden explained to his wife without delay.

Existence in an English country house was quite new to her, and but for the abominable weather for which that year remained famous, she would at first have enjoyed it very much. The rain, however, seemed inexhaustible. Day after day it poured, night after night the heavy mists rose from park, and woodland, and meadow, and moor. It seemed as though the sun would never shine again. Arden never grew weary of those long days spent with Laura, nor indeed was she ever tired of being with the man she loved. But being young and strong, she would gladly have breathed the bright air again, while he, on his part, lost appetite, caught cold continually, and grew daily paler and more languid. Little by little Laura became anxious about him and her care redoubled. He

had never looked as he looked now, even when most worn
and wearied out with the life of society he had led in
Rome before his marriage. His face was growing thin,
almost to emaciation, and his hands were transparent.
Laura made up her mind that something must be done at
once. It was clear that he longed for the south again,
and it was probable that nothing else could restore him
to comparative strength.

"Let us go away, Herbert," she said one day. "You
are not looking well, and I believe we shall never see the
sun again unless we go to the south."

"No," answered Arden, "I am not well. I shall be
all right again as soon as we get to Rome."

He seemed to take it for granted that Rome should be
their destination, and on the whole Laura was glad of it.
She would be glad to see her mother, too, after so many
months of separation. So it was decided, and before
long they were once more on their way.

It was not an easy journey for either of them. Arden
was now decidedly out of health, and needed much care
at all times, while Laura herself was so nervous and anxious about him that she often felt her hand tremble violently when she smoothed his cushion in the railway
carriage, or poured him out something to drink. She
would not hear of being helped, when her husband's man,
who had been with him since his boyhood, privately entreated her to take a nurse, and to give herself rest from
time to time, especially during the journey.

"We must not let his lordship know how ill he is,
Donald," she answered gently. "You must be very careful about that, too, when you are alone with him. He
will be quite well again in Rome," she added hopefully.

Donald shook his head wisely, and refrained from further expostulation. He had discovered that his new
mistress did not easily change her mind upon any subject,
and never changed it at all when she thought she was
right in regard to Lord Herbert's health.

And in due time they reached the end of their journey,

and took up their quarters in the old house known as the Tempietto, which stands just where the Via Gregoriana and the Via Sistina end together in the open square of the Trinità de' Monti — a quarter and a house dear to English people since the first invasion of foreigners, but by no means liked or considered especially healthy by the Romans.

CHAPTER VI.

MEANWHILE, the lives of some of the other persons concerned in this history were less idyllic, and very probably more satisfactory to themselves. Having survived the season, and having borne the severe Lenten mortification implied in not capering nightly to the tune of two or three fiddles and a piano, the world arose after Easter like a giant refreshed with wine, and enjoyed a final fling before breaking up for the summer. Having danced with the windows shut, it now danced with the windows open, and found the change delightful, as indeed it is. Instead of sitting in corners together, the couples who had anything to say to one another now stood or sat in the deep embrasures, glancing up at the starlit sky to see whether the dawn were yet breaking. As for the rest, there was little change at all. The little Vicomte de Bompierre had transferred his attentions from the Marchesa di San Giacinto to Donna Maria Boccapaduli, and the Marchesa, who was in love with her husband, did not seem to care at all, but remained on the best of terms with Donna Maria, to the latter's infinite satisfaction. The Contessa dell' Armi attracted more attention because some one had started the report that dell' Armi himself was in a state of jealousy bordering upon delirium, that he had repeatedly struck her, and that he spent the few hours he could spare from this unwholesome exercise and from his parliamentary duties in tearing out his hair by the handful.

The picture of dell' Armi evoked by these stories was striking, dramatic, and somewhat novel, so that every one was delighted. As a matter of fact, the Count did not care a straw for his wife, rarely saw her at all, and then only to discuss the weather. He had married her in order that her fortune might help him in his political career, he had got what he wanted, and he was supremely indifferent to the rest. The sad part of the matter was — if any one had known the truth — that poor Maddalena dell' Armi had been married out of a convent, and had then and there fallen madly in love with him, her own husband. He had resented her excessive affection, as it interfered with his occupations and amusements, and after an interval of five years, during which the unhappy young wife shed endless tears and suffered intensely, he had the satisfaction of seeing that she no longer loved him in the least, and rather avoided him than otherwise. In taking a fancy to Pietro Ghisleri he thought she had shown considerable discrimination, since every one knew that Ghisleri was a very discreet man. The amazing cynicism of his view altogether escaped him. He was occupied in politics. If he had observed it, he would have undoubtedly laughed as heartily as he did when a lady on the outskirts of society told him that he was supposed to be a jealous husband.

But the rest of the world watched Maddalena and Pietro with great interest. They had quarrelled — or they had made it up — they had not danced together during one whole evening — they had danced a waltz and then a quadrille, the one after the other — Maddalena had been crying — by a coincidence, Ghisleri looked unusually strong and well — Pietro, again, was looking somewhat haggard and weary, and the Contessa met the world that evening with a stony stare. There was endless matter for speculation, and accordingly the world speculated without end, and, as usual, to no puprose. Ghisleri was absolutely reticent, and Maddalena was a very proud woman, who, in spite of her past sufferings, did her best not to let any one suspect that she and her husband were on bad terms. She was also unhappy in the present about a very different matter, concerning which she was not inclined to speak with any one. Donna Adele's last decided attempt to defame Lord Herbert Arden had, to a certain extent, been successful, but it had also produced another result of which Adele did not know, but which would have given her even greater satisfaction. It had almost caused a quarrel between Ghisleri and the Contessa.

It will be remembered that the latter heard the story from Donna Maria Boccapaduli on the steps of a church in Holy Week. She was at the time more unhappy than usual. Something had touched the finer chords of her nature, and she felt a sort of horror of herself and of the life she was leading — very genuine in its way, and intensely painful. Donna Maria's story was revolting to her, for just then everything and everybody seemed to be false — even Ghisleri. She did not even stop, as she would have done at any other time, to weigh the value of the story, and to ask herself whether it were likely that he could thus deliberately betray his friend, and especially to Adele Savelli whom she believed he disliked. Even with her he was reticent, and she had never quite assured herself of his opinion concerning Adele, but she had watched him narrowly and had drawn her own conclusions. And now, if he had betrayed the man whom he called his friend, he must be capable of betraying the woman he loved.

"Is it true that you have been talking to Donna Adele Savelli about your friend Arden?" she asked, when they met later on the same afternoon.

"Quite true," answered Ghisleri, indifferently. "We were talking about him yesterday afternoon."

"Do you mind telling me what you said?" asked the Contessa, her eyes hardening and her whole face growing scornful.

"I have not the least objection," said Ghisleri, coldly.

He at once gave her all the details of the conversation as far as he could remember them; his memory was accurate in such matters and he scarcely omitted a word.

"Am I to believe you or her?" asked the Contessa when she had listened to the end.

"As I am speaking the truth, it might be as well to believe me."

"And how am I to know that you are speaking the truth, now or at any other time? You would not change colour, nor look at me less frankly, if you were telling me the greatest falsehood imaginable. Why should I believe you?"

"I am sure I do not know," answered Ghisleri. "I would only like to be sure whether, as a general rule, you mean to believe me in future, or not. If you do not, I need not say anything, I suppose. Conversation would be singularly simplified."

"You would not be so angry with me now, if your story were true," said the Contessa, with a forced laugh.

"A man may reasonably be annoyed at being called a liar even by a lady," retorted Ghisleri.

"And you do not take the least trouble to defend yourself—"

"Not the least. Why should you believe my defence any more than my plain statement? You have rather a logical mind—you ought to see that."

"Are you trying to quarrel with me? You will succeed if you go on in this way."

"No. I am doing my best to answer your questions. I should be very sorry to quarrel with you. You know it. Or are you going to doubt that too?"

"From the tone in which you say it, and from the way you act, I am inclined to."

"You are in a very unbelieving humour to-day."

"I have reason to be."

"Am I the cause?"

"Yes." The Contessa was not quite sure why she said it, but for the moment she felt that it was true, as perhaps it was in an indirect way.

"Do you know that although you have asked me a great many questions which I have answered as well as I could, you have not told me what it is I am accused of saying?"

"You are accused of saying," answered the Contessa, looking straight into his eyes, "that your friend Lord Herbert Arden is in the habit of taking too much wine. Is that so nice a thing to have said?"

Ghisleri's face darkened, and the blood throbbed in his temples.

"As I have told you precisely what I really said," he replied, "I shall say nothing more. Only this — if you have any sense of justice left, which I begin to doubt, you will ask San Giacinto whether he thinks it probable that I would say such a thing. That is all. I suppose you will believe him."

"I do not think I believe any one. Besides, as you say, he can only testify to your character, and say that the thing is improbable. Of course he would do that. Men always defend each other against women."

"He can tell you something more if he chooses," answered Ghisleri.

"If he chooses!" The Contessa's scornful expression returned. "If he tells me nothing you will remind me of that word, and say that he did not choose. How you always arrange everything beforehand to leave yourself a way of escape."

"I am sorry you should think so," said Ghisleri, gravely.

"I am sorry that I have to think so. It does not increase my self-respect, nor my vanity in my judgment."

They parted on very bad terms that day, and two or three days more passed before they saw each other again. The Contessa had almost made up her mind that she would not speak to San Giacinto at all, and Ghisleri began to think that she wished to break with him permanently. Far more sensitive than any one supposed, he had been deeply wounded by her words and tone, so deeply indeed that he scarcely wished to meet her for the present. The world did not fail to see the coldness that had come between them, and laughed heartily over it. The Contessa, said the world, thought that the way to keep Ghisleri was to be cold to him and encourage Pietrasanta, but she did not know dear Ghisleri, who did not care in the very least, who had not a particle of sensitiveness in him, and had never really loved any one but the beautiful Princess Corleone who died of fever in Naples five years ago, and of whom he never spoke.

But as chance would have it, the Contessa found herself talking to San Giacinto one evening, when she was feeling very lonely and unhappy, and her half-formed resolution broke down as suddenly as it had presented itself. The giant looked at her keenly for a moment, bent his heavy black brows, and then told her the story of what had taken place at the club. He, who saw most things, and talked little of them, noted the gradual change in her face, and how the light came back to it while he was speaking. She understood that the man whom she had accused of betraying his friend had faced a roomful of men in his defence, and on the very ground now under discussion, and she repented of what she had done. Then she swore vengeance on Adele Savelli.

The world saw that a reconciliation had taken place, and concluded that Maddalena dell' Armi had abandoned her foolish plan of trying to attract Ghisleri by being cold to him. Ghisleri, indeed! As though he cared!

"But I have no particular wish to be revenged on Donna Adele," objected Ghisleri, when the Contessa spoke to him on the subject. "That sort of thing is a disease of the brain. There are people who cannot see things as they are. She is one of them."

"How indifferent you are!" sighed Maddalena. "I wonder whether you were always so."

"Not always," answered Pietro, thoughtfully.

In due time the short Easter season was over, the foreigners departed, and many of the Romans followed their example, especially those whose country places were within easy reach of the city, by carriage or by rail. The Contessa went to pay her regular annual visit at her

G

father's, near Florence,— her mother had long been dead,
—and Ghisleri remained in Rome, unable to make up
his mind what to do. Something seemed to bind him to
the town this year, and though he went away for a day
or two from time to time, he always came back very soon.
Even his damaged old castle did not attract him as it
usually did, though he had begun to restore it a little
during the last few years, a little at a time, as his modest
fortune allowed. There was an odd sort of foresight in
his character. He laughed at the idea of being married,
and yet he had a presentiment that he would some day
change his mind and take a wife. In case that should
ever happen, Torre de' Ghisleri would be at once a beautiful and an economical retreat for the summer months.
Though he had a reputation for extravagance and for
living always a little beyond his income, he was in reality
increasing his property. He was constantly buying small
bits of land in the neighbourhood of his castle, with a
vague idea that he might ultimately get the old estate
together again. He generally bought on mortgage, binding himself to pay at a certain date, and as he was a very
honourable man in all financial transactions, he invariably paid, though sometimes at considerable sacrifice.
He said to himself that unless he were bound he would
inevitably throw away the little money he had to spare.
It was a curiously practical trait in such an unruly and
almost lawless character, but he did such things when he
could, and then thought no more about them until a fresh
opportunity presented itself. He was a man whose life
and whole power of interest in life were almost constantly
absorbed by the two or three persons to whom he was
sincerely attached, a fact never realised by those who
knew him — a passionate man at heart, and one who
despised himself for many reasons — a man who would
have wished to be a Launcelot in fidelity, a Galahad in
cleanness of heart, an Arthur for justice and frankness,
but who was indeed terribly far from resembling any of
the three. A man liable to most human weaknesses, but
having just enough of something better to make him hate

weakness in himself and understand it in others without condemning it too harshly in them.   He had the wish to overcome it in his own character and life, but when the victory looked too easy it did not tempt him, for his vanity was of the kind which is only satisfied with winning hard fights, and rarely roused except by the prospect of them, while quite indifferent to small success of any kind — either for good or evil.

And this year, for some reason which he did not attempt to explain to himself, he lingered on in Rome, living a lonely life, avoiding the club where many of his acquaintances still congregated, taking his meals irregularly at garden restaurants, and spending most of his evenings in wandering about Rome by himself.   The old places attracted him strongly.   Many associations clung to the shady streets, the huge old palaces, and the dusky churches.   Ten years of such a life as he had led had left many traces behind them, many sensitive spots in his complicated nature which inanimate things had power to touch keenly and thrill again with pain or pleasure. There was much that was sad, indeed, in these recollections, but there were also many memories dear and tender and almost free from the sting of self-reproach.   He was not one to crave excitement for its own sake, nor to miss it when it was past.   It often chanced, indeed, that he could find the few things that pleased him, the few people he liked, in the midst of the world's noisiest fair, but he would always have preferred to be alone with them, to meet with them when he was quite sure of being altogether himself and not the overwrought, nervous being which he came to be during the rush of the season, in spite of his undeniable physical strength.   Those who need excitement most are either those who have never lived in it, or those unhappily morbid beings who cannot live without it, because by force of habit it has become the only atmosphere which their lungs can breathe and in which they can act more or less normally.

Ghisleri followed the Ardens in imagination as they pursued their wedding trip.   He rarely knew exactly where they were, but he was familiar with all the places they were visiting, and he liked to fancy them enjoying together all there was to be seen and done. Had he not himself still been young, he would almost have fancied that he felt a fatherly interest in their doings. Then he heard that they were in England, and at last, when he had made up his mind to go away for a month or two, he learned that Arden was in bad health. He was distressed by the news, and wished he could see his old friend, if only for a day, to judge for himself of his condition. But that was impossible at present. He was not always free to dispose of his time as he pleased, and as he had been during the past months. Moreover, the world was not quite just when it said that Ghisleri did not "care," as it expressed the state of mind it attributed to him. Between going to England, and going to Vallombrosa, near Florence, he did not hesitate a moment.

So the autumn came round again, and when he returned to his lodging in Rome, he found that the Ardens were already installed in the Tempietto. The Savelli couple were still out of town at the family castle in the Sabines, but the Prince and Princess of Gerano had come back.

Ghisleri found both Laura and Arden greatly changed. The latter's appearance shocked him especially, and he felt almost from the first that his friend was doomed. The man who was not supposed to care spent at least one sleepless night, turning over in his mind the various possibilities of life and death. On the following morning at twelve o'clock, he climbed the steps to the Trinità de' Monti, and asked to see Lady Herbert Arden alone, a request which was easily granted, as her husband now rarely rose until one, and then only for a few hours.

Laura's eyes looked preternaturally large and deep — almost sunken, Ghisleri thought — and she had grown thin, and even paler than she usually was when in good health. He took the seat she pointed to, by the open fire, and stared into the flames absently for some seconds. It was a rather dreary morning early in November, and the air in the streets was raw and damp. At last he looked up.

"You are anxious about your husband, Lady Herbert?" he said.

Laura sighed, and opened her white hands to the warmth, as she sat on the other side of the fireplace. But she said nothing. She could not deny what he had told her, for she was in mortal anxiety by day and night.

"It is very natural," said Ghisleri, trying to speak more cheerfully. "But I do not think there is any very serious reason for anticipating danger. I have known Arden many years, and I have often known him to be ill before now."

Laura glanced nervously at Pietro, and looked away again almost instantly. There was a frightened look in her face as though she feared something unexpected. Perhaps she was afraid of believing too readily in Ghisleri's comforting view.

"All the same," he continued, "there is no denying that he is in very bad health. Forgive me if I seem officious. I do not love him as you do, of course, but we have been more or less good friends these many years — since very long before you knew him."

"More or less good friends!" repeated Laura, in a disappointed tone. "Herbert calls you his best friend."

"I dare say he has many better than I am," answered Ghisleri, quietly. "But I have certainly never liked any man as much as I like him. That is why I come to you to-day. Do you not think that he should be taken care of, or, at least thoroughly examined by the best specialist to be found?"

"I have thought of it," said Laura, after a short pause. "Of course the doctor comes regularly, but I do not think he is a really great authority. I am afraid that anything like a consultation might alarm Herbert. I see how determined he is to be cheerful, but I cannot help seeing also that he is despondent about himself."

"There need be nothing like a consultation. Will you trust me in this matter?"

Laura looked at him. She felt, on a sudden, the old, almost inexplicable, timid dislike of him with which she had long been familiar, and she hesitated before she answered.

"Could I not manage it myself?" she asked abruptly. "It would seem more natural."

Ghisleri's face grew slowly cold, and his eyes fixed themselves on the fire.

"I thought I might be able to help you," he said. "Have you any particular reason for distrusting me as you do, Lady Herbert?"

Laura's face contracted. She was not angry, but she was sorry that she had shown him what she thought, and it was hard to answer the question truthfully, for she was not really sure whether she had any excuse for doubting his frankness or not. In the present instance she assuredly had none.

"I should certainly never distrust you where Herbert is concerned," she said, after a short pause. "It is only that it seems more natural, as I said, that I should be the one to speak to him and to arrange about the specialist's visit."

"Very well. Forgive me, as I begged you to at first, if I have seemed officious. I will come and see your husband this afternoon."

The consequence of this conversation was that Laura, being even more seriously alarmed than before, since she realised that Ghisleri himself was anxious, spoke to Arden about the necessity for seeing a better doctor, breaking it to him with all the loving gentleness she knew how to use with him, and Arden consented without much apparent reluctance to being examined by a man who had a great reputation. The latter took a long time before he gave an opinion, and ultimately declared to Laura that her husband was consumptive and would probably not live a year. Laura suffered in that moment as she would not have believed it possible to suffer, and it was long before she could compose herself enough to go to Arden. It was of course impossible to tell him all the doctor had said. She told him that his lungs were delicate, and that he must be very careful.

"It seems to me I am always very careful," said Lord Herbert, patiently.

She looked at him and saw for the hundredth time how ill he seemed. She tried to turn quickly and leave the room, but she could not. Suddenly the passionate tears broke out, and she fell on her knees beside his chair and clasped the poor little body in her arms.

"Oh, Herbert, my love, — my love!" she sobbed.

Then he felt that he was doomed. Had she loved him less, she could have kept the secret better. But he was brave still.

"Hush, darling, hush!" he said, gently stroking her coal-black hair with his transparent hand. "You must not believe these foolish doctors. I have been just as ill before."

But the mischief was done, and she felt that she had done it, and her remorse knew no bounds. In spite of his courage, Arden lost heart. The next time Ghisleri saw him he was much worse. Laura went out and left the two together.

"Has anything worried you?" asked Ghisleri. "You look tired."

Arden was silent for a long time, and his friend knew that he was carefully weighing his answer.

"Yes," he said at last, "something has worried me very much. I can trust you not to speak — never to speak, even to my wife, of what I am going to say — especially if anything should happen," he added, as though with a painful afterthought.

"I will never speak of it," replied Pietro, gravely.

"I know you will not. We had a consultation the other day. Of course they were very careful not to tell me what they thought, but I could not help guessing it. You know how truthful my wife is — she could not deny it when I put the question directly. It is all up with

me, my dear fellow, and I know it. I am consumptive.
It will last a year at the most."

"I do not believe a word of it!" exclaimed Ghisleri,
with unusual heat. "You are not in the least like a consumptive man!"

"The doctor is a good specialist," said Arden, quietly.
"But that is not all. I have been so happy — I am so
happy in many ways still — that I am weak enough to
cling to my life, such as it is. But there is something
else, Ghisleri. I knew I was ill, and I knew there was
danger — but this is different. I had hoped to see my
child, even if I were to die. I do not hope to see it now
— you understand? Those things are always inherited."

A deadly paleness came over Arden's face, and his clear
brown eyes seemed unsteady for a moment. His face
twitched nervously, and his hands were strained as they
grasped the arms of his chair. Ghisleri looked very
grave.

"I repeat that I believe the doctor to be wholly mistaken. It would hardly be the first time that doctors
have made such mistakes. Consumptive people do not
behave as you do. They always feel that they are getting
well, until the very last, and they have a regular cough,
not to be mistaken, and they eat a great deal. You are
quite different."

"But he examined me so carefully," objected Arden,
though he could not help seeing a ray of hope.

"I cannot help that. He was mistaken."

That afternoon Ghisleri telegraphed to a great Euro-
pean celebrity whom he knew in Paris, to come if possible at once, no matter at what sacrifice of money. Forty-
eight hours later the man of genius was breakfasting
with Pietro in his rooms.

"I will ask leave to bring you as a friend," said the
latter. "I have begged you to come on my own responsibility."

He wrote a note to Laura, explaining that an old
acquaintance, a man of world-wide fame, was spending a

couple of days with him, and begged permission to introduce him. He might amuse Arden, he said. He did not mention the doctor's profession. It was just possible that neither Arden nor Laura had ever heard of the man who was so great in a world not theirs. Laura asked them both to tea by way of answer.

As it turned out, the Ardens had a very vague idea that the Frenchman was a man of science. In the course of conversation he admitted that he had studied medicine, and then went on to talk about the latest news from Paris, social, artistic, and literary. Arden was charmed with him, and Laura was really grateful to Ghisleri for helping to amuse her husband.

Would they both come to luncheon the next day? They would, with pleasure, and they went away together.

"Well?" asked Ghisleri, as they walked towards the Pincio in the early dusk, just to breathe the air.

"I think he may live," answered the great man. "I believe it is a trouble of the heart with an almost exhausted vitality."

Laura was left alone with her husband. Whether it was the doctor's personal influence, or whether Arden was really momentarily better, she could not tell, but he looked as he had not looked for two months.

"That man delights me," he said dreamily. "I do not know what there is about him, and it is very foolish — but I fancy that if he were a doctor, he might cure me — or keep me alive longer," he added, with a sort of reluctant sadness.

Laura looked at him in surprise.

"He said he had studied medicine," she answered. "Shall I ask Signor Ghisleri, if, as a friend, he would come and give his opinion?"

"It is too much to ask of a stranger."

"Nothing is too much to ask," she said quietly. In her own room she wrote a note to Pietro.

With many apologies, she explained to him that her husband was so delighted with Ghisleri's friend, that she

believed it might make a difference if, as a doctor — since he was one — the latter would be willing to see him once and give his opinion.

Pietro smiled when he read the note.   On the following day the great man went again to the Tempietto, and with many protestations of incompetence did as he was requested, assuring Lady Herbert that it was only in deference to her wishes that he did so.

"You are not consumptive — in the least, and you may even become strong," he said, after a very long and thorough examination.   "That, at least," he added, "is my humble opinion."

Arden's face brightened suddenly.   But Laura and Ghisleri remained alone together for a moment afterwards, while the doctor was already putting on his coat.

"After all," said Laura, despondently, "it was to please Herbert.   The man says that his opinion is not worth very much."

"He is the greatest living authority on the subject," answered Ghisleri.   "You may safely take his opinion."

Laura's face expressed her surprise, and at the same time, an unspeakable relief.

"Are you sure?" she asked, in trembling tones.

"Ask your doctor.   He will tell you.   Will you forgive me my little trick, Lady Herbert?   As he was here, I thought you might like to see him."   Ghisleri put out his hand to take his leave, and Laura pressed it warmly.

"If I had ever had anything to forgive, I would forgive you — for your great kindness to me," she said, and the tears were almost in her eyes.   "It is you who should forgive me for not trusting you when you first spoke. How wrong I was!"

"Nonsense!" exclaimed Ghisleri.   "It was very natural."

And so it seemed to him, perhaps.   But such little tricks, as he called what he had done, cost money, and that year Ghisleri did not buy the bit of land which stood next on the list in his scheme for reacquiring the old estate.

CHAPTER VII.

ARDEN's health improved, at first very rapidly, and then more slowly, as he seemed to approach what, for him, was a normal condition of strength. The month of December was fine, and he was able to drive out constantly, to be up most of the day, and to talk with acquaintances without any great fatigue. As a natural consequence, too, Laura regained in a very short time all that she had lost, and her eyes no longer looked sunken and haggard nor her face unnaturally pale.

Her gratitude to Ghisleri was boundless, and as the days went on and Arden had no relapse, she began to wonder how she could ever have felt anything approaching to dislike for the man to whom she almost owed her husband's life. Pietro, on his part, came often to the house and saw the change that had taken place in her manner towards him. He was pleased, though he had not thought of producing any impression upon her by what he had done solely for Arden's sake, for he had long admired her, and felt that she was very like a certain ideal of woman of which he never talked. But his pleasure was not very genuine, after all. He hardly believed that Laura's mood would last, because he had hitherto had little experience of lasting moods in women. For the present, at least, she believed in him and was grateful.

About this time Donna Adele, her husband, and his father and mother all came back from the country, and at or near the same period the great majority of the old society stagers appeared again as forerunners of the coming season. The gay set was not yet all assembled, and it was even reported that some of them would not come at all, for there was financial trouble in the air, and many people had lost money, or found their incomes diminished by the general depression. Nevertheless, when Christmas came, few of the familiar faces of the previous year were missing, and those few have not been seen in this history.

"This is the beginning," said Gouache to Ghisleri. "You may remember that charming description of chaos in the sacred writings: 'in the beginning darkness was over all the earth' — very like Rome before the season begins. The resemblance ends there, my dear friend. The sentence which follows would hardly be applicable. Are we to have another Shrove Tuesday feast this year for the sake of giving sin a last chance? Have you another diabolical production ready?"

"I am afraid not," answered Ghisleri. "Besides, one should never repeat a good thing."

"That is what my wife says," observed Anastase, thoughtfully. "That dear woman! But for her, I should do nothing but repeat my successful pictures — if possible by a chemical process. It would be so easy! That is the way the modern galleries of old masters are formed. There is a little man in the Via da' Falegnami who turns out the article at a fixed price, including the cost of the green wood for smoking the Rembrandts, and the genuine old panels for doing the Botticellis. I often go to see him. He knows more about grinding colours, and about vehicles and varnishes, and the price of lamp-black than any artist I ever knew. He painted that portrait of Raphael by himself — by Raphael, I mean, for Prince Durakoff last year, and found the documents to prove its existence among his papers. It took him six months, but it was well done, especially the parchments. There was even the receipt for the money paid to Raphael for the picture by the Most Excellent House of Frangipani, signed by the painter himself — I mean by Raphael. Cheap, at ten thousand francs. Durakoff paid the dealer eighty thousand without bargaining. He did not reflect that if it had been genuine it would have been worth five hundred thousand, and, if not, that it was not worth fifty centimes."

"Rather like a friend," observed Ghisleri.

"Friendship is a matter of fortune," said Gouache, "as love is a question of climate."

"You are not usually so cynical. What has happened?"

"My wife has been amusing me, this morning, with an account of society's opinions on various subjects. One-half of her friends assure her that black is white, and the other half tell her it is a vivid yellow. That is called conversation. They give it you with tea, milk, and sugar, between five and seven in the afternoon."

Gouache seemed to be in a somewhat communicative frame of mind. As a matter of fact he often was with Ghisleri, whom he trusted more than most men.

"What was it all about?" inquired the latter.

"People, people, and then people again. What does everybody talk about? Silly stories about Lady Herbert Arden and Savelli, and about Lord Herbert himself, and his dissipated life. The Ardens do not seem to be liked. He is a great friend of yours, is he not?"

"Yes, we have known each other almost ten years." Ghisleri began to smoke, rather gloomily, for he perceived that there was trouble in store for Laura.

"It is Donna Adele who does all the mischief," continued Gouache, putting a dash of bright blue into the face of the portrait he was painting, a proceeding which, as Ghisleri noticed with some surprise, improved the likeness. "It is Donna Adele. You know the old story. Savelli loved Miss Carlyon but could not marry her. Donna Adele never forgave her, and she will end by doing her a great deal of harm. She pretends that Savelli has told her that Lady Herbert is already talking to him and to everybody of her own wretched married life — rather hinting that if Savelli would care to depart this life of respectability she would go with him, a proposition which, of course, Savelli scorns in the most virtuous and approved fashion, rolling his fine paternal language as in the fourth act of a tragedy at the Comedie Française. I suppose you cannot stop this sort of thing, can you?"

"I will try," said Ghisleri, in a tone that made Gouache look round from his painting. He had not often witnessed even such a slight manifestation of real anger on Pietro's part, as was apparent in the enunciation of the three words.

"You might, perhaps, better than any one else," observed Gouache. "From other things she has said, it is quite apparent that she would like to see you at her feet."

Ghisleri looked at Anastase rather sharply, but said nothing. It was not the fact that Donna Adele wished him to pay her more attention that struck him; he was wondering what the other remarks might have been, to which Gouache alluded. They might have been directed against the Contessa — or they might have been such as to show that Adele suspected Ghisleri of an attachment for Laura Arden since he now went so often to the house. As Gouache did not volunteer any further information, however, Ghisleri thought it wiser to ask no questions, and he was inclined to infer that the aforesaid observations had been directed against Maddalena dell' Armi.

Ghisleri went away in a very bad humour. So long as the gossip came from the men, he had a very simple and definite course open to him, and he knew that his personal influence was considerable. But when the worst things said were said by women, there seemed to be no remedy possible. It would not be an easy matter to go to Adele and tax her with lying, slandering, and evil speaking. She would very properly be angry, and would of course deny that she had ever spoken on the matter, her friends would support her in her denial, and he would be no further advanced than before. He could not possibly go to Francesco Savelli and demand of the latter an explanation of Donna Adele's conduct. That was out of the question. To let Donna Adele know that both Laura and Arden were quite unconscious of her attacks and, in their present life of almost enforced retirement, were likely to remain in ignorance of them, might annoy Donna Adele, but could do no good. It would be positively unkind to speak to the Princess of Gerano and ask her to use her influence with her step-daughter, but Ghisleri thought he had struck a possibility at last — he could go to old Gerano himself and explain matters. After all, Gerano was Adele's father and had some authority over her still. Ghisleri came rather hastily to the conclusion that this would be the wisest course to follow, and acted almost immediately upon his decision, for it chanced that he found the Prince at the club, and had the opportunity he needed within half an hour after forming his plan of action.

He approached the subject coolly and diplomatically, while Gerano blandly listened and puffed at a cigarette. Donna Adele, he said, had of course no intention of injuring her step-sister, but she was too young to know the weight a careless tale often carried with it in the world, and had no idea of the harm she was doing. No one, not even the Prince himself, was ignorant of the fact that Don Francesco Savelli's first inclination had been rather for Miss Carlyon than for Donna Adele, but that it had been a mere young man's fancy, without any importance, and that having yielded to parental authority, Don Francesco was now a perfectly happy man. Perhaps Donna Adele had not been able to forget this apparent slight upon her beauty and charm, as far as her step-sister was concerned, though well aware that her husband thought no more about Lady Herbert. It was natural and womanly in her to resent it. But that was not a good reason why she should say — as she seemed to be saying constantly — that Lady Herbert was very much in love with Don Francesco.

Here Ghisleri paused, and the Prince opened his eyes very wide at first, and then almost shut them as he scrutinised his companion's face. He knew the man well, however, and guessed that the matter must be serious indeed, since he took the trouble to treat it in such earnest.

"I suppose," said Gerano, "that you are quite prepared

to support your words if any question arises. This is a strange tale."

"Yes," answered Ghisleri. "I am always ready." He spoke with such gravity that the Prince was impressed.

Pietro went on to say that Donna Adele, doubtless out of pure carelessness, had certainly, by a foolish jest, suggested the story that Lord Herbert was very intemperate, a story which Ghisleri had last year been obliged to deny in the most formal manner in the very room in which they were now talking, to a number of men. The tale had of late been revived in a form even more virulent than before, and such untruths, even when they have originated in a harmless bit of fun, could damage a man's reputation for life.

"Of course they can, and they do," asserted the Prince, who was becoming rather anxious.

"As, for instance," continued Ghisleri, "it is now said that Lady Herbert Arden, your step-daughter, now talks to Don Francesco and to everybody — which probably means the few persons who circulate the myth — about her wretched married life, and other suggestions which I will not repeat are added, which are very insulting to her. For my part, my business is to defend Arden, who is my friend, and who is unfortunately too ill to defend himself should all this come to his ears. I do not say that this last addition concerning Lady Herbert's confidences comes from Donna Adele Savelli. But it is undoubtedly current, and proceeds directly from the former gossip, as its natural consequence."

"Evidently," said the Prince, who kept his temper admirably, in consideration of the gravity of the case. "And now what do you expect me to do?"

"You are Donna Adele's father," answered Ghisleri. "She is assuredly ignorant of the harm she has caused. It would seem quite natural if you suggested to her that it is in her power to undo what she has unintentionally done."

"How, may I ask? By an apology?" Gerano did not like the idea, but Ghisleri smiled.

"That would make matters worse," he said. "She could put everything right merely by saying a few pleasant things about the Ardens to half a dozen people of her acquaintance — at random. Donna Maria Boccapaduli, the Marchesa di San Giacinto, the Contessa dell' Armi — even Donna Faustina Gouache. She might ask the Ardens to dinner —"

"I observe that you do not name any men," observed the Prince.

"It is not the men who have been talking, so far as I know — nor if they did, would their gossip do so much damage."

"That may be. As for the rest, I will say this. You have said some exceedingly unpleasant things to me this afternoon, but I know you well enough to be sure that you are not only in earnest, but wish to avert trouble rather than cause it. Otherwise I should not have listened to you as I have. I am very deeply attached to my only child, though I am also very fond of my stepdaughter. However, I will take this question in hand and find out the truth, and do what I can to mend matters. If I find you have been misinformed, I will ask the favour of another interview."

"I shall always be at your service."

They parted rather stiffly, but without any nearer approach to hostility than was implied in the last formal words they exchanged. Gerano walked slowly homeward, revolving the situation in his mind, and wondering how he should act in order to get at the truth in the case. Being very fond of his wife, his first impulse was to tell her the whole story, and to take counsel with her before doing anything definite. It would have been better had he gone directly to Donna Adele, though he might not have accomplished anything at all, and might have believed her, and might also have quarrelled with Ghisleri afterwards. But he did not foresee the consequences.

The Princess was very much overcome by the account he gave her of his interview with Ghisleri, of whom she

had a high opinion as a man of truthful character, bad
as he seemed to be in other respects. She knew instinctively and at once that every one of his statements must
have been perfectly well founded, and that if he had
erred it had assuredly not been in the direction of exaggerating the facts. She was in much the same position
as her husband, except that her own daughter was the
victim, while his was the aggressor. It was strange that
in so many years neither should have understood Adele's
character well enough to suspect that she could be capable of any treachery, and yet both were now convinced
that the case against her was not by any means a fiction.
The Princess was now in the gravest distress, and she
could not keep back her tears as she tried to find argu-
ments in Adele's favour, wishing to the last to defend her
husband's child, while never for a moment losing sight
of her own.

She was an eminently good woman, but very far from
worldly-wise. Indeed, as events proceeded that day,
there seemed to be a diminution of wisdom in the action
of each in turn as compared with that of the last person
concerned. Ghisleri had not really allowed himself time
to consider the situation in all its bearings before speaking to Gerano, or he might not have spoken at all. Gerano, next, had scarcely hesitated in confiding the whole
affair to his wife, and she, in despair, turned to the one
person of all others with whom she was really most in
sympathy, to Laura Arden herself, regardless of the
consequences to every one concerned. Lord Herbert was
resting before dinner, and she found her daughter alone.

Her heart was almost bursting, and she poured out the
story in all its details, accurately, as she had heard it,
though hardly knowing what she said. At first Laura
was tempted to laugh. She had been so much happier
of late that laughing had grown easy, but she very soon
saw the real meaning of the situation, and she grew pale
as she silently listened to the end. Then her mother
broke down again.

"And I have loved her so!" cried the poor lady. "Almost as I have loved you, my child! To think of it all — oh, it is not to be believed!"

Laura was not at that moment inclined to shed tears. It was almost the first time in her life when she was really angry, for her temper was not easily roused. It was not destined to be the last. Dry-eyed and pale, she sat beside the Princess, holding her hands, then drying her fast flowing tears, then caressing her, and saying all she could to soothe and calm her, while almost choking herself to keep down the rage she felt. Her eyes had been opened at last, and she saw what the story really was at which Arden had made such a poor guess. As the Princess grew more calm, she began to look at her daughter in surprise.

"What is the matter, darling?" she asked anxiously. "Are you ill, dear, you look so changed!"

"I am angry, mother," answered Laura, quietly enough. "I shall get over it soon, I dare say."

Even her voice did not sound like her own. It was hollow and strange. Her mother was frightened.

"I have done very wrong to tell you, Laura," she said, realising too late that the revelation must have been startling in the extreme.

"I do not know," answered Lady Herbert, still speaking in the same peculiar tone, and with an effort. "Adele and I meet constantly. Of course we have been brought up like real sisters, and though we were never intensely fond of one another we talk about everything as if we were. I will be careful in future. This may not be all true, but there is truth in it, if you have remembered exactly what Signor Ghisleri said — or rather, if the Prince has."

The Princess started slightly. Laura had always called Gerano father, as though she had really been his daughter, but the shock had been very sudden, and she found it hard to call by that name the man whose daughter was Adele Savelli.

"I hope it will turn out to be all a mistake!" exclaimed the Princess, weakly, and on the point of bursting into tears again.

"Until we are sure of it, I shall try and behave as usual to Adele, if we have to meet," said Laura. "After that, if it is all true — I do not know — "

When the Princess went home, she was a little frightened at what she had done, and repented bitterly of having yielded to her own unreasoning longing to talk the matter over with Laura — natural enough indeed, when it is remembered that the two loved one another so dearly. It had been a mistake, she was sure, and she would have given anything to undo it. She only hoped that she should not be obliged to explain to her husband.

Laura sat alone by the fireside. Herbert was lying down and would not appear until dinner time, so that she had almost an hour in which to think over the situation. She determined to master her anger and to look the matter in the face calmly. After all, it was only gossip, town-talk, insignificant chatter, which must all be forgotten in the light of the true facts. So she tried to persuade herself, at least, but she found it a very hard matter to believe her own statement of it all. The more she thought it over, the more despicable it all seemed in her eyes, the more savagely she hated Adele. She could have borne the story about herself better, if it had come alone, but she could neither forgive nor find an excuse for what had been said against her husband. To know that people openly called him intemperate — a drunkard, that would be the word! Him, of all living men! The assertion was so monstrous that all Laura's resolution to control herself gave way suddenly, and she, in her turn, burst into a flood of tears, hot, angry, almost agonising, impossible to check.

She might have been proud to shed them, for they showed how much more she loved her husband than she cared for herself, but she was conscious only of the intense desire to face Adele, and do her some grievous bodily

hurt and be revenged for the foul slander cast on Herbert
Arden. She opened and shut her hands convulsively, as
though she were clutching some one and strangling the
breath in a living throat. Every drop of blood in her
young body was fire, every tear that rolled down her pale
cheek was molten lead, every beat of her angry pulse
brought an angry thought to her brain. How long she
remained in this state she did not know.

She did not hear her husband's laboured, halting step
on the soft carpet, and before she was aware of his presence he was standing before her, with a look of pain and
almost of horror in his delicate face. That was the most
terrible moment in his life.

Highly sensitive as he was, loving her almost to distraction as he did, he had always found it hard to understand her love for him. To suspect that all of it was
pity, or that a part of it had grown weak of late, was
almost impossible to him, and yet the possibility of doubt
was there. He had entered the room as usual, without
any precaution, but she had not heard him; he had seen
her apparently struggling with herself and with some un-
seen enemy, in a paroxysm of grief and rage. Instantly
the doubt rose supreme and struck him, like a sudden
blow in the face.

"She has found out her mistake too late — she does
not love me, and she longs to be free." That was what
Herbert Arden said to himself as he stood before her, and
the horror of it was almost greater than he could bear.
Yet there was a great and manly courage in his narrow
breast. He felt that he must die, but she should not
suffer any more than was necessary until then. He drew
the best breath he could, as though it were his last. She
started, wild-eyed, as he spoke.

"Laura darling — it has been a terrible mistake — and
it is all my fault. Will you forgive me, dear one? I
thought that you would love me — I see how it is when
you are alone. No woman could have borne this bond-
age of yours as you have borne it since you have found
out — "

"Herbert! Herbert!" cried Laura, in sudden agony. She thought he was going mad before her eyes.

"No, dear," he said, with an immense effort, and making a gesture with his hand as though to keep her in her place. "It is better to say it now, and it need never be said again. Perhaps I should not have the strength. I see it all. You are so kind and good that you will never show it to me — but when you are alone — then you let yourself go — is it any wonder? Are you to blame? You see that you have made the great mistake — that it was all pity and not love — and you long to be free from me as you should be, as you shall be, dear."

A wild cry broke from Laura's very heart when she realised what he meant.

"Love! Darling — Herbert! I never loved you as I love you now!"

She did not know that she spoke articulate words as she sprang to her feet and clasped him in her arms, half mad with grief at the thought of what he must have suffered, and loving him as she said she did, far beyond the love of earlier days. But he hardly understood yet that it was really love, and he tried to look up into her face, almost fainting with the terrible strain he had borne so bravely, and still struggling to be calm.

"Laura darling," he said, in a low voice, "it was all too natural. Unless you tell me what it was that made you act as I saw you just now, how can I understand?"

She turned her deep eyes straight to his.

"Do you doubt me still, Herbert?" she asked. And she saw that he could not help doubting.

"But if I tell you that what I was thinking of would pain you very much, and that it would be of no use — "

"It cannot be like the pain I feel now," he answered simply.

She realised that what he said was true. Then she told him the whole story, as she knew it. And so, in a few hours, the conversation Ghisleri had held with Gouache began to bear fruit in a direction where neither of them had suspected it possible that their words could penetrate.

Arden had allowed himself to sink into a chair at Laura's side, and he listened with half-closed eyes and folded hands while she spoke. Under ordinary circumstances he would probably have betrayed some emotion, and might have interrupted her with a question or two, but the terrible excitement of the last few minutes was followed by a reaction, and he felt himself growing colder and calmer every moment, while his heart, which had been beating furiously when he had first spoken to her, seemed now about to stand still. As she proceeded, however, he was aware of the most conflicting feelings of happiness and anger — the latter of the quiet and dangerous sort. He saw at once that he had been utterly mistaken in doubting Laura's love, and from that direction peace descended upon his heart; but when he heard what the world was saying of her, he felt that weak as he was, he had the sudden strength to dare and do anything to avenge the insult. He was human enough, too, to resent bitterly the story about himself, though that, after all, was but a secondary affair in comparison with the gossip about Laura.

When she had finished, he rose slowly, and sat upon the arm of her easy-chair, drawing her head to his shoulder. He kissed her hair tenderly.

"My beloved — can you forgive me?" he asked, in a very gentle voice. "My darling — that I should have doubted you!"

"I am glad you did, dear — this once," she answered. "You see how it is. You are all the world to me — the mere thought that any one can hurt you by word or deed — oh, it drives me mad!"

And she, who was usually so very calm and collected, again made that desperate gesture with her hands, as though she had them on a woman's throat and would strangle out the life of her in the grip of her firm fingers.

"As for me, it matters little enough," said Arden,

taking her hands and stroking them as though to soothe her anger. "Of course it is an absurd and disgusting story, and I suppose some people believe it. But what they say of you is a very different matter."

"I do not think so," broke in Laura, indignantly. "Of course every one knows that we love each other, and that it is all a lie — but when such a tale is started about a man — that he drinks — oh, it is too utterly vile!"

"Dear — shall we try and forget it? At least for this evening. Let us do our best. You have made me so happy in another way — I suffered in that moment very much."

She looked up into his face as he sat on the arm of the chair, and she saw that he looked very ill. The scene had been almost too much for him, and she realised that when he spoke of forgetting it was because he could bear no more.

"Yes, love," she said, "we will put it all away for this evening and be happy together as we always are."

Each was conscious, no doubt, that the other was making a great effort, but neither of them referred to the matter again that night. They talked of all manner of subjects, rather nervously and resolutely at first, then naturally and easily as ever, when the deep sympathy which existed between them had asserted itself. During two hours, at least, they nearly forgot what had so violently moved them both.

When Arden laid his head upon his pillow, his anger had not subsided, but he knew that his love had taken greater strength and depth than ever before. He spent a sleepless night indeed, but when he rose in the morning he did not feel tired. Something within him which was quite new seemed to sustain him and nourish him. He could not tell whether it was love for Laura, or anger against the woman who slandered her, or both acting at once, and he did not waste much time in speculating upon his mental condition. He had formed a resolution upon which he meant to act without delay.

It was a rainy morning, chilly and raw again, as the weather had been earlier in the year.

"Give me warm clothes, Donald," he said to his man. "I am going out."

"Going out, my lord! In this weather!" Donald's face expressed the greatest anxiety.

"Never mind the weather," said Arden. "Give me warm clothes, and send for a closed carriage."

Donald obeyed, shaking his head, and muttering in detached expressions of disapproval. He was a privileged person.

CHAPTER VIII.

ARDEN, for the first time in his life, paid no attention to Laura's remonstrances when she tried to prevent him from going out in the rain, and he would not hear of her accompanying him on any condition. He assured her that with his fur coat, and in a closed carriage with a foot-warmer, he was as safe as at home in the drawing-room, and he gave her to understand that he had a small surprise in store for her, of which all the effect would be spoiled if she went with him. Very reluctantly she let him go. Even after he was gone, when she heard the brougham rattling down the Via Gregoriana, she was tempted to open the window and call the driver back. Then she reflected that she was probably foolish in being so anxious, since he now seemed almost as well as ever.

When he left the house, Arden drove to a certain studio, and then and there bought a small picture which Laura had admired very much, and had been two or three times to see. To the artist's surprise, he insisted upon carrying it away with him at once, just as it was. Then he told the coachman to drive to the Palazzo Savelli. He sent up his card and asked to see Don Francesco, and at once received an answer, begging him to go up stairs.

Francesco was very much surprised by the visit, and could not conceive what had brought Lord Herbert Arden to him at eleven o'clock in the morning. He awaited him in a vast and gloomy drawing-room in which there was no fire. The walls were hung with old portraits of the Savelli in armour, the carpet was of a sombre hue, and the furniture consisted of three superb marble tables with carved and gilt feet, and sixteen chairs of the style of Louis the Fourteenth's reign, all precisely alike, and standing side by side against the walls. Francesco Savelli stood facing the door, his yellow hair, blue eyes, and fresh complexion contrasting strongly with the dark background. He was a fine-looking fellow, with a mild face, a quiet manner, and a good deal of old-fashioned formality, which latter, however, seemed to wear off every evening in society, coming back as soon as he returned to the dim and shadowy halls of his home.

The connexion between him and Arden was in reality so distant, that they had never assumed even the outward forms of intimacy, though their wives called each other sister. Savelli disliked Lord Herbert because he was a cripple, and chiefly because he had married Laura Carlyon. Arden, on his side, was more or less indifferent to Francesco, but treated him always with a shade more warmth than an ordinary acquaintance, as being, in a sense, a member of his wife's family.

Savelli came forward as Arden entered. The servant allowed the heavy curtain to drop, closed the door, and went out, and the two men were left alone.

"Good morning, my dear Arden," said Savelli, taking his hand. "I hope you are quite well. Pray be seated."

"Good morning. Thanks." Both spoke in French.

They sat down, side by side, on the stiff, high-backed gilt chairs, and each looked at the other.

"I have something especial to say to you," began Arden, in his calm and even voice — a man quicker-witted than Savelli would have noticed the look of determination about the smooth-shaven lips and the prominent chin

—the look of a man who will not be trifled with, and will say what he means in spite of all difficulties and all opposition.

"I am entirely at your service," answered Don Francesco, politely.

"Thanks. I have thought it best to come to you directly, because my business concerns your wife and mine, and it is better that we should settle such matters between us without the intervention of others."

Savelli opened his eyes in surprise, but said nothing, only making a slight inclination of the head in answer. Arden continued in the cool and collected manner with which he had begun.

"A number of outrageous lies," he said slowly, "are in circulation concerning my wife, and some of them concern myself. May I inquire whether you have heard them?"

"It would facilitate matters, if you would tell me something of their nature," observed Savelli, more and more astonished.

"There is no difficulty about that. I can even repeat them to you, word for word, or nearly so. It is said, in the first place, that my wife is very much in love with you —"

"With me?" cried Savelli, startled out of his formality for once.

"Yes — with you — and that she has loved you long. Secondly, it is said that I am a confirmed drunkard, and that my wife leads a most unhappy existence with me in consequence. It is further stated that she makes no secret of this supposed fact, but complains loudly to her friends, and especially selects you for her confidence in the matter."

"That is totally untrue," said Don Francesco, gravely. "She has never spoken of you to me except in terms of the highest praise."

"I am aware that it is not true, but I am much obliged to you for your very plain statement. I will go on. It is asserted that my wife has given you to understand that she loves you, and that, if you would consent, she would be ready to leave me and Rome in your company. These things, it appears, are current gossip, and are confidently stated as positive truths."

"I have not heard any of them, except some vague reports about yourself, to the effect that you once took too much wine at the Gerano's house. But Ghisleri made a scene about it at the club, and I have heard no more of the absurd story."

"I did not know that Ghisleri had actively taken my part," answered Arden. "But the story has now reached the form in which I repeated it. For myself, I care very little. It is on account of its connexion with the tales about my wife that I have told it to you."

"May I ask who your informant is?"

"My wife."

"And hers?"

"A reliable and truthful person, whom I shall not name at present. The affair concerns you and me. I have not come to the most important point, which will explain why I came to you."

"I supposed that you came, as to a connexion of the family, to ask advice or assistance."

"No. That is not it. I do not need either, thank you. I come to you because all these stories are distinctly traceable to Donna Adele Savelli."

Francesco started violently, and almost rose from his seat, his face flushing suddenly.

"Lord Herbert — take care!" he cried in a loud and angry voice, and with a passionate gesture.

"Be calm," said Arden, in an unnaturally quiet tone. "If you strike me, you will be disgraced for life, because I am a cripple. But I assure you that I am not in the least afraid of you."

"You are wrong!" exclaimed Savelli, still furious, and turning upon him savagely.

"Not at all," returned the Englishman, unmoved. "I

came here to settle this business, and I have not the smallest intention of going away until I have said all I meant
to say. After that, if you are inclined to demand satisfaction of me, as is the custom here, you can do so. I will
consider the matter. I shall probably not exchange shots
with you, because I believe that duelling is wrong. But
let me say that I do not in the least mean to insult you,
nor, as I think, have I been lacking in civility to-day.
I have given you a number of facts which I have every
reason for believing to be true. You will in all likelihood have no difficulty in finding out whether they are
true or not. If we, jointly, are convinced that the statements are false, I shall be happy to offer you my best
apologies; if not, and if you are convinced that Donna
Adele has been slandering my wife, I shall expect you to
act upon your conviction, as a man of honour should, and
take measures to have these reports instantly and fully
denied everywhere by Donna Adele herself. I think I
have stated the case plainly, and what I have said ought
not to offend you, in my opinion."

"It is certainly impossible to be more plain," answered
Savelli, regaining something of his outward calm. "As
to what may or may not give offence, opinions may differ
in England and in Italy."

"They probably do," returned Arden, coolly. "It is
not my intention to offend you."

Francesco Savelli looked at the shrunken figure and the
thin hands with an odd sensation of repulsion and respect.
He had been very far from supposing that Herbert Arden
possessed such undeniable courage and imperturbable
coolness, and not being by any means a coward himself,
he could not help admiring bravery in others. He was
none the less angry, however, though he made a great
effort to keep his temper. He did not love his wife, but
he had all the Roman traditions concerning the sacred-
ness of the family honour, which he now felt was really
at stake, and he had all a Roman's dread of a public
scandal.

"I must beg you once more to tell me by whom these stories were told to Lady Herbert," he said, after a pause.

"I cannot do so, without consulting that person," answered Arden. "I do not wish to drag other people into the affair. You will be able to find out for yourself, and probably through members of your own family, how much truth there is in it all."

"You positively refuse to tell me?"

"I have said so. If you wish to be confronted with the person in question, I will consult that person, as I said before."

"And if I then, on my side, positively refuse to do anything without having previously spoken to that person — to him or to her — what then?"

"In my opinion, you will be allowing a state of things to continue which will not ultimately reflect credit upon you or yours. Moreover, you will oblige me to take some still more active measures."

"What measures?"

"I do not know. I will think about it. And now I will wish you good morning."

He got upon his feet, and stood before Savelli.

"Good morning," said the latter, very stiffly. "Allow me to accompany you to the hall."

"Thanks," said Arden, as he began to move towards the door in his ungainly, dislocated fashion, while Savelli walked slowly beside him, towering above him by a third of his own height.

Arden shivered as he slipped on his fur coat in the hall, for it had been very cold in the drawing-room though he had scarcely noticed the fact in his preoccupied state of mind. While driving homeward, he looked at the little picture as it stood opposite to him on the seat of the carriage. It was one of those exquisite views of the Campagna, looking across the Tiber, which Sartorio does so wonderfully in pastel.

"She will be glad to have it," said Arden to himself, "and she will understand why I went out alone."

He was tolerably well satisfied with the morning's work. It had seemed to him that there was nothing else to be done under the circumstances, and he certainly did not choose the least wise course, in going directly to Savelli. He did not regret a word of what he had said, nor did he feel that he had said too little. As he anticipated, Laura suspected nothing, and was delighted with the picture. She scolded him a little for having insisted upon going out on such a morning, especially for her sake, but as the clouds just then were breaking and the sunshine was streaming into the room, she felt as though it could not have been a great risk after all. Before they had finished luncheon, a note was brought in. Laura laughed oddly as she read it.

"It is an invitation to dinner from Adele," she said. "It is for the day after to-morrow, shall we accept?"

Arden's face grew thoughtful. He could not be sure whether the invitation had been sent before his interview with Savelli, or since. It was therefore not easy to decide upon the wisest course.

"Better to accept it, is it not?" asked Laura. "It is of no use to make an open breach."

"No. It is of no use. Accept, dear. It is more sensible."

Neither of them liked the thought of dining at the Palazzo Savelli just then, and Laura, at least, knew that she would find it hard to behave as though nothing had happened. Both would have been very much surprised, could they have known why they were asked, and that the idea had originated with Pietro Ghisleri.

On the previous evening, Gerano had taken pains to see his daughter alone at her own house, on pretence of talking to her about business. With considerable skill he had led the conversation up to the required point, and had laid a trap for her.

"Do you see much of the Ardens just now?" he asked.

"No. We do not meet often," answered Adele, with a little movement of the shoulders.

"I wish you did. I wish you saw them every day," observed the Prince, more gravely.

"Do you, papa? Why?"

"You might find out something that I wish very much to know. It would not be hard at all. We are rather anxious about it."

"What is the matter?" asked Adele, with sudden interest.

"That is it. There is a disagreeable story afloat. More than one, in fact. It has reached my ears on good authority that Arden drinks far too much. You know what a brave girl Laura is. She hides it as well as she can, but she is terribly unhappy. Have you any idea whether there is any truth in all this?"

Adele hesitated a moment, and looked earnestly into her teacup, as though seeking advice. The moment was important. Her father had brought her own story back to her for confirmation, as it were. It might be dangerous to take the other side now. Suddenly she looked up with a well-feigned little smile of embarrassment.

"I would rather not say what I think, papa," she said, with the evident intention of not denying the tale.

"But, my dear," protested her father, "you must see how anxious we are on Laura's account. Really, my child, have a little confidence in me — tell me what you know."

"If you insist — well, I suppose I must. I am afraid there is no doubt about it. Laura's husband is very intemperate."

"Ah me! I feared so, from what I had heard," said the Prince, looking down, and shaking his head very sadly.

"You see, the people first began to talk about it last year, when he was in such a disgraceful condition in your house, and Pietro Ghisleri had to take him home."

"Yes, yes!" Gerano still shook his head sorrowfully. "I ought to have known, but they told me it was a fainting fit. And the worst of it is, my dear Adele, that there are other stories, and worse ones, too, about Laura. I hear that she is seriously in love with Francesco. Poor thing! it is no wonder — she is so unhappy at home, and Francesco is such a fine fellow, and always so kind to her everywhere."

"No, it is no wonder," assented Adele, who felt that she was launched, and must go to the end, though she had no time to consider the consequences.

"I suppose there is really some evidence about Arden's habits," resumed the Prince. "Of course he will deny it all, and I would like to have something to fall back upon — to convince myself more thoroughly, you understand."

Adele paused a moment.

"Arden has a Scotch servant," she said presently. "It appears that he is very intimate with our butler, who has often seen him going into the Tempietto with bottles of brandy hidden in an overcoat he carries on his arm."

"Dear me! How shocking!" exclaimed the Prince. "So old Giuseppe has actually seen that!"

"Often," replied Adele, with conviction. "But then, after all — so many men drink. If it were not for Laura — poor Laura!"

"Poor Laura, — yes, as I said, it is no wonder if she has fallen in love with Francesco — such a handsome fellow, too! She has shown good taste, at least." The Prince laughed gently. "At all events, you are not jealous, Adele; I can see that."

"I?" exclaimed Adele, with indignant scorn. "No, indeed!"

Gerano began to feel his pockets, as though searching for something he could not find. Then he rang the bell at his elbow.

"I have forgotten my cigarettes, my dear, I must have left them in my coat," he said.

The old butler answered his summons in person, for Gerano knew the usage of the house and had pressed the button three times, unnoticed by Adele, which meant that Giuseppe was wanted.

I

"I have left my cigarettes in my coat, Giuseppe," said the Prince. Then as the man turned to go, he called him back. "Giuseppe!"

"Excellency!"

"I want you to do a little commission for me. I have a little surprise for Donna Laura, and I do not want her to know where it comes from. It must be placed on her table, do you see? Now Donna Adele tells me that you are very intimate with Lord Herbert's Scotch servant—"

"I, Excellency?" Giuseppe was very much astonished.

"Yes—the man with sandy grey hair, and a big nose, and a red face—a most excellent servant, who has been with Lord Herbert since he was a child. Donna Adele says you know him very well—"

"Her Excellency must be mistaken. It must have been some other servant who told her. I never saw the man."

"You said Giuseppe, did you not?" asked the Prince very blandly, and turning to Adele. She bit her lip in silence. "Never mind," he continued. "It is a misunderstanding, and I will manage the surprise in quite another way. My cigarettes, Giuseppe."

The man went out, and Adele and the Prince sat without exchanging a word, until he returned with the case, Gerano all the time looking very gentle. When the servant was gone a second time, the Prince's expression changed suddenly, and he spoke in a stern voice.

"Now that you have sufficiently disgraced yourself, my daughter, you will begin to make reparation at once," he said.

Adele started as though she had been struck, and stared at him.

"I am in earnest," he added.

"What do you mean, papa?" she asked, frightened by his manner. "Disgraced myself? You must be mad!"

"You know perfectly well what I mean," answered her father. "I have been playing a little comedy with you,

and I have found out the truth. You know as well as I
that everything you have repeated to me this evening is
absolutely untrue, and there is some reason to believe
that you have invented these tales and set them going in
the world out of jealousy, and for no other reason, with
deliberate intention to do harm. Even if it were not you
who began, it would still be disgraceful enough on your
part to say such things even to me, and you have said
them to others. That last vile little invention about the
bottles was produced on the spur of the moment — I saw
you hesitate. You are responsible for all this, and no
one else. I will go into the world more in future than I
have done hitherto, and will watch you. You are to make
full reparation for what you have done. I insist upon it."

"And if I deny that I originated this gossip, and refuse
to obey you, what will you do?" asked Adele, defiantly.

"You are aware that under the present laws I can dispose of half my property as I please," observed the Prince.
"Laura has nothing — " He stopped significantly.

Adele turned pale. She was terrified, not so much at
the thought of losing the millions in question, but at the
idea of the consequence to herself in her father-in-law's
house. Casa Savelli counted upon the whole fortune as
confidently as though it were already theirs. She knew
very well how she should be treated during the rest of
her life, if one-half of the great property were lost to her
husband's family through her fault.

"You are forcing me to acknowledge myself guilty of
what I never did," she said, still trying to make a stand.
"What do you wish me to do?"

"You will everywhere say nice things about Laura and
her husband. You will say that you are now positively
sure that Arden does not drink. You will say that there
is no truth whatever in the report that Laura is in love
with Francesco, and that you are absolutely certain that
the Ardens are very happy together. Those are the principal points, I believe. You will also at once ask them
to dinner, and you will repeat your invitation often, and
behave to both in a proper way."

Adele laughed scornfully, though her mirth had something of affectation in it.

"Say pretty things, and invite them to dinner!" she exclaimed. "That is not very hard. I have not the slightest objection to doing that, because I should do it in any case, even if you had not made me this absurd scene."

"In future, my child, before you call anything I do or say absurd, I recommend you to think of the law regarding wills, to which I called your attention."

Adele was silent, for she saw that she was completely in her father's power. Being really guilty of the social misdeeds with which she was charged, she was not now surprised by his manner. What really amazed her was the display of diplomatic talent he had made, while entrapping her into what amounted to a confession. She had never supposed him capable of anything of the kind. But he was a quiet man, much more occupied in dealing with humanity in the management of his property than most people realised. No genius — certainly, — for if he had been, he would not have told the whole story to his wife, as he had done on the previous evening, but possessing the talent to choose the wise course at least as often as not, which is more than can be said for most people. There was something of the old-fashioned father about him, too, and he showed it in the little speech he made before leaving Adele that evening.

"And now, my dear daughter," he said, rising and standing before her as he spoke, "I have one word more to say before I go. You are my only child, and, in spite of all that has happened, I love you very much. I do not believe that you have ever done anything of the kind until now, and I do not think you will fall into the same fault in the future. If you do all that I have told you to do, I shall never refer to the matter after this, and we will try and forget it. But you have learned a lesson which you will remember all your life. Jealousy is a great sin, and slander is not only vile and degrading, but is also the greatest mistake possible from a worldly point of view. Remember that. If you wish to be successful in society, never speak an unkind word about any one. And now good night, my dear. Do what I have bidden you, and let us think no more about it."

Having concluded his sermon, Gerano kissed Adele on the forehead, as he was accustomed to do. She bent her head in silence, for she was so angry that she could not trust herself to speak, and he left her at the door and went home. All things considered, she knew that she had reason to be grateful for his forbearance. She was quite sure that her father-in-law would have behaved differently, and the stories she had heard of old Prince Saracinesca's temper showed clearly that the race of violent fathers was by no means yet extinct. She was not even called upon to make a formal apology to Laura in her father's presence, which was what she had at first expected and feared. Nothing, in fact, was required of her except to avoid gossip and treat the Ardens with a decent show of sisterly affection. She could scarcely have got better terms of peace, had she dictated them herself.

But she was far too angry to look at the affair in this light and far too deeply humiliated to forgive her father or the Ardens. If anything were necessary to complete her shame, it was the knowledge that she was utterly unable to cope with Gerano, who could disinherit her and her children of an enormous sum by a stroke of the pen, if he pleased; and he would please, if she did not obey him to the letter.

With a trembling hand she wrote the invitation required of her and gave it to be taken in the morning. Then she sat down and tried to read, taking up a great French review and opening it hap-hazard. The article chanced to be one on a medical subject, written by a very eminent practitioner, but not at all likely to interest Adele Savelli. But she felt the necessity of composing herself before meeting her husband when he should come home from the club, and she followed the lines with a sort of resolute

determination which belonged to her character at certain
moments. It was very hard to understand a word of
what she was reading, but she at last became absorbed in
the effort, and ultimately reached the end of the paper.

In the meantime, Francesco Savelli had spent his day in
deliberately thinking over the situation, and he had determined, very wisely, that it would be a great mistake to
speak to his wife on the subject. He went over in his
mind all the men of his acquaintance whom he might consult with safety and with some prospect of obtaining a
truthful answer to his question, and he saw that they
were by no means many. Wisdom and frankness are rare
enough separately, but rarer still in combination in the
same person, though a few are aware that the truest wisdom is the most consistent frankness. Most of those of
whom Savelli thought were men considerably older than
himself, and not men with whom he had any great intimacy. The Prince of Sant' Ilario and his cousin, the
Marchese di San Giacinto, Spicca, the melancholy and sarcastic, and perhaps Pietro Ghisleri — there were not many
more, and the last named, who was the nearest to him
in point of age, was not, as Savelli thought, very friendly
to him. On the whole, he determined to wait and bide
his time, watching Adele carefully, and collecting such
evidence as he could while studiously keeping his own
counsel. He saw very little of his wife on that day, and
when he next spoke to her about the Ardens, her manner
was so cordial and apparently sincere, that he at once
formed an opinion in her favour, as indeed he desired to
do, though it was more for the sake of his family as a
whole, than for her own.

"I have asked them to dinner," she said, "because we
never see anything of them, any more than if they were
not in Rome. Shall we have my father and the Princess,
too? It will make a family party."

"By all means," answered Savelli, who did not enjoy
the prospect of having the Ardens as the only guests,
after what had recently passed between himself and Lord

Herbert. "By all means — a family party — a sort of rejoicing over Arden's recovery."

"Dear Arden!" exclaimed Adele. "I like him now. I used to have the greatest antipathy for him because he is a cripple, poor fellow! I suppose that is natural, but I have quite got over it."

"I am very glad," observed Francesco. "You and Laura were brought up like sisters — there ought never to be any coldness between you."

"Oh, as for Laura, there never has been the least difference since we were children. We are sisters still, just as we used to be when you first came to the house. Do you remember, Francesco — four years ago? I used to think you liked Laura better than me. Indeed I did! It was so foolish, and now you are always so good to me that I see how silly I was. It never was true, carissimo, was it?"

"No, indeed!" answered Savelli, with an awkward laugh, and turning away his face to hide the colour that rose in his cheeks.

"Of course not. And as for Laura, she is so much in love with her husband that I believe she was dreaming of him even then, before she had ever seen him, and long before she was old enough to think of marrying any one. How she loves him! Is it not wonderful?"

Francesco glanced at his wife, and he believed that he was not mistaken in her. There was a look of genuine admiration almost amounting to enthusiasm in her face. He suppressed a slight sigh, for he still loved Laura in his helpless and hopeless way.

"Yes," he said, "it is wonderful, all things considered."

"But then," concluded Adele, "with Arden's beautiful character — well, I am not surprised."

CHAPTER IX.

ADELE SAVELLI was a very good actress, and she deceived her husband without much trouble, making him believe that she had never felt ill-disposed towards Laura, and that the repulsion she had felt for Arden had depended upon his deformity, to which she had now grown accustomed, as was quite natural. She had aways been careful not to speak out her mind upon the subject to Francesco, and had been more than cautious in other respects. She was far too clever a woman to let him hear the gossip she had originated except through outsiders, in the way of general conversation, and now she found it easy to change her tactics completely without doing anything to rouse his suspicion. She seemed very much preoccupied, however, in spite of her efforts to seem cheerful and agreeable during the two days which preceded the dinner party her father had obliged her to give. There were domestic details, too, which gave her trouble, and she had more than enough to occupy her. Her maid had been very ill, too, and was barely beginning to recover. Every woman of the world knows what it means to be suddenly deprived of a thoroughly good maid's services just at the opening of the season. That was one more annoyance among the many she encountered, and, in her opinion, not the smallest.

There was, of course, no open humiliation in what she was now forced to do, but she felt the shame of defeat very keenly whenever she thought of her interview with her father. It was not surprising that her hatred of the Ardens should suddenly take greater proportions under circumstances so favourable to its growth. And she hated them both with all her heart, while preparing herself to receive them with open arms and protestations of affection. But she did everything in her power to make the meeting effective. She even went so far as to buy pretty

little gifts for the Prince and Princess of Gerano, and for
Laura and Arden, which she took the trouble to conceal
with her own hands in the folds of each one's napkin
just before dinner; pretty little chiselled silver sweet-
meat boxes for the two ladies, and tiny matchboxes for
the men. Both the elder Savelli being away at the time,
she arranged everything according to her own taste, which
was excellent, thus taking advantage of her position as
temporary mistress of the house. There were flowers
scattered on the table, a form of decoration of which the
old butler disapproved, shaking his head mournfully as
he carried out Adele's directions.

She did not over-act her part when the evening came,
for she knew how to be very charming when she pleased,
and she meant on the present occasion to produce a very
strong impression upon every one present at dinner. She
succeeded well. The Ardens themselves were surprised
at the pleasant feeling which seemed to pervade everything. Gerano looked at his daughter approvingly,
repeatedly smiled, nodded to her, and at last drank her
health. Don Francesco was delighted, for he saw in his
wife's manner the strongest refutation of all that Arden
had told him two days earlier. Moreover, he had Laura
Arden on his left and was at liberty to talk to her as
much as he pleased, which was in itself a great satisfaction, especially as she herself was more than usually
cordial, being determined not to betray herself. Francesco looked across the table at Arden more than once,
with a significant glance, and inwardly congratulated
himself upon having said nothing to his wife about the
difficulty.

Arden looked ill. He had caught cold during that
interview with Savelli in the icy drawing-room, and even
an ordinary cold told quickly upon his appearance in his
weak state of health. But he did all in his power to seem
cheerful and talked more than usually well, so that his
wife alone knew that he was making an effort.

So the dinner passed off admirably — so well, indeed,

that when all were going home, Laura and her mother looked at one another as though they could hardly believe what they had seen and heard. The Princess of Gerano began to doubt the truth of the accusations against Adele, and even Laura fancied that they must have been very much exaggerated. The Prince, himself, the only one of the party who had heard the slander from Adele's own lips, sentence by sentence, and almost word for word as Ghisleri had repeated it to him, wisely held his peace, while by no means so wisely believing that his daughter had repented and was carrying out his instructions in all sincerity. He kissed her affectionately on the forehead when he went away, and she felt that she had won a victory.

"You look a little pale, my child," he said. "I have noticed it all the evening. Be very careful of your health, my dear."

"Yes, papa—but I am quite well, thank you," answered Adele.

Yet she did not look well. There was an odd, half-frightened look in her eyes when they were all gone and she was left alone with her husband. But he did not notice it, and made it easy for her, bestowing infinite praise upon her tact and talent as a hostess. Though she did not hear all he said, she was vaguely pleased, that, after spending the whole evening at Laura's side, he should stay at home instead of going to the club, and find so many pleasant things to say. In spite of her success, however, she spent a restless night.

Laura looked anxiously at Arden's face when they got home. He looked worse, and coughed two or three times in a way she did not like.

"You are very tired, dear," she said. "You had better not get up to-morrow. The rest will do you good."

"I think you are right," he answered. "I need rest."

The next morning his cold was worse, and he did not rise. He seemed restless and nervous, too, perhaps from the fatigue of the previous evening. The doctor came and said there was no danger, as the cold was not on the lungs, and that the best thing to be done was to stay in bed two or three days. Later in the afternoon Pietro Ghisleri called, and Laura, at Arden's express desire, received him alone, promising to bring him into the bedroom afterwards. Several days had passed since they had met. Ghisleri was looking fresher and less nervous than the last time Laura had seen him. He, on his part, saw that she was anxious again, for there were dark shadows under her eyes as there had been when she had first returned from England.

"Is there anything wrong?" he asked, as soon as they met.

"Herbert has a bad cold," she answered. "The doctor says it is nothing serious, but he coughs, and I am worried about him."

Ghisleri reminded her that there was nothing the matter with Arden's lungs, and that a cough might be a very insignificant affair, after all. Then she told him of the dinner party on the previous evening, dwelling at length on the tact and amiability Adele had displayed. Pietro was inclined to smile, when he understood that what he had said to Gerano had borne fruit so soon. He was quite sure that before night he should hear of some even more amiable doings on Adele's part, for he guessed at once that the Prince had forced her to change her behaviour. But he kept his reflections to himself. There was no reason why any one but Gerano should ever know that he had been concerned in the matter. He had no idea that everything had been repeated through the family, till it had reached Laura herself.

"Donna Adele has great social talent," he remarked, finding, as usual, the one thing to be said in her favour.

"Indeed she has!" assented Laura, with a constrained little laugh, and looking into his blue eyes.

Ghisleri made no sign, however, and presently began to talk of other matters. He always felt a singular satisfaction in being with Laura, and this year he noticed that it was growing upon him. The impression he had first formed of her, when she had appeared in society, was confirmed year by year, and appealed to ·a side of his nature of which few people suspected the existence. It depended largely on Laura's looks, no doubt, which strongly suggested the high predominance of all that was good over the ordinary instincts of average human nature. He felt a sort of reverence for her which he had never felt for any one; he knew that she was good, he imagined that she was almost saintly in her life, and he believed that she might, under certain circumstances become, in the best religious sense, a holy woman. Had he seen her on that evening when Arden had found her strangling an imaginary enemy in a fit of exceedingly human anger, he could hardly have accepted the evidence of his senses. All that was good in her appealed directly through all that was bad in him to the small remnant of the better nature which had survived through his misspent life. It did not, indeed, rouse in him the slightest active desire to imitate her virtues. The very idea that he could ever be virtuous in any sense, brought a smile to his face. But he could not help admiring what he knew to be so very far beyond his sphere — what he believed, perhaps, to be even further from his reach than it actually was. He had reached that almost morbid stage of self-contempt in which a man, while still admiring goodness in others, checks even the aspiration towards it in his own heart, because he is convinced that it cannot be really genuine, and looks upon it as one of the affectations most to be despised in himself. He had got so far sometimes as to refuse a very wretched beggar a penny, merely because he doubted the sincerity of the charitable impulse which impelled his hand towards his pocket — laughing bitterly at himself afterwards when he thought of the poor wretch's disappointed face, and going back to find him again, perhaps, and to bestow a silver coin, simply because he could not resist the temptation to be kind.

Such unhealthy conditions of mind may seem inconceivable and incomprehensible to men of other nature, all whose thoughts are natural, logical, and sound. They exist, none the less, and not by any means necessarily in persons otherwise weak or morbid. The very absurdity of them, which cannot escape the man himself, makes him seem still more despicable in his own eyes, increases his distrust of himself and gives rise, completing the vicious circle, to conditions each time more senselessly self-torturing than the last. It is hard to bring such men to see how untenable their own position is. They will not even believe that a good instinct underlies the superstructure of morbid fancy, and that the latter could not exist without it.

Ghisleri looked long at Laura and admired her more than ever, realising at the same time how deeply her personality was impressed in his thoughts, and how vividly he was able at all times to evoke her outward image, and the conception he had formed of her character. He almost hated old Spicca for having said that no one could possibly be as good as she looked. In her own self she was the most overwhelming refutation of that remark; but then, he reflected, Spicca did not know her well enough, and habitually believed in nothing and in nobody. At least every one supposed that was Spicca's view of the world.

Before long Laura took Pietro to see Arden, and left the two together.

"There is something seriously wrong with me, Ghisleri," said his friend. "I am going to be very ill. I feel it."

It was not like him to speak in that way, for he was brave and generally did his best to hide his sufferings from every one. Ghisleri looked at him anxiously. His face was drawn and pinched, and there were spots of colour on his cheeks which had not been there a few hours earlier.

"Perhaps you have a little fever with the cold," suggested Pietro, in a reassuring tone. "It often happens in this country."

"I dare say," replied Arden. "It may be so. At all events, your specialist was right about the main thing, and I am no more consumptive than you are. But I feel — I cannot tell why — that I am going to be very ill indeed. It may be an impression, and even if I am, I shall probably weather it."

"Of course you will." But Ghisleri was in reality alarmed.

"I am so glad you came to-day," continued Arden, speaking more rapidly. "If I should get worse to-morrow, really ill, you know — you must write to my brother. I would not ask my wife to do it for worlds. Do you understand?"

"Perfectly — but I do not believe there will be any reason —"

"Never mind that!" exclaimed Arden, interrupting him almost impatiently. "If there is any reason, you will write. I cannot tell you all about it. Of course I may not be delirious, you know, but again, I may be — one is never sure, and then it would be too late. Uncle Herbert is alive still, thank God, and quite well, and if anything should happen to me, his will would be worth nothing. Laura would not get a penny and would be dreadfully poor. Henry must do something for her. Do you understand me? He must. You must see to it, too, or he will never think of it — kind as he is. Those things do not strike him. You see I have only my small portion — which is little enough, as you know, because there are so many sisters — and they are not all rich, either. We could not go on living in this way long — but Henry was very generous. He sent me two thousand pounds when we were married, and the yacht too, so that we spent very little —"

"You are exhausting yourself, my dear fellow," said Ghisleri, growing more anxious as he listened to the sick man's excited talk. "You have told me all this before, and your brother knows it too; he will not allow Lady Herbert — "

"One never can tell what he will do," broke in Arden, raising himself a little on his elbow, and facing his friend. His eyes were unnaturally brilliant. "He is so eccentric. And Laura must have money — she must have plenty — not that she is extravagant, but you know how she was brought up in the Gerano's house, and I should never have thought of marrying her, but for Uncle Herbert's money."

"You would both have been perfectly happy on a hundred a year," observed Pietro. "People are when they love each other as you do."

Arden's face softened at once, and Ghisleri saw that he was thinking of his wife. He was silent for a few moments.

"That is all very well," he said, suddenly rousing himself again. "That might do so long as I should be there to make life smooth for her. But when she is left alone — especially here — Ghisleri, I do not like to think that she must live here after I am gone — "

"For Heaven's sake do not begin to talk in that way, Arden! It is perfectly absurd. You only have a cold, after all!"

"Perhaps so. I believe I have something worse. Never mind! I was saying that I could not bear to think of her living here without me. It is quite true. No — it is not sentiment — something much more reasonable and real. There are people here who hate us both, who positively hate us, and who will make her life unbearable when there is no one to protect her — the more so, if she is poor. And besides, you know what will happen before long — oh, I cannot think of it!"

Ghisleri did not answer at once, for it was not clear to him how Arden had discovered that he had enemies. But the latter waited for no answer, and went on after a few seconds, still speaking excitedly.

"You see," he said, "how necessary it is that Harry

should come — that you should write to him — that he
should be made to understand — he must do something
for Laura, Ghisleri — he really must."

There was something painful in the persistent repeti-
tion of the thought, and then, oddly enough, Pietro started
as he heard his own name pronounced almost without an
interval, immediately after that of Laura. It sounded
very strangely — Laura Ghisleri — he had never thought
of it before. A moment later he scorned himself for
thinking of it at all.

"My dear Arden," he said, "you are really making
yourself ill about nothing. Put it all out of your mind
for the present, and remember that I am always ready if
you need anything. You have only to send for me, and
besides, I shall come every day until you are quite well."

"Thank you, my dear fellow, you are a good friend.
Perhaps you are right. But as I lie here, thinking of all
the possibilities — "

"You are beginning again," interrupted Ghisleri. "I
must go away or you will talk yourself into a fever."

At that moment Laura re-entered the room. She started
a little when she saw her husband's face.

"How do you find him?" she asked quickly of Ghisleri.

"He has a cold," answered the latter, cheerfully, "and
perhaps there is a little fever with it. I am going to
leave him, for he ought to keep quiet and not tire himself
with too much talking."

He shook hands with Arden. Laura followed him out
into the passage beyond.

"He is very ill!" she exclaimed, in a low voice, touching his sleeve in her excitement. "I can see it. He
never looked like that."

"It may not be anything serious," answered Ghisleri.
"But he ought to see the doctor at once. I have a cab
down stairs, and I will go and find him and bring him
here. Keep him quiet; do not let him talk."

"Yes. You are so kind."

She left him and went back to Arden's bedside. He was tossing uneasily as though he could not find rest in any position, and the great round spots on his cheeks had deepened almost to a purple colour. He scarcely seemed to notice her entrance, but as she turned to move something on the table, after smoothing his pillow, he caught her suddenly by the skirt of her frock.

"Laura! Laura! do not go away!" he cried. "Do not leave me alone."

"No, love, I am not going," she answered gently, and sat down by his side.

Ghisleri was not gone long. By a mere chance he found the doctor at home, and brought him back. Then he waited in the drawing-room to hear the result of the visit. The physician's face was graver when he returned, and Laura was not with him.

"Is it anything serious?" asked Ghisleri.

"I am afraid so. I shall be better able to tell in a couple of hours. The fever is very high, the other symptoms will develop before long, and we shall know what it is."

"What do you think it might be?"

"It might be scarlet fever," answered the doctor. "I am afraid it is. But say nothing at present. You should get a nurse at once, for some one must sit up with him all night. I will send him something to take immediately, and I will come back myself in about two hours."

. They went away together, but when the doctor returned, he found Ghisleri waiting for him in the street. It was now five o'clock and quite dark. Pietro remained down stairs while the visit lasted.

"Well?" he asked, when the physician came down again.

"It is scarlet fever, as I was afraid — one of the most sudden cases I ever knew. They have not got a nurse yet, the idea seems to frighten Lady Herbert."

"I will see to it," said Ghisleri. "By the bye, it is contagious, is it not? I have a visit to pay before dinner; ought I to change my clothes?"

K

The doctor smiled. He did not know Ghisleri, and fancied that he might be timid.

"It is not contagious yet," he answered, "or hardly at all. I do not think there is any danger."

"There might be a little — even a very little, you think?" asked Pietro, insisting.

"Of course it can do no harm to change one's clothes," replied the other, somewhat surprised.

"You have told Lady Herbert exactly what must be done, I suppose. In that case I shall not go up."

The doctor was confirmed in his suspicion that Ghisleri was afraid of catching the fever, and got into his carriage, musing on the deceptive nature of appearances. Pietro wrote a few words on his card, telling Laura that he would be back before dinner time with the best nurse to be found, and sent it up by the porter. Then he drove home as quickly as possible, dressed himself entirely afresh, and went to see the Contessa dell' Armi.

"I have come," he said, after the first greeting, "to tell you that you will not see me for several days. Arden has got the scarlet fever, and I shall be there taking care of him, more or less, until he is out of danger."

"Can they not have a nurse for him?" asked Maddalena, raising her eyebrows.

"There will be a nurse, too. I am going to get one now and take her there."

"You do not seem anxious to consult me in the least," said the Contessa. "You never do nowadays."

"What do you mean? Do you think this is a case of consulting any one? I do not understand."

"Do you think you have any right to risk your life in this way? Do you think you contribute to my happiness by doing it? And yet I have heard you say that my happiness is first in your thoughts. Not that I ever believed it."

"You are wrong," answered Ghisleri, gently. "I would do almost anything for you."

"What a clever reservation — 'almost' anything. You

know that if you did not put it in that way, I should tell you not to go near the Ardens until there is no danger of catching the fever."

"Of course," assented Pietro.

"You ought not to be so diplomatic. You used to talk very differently. Do you remember that evening by the waterfall at Vallombrosa? You have changed since then."

Her classic face began to harden in the way he knew so well.

"There is no question of diplomacy," he said quietly. "Arden has been my friend these ten years, and he is in very great danger. I mean to take care of him as long as I am needed because I do not trust nurses, and because Lady Herbert is anything but strong herself at the present time, and may break down or lose her head. As for risking my life, there is no risk at all in the matter. I have very little belief in contagion, though the doctors talk about it."

"I suppose you have just seen him," observed the Contessa, who was determined to find fault. "You do not seem to ask yourself whether I share your disbelief."

"Since you ask," said Ghisleri, with a smile, "I admit that I changed my clothes before coming to see you, for that very reason. Some people do believe in danger of that kind."

"I am glad you admit it. So I am not to see you until Lord Herbert is quite well again. I will not answer for the consequences. I have something to say to you to-day. Are you in a hurry?"

"Not in the least."

"It will not take long. I have discovered another proof of your desertion. You know what pleasant things Adele Savelli says about me — and you, too. I have told you more than once exactly what was repeated to me. Did you ever take any steps to prevent her talking about me?"

"No, I never did. I do not even see how I could. Can I quarrel with Francesco Savelli, because his wife spreads scandalous reports about you? It would look singularly like fighting your battles."

"And yet," retorted the Contessa, speaking slowly, and fixing her eyes on his, "there is no sooner something said against Lady Herbert Arden, than you show your teeth and fight in earnest. Can you deny it?"

"No, I do not lie," answered Ghisleri. "But I did not know that you were aware of the fact. Some one has been indiscreet, as usual."

"Of course. That sort of thing cannot be a secret long. All Rome knows that there was a dinner of reconciliation at the Palazzo Savelli last night, that every one embraced every one else, that Adele looks like death to-day, and is going about everywhere saying the most delightful things about the Ardens, in the most horribly nervous way. You see what power you have when you choose to use it."

She spoke bitterly, though she was conscious that the right was not all on her side, and that Ghisleri, as he said, could defend the Ardens without fear of adverse criticism, whereas it would be a very different matter if he entered the lists in her defence.

"You are not quite just to me, my dear lady," he said, after a moment's reflection. "You are not the wife of my old friend, and an otherwise indifferent person —"

"Quite indifferent?" She looked keenly at him.

"Quite," he answered, with perfect sincerity. "A person is indifferent whom one neither loves nor calls an intimate friend. Yet Lady Herbert is beautiful and good, and is admirable in many ways. But the world knows that I am no more in love with her than with Donna Adele, and I am quite free, therefore, to defend her."

"Of course you are. The only thing that surprises me is your alacrity in doing so. You do not generally like to give yourself trouble for indifferent people. But then, as Arden really is your friend —" She stopped, with a little impatient movement of the shoulders.

"I wish you could bring yourself for once to believe that I am not altogether insincere and calculating in everything I do," said Ghisleri, weary of her perpetual suspicion.

"I wish I could," she answered coldly. "But how can I? There are such extraordinary inconsistencies in your character, such contradictions — it is very hard to believe in you. And yet," she added sadly, "God knows I must — for my own sake."

"Then do!" exclaimed Pietro, with energy. "Make an end of all this doubting. Have I ever lied to you? Have I ever made a promise to you and not kept it? How have I deceived you? And yet you never trust me altogether, and I know it."

"It is not that — it is not that!" repeated Maddalena. "What you say is all true, in its way. It is — how shall I say it — you did not deceive me, but I was deceived in you. You are not what I thought you were. You used to say that you would stand at nothing — that my word was your law — all those fine phrases you used to make to me, and they all seem to come to nothing when reality begins."

"If you would tell me what you expect me to do, you would not find me slow in doing it."

"That is the thing. If you loved me as you say you do, would you need any direction? Your heart would tell you."

"You are angry with me now, because you do not wish me to take care of Arden — "

"Can I wish that you should be willing to cut yourself off from me for a week — or two weeks? I suppose that is your idea of love. It is not mine."

"Then be frank in your turn. You have the right to ask what you please of me. Say plainly that you wish me to give up the idea, to leave Arden to the doctors and the nurses, and I will obey you unhesitatingly."

"I would not have the sacrifice now — not as a gift," murmured Maddalena, passionately. "If you could think of doing it, you shall do it. I will force you to it now. I will not see you until Arden does not need you any more — not even if you never go near him. If you do not think of me naturally, I would rather that you should never think of me again."

Ghisleri rose and went to the fireplace, and looked at the objects on the mantelpiece for a long time, without seeing them. There was a strange conflict in his heart at that moment. He could not tell whether he loved her or not — that he had loved her a very short time since, he was sure. At the present juncture it would be very easy to tell her the truth, if his love were no longer real, and to break with her once and for ever. Did she love him? Cruelly and coldly he compared her love with that of another whom he had sacrificed long ago — a memory that haunted him still at times. That had been love indeed. Was this also love, but of another kind? Then, suddenly, he despised himself for his fickleness, and he thought of what Maddalena had done and risked for him, and for him alone.

"Maddalena," he said, and his voice shook as he came to her side, and took her small white hand. "Forgive me, forgive me all there is to forgive. I am a brute sometimes. I cannot help it."

Her lip trembled a little, but her face did not relax.

"There is nothing to forgive," she said. "It is I who have been mistaken."

CHAPTER X.

GHISLERI left the Contessa's house anything but calm. To hate himself and the whole world in general, with one or two unvarying exceptions, was by no means a new sensation. He was quite familiar with it and looked upon it as a necessary condition of mind, through which he must pass from time to time, and from which he was never very far removed. But he had rarely, in his ever-changing life, been in such strange perturbation of spirit as on this particular evening. He was almost beyond reasoning, and he seemed to be staring at the facts that faced him in a day-dream horribly like reality. He knew that if he really loved Maddalena, he would sacrifice his friend, even after what the Contessa had said, and that, after a day or two, she would probably relent. Nor did the sacrifice seem a very great one. People were ill all the year round, were taken care of by the members of their own family and by nurses, and recovered or died as the case might be. He had no especial knowledge to help him in watching over Herbert Arden, though he believed himself quiet and skilful in a sick-room, and had more than once done what he could in such cases. He felt, indeed, that he was more deeply attached to the man than he had supposed himself to be, but he had not imagined that, at the critical moment, that attachment would outweigh all consideration for Maddalena dell' Armi. And yet, he not only clung to the belief that he loved her, but was conscious that there was a broad foundation of truth for that belief to rest upon. He asked himself in vain why he was at that moment going from her house to Arden's, and he found no answer. That Laura herself contributed in any way to strengthen his resolve was too monstrous to be believed, even by himself, against himself. He was not so bad as that yet. He laughed bitterly at his inability to comprehend his own motives and impulses, as he drove to the little convent of the French Sisters of the " Bon Secours," to ask for the best nurse they could give him. It was strange, too, that he should be coming directly from Maddalena's side to the habitation of a community of almost saintly women — stranger still, that he should be on his way to a house where, during the next few days, he expected to spend his time in the society of a woman who ranked even higher than they in his exalted estimate of her character.

He got the nurse, and she was despatched in the company of another sister in a separate cab, while

Ghisleri followed in his own.   When they reached the house, they found that Arden was much worse.   His mind was wandering, and, though he constantly called for Laura, he did not know her when she came to his side, trying to keep back the scalding tears, lest they should fall on him as she bent down to catch his words. The doctor had been sent for a third time in great haste. Meanwhile, the sister went about her duties silently and systematically, making herself thoroughly familiar with the arrangements of the room, and preparing all that could be needed during the night, so far as she could foresee the doctor's possible instructions.   She smoothed Arden's pillows with a hand the practised perfection of whose touch told a wonderful tale of life-long labour among the sick.

"Madame should not be here," she said to Ghisleri, in a quiet, even voice.   "It may soon be contagious."

Laura heard the words as she stood on the other side of the bed, watching every passing expression on Arden's flushed face.

"I will not leave him," she said simply.

The sister did not answer.   She had done her duty in giving the warning, and she could do no more.   When she had finished all her arrangements, she sat down, accustomed to husband her strength always, against the strain that must inevitably fall upon it day by day. She took out her small black book and began to read, glancing at Arden at regular intervals of about a minute.

Ghisleri entreated Laura to take some rest, or at least to follow the sister's example and sit down, since nothing could be done.   She did not seem to understand.   He was glad he had come, for he fancied she was losing her head already.   He stood beside her watching his friend and waiting for the doctor, who appeared before long.

"It is one of the most extraordinarily virulent cases I ever knew," he said to Ghisleri, when the two were alone together in the drawing-room, for Laura would not leave her husband's side for a moment.   "I hardly know

what to make of it, though of course there can be no
doubt as to what it is. It is better that you should know
how serious the case is. I presume you are an intimate
friend of Lord Herbert Arden's ? "

" Yes, an old friend."

" And you are not afraid of catching the fever ? "
asked the doctor.

" Not in the least."

" Oh, I thought from a question you asked—" He
hesitated.

" I was going to see a friend, and I wanted to be on
the safe side," said Ghisleri.

" I am glad of that ; it is just as well that there should
be a man at hand. Shall you spend the night here ? "

" Yes," replied Ghisleri.

" Very good. I have told the sister to send for me
if the temperature rises more than two-tenths of a degree
centigrade higher than it is now. It ought to go down.
If I am called anywhere I will leave the address at
my lodgings, where one of my servants will sit up all
night. I confess that I am surprised by the case. In
Rome the scarlet fever is rarely so dangerous."

Thereupon the doctor took his leave and Ghisleri
remained alone in the drawing-room. He sat down and
took up a book. For the present it seemed best not to
go back to Arden's room. His constant presence might
be disagreeable to Laura, since she could not be induced
to leave her husband as yet. Ghisleri's turn would come
when she was exhausted, or when he had an opportunity
of persuading her to take some rest. Until then there was
nothing to be done but to wait. A servant came in and
put wood on the fire and turned down a lamp that was
smoking a little. He inquired of Ghisleri whether her
ladyship would wish any dinner served, and Pietro told
him to keep something in readiness in case she should
be hungry. He himself rarely had much appetite, and
to-night he had none at all. He tried to read, without
much success, for his own thoughts crowded upon each

other so quickly and tumultuously that he found it impossible to concentrate his attention.

The clocks struck half-past eight, nine, ten, and half-past ten, and still he sat motionless in his place. Again the Italian servant came in, put wood on the fire and looked to the lamps. Did the Signore know what orders were to be given for the night? The Signore did not know, as her ladyship was still with his lordship, and was not to be disturbed, but some food must be kept ready in case she needed it. Eleven, half-past, twelve. Again the door opened. There was something awful in the monotony of it all, Ghisleri thought, but this time Donald appeared instead of the Italian, who had been sent to bed. After making very much the same inquiries as the latter, Donald paused.

"His lordship is very ill, sir, as I understand," he said. He had known Ghisleri as his master's friend for years.

"Yes, Donald, he is very ill," answered Ghisleri, gravely. "It is scarlet fever, the doctor says. We must all help to take care of him."

"Yes, sir."

The few insignificant words exchanged with the servant seemed to rouse Ghisleri from the reverie in which he had sat so many hours. When Donald was gone he rose from the chair and began to walk up and down the drawing-room. The inaction was irksome, and he longed to be of use. He would have gone to Arden's room, but he fancied it would be better to let Laura stay there without him, until she was very tired, and then to take her place. She would be more likely to rest if she had a long watch at first, he thought. As a matter of fact, an odd sort of delicacy influenced him, too, almost without his knowing it,—an undefined instinct which made him leave her with the man she so dearly loved in the presence only of a stranger and a woman, rather than intrude himself as the third person and the witness of her anxiety.

As he turned for the fiftieth time in his short, monotonous walk, he saw Laura entering at the opposite end of the room. She was dressed all in white, in a loose robe of some soft and warm material, gathered about the waist and hanging in straight folds. Her heavy black hair was fastened in a great knot, low at the back of her head. The light fell full upon her pale face and deep, dark eyes as she caught sight of Ghisleri, and stood still at the door, her hand upon the curtain as she thrust it aside from before her. She was so really beautiful at that moment that Pietro started and stared at her.

"I did not know you were here," she said softly. He came forward to meet her.

"I will take my turn when you are willing to go and rest," he answered. "I have waited for that reason. How is he now ?"

"Much more quiet," answered Laura. "The sister persuaded me that my being there perhaps prevented his going to sleep, and so I came away. She will call me if there is any change. Oh! if he could only sleep!"

Ghisleri knew how very improbable such a fortunate circumstance was at the outset of such a severe illness, but he said nothing about it. Any idea which could give Laura hope was good in itself. She sank into a deep chair by the fire and watched the flames, her chin resting on her hand. She seemed almost unconscious of Ghisleri's presence as he stood leaning against the mantelpiece and looking down at her.

"I will go and see how he is," he said at last, and went towards the door. Just as he touched the handle she called him in an odd tone as though she were startled by something.

"Signor Ghisleri! Please come back."

He obeyed, and resumed his former attitude.

"I am very nervous," she said, with a little shiver. "Please do not leave me — I — I am afraid to be alone. If you wish to go, we will go together."

Ghisleri concealed his surprise, which was considerable.

The wish she expressed was very foreign to her usually quiet and collected nature. He saw that her nerves were rudely shaken.

"It is very weak of me," she said presently, in an apologetic tone. "But I see his face all the time, and I hear that dreadful wandering talk — I cannot bear it."

"I do not wonder," answered Pietro, quietly. "You must be very tired, too. Will you not lie down on the sofa, while I sit here and wait? It would be so much better. You will need your strength to-morrow."

"That is true," she said, as though struck by the truth of the last words.

She crossed the room and lay down upon a large sofa at a little distance from the fire, arranged the folds of her dress with that modest, womanly dignity some women have in their smallest actions, clasped her hands, and closed her eyes. Pietro sat down and looked at her, musing over the strange combination of circumstances which formed themselves in his life. It seemed odd that he should be where he was, towards the small hours of the morning, watching over one of the women he admired most in the world, keeping his place at her especial request, when he had in reality come to help in taking care of her husband. How the world would wag its head and talk, he thought, if it could guess where he was!

For a long time Laura did not move, and he was sure that she was still awake. Then, all at once, he saw her hands relax and loosen from each other, her head turned a little on the dark velvet cushion, and she sighed as she sank to sleep. She was less quiet after that. Her lips moved, and she stirred uneasily from time to time, evidently dreaming over again the painful scenes of the evening. Ghisleri rang the bell, crossed the room swiftly, and opened the door without noise. Donald appeared in the hall outside.

"Her ladyship has fallen asleep on the sofa," said Pietro. "She does not wish to be left alone. Is there any woman servant awake in the house?"

"No, sir. Her ladyship sent her maid to bed."

"Never mind. Go and sit quietly in the drawing-room, in case she should need anything, while I go and see how Lord Herbert is."

"Very good, sir."

The world would have been even more surprised now than before, especially if it could have understood the meaning of what Ghisleri did, and the refined reverence implied in his unwillingness to remain in the drawing-room longer than necessary. It would not have believed in his motive, and it would have added that he was very foolish not to enjoy the artistic pleasure of watching over the beautiful woman in her sleep as long as he could, more especially as she had gone to the length of asking him to do so. But Ghisleri thought very differently.

He entered the sick-room, and sat down by the bedside. Arden was in a restless state between waking and unconsciousness, moaning aloud without articulating any words, his face flushed to a deep purple hue, his eyes half open and turned up under the lids, so that only the white was visible. The sister was seated by the table, on which stood a small lamp, the light being screened from Arden by a makeshift consisting of the cover of a bandbox supported by a few heavy books. When Ghisleri had entered she had glanced at him, and explained by a sign that there was no change. Neither he nor she thought of speaking during the hour that followed. The sister had a watch before her on the table, and at regular intervals she rose, poured a spoonful of something into Arden's mouth, smoothed his pillow, saw that he was as comfortable as he could be, and went back to her seat. At the end of the hour she took Arden's temperature with the fever thermometer, and wrote down the result on a sheet of paper. It had fallen one-tenth of a degree since midnight.

"It generally does towards morning," said the sister, in a low voice, in answer to Ghisleri's inquiry as to whether this was a really favourable symptom of a change for the better.

The night passed wearily. Pietro felt that he was of little use, unless his presence in the house afforded Laura some sort of moral support. So far as the nursing was concerned, the sister neither needed nor expected any assistance. Towards five o'clock, Laura entered the room. On waking from her sleep, she had seen Donald seated in Ghisleri's place, and had wondered why the latter had gone away.

"He seems better," she whispered, bending over her husband, and softly smoothing the thick brown hair from his forehead.

"The temperature has fallen," answered Ghisleri, giving her the only encouragement he could.

"Thank God!" Laura sat down by the opposite side of the bed. Presently, by a sign, she asked Ghisleri whether he would not go home.

"I will wait in the drawing-room until the doctor comes, and the other sister has arrived for the day," he said, coming to her side.

She merely nodded, and he quietly went out. Before long, Donald brought him some coffee, and he sat where he had sat in the early part of the night, anxiously awaiting the doctor's coming.

There was little enough to be learned, when the latter actually came. A very bad case, he said, so bad that he would not be averse to asking the opinion of a colleague, — and later, the same colleague came, saw Arden, shook his head, and said that it was the worst case he had ever seen, but that the treatment so far was perfectly correct.

There was nothing to be done, but to take the best care possible of the patient. Ghisleri had no hope whatever, and Laura became almost totally silent. She could not be paler than she was, but Pietro almost fancied that she was growing hourly thinner, while the sad eyes seemed to sink deeper and deeper beneath the marble brow. He went home for a few hours to dress, and returned at midday. The loss of one night's rest had not even told upon his face, but his expression was grave and reserved in the

extreme, and his manner even more than usually quiet.
Laura had not slept since her nap in the drawing-room,
and looked exhausted, though she was not yet really
tired out. Ghisleri thought it was time to speak seriously to her.

"My dear Lady Herbert," he said, "forgive me for
being quite frank. This is not a time for turning phrases.
You must positively rest, or you will break down and
you may be dangerously ill yourself."

"I do not feel tired," she said.

"Your nerves keep you up. I entreat you to think of
what I say, and I must say it. You may risk your own
life, if you please; it is natural that you should run
at least the risk of contagion, but you have no right to
risk another life than your own by uselessly wearing out
your strength. Besides, Arden is unconscious now;
when he begins to recover he will need you far more, and
will not need me at all."

A very slight blush rose in Laura's pale cheeks, and
she turned away her face. A short pause followed.

"I think you are right," she said at last. Then, without looking at him, she left the room.

Ghisleri watched her until she disappeared, and there
was a strange expression in his usually hard blue eyes.
It seemed as though the woman could do nothing without touching some sensitive, sympathetic chord in his
inner nature, though her presence left him apparently
perfectly cold and indifferent. Yet he had known himself so long, that he dreaded the sensation, and his ever-
ready self-contempt rose at the idea that he could possibly find himself capable of loving his friend's wife, even
in the most distant future. Besides, there was nothing
at all really resembling love in what he felt, so far as he
could judge. If it ever developed into love, it would
turn out to be a love so far nobler than anything there
had been in his life, as to be at present beyond his
comprehension.

He did not see Laura again for several hours. He

spent the day in Arden's room, and for the first time felt that he was of use when his strength was needed to lift the frail body from one bed to the other. Arden grew rapidly worse, Ghisleri thought, and the doctor confirmed his opinion when he came for the third time that day.

"To be quite frank," he said gravely, as he took leave of Pietro in the hall, "I have no hope of his recovery, and I doubt whether he will last until to-morrow night."

This was no surprise to Ghisleri, who knew how little strength of resistance lay in the crippled frame. He bent his head in silence as the physician went out, and he almost shivered as he thought of what was before him. He knew now that he must stand by Laura's side at the near last moment of great suffering, when she was to see the one being she loved pass away before her eyes. He was more than ever glad that he had induced her to rest. Arden's mind was still wandering, and she could be of no immediate use.

So the day ended at last and the night began and wore on, much like the previous one, saving that the anxiety of all was trebled. The other sister had returned, and Ghisleri saw by her face that she had no hope. With the same faultless regularity she performed her duties through the long hours.

Towards midnight Laura and Ghisleri met in the drawing-room. For several minutes she stood in silence before the fire. Pietro could see that her lips were trembling as though she were on the point of bursting into tears. He knew how proud she must be, and he moved away towards the door. She heard his step behind her, and without turning round she beckoned to him with her hand to stay. He came back and stood at a little distance from her. Still she was silent for a moment; then she spoke.

"It is coming," she said unsteadily. "You must help me to bear it."

"I will do my best," answered Ghisleri, earnestly.

Another pause followed. Then again she made a gesture, hurried and almost violent, bidding him leave her. Before he could reach the door he heard her first sob, and as he closed it behind him the storm of her passionate grief broke upon the silence of the night. He was not a man easily moved to any outward demonstration of feeling, but the tears stood in his eyes as he went back to Arden's bedside, and they were not for the friend he was so soon to lose.

The sick man was unconscious and lay quite still on his back with closed lids. The sister was on her feet, watching him intently. She shook her head sadly when Ghisleri looked at her. The end was not far off, as she in her great experience well knew. In hot haste Pietro sent for the doctor, with a message saying that Lord Herbert was dying. But when he came he admitted reluctantly that he could do nothing; there was no hope even of prolonging life until morning.

"Lady Herbert should be told the truth," he said. "If you wish it I will wait in another room until the end."

"I think it would be better. Lady Herbert knows that there is no hope, but she will feel less nervous if you are at hand. How long do you expect — ? "

"He will not live many minutes after he comes to himself, I should say. The little strength there was is all gone. There will be a lucid interval of a few moments, and then the heart will stop. It was always defective."

"Then Lady Herbert ought to be with him now, in case it comes," said Ghisleri.

He left the doctor in the little room which Arden had used as a study, and went back to the drawing-room, feeling that one of the hardest moments of his life had come. Laura was seated in a deep chair, leaning back, her eyes half-closed and her cheeks still wet with tears. She started as Ghisleri entered.

"The doctor has seen him again," he said. "If you are able, it would be better —" He stopped, for he saw that she understood.

L

They went back together. As they entered the room they heard Arden's weak voice.

"Laura, darling, where are you?" he was asking. Ghisleri saw that he was quite in possession of his faculties and went quietly out, leaving him with his wife and the sister.

"I am here, love," Laura answered, coming swiftly up to his side and supporting him as he tried to sit up.

"It was so long," he said faintly. "I am so glad you have come, dear."

"You must not try to talk. You must not tire yourself."

"It can make no difference now," he answered, letting his head rest upon her shoulder. "I must speak, dear one — this once before I die. Yes, I know I am dying. It is better so. I have had in you all that God has to give, all the happiness of a long life, in these short months."

He paused and drew a painful breath. Laura's face was like alabaster, but she did not break down again now until all was over.

"I owe it all to you — my life's love. You have given me so much, and I have given you so little. But God will give it all back to you, dear, some day. There is one thing I must say — oh, my breath!"

He gasped in an agonised way, and almost choked. Laura thought it was the end, but he rallied again presently.

"One thing, darling — you must remember, if you have loved me — ah, and you have, dear — that no promise binds you. You must try and think that if you forego any happiness for the memory of me, you will be taking that same happiness from me as well as from yourself. It will be right and just that you should marry if you wish to."

"Oh, Herbert! Herbert!" cried Laura, pressing him to her, "do not talk so!"

"Promise me that you will never think yourself

bound," he said earnestly, speaking with more and more effort. " I shall not die happily unless you do."

Laura bowed her head.

" I promise it, dear, because you wish it."

" Thank you, love."

He was silent for some time. He seemed to be thinking, or at least trying to collect his last thoughts.

" If it is a little girl, call her Laura," he said, in a breaking voice. " Then I shall know her in heaven, if she comes to me before you."

" Or else Herbert," said Laura, softly.

He moved his head a little in assent.

" Darling," he said presently, " always remember that my last breath is a blessing for you."

Very tenderly she pressed him to her heart and kissed him. Not till long afterwards did she realise the perfect unselfishness of the man's end, nor how every word so painfully spoken was meant to forestall and soothe her coming sorrow.

" Say a prayer for me, darling — it is not far off. Say something in your own words — they will be better heard."

Still supporting him against her breast, Laura raised her eyes heavenwards. The sister, little used to seeing men die without comfort of Holy Church, knelt down by the table. Then Laura's soft voice was heard in the quiet chamber.

" Almighty God, I beseech Thee to receive the soul of this pure and true-hearted man amongst the spotless ones that are with Thee, to forgive all his sins, if any are yet unforgiven, and to render to him in heavenly joy all the happiness he has brought her who loves him on earth, through our Lord Jesus Christ, Amen."

She ceased, forcing back the tears. He moved his head a little and kissed the hand that supported him. A long silence followed.

" I thought Ghisleri came to the door with you and went out again," he said very feebly.

"Would you like to see him, darling?"

"Yes. He is a dear friend —better in every way than any one knows."

At a word from Laura the sister rose and called Pietro. He was waiting in the passage. He came to the bedside and stood opposite to Laura, bending down and pressing Arden's wasted hand; he was very pale.

"Ghisleri—dear old friend—good-bye—I am going. Take care of her—you and Harry—" He gasped for breath.

"So help me God, I will do my best," answered Pietro, solemnly.

Arden gave him one grateful look. Then with a last effort he drew Laura's face to his and kissed her once more.

"Love—love—love—"

The light went out in his eyes and Herbert Arden was dead, dying as he had lived of late, and perhaps all his life, unselfish in every thought and deed.

With a cry that seemed to break her heart, Laura fell forward upon the shadowy form that seemed so unnaturally small as it lay there under the white coverlet. Ghisleri knelt in silence a few minutes beside his dead friend, and then rose to his feet.

"She has fainted," said the sister softly. "If you could lift her with me—"

But Ghisleri needed no help as he lifted the unconscious woman in his arms and carried her swiftly from the room. He laid her upon the very sofa on which he had seen her fall asleep on the previous night, and rang for Donald as he had then done.

"His lordship is dead," he said in a low voice, as the Scotchman entered. "Her ladyship has fainted. Please send me her maid."

Donald turned very white and left the room without a word. When Laura came to herself the women were with her and Ghisleri was gone. With an experienced man's coolness he gave all necessary orders, and foresaw details which no one else would have remembered. Then he went back to the chamber of death. No strange, unloving hands should touch the frail body of the man he had known so well. Pietro Ghisleri, who, as the world said, "never cared," was oddly sensitive at times. On that memorable night he would let no one help him in performing the last offices for Herbert Arden. When Laura next saw her husband, the calm and beautiful face lay on its snowy pillow surrounded with masses of white flowers. That was at daybreak.

Late on the following night Ghisleri followed the men who bore the heavy burden down the stairs. A quiet-looking woman of middle age met them and crossed herself as she waited for them to pass her on the landing. She came to take care of Herbert Arden's son.

CHAPTER XI.

THE season had begun, but Pietro Ghisleri had little heart for going into the world. Apart from the very sad scenes of which he had been a witness so recently, he really mourned the loss of his friend with a sincerity for which few would have given him credit. It would, of course, have been an exaggeration to act as though Arden had been his brother and to cast himself off from society for several months; but during a fortnight after he had laid Lord Herbert in the Protestant Cemetery at Monte Testaccio, he was seen nowhere. He went, indeed, to the house of the Contessa dell' Armi, but he made his visits at hours when no one else was received, as everybody knew, and he consequently saw none of his acquaintances except in the street. Twice daily at first, and then once, he went to the door of the Tempietto and sent up for news of Laura and the child. Strange to say, after the first three or four days the news became uniformly good.

Ghisleri learned that the little boy had come into the world sound and strong at all points, without the slightest apparent tendency to inherit his father's physical defects which, indeed, had been wholly the result of accident. The Princess of Gerano who, by Laura's express wish, had been kept in ignorance of Arden's illness on the first day and had not learned that he was seriously ill until he was actually dead, had now established herself permanently at the Tempietto, and her presence doubtless did much towards hastening her daughter's recovery. It was wonderful that Laura should have escaped the fever, still more so that she should rally so rapidly from a series of shocks which might have ruined an ordinary constitution; but Laura was very strong.

The Princess told Ghisleri that the child seemed to have taken Herbert's place. He was to he called Herbert too, and the other dearly loved one who had borne the name was never spoken of. No one would ever know what Laura felt, but those who knew her well guessed at the depth of a sorrow beyond words or outward signs of grief. In the meanwhile life revived in her and she began to live for her child, as she had lived for her husband, loving the baby boy with a twofold love, for himself and for his father's sake.

Ghisleri had written to the Marquess of Lulworth, Arden's brother, but a letter from him to Arden himself arrived on the day after the latter's death, telling him that Lord and Lady Lulworth were just starting to go round the world in their yacht. The Lulworths were people whose movements it was impossible to foretell, and after sending a number of telegrams to ports they were likely to touch at, Ghisleri abandoned all hope of hearing from them for a long time.

Meanwhile, he ascertained that Laura was likely to be hampered for ready money. Her mother's private resources were very slender, and Laura was far too proud to accept any assistance from Adele Savelli's father. She could not dispose, as a matter of fact, of anything which

her husband had left her except the actual ready money
which happened to be in the house; for she could not
even draw upon his letters of credit until the will was
proved and the legal formalities all carried out. It was
natural, too, that at such a time she should neither be
aware of her position nor give a thought to such a trivial
matter as household expenses.

One morning Donald came to Ghisleri's rooms in considerable distress, to ask advice of his master's old friend.
He would not disturb Lady Herbert, he said, and he was
ashamed to tell the Princess that there was no money in
the house. Ghisleri's first impulse was to give him all
the cash he had; but he reflected that in the first place the
sum might not be sufficient, for Donald, in a rather
broken voice, had referred to "the necessary expenses
when his lordship died," and which must now be met:
and secondly, Pietro felt that when Laura came to know
the truth she would not like to find herself under a serious obligation to him.

"Donald," he said, after a few moments' reflection, "it is
none of my business, but you have been a long time with
Lord Herbert, and you are a Scotchman, and the Scotch
are said to be careful; have you saved a little money?"

"Well, yes sir," answered Donald; "since you ask me,
I may say that I have saved a trifle. And I am sure, sir,
it would be most heartily at her ladyship's disposal if I
could go home and get it."

"You need not go for it, Donald. I will lend you the
equivalent, in our money, of a couple of hundred pounds.
You can then pay everything, and when the law business
is finished and you come to settle with her ladyship, you
can say that you advanced the sum yourself. That will
be quite true, because I lend it to you, personally, as
money for your use, and when you get it back you will
pay it to me. Do you see?"

"Yes, sir; it is a good way, too. But if you will excuse me, sir, you might very well lend the money to her
ladyship's self without pretending anything."

"No, Donald, I would rather not. Do you understand? Lady Herbert would much rather borrow from you than from a stranger."

"A stranger, sir! Well, well, if his poor lordship could hear you call yourself a stranger, sir!"

"One who is no relation. She might feel uncomfortable about it, just as you would rather come to me than go to the Princess of Gerano."

"Yes, sir. When you put it in that way. I see it."

So Ghisleri took Donald with him to a banker's and drew upon his slender resources for five thousand francs, which he gave to the Scotchman in notes. It had seemed to him the simplest way of providing for Laura's immediate necessities, while keeping her in ignorance of the fact that any necessity at all really existed. The sensation of helping her with money was an odd one, he confessed to himself, as he sent Donald home and walked idly away in the opposite direction through the crowded streets.

As he strolled down the Corso thinking of Laura's position, he came suddenly upon Donna Adele Savelli, alone and on foot. Even through the veil she wore he could see that she was very much changed. She had grown thin and pale, and her manner was unaccountably nervous when she stopped and spoke to him.

"Have you been ill?" he inquired, scrutinising her face.

"No, not ill," she answered, looking restlessly to the right and left of him and avoiding his eyes. "I cannot tell what is the matter with me. I cannot sleep of late — perhaps it is that. My husband says it is nothing, of course. I would give anything to go away for a month or two."

"You, who are so fond of society! Just at the beginning of the season, too! How odd. But you should be careful of yourself if you are losing your sleep. Insomnia is a dangerous disease. Take sulphonal in small doses. It does real good, and it never becomes a habit, as chloral does."

"Sulphonal? I never heard of it. Is it really good? Will you write it down for me?"

Ghisleri took one of his cards and wrote the word in pencil.

"Any good chemist will tell you how much to take. Even in great quantities it is not dangerous."

"Thanks."

Donna Adele left him rather abruptly, taking the card with her and holding it in her hand, evidently intending to make use of it at once. Ghisleri had good cause for not liking her and wondered inwardly why he had suggested a means of alleviating her sufferings. It would have been much better to let her bear them, he thought. Then he laughed at himself — any doctor would have told her what to take and would probably have given her a store of good advice besides.

Nearly a month had passed when Ghisleri was at last admitted to see Laura. He found her lying upon the same sofa on which she had slept a few hours during the memorable night before her husband died. She was even thinner now, he thought, and her eyes seemed to be set deeper than ever, while her face was almost transparent in its pallor. But the look was different — it was that of a person growing stronger rather than of one breaking down under a heavy strain. She held out her hand to him and looked up with a faint smile as he came to her side. The greeting was not a very cordial one, and Ghisleri felt a slight shock as he realised the fact.

She could not help it. As Herbert Arden breathed his last, the old sense of vague, uneasy dislike for Pietro returned almost with the cry she uttered when she lost consciousness. It was quite beyond her control, although it had been wholly forgotten during those hours of suffering and joint nursing which preceded her husband's death. Ghisleri was quite conscious of it, and was inwardly hurt. It was hard, too, to talk of indifferent subjects, as he felt that he must, carefully avoiding any allusion to the time when they had last been together.

"How do you pass the time?" he asked, after a few words of commonplace greeting and inquiry. "It must be very tiresome for you, I should think."

"I never was so busy in my life," Laura answered. "You have no idea what it is to take care of a baby!"

"No," said Ghisleri, with a smile, "I have no idea. But your mother tells me he is a splendid child."

"Of course I think so, and my mother does. You shall see him one of these days — he is asleep now. Would you like to know how my day is passed?"

And she went on to give him an account of the baby life that so wholly absorbed her thoughts. Ghisleri listened quietly as though he understood it all. He wished, indeed, that it were possible to talk of something else, and he felt something like a sensation of pain as Laura constantly called the child "Herbert," just as she had formerly been used to speak of her husband. Nevertheless, he was conscious also of a certain sense of satisfaction. During the month which had elapsed she had learned to hide her great trouble under the joy of early motherhood. There was something very beautiful in her devotion to the child of her sorrow, and hurt though Ghisleri was by her manner to him, she seemed more lovely and more admirable than ever in his eyes. He said so when he went to see Maddalena dell' Armi late in the afternoon.

"I have seen Lady Herbert to-day," he began. "It is the first time since poor Arden died."

"Is she very unhappy?" asked the Contessa.

"She must be, for she never speaks of him. She talks of nothing but the child."

"I understand that," said Maddalena, thoughtfully. "And then, it is such a compensation."

"Yes." Ghisleri sighed. He was thinking of what her life might have been if children had been born to her, and he guessed that the same thoughts were in her mind at the time.

"Did you ever think," she asked after a short pause, "what would become of me if you left me? I should be quite alone; do you realise that?"

Ghisleri remembered how nearly he had broken with her more than once and his conscience smote him.

"I would rather not think of it," he said simply.

"You should," she answered. "It will come some day. I know it. When it does I shall turn into a very bad woman, much worse than I am now."

"Please do not speak so; it hurts me."

"That is a phrase, my dear friend," said Maddalena. "I always tell you that you are too fond of making phrases. You ought not to do it with me. You are not really at all sensitive. I do not even believe that you have much heart, though you used to make me believe that you had."

"Have I shown you that I am heartless?"

"That is always your way of answering. You are a very strange compound of contradictions."

"Do you know, my dear lady, that you are falling into the habit of never believing a word I say?"

"I am afraid it is true," assented Maddalena, sadly. "And yet I would not be unjust to you for the world. You have given me almost the only happiness I ever knew, and yet, from having believed too much, I know that I am coming to believe too little."

"And you even think it is a mere phrase when I tell you that your distrust hurts me."

"Sometimes. You are not easily hurt, and I do not believe either —" She stopped suddenly in the midst of her speech.

"What?" asked Ghisleri.

"I will not say it. I say things to you occasionally which I regret later. I told you that I would not be unjust, and I will try not to be. Be faithful, if you can, but be honest with me. Do not pretend that you care for me one hour longer than you really do. It would be dreadful to know the truth, but it is much worse to doubt. Will you promise?"

"Yes," answered Pietro, gravely. "I have promised it before now."

"Then remember it. Be sure of what you mean and of yourself, if you can, — be quite, quite sure. You know what it would mean to me to break. I have not even a little child to love me, as Laura Arden has. I shall have nothing when you are gone — nothing but the memory of all the wrong I have done, all that can never be undone in this world or the next."

Ghisleri was moved and his strong face grew very pale while she was speaking. He had often realised it all of late, and he knew how greatly he had wronged her. It was not the first time in his life that he had been so placed, and that remorse, real while it lasted, had taken hold of him even before love was extinct. But he had never felt so strongly as he felt to-day, and he did his best to comfort himself with the shadowy medicine of good resolutions. He had honestly hoped that he might never love woman again besides Maddalena dell' Armi, and as that hope grew fainter he felt as though the very last poor fragments of self-respect he had left were being torn from him piecemeal. She, on her part, was very far from guessing what he suffered, for she was unjust to him, in spite of her real desire not to be so, and it was in a measure this same injustice which was undermining what had been once a very sincere love — good in that one way, if sinful and guilty in all other respects. Unbelief is, perhaps, what a man's love can bear the least; as a woman's may break and die at the very smallest unfaithfulness in him she loves, and as average human nature is largely compounded of faithlessness and unbelief, it is not surprising that true love should so rarely prove lasting.

Ghisleri saw no one after he left Maddalena on that day. He went home and shut himself up alone in his room, as he had done many times before that in his life, despairingly attempting to see clearly into his own heart, and to distinguish, if possible, the right course from the

wrong in the dim light of the only morality left to him
then, which was his sense of honour. And the position
was a very hard one. He knew too well that his love
for Maddalena was waning, and he even doubted whether
it had ever been love at all. Most bitterly he reproached
himself for the evil he had already brought into her
existence, and for the suffering that awaited her in the
future. Again and again he went over in his mind the
hours of the past, recalling vividly each word and gesture
out of the time when the truest sympathy had seemed to
exist between them, and asking himself why it might
not take a new life again and be all that it once had
been. The answer that suggested itself was too despicable in his eyes for him to accept it, for it told him that
Maddalena herself had changed and was no longer the
same woman whom he had once loved, and whom he
could love still, he fancied, if she were still with him.
It seemed so utterly disloyal to cast any of the blame on
her that the lonely man put the thought from him with
an angry oath. Of that baseness at least he would not
have to accuse himself. He would never, by the merest
suggestion, suffer himself to think one unkind thought of
Maddalena dell' Armi.

But the great question remained unsolved. Was
what was now left really love in any sense, or not, and
if not must he keep his promise and tell her the truth,
or would it be more honourable to live for her sake by a
rule of devotion and faithfulness which his strong will
could make real in itself and in the letter, if not in the
spirit? He knew that she was in earnest in what she
had said. If she knew that he had ceased to love her,
she would feel utterly alone in the world, and might
well be driven to almost any lengths in the desperate
search for distraction. She had not said it, but he knew
that in her heart she would lay all the sins of her life at
his door and that in this at least she would not be
wholly unjust.

With such a character as Ghisleri's it is not easy to

foresee what direction impulse will take when it comes at last. He was quite capable of giving up the attempt to understand himself and of leaving the whole matter to chance, with a coolness which would have seemed cruel and cynical if it had not been the result of something like despair. He was capable, if he failed to reach a conclusion by logical means, of tossing up a coin to decide whether he should tell poor Maddalena dell' Armi that he did not love her, or else stand by her in spite of every obstacle and devote his whole life to the elaborate fiction of an unreal attachment. Strangely enough Laura Arden played a part, and an important one, in bringing about his ultimate decision. He assuredly had no thought of loving her, nor of the possibility of loving her at that time. He would even have thought it an exaggeration to say that he was devotedly attached to her in the way of friendship. And yet he felt that she exercised a dominating influence over his mind. He found himself laying the matter before her in imagination, as he should never be likely to do in fact, and submitting it to her judgment as to that of a person supremely capable of distinguishing right from wrong and false from true. It was singular, too, that he should make no comparison between her and Maddalena, though possibly no such comparison could have been made. But he compared himself with her — the depth of his moral degradation in his own eyes with the lofty purity of thought and purpose which he attributed to her. The consequence could hardly fail to be a certain aspiration, vague and almost sentimental, to become such a man as might not seem to her wholly unworthy of trust. This did not help him much, however, and when at last he went to bed, having forgotten to go out and dine, and weary of the hard problem, he was not much further advanced than when he had sat down to think of it last in the afternoon.

In the morning everything seemed simpler, and the necessity for immediate decision disappeared. He had

not yet by any means reached the point of not loving
Maddalena at all, and until he did there was no reason
why he should form any plan of action. It would in
any case be very hard to act upon such a plan, for the
dreaded moment would in all likelihood be a stormy one,
and he could not foresee in the least what Maddalena
herself would do.

After that he felt for a long time much more of the old
sympathy with her than he had known of late, and he
tormented himself less often with the direction of his own
motives and thoughts. He saw much of Laura, too, in
those days, and spent long hours beside her as she lay
upon her sofa. He always left her with a sensation
of having been soothed and rested, though he could not
say of her that she was much inclined to talk, or
showed any great satisfaction at his coming. Probably,
he thought, she was willing to see him so often because
he had been Arden's friend. He did not understand
that she did not quite like him and that his presence
was often irksome to her, for she was far too kind by
nature to let him suspect it. He only thought that he
was in her eyes a perfectly indifferent person, and he
saw no reason for depriving himself of her society so
long as she consented to receive him. They rarely
talked of subjects at all relating to themselves, either,
and their conversation turned chiefly upon books and
general topics. Ghisleri read a good deal in a desultory way, and his memory was good. It interested him,
too, to propound problems for her judgment and to see
how nearly she would solve them in the way he expected
her to choose. He was rarely mistaken in his expectations.

Little by little, though Laura's principal feeling in
regard to him did not change perceptibly, she became
interested in his nature, beginning to perceive that there
were depths in it which she had not suspected.

" Are you a happy man ? " she once asked him rather
abruptly, and watching the expression of his face.

"Certainly not at present," he answered, looking away from her as though to hinder her from reading his thoughts. "Why do you ask that?"

"Forgive me. I should not put such a question, I suppose. But you interest me."

"Do I?" He glanced quickly at her as he spoke, and she saw that he was pleased. "I am very glad that you should take any interest in me, — of any kind whatever. Would you like to know why I am unhappy?"

"Yes."

"I can only tell you in a general way. I make no pretence to any sort of goodness or moral rectitude, beyond what we men commonly include in what we call the code of honour. But I am perpetually tormented about my own motives. Knowing myself to be what I am, I distrust every good impulse I have, merely because it is not a bad one, because my natural impulses are bad, and because I will not allow myself to act any sort of comedy, even in my own feelings. That sort of honesty, or desire for honesty, is all I have left — on it hangs the last shred of my tattered self-respect."

"How dreadful!" Laura's deep eyes rested on him for the first time with a new expression. There was both pity and wonder in their look — pity for the man and wonder at a state of mind of which she had never dreamed.

"Does it seem dreadful to you?" he asked.

"If you really feel as you say you do," answered Laura, "I can understand that you should be very unhappy."

"Why do you doubt that I feel what I have told you?" Ghisleri wondered, as he asked the question, whether he was ever to be believed again by any woman. "Do you think I am untruthful?"

"No," said Laura, quickly. "Indeed I do not. On the contrary, I think you very scrupulously exact when you speak of things you know about. But any one may be mistaken in judging of himself."

"That is precisely the point. I am afraid of finding myself mistaken, and so I do not trust my own motives."

"Yes — I see. But then, if you do what is right, you need not let your motives trouble you. That seems so simple."

"To you. Do you remember? I once told you that you were horribly good."

"I am not," said Laura, "but if I were, I should not see anything horrible in it."

"I should, and I do. When I see how good you are I am horrified at myself. That is what I mean."

"Why do you so often talk about being bad? You will end by making me believe that you are — if I do not believe it already."

"As you do, I fancy. What difference can it make to you?"

"Everything makes a difference which lowers one's estimate of human nature," Laura answered, with a wisdom beyond her age or experience. "After all, to go back to the point, the choice lies with you. You know what is right; do it, and give up wasting time on useless self-examination."

"Useless self-examination!" repeated Ghisleri, with rather a sour smile. "I suppose that is what it really is, after all. How you saints bowl over our wretched attempts at artificial morality!"

"No; do not say that, please, and do not be so bitter. I do not like it. Tell me instead why you cannot do as I suggest. If a thing is right, do it; if it is wrong, leave it undone."

"If I could tell you that, I should understand the meaning of this life and the next, instead of being quite in the dark about the one and the other."

Laura was silent. She was surprised by the result of the question she had at first put to him, and was at the same time conscious that she did not feel towards him as she had hitherto felt. Not that she liked him any better. She was perhaps further than ever from that, though her

M

likes and dislikes did not depend at all upon the moral estimate she formed of people's characters. But she understood what he meant far better than he guessed, and she pitied him and wished that she could say something to make him take a simpler and more sensible view of himself and the world. He interested her much more than half an hour earlier.

They did not return to the subject the next time they met, and Ghisleri fancied she had forgotten what he had said, whereas, in reality, she often thought of it and of him. Before long she was able to go out, and they met less frequently. She began to lead the life which she supposed was in store for her during the remainder of her existence. The only difference in the future would be that by and by she would not wear black any longer, that next year she would move into a more modest apartment, and that as time went on little Herbert would grow up to be a man and Laura would be an elderly woman.

Matters had been settled at last in England, and the momentary embarrassment which so much distressed Donald had ceased. The good man had felt somewhat guilty when Laura had thanked him for using what she supposed to be his savings in order to save her trouble. But he remembered what Ghisleri had told him and held his tongue, afterwards going early in the morning to Pietro's lodgings to repay the loan.

Laura had heard from the Lulworths, too. Ghisleri's letter and one of his telegrams had reached them at the same time somewhere in South America. Lulworth wrote himself to Laura and there was a deep, strong feeling in his few words which made her like him better than ever. He did not speak of coming back, and she thought it quite natural that he should stay away. He only said in a postscript that if she chose to go to England his house was at her disposal, but that he himself might be in Rome during the following winter.

But she would not have gone to England for anything. Her mother's presence was a quite sufficient reason for

staying where she was, and she knew also that her modest income would seem less restricted in Italy. The
Princess of Gerano had proposed to her to come and live
in the palace, but Laura would not do that — she would
never put herself under any obligation to Adele's father,
much as she herself was attached to him. Her mother
represented to her that she was too young to live quite
alone, but Laura remained unshaken in her determination.

"Herbert protects me," she said quietly, but the
Princess did not feel sure what she meant by the words,
nor whether the Herbert in question was poor Arden, or
the baby boy asleep in his cradle in the next room.

There was in either case a certain amount of truth in
what she said. Great sorrow is undeniably a protection
to a woman, and so is her child, under most circumstances.

"And as for my living alone," added Laura, "Signor
Ghisleri is the only man I receive, and people would be
ingenious to couple his name with mine."

CHAPTER XII.

ADELE SAVELLI followed Ghisleri's advice, and took
the new medicine he had so carelessly recommended.
At first it did her good and she regained something of
her natural manner. But her nerves seemed to be mysteriously affected and terribly unstrung. Her husband,
watching her with the cool judgment of a person neither
prejudiced by dislike nor over-anxious through great affection, came to the conclusion that she was turning into one
of those nervous, hysterical women whom he especially
disliked, and whom she herself professed to despise. The
world, for a wonder, was at a loss to find a reason for her
state, and contented itself with suggesting that the family
skeleton in Casa Savelli had probably grown restless of
late, and was rattling his bones in his closet in a way

which disturbed poor dear Adele, who was such a delicately organised being. To what particular tribe the Savellis' skeleton belonged, the world was not sure. Some said that he was called Insanity, some whispered that his name was Epilepsy, and not a few surmised that his nature was financial. As a matter of fact, no one knew anything about him, though every one was sure that he was just now in a state of abnormal activity, and that his antics accounted for Adele's pale face and startled eyes.

There was no doubt of the fact that she was ill, though she would scarcely admit it, and went through the season with a sort of feverish, unnatural gaiety. Being in reality no relation at all to Laura, she merely wore black for three weeks as a token of respect, but did not especially restrict herself in the matter of amusements even during that time, and when it was over, she threw herself into the very central whirl of the gay set with a sort of desperate recklessness which people noticed and commented upon. They were careful, however, not to speak too loud. Adele Savelli was very popular in society, and a very important person altogether, so that the world did not dare to talk about her as it discussed poor Laura Arden. And it found much good to say of Adele. It was so nice of her, it remarked, to change completely in her way of speaking of her step-sister, since the latter had lost that wretched little husband of hers. He, of course, as every one knew, had fallen a victim to his abominable habit of drinking brandy. It was all very well to call it scarlet fever — the world was well aware what that meant. The name of the thing was delirium tremens, and they said the last scene was quite appalling. The cripple, in the violence of the crisis, had twice sprung up and thrown down Ghisleri, who was a very strong man, nevertheless, and who had behaved in the most admirable way. He had not allowed any one to be present except the doctor, and it was impossible to extract a word of the truth from him. That was how it happened and, well — after all, it was a great mercy, and it was no wonder that Laura should have recovered so easily from the shock, and should already be beginning to amuse herself with Ghisleri. There was no doubt about that, either, for he went there every day, as regularly as he went to see the Contessa dell' Armi. And it was really angelic of Adele to stand up so resolutely for her step-sister, considering how the latter had always behaved. Adele took so much trouble to deny the stories that were circulated, that some people learned them for the first time through her denial.

In this, as in many other things, Adele was consistent. She denied everything.

"It is not even true," she said to Donna Maria Boccapaduli, "that Laura has the evil eye."

But as she said it, she quickly folded her two middle fingers over her bent thumb, making what Italians call "horns" with the forefinger and little finger. Donna Maria saw the action, instinctively imitated it, and fell into the habit of repeating it whenever Laura was mentioned.

"Why do you do that?" asked the Marchesa di San Giacinto of her the next day.

"Eh — my dear! Poor Laura Arden is a terrible jettatrice, you know. Adele says it is not true, but she makes horns behind her back all the same, just as every one else does."

Thereupon the Marchesa did the same thing, wondering that she should so long have been ignorant that Laura had the evil eye. In a week's time all Rome made horns when Laura was mentioned. At a dinner party a servant broke a glass when she was being discussed, and at once every one laughed and stuck up two fingers. San Giacinto, who, lean as he was, weighed hard upon sixteen stone, sat down upon a light chair in Casa Frangipani, just as he was saying that this new story about Laura was all nonsense, and the chair collapsed into a little heap of straw and varnished sticks under his weight. It was no wonder, people said, that Arden should have fainted that night at the Palazzo Braccio, for Laura had just accepted him. They seemed to have forgotten how they had interpreted that very scene hitherto. The world was not at all surprised that he should have died in the first year of his marriage, considering that he had married a notorious jettatrice. Look at poor Adele herself! She had never been well since that dinner at which the reconciliation with Laura was sealed and ratified. Pietro Ghisleri should be careful. It was very unwise of him to go and see her every day. Something awful would happen to him. Indeed it had been noticed that he was not looking at all well of late. That dreadful woman would kill him to a certainty.

Ghisleri was furious when the tale reached him, as it did before long. He knew very well how dangerous a thing it was to have the reputation of possessing the evil eye. It is a strange fact that at the present day such things should be believed, and well-nigh universally, by a cultured society of men and women. And yet it is a fact, and an undeniable one. Let it once get abroad that a man or a woman "projects" — to translate the Italian "jetta" — the baneful influence which causes accidents of every description, and he or she may as well bid farewell to society forever. Such a person is shunned as one contaminated; at his approach, every hand is hidden to make the sign of defence; no one will speak to him who can help it, and then always with concealed fingers kept rigidly bent in the orthodox fashion, or clasped upon a charm of proved efficacy. Few, indeed, are those brave enough to ask such a man to dinner, and they are esteemed almost miraculously fortunate if no misfortune befalls them during the succeeding four and twenty hours, if their houses do not burn, and their children do not develop the measles. Incredible as it may appear to northern people, a man or woman may be socially ruined by the imputation of "projecting," when it is sustained by the coinciding of the very smallest accident with their presence, or with the mention of their names, and quite enough of such coincidences were actually noted in Laura's case to make the reputation of being a jettatrice cling to her for life. Ghisleri knew this, and his wrath was kindled, and smouldered, and grew hot, till it was ready to burst out at a moment's notice and do considerable damage.

"It is an abominable shame," he said to Maddalena dell' Armi. "It is all Adele Savelli's doing. She has taken a new departure. Instead of starting bad reports as true, she begins by denying things of which nobody ever heard. I am quite sure she is at the bottom of it, but I do not see how I can stop the story."

"You seem to care a great deal," said Maddalena.

"Yes. I do care. If it would do any good, I would call out Francesco Savelli and fight about it."

"For Laura Arden's sake?" It was the first time she had ever heard Ghisleri even hint that he would do so much for any one, though she knew that he would for herself.

"No," he answered, with sudden gentleness. "Not for Lady Herbert's sake, my dear lady. I would do it because, just when he was dying, Arden told me that I must take care of her, and I mean to do my best, as I promised him."

"You are quite right," answered Maddalena, taking his hand and pressing it a little. "I would not have you do otherwise, if I could — if I had all the influence over you which I have not. But oh — if you can help fighting — please — for my sake, if you care — "

Maddalena's cold face and small classic features expressed a great deal at that moment, and there were bright tears in her violet eyes. In her own way she loved him more than ever. He was deeply touched as he tenderly kissed the hand that held his.

"For your sake, I will do all that a man can do to avoid a quarrel," he said earnestly.

"I know you will," she answered.

During a few moments there was silence between them, and Maddalena recovered control of herself.

"That is the true reason why I ask you," she said. "There are plenty of others which you may care for more than I. You would not care to have it said that you were fighting her battles. Will you promise not to be angry if I tell you something you will not like — something I know positively?"

"Yes. I promise. What is it?"

"People are beginning to say already that you are making love to her, and that you are always at the house."

"The brutes!" exclaimed Ghisleri, fiercely. "Who says that?"

"The women, of course. The men are much too sensible, and none of them care to quarrel with you."

"Oh!" Pietro contented himself with the exclamation, and controlled his anger as best he could.

"Was I wrong to tell you?" asked Maddalena.

"No, indeed. I am very glad you have told me. I shall be more careful in future."

"It will make very little difference. You know the world as well as I do, and better. People have begun to say that you go to see Lady Herbert every day — they will still say it after you have not been to her house for months."

"Yes. That is the way the world talks. I hope this will not reach her ears — though I suppose it ultimately will. Some dear kind friend will go and tell her in confidence, and give her good advice."

"Probably. That is generally the way. Only, as she is in deep mourning and receives very few people, it may be a little longer than usual in such cases before the affectionate friend gets at her. Then, too, the idea that she is a jettatrice will keep many of her old acquaintances away. You know how seriously they take those things here."

It will be remembered that both Maddalena and Ghisleri were from the north of Italy, where the superstition about the evil eye is much less general amongst the upper classes than in Rome and the south. Pietro himself had not the slightest belief in it, and he had so often laughed at it in conversation with the Contessa that if she had ever had any vague tendency to put faith in the jetta-tura, it had completely disappeared. But both of them were thoroughly familiar with the society in which they lived, and understood the position in which Laura was placed.

"I will help you as much as I can," said Maddalena, "though I cannot do much. At all events, I can laugh at the whole thing and show that I do not believe in it. But as for the rest, — placed as I am, I can hardly make an intimate friend of Lady Herbert Arden, much as I like her."

She spoke sadly and a little bitterly. Ghisleri made no reference to the last remark when he answered her.

"I shall be very sincerely grateful for anything you can do to help the wife of my old friend," he said. "And I think you can do a good deal. You have great influence in the gay set — and that means the people who talk the most — Donna Adele, Donna Maria Boccapaduli, the Marchesa di San Giacinto, and all the rest, who are, more or less, your intimates. It is very good of you to help me — Lady Herbert needs all the help she can get. Spicca is a useful man, too. If he can be prevailed upon to say something particularly witty at the right moment, it will do good."

"I rarely see him," said Maddalena. "He does not like me, I believe."

"He admires you, at all events," answered Ghisleri. "I have heard him talk about your beauty in the most enthusiastic way, and he is rarely enthusiastic about anything."

Maddalena was pleased, as was natural. She chanced to be in one of her best humours on that day, and indeed of late she had been much more her former self when she was with Ghisleri. A month earlier, the discussion about Laura Arden could not have passed off so peaceably, for the Contessa would then have resented anything approaching to the intimacy which now appeared to exist between Lady Herbert and Pietro. The latter wondered what change had taken place in her character, but accepted her gentle behaviour towards him very gratefully as a relief from a former phase of jealous fault-finding which had cost him many moments of bitterness. As he saw, from time to time, how her cold face softened, he almost believed that he loved her as dearly as ever, though the illusion was not of long duration. He left her, on that afternoon, with a regret which he had not felt for some time at the moment of parting, and he would gladly have stayed with her longer. They agreed to meet in the evening at one of the embassies, where there was to be a dance. In the mean time, they were to dine out at different houses, and the Contessa had a visit to make before going to the ball.

Pietro was sorry that he had promised not to quarrel about the story of the evil eye. The affair irritated him to an extraordinary degree, and though he had grown calmer under Maddalena's influence, his anger revived as he walked home and thought over it all. He dined that evening in Casa San Giacinto, and found himself placed between Donna Maria Boccapaduli and Donna Christina Campodonico. The latter was a slim, dark, graceful woman of five and twenty, remarkably quiet, and reported to be very learned, a fact which contributed less to her popularity than her own beauty and her husband's rather exceptional reputation. Gianforte Campodonico was a man whom Ghisleri would have liked if they had not known each other some years previously in circumstances which made liking an impossibility. He respected him more than most people, for he had fought a rather serious duel with him in days gone by, and had seen the man's courage and determination. Campodonico was the brother of the beautiful Princess Corleone who had died in Naples shortly after the above-mentioned duel, and who was said to have been the love of Ghisleri's life. Gianforte, for his sister's sake, had made up his mind to kill Ghisleri or to die in the attempt, with a desperate energy of purpose that savoured of earlier ages. He was, moreover, a first rate swordsman, and the encounter had remained memorable in the annals of duelling. Ghisleri had done all in his power to avoid the necessity of fighting at all, but Campodonico had forced him into it at last, and the weapons had been foils. The world said that Ghisleri was not to be killed so easily. He was as good a fencer as his adversary, and was left-handed besides, which gave him a considerable advantage. The result was that he defended himself successfully throughout one of the longest duels on record, until at last he almost unintentionally ran Gianforte through the sword arm and disabled him. The latter, humiliated and furious at his defeat, had demanded pistols then and there, and Ghisleri had professed himself ready, and had placed himself in the hands of his seconds. But both his own friends and Gianforte's decided that honour was satisfied, and refused to be parties to any further fighting, so that Campodonico had been obliged to accept their verdict. He sought an opportunity of quarrelling again, however, for he was a determined man, and he would probably have succeeded in the end; but at this juncture the Princess died after a short illness, and after exacting a solemn promise from both men that they would never fight again. That was the last act of her brief life of love and unhappiness, and it was at least a good one. Loving her with all their hearts, in their different ways, both Ghisleri and Campodonico respected the obligation they had taken as something supremely sacred. Ghisleri went and lived alone in a remote village of the south for more than a year afterwards, and Gianforte spent an even longer period in almost total seclusion from the world, and in the sole society of his widowed mother. Three years before the time now reached in this chronicle, he had married, as people said, for love, and for once people were right.

His elder brother bore the title, and as there was another
sister besides the Princess Corleone, Gianforte's portion
had been small, for the family was not rich, and he and
his wife lived very modestly in a small apartment in the
upper part of the city, the Palazzo Campodonico having
long ago passed into the hands of the Savelli.

And now, at the San Giacinto's dinner table, Ghisleri
found himself seated next to Donna Christina, and nearly
opposite to her husband. It had long been known and
generally understood that Pietro and Gianforte had buried their enmity with the beautiful woman about whom
they had fought, and that they had no objection to meeting in the world, and even to conversing occasionally on
general subjects, so that there was nothing surprising in
the fact that at a dinner of eighteen persons they should
be asked together. It chanced that, by the inevitable
law of precedence, Ghisleri sat where he did. Donna
Christina of course knew the story above related, and in
her eyes it lent Ghisleri a somewhat singular interest.   .

Now it happened, towards the end of dinner, that some
one mentioned Lady Herbert Arden. Instantly Donna
Maria, on Pietro's right, made the sign of the horns with
both hands, laughing in a foolish way at the same time.
Ghisleri saw it, and a glance round the table showed him
that the majority of the guests did the same thing.

"How can you believe in such silly tales?" he asked,
turning to Donna Maria.

"Everybody does," answered the sprightly lady. "Why
should not I?   And besides, look at the facts — San
Giacinto had the name of the lady we do not mention on
his lips when he broke that chair the other day — there,
I told you so!" she exclaimed suddenly.

Young Pietrasanta, who, as it happened, had been the
one to speak of Laura Arden, had upset a glass, which,
being very delicate and falling against a piece of massive
silver, was shivered instantly. The claret ran out in a
broad stain.

"Allegria — joy!" laughed the lady of the house.

Italians very often utter this exclamation when wine is spilled. It is probably a survival of some primeval superstition.

"Joy!" repeated Pietrasanta, with quite a different intonation. "If ever I mention that name again!"

"You see," said Donna Maria triumphantly to Ghisleri. "There is no doubt about it."

"I beg your pardon for contradicting you," answered Ghisleri, coldly, "but I think there is so much doubt that I do not believe in the possibility of the evil eye at all, much less in the ridiculous story that Lady Herbert Arden's name can upset a glass of wine or break a chair."

"I agree with you," said Donna Christina, in her quiet voice, on Pietro's other side. "It is almost the only point on which my husband and I differ — is it not true, Gianforte?" she asked, speaking across the table to Campodonico. There had been a momentary lull in the conversation after the little accident, so that he had heard what had been said.

"It is quite true," he answered. "I believe in the jettatura, just as most people do, but my wife is a sceptic."

"And do you really believe that Pietrasanta upset his glass because he mentioned Lady Herbert?" asked Pietro.

"Yes, I do." Their eyes met quietly as they looked at each other, but the whole party became silent, and listened to the remarks exchanged by the two men who had once fought such a memorable fight.

Gianforte Campodonico was a very dark man, of medium height, strongly built, and not yet of an age to be stout, with bold aquiline features, keen black eyes, and a prominent chin. A somewhat too heavy moustache almost quite concealed his mouth. At first sight, most people would have taken him for a soldier. Of his type he was very handsome.

"Can you give any good reason for believing in anything so improbable?" asked Ghisleri.

"There are plenty of facts," answered Campodonico, calmly. "Any one here will give you fifty — a hundred

instances, so many indeed, that you cannot attribute them all to coincidence. Do you not agree with me, Marchese?" he asked, appealing to the master of the house, whose opinion was often asked by men, and generally accepted.

"I suppose I do," said the giant, indifferently. "I never took the trouble to think of it. Most of us believe in the evil eye. But as for this story about Lady Herbert Arden, I think it is nonsense in the first place, and a malicious lie in the second, invented by some person or persons unknown — or perhaps very well known to some of you. Half of it rests on that absurd story about the chair I broke in Casa Frangipani. If any of you can grow to be of my size, you will know how easily chairs are broken."

There was a laugh at his remark, in which Campodonico joined.

"But it is true that you were speaking of the lady one does not mention at the moment when the chair gave way," he said.

"Yes," said San Giacinto, "I admit that."

"I agree with San Giacinto, though I do not believe in the evil eye at all," said Ghisleri. "And I will go a little further, and say that I think it malicious to encourage the story about Lady Herbert. She has had trouble enough as it is, without adding to it gratuitously."

"I do not see that we are doing her any harm," observed Campodonico.

"The gossip may be perfectly indifferent to her now," said Ghisleri. "She is most probably quite ignorant of what is said. But in the natural course of events, two or three years hence she will go into the world again, and you know what an injury it will be to her then."

"You are looking very far ahead, it seems to me. As for wishing to do her an injury, as you call it, why should I?"

"Exactly. Why should you?"

"I do not."

"I beg your pardon. I think every one who contributes to the circulation of this fable does harm to Lady Herbert, most distinctly."

"In other words, we are not of the same opinion," said Campodonico, in a tone of irritation.

"And I express mine because poor Arden was my oldest friend," answered Ghisleri, with the utmost calm. "If I cannot persuade you, let us agree to differ."

"By all means," replied Gianforte, and he turned and began to talk with the lady on his right.

Donna Christina leaned towards Ghisleri and spoke to him in a very low voice, quite inaudible to other ears than his, as the hum of general conversation rose again.

"Is it true," she asked, "that you and my husband agreed, years ago, that you would never quarrel again?"

Ghisleri looked at her in cold surprise. He was amazed that she should refer to that part of his past life, of which no one ever spoke to him.

"It is true," he answered briefly.

"I am very glad," said Donna Christina. "I thought you were near a quarrel just now about this absurd affair. You hate each other, and Gianforte is very hot-tempered."

"There is no danger. But I am sorry you think that I hate your husband. He is one of the few men whom I really respect. There are other reasons why I should not hate him, and why I should not be surprised if he hates me with all his heart, as I dare say he does, from what you say."

He glanced at her, but she did not answer at once. She was still young and truthful, and it did not occur to her to be tactful at the expense of veracity.

"I am glad you defended Lady Herbert as you did," she said, after a short pause. "It was nice of you." Then she turned and talked with the man on her other side.

Donna Maria Boccapaduli had been waiting for her opportunity and attacked Ghisleri as soon as he had ceased talking with his other neighbour.

"Tell me," she said, "you like Laura Arden very much, do you not?" Of course she made the sign at Laura's name.

"Yes. She is a very charming woman."

"She ought to be grateful to you. She would be, if she knew how you stood up for her just now."

"I should be sorry if she ever came to know that she needed to be defended," answered Ghisleri, almost indifferently.

"She will, of course. It will be all over Rome to-night that you and Campodonico almost quarrelled about her. She is sure to hear about it. Why do you take so much interest in her?"

"Because her husband was my friend," Pietro replied, rather wearily. "I just said so."

"You need not be so angry with me because I ask questions," said Donna Maria with a laugh. "I always do — it is the way to find out what one wants to know."

"And what do you want to know?"

"You will be angry if I ask you."

"Then ask me something else."

"But I want to know so much," objected Donna Maria, with an expression that made Ghisleri smile.

"Then you must take the risk," he said. "It is not very great."

"Well, then, I will." She dropped her voice almost to a whisper. "Is the lady in question — I mean — is she the sort of woman you can imagine falling in love with?"

"I do not think I should ever fall in love with her," answered Ghisleri, without betraying emotion or surprise.

"Why not? There must be some reason. So many men have said the same thing about her."

"She is too good a woman for any of us to love. We feel that she is too far above us to be quite human as we are."

"What a strange man you are, Ghisleri! I should never have dreamt that you could say such a thing as that. It is not at all like your reputation you know, and

not in the least like those delightfully dreadful verses
you addressed to the saint last year on Shrove Tuesday
at Gouache's studio. I should think that Mephistopheles
would delight in making love to saints."

"In real life Mephistopheles would get the worst of
it, and be shown to the door with very little ceremony."

"I doubt that. Every woman likes a spice of devilry
in the man she loves — and as for being shown to the
door, that is ridiculous. Is there any reason in the
world why you should not fall in love with a woman exactly like the unmentionable lady and marry her, too,
if you love her enough — or little enough, according to
your views of married life? You are quite free, and so
is she, and you said yourself that in the course of time
she would naturally come back to the world."

"No," said Ghisleri, thoughtfully, "I suppose there is
no reason why I should not ask Lady Herbert Arden to
marry me in four or five years, except that I do not love
her in the least, and that she would most certainly refuse
me. And those are two very good reasons."

The dinner was over and the party returned to the
drawing-room. Ghisleri stood a little apart from the rest,
examining a painting with which he had long been familiar, and slowly inhaling the smoke of a cigarette. It was
a small copy of one of Zichy's famous pictures illustrat-
ing Lermontoff's "Demon" — the one in which Tamara
yields at last, in the convent, and throws her arms round
the Demon's neck. Prince Durakoff had ordered the copy
and had presented it to the Marchesa di San Giacinto.
Ghisleri had always liked it, and had a photograph of
the original in his rooms. He now stood looking at it
and recalling the strange, half allegorical romance of
which the great Russian made such wonderful poetry.

Presently he was aware that some one was standing at
his elbow. He turned to see who it was, and found himself face to face with Gianforte Campodonico, who was
looking at him with an expression of indescribable hatred
in his black eyes.

CHAPTER XIII.

PIETRO at once realised the situation and the meaning
of the look he saw. Something was passing in his old
enemy's mind which had passed through his own while
he was looking at the picture, for Campodonico and Ghisleri were both thinking of the extraordinary resemblance
between poor Bianca Corleone and the Tamara of Zichy's
painting. That resemblance, striking in a high degree,
was the reason why Ghisleri liked it, and had a photograph of it at his lodging. He regretted now that he
should have been so tactless as to stand long before it
when Campodonico was in the room. It was too late,
however, and there was nothing to be done but to meet
the man's angry look quietly, and go away. It was
unfortunate that there should have been any discussion
between them at dinner, too, for Campodonico, as his
wife said, was hot-tempered in the extreme, and Ghisleri, though outwardly calm, had always been liable to
outbreaks of dangerous anger. There was, indeed, in
the present instance, a very solemn promise given to a
dying woman beloved by both, to keep them from quarrelling, and both really meant to respect it as they had
done in past years. But to see Ghisleri calmly contem-
plating a picture which seemed intended to represent
Bianca Corleone falling into the arms of a demon lover,
was almost too much for the equanimity of Gianforte,
which was by no means at any time very. stable. Moreover, he not only hated Ghisleri with his whole heart as
much as ever, but he despised him quite as much as
Pietro despised himself, and probably a little more. He
would never have forgiven him, at the best; but he might
have respected him if Ghisleri had honoured Bianca's
memory by leading a different life. It made his blood
sting to think that a man who had been loved to the latest
breath by such a woman as Bianca should throw himself

at the feet of Maddalena dell' Armi — not to mention
any of the others for whom Pietro had felt an ephemeral
passion during the last six years and more. And Pietro,
on his side, knew that Campodonico was right in judging
him as he judged himself, harshly and without mercy.
Unfortunately, Pietro's judgments on himself generally
came too late, when the evil he hated had already been
done, and self-condemnation was of very little use. He
had great temptations, too — far greater than most men,
and was fatally attracted by difficulty in any shape.

On the present occasion he really desired to avoid
doing the least thing which could irritate Campodonico,
and if the latter had not done what he did Pietro would
certainly have gone quietly away. He could not help
being a little surprised at the persistent stare of his old
adversary, considering that for years they had met and
acted with perfectly civil indifference towards one another. Nevertheless, he relit his cigarette which had
gone out, and made a step towards the other side of the
room. To Campodonico, the calm expression of his face
seemed like scorn, and he became exasperated in a moment. He called the other back. They were at some
distance from the other guests, and out of hearing if they
spoke in low tones.

"Ghisleri!" Campodonico pronounced the name he
detested with an almost contemptuous accent. Pietro
knew that an exchange of unfriendly words was inevitable. He turned instantly and came close to Gianforte,
standing before him and looking down into his fierce eyes,
for he was by far the taller man.

"What is it?" he asked, controlling his voice wonderfully.

"Do you not think there are circumstances under which
one is justified in breaking a solemn promise?" asked
Campodonico.

"No. I do not."

"I do."

"I am very sorry. I suppose you mean to say that you
wish to quarrel with me again. Is that it?"

"Yes."

"You will find it hard. I shall do my very best to be patient whatever you do or say. In the first place, I begin by telling you that I sincerely regret having irritated you twice, as I have done this evening, the second time, as I know, very seriously."

"I did not ask you for an apology," said Gianforte, with contempt.

"But I have offered you one which you will find it hard not to accept."

"You were not formerly so ready with excuses. I dare say you have grown cautious with age, though you are not much older than I."

"Perhaps I have." Ghisleri grew slowly pale, as he bore one insult after the other for the dead woman's sake.

"In other words, you are a coward," said Campodonico, lowering his voice still more.

Pietro opened his lips and shut them without speaking. He glanced at the passionate white face of the woman in the picture before he answered.

"I do not think so," he said. "But I make no pretence of bravery. Have you done?"

"No. You make a pretence of other things if not of courage. You pretend that you will not quarrel now because of the promise you gave."

"It is true."

"I do not believe you."

"I am sorry for it," answered Pietro.

"And do you mean to tell me that the promise binds us? If you had acted as a man should, if you had led a life that showed the slightest respect for that memory, it might be binding on me still."

"I think it is." Ghisleri was trembling with anger from head to foot, but his voice was still steady.

"I do not," answered Gianforte, scornfully. "If she were here to judge us, if she could see that the man who was loved to the last by Bianca Corleone — God give her rest! — would live down to such a level, would live to

throw himself at the feet of a Maddalena dell' Armi —
ah, I have touched you now! — she would — "

Ghisleri's face was livid.

"She whose name you are not more worthy to speak
than I, never meant that I should not defend a good and
helpless woman because the liar who accuses her chances
to be called Gianforte Campodonico."

"And the one who defends her, Pietro Ghisleri,"
retorted Gianforte. "Where can my friends find yours?"

"At my lodging, if that suits them."

"Perfectly."

Campodonico turned on his heel and slowly went
towards the group at the other end of the room. Ghisleri followed him at a distance, lighting a fresh cigarette
as he walked. He had recovered his composure the
moment he had felt himself freed from the obligation to
bear the insults heaped upon him by Bianca Corleone's
brother.

It must not be supposed that no one had watched the
two as they stood talking before the picture. More than
one person had noticed the fierce look in Campodonico's
eyes, and the unnatural paleness of Ghisleri's face. One
of these was Donna Maria Boccapaduli.

"I suppose you have been discussing that painting,"
she said carelessly to Pietro. "People always do."

"Yes," answered Ghisleri, as indifferently as he could.

"And what was the result of the discussion?"

"We agreed to differ." Pietro laughed a little harshly.

As soon as possible he excused himself and got away,
for he had only just the time necessary to find a couple
of friends and explain matters, before going to the ball to
meet the Contessa, as he had promised to do. He had
forgotten an important detail, however, and as he passed
Campodonico who was also going away, and without his
wife, on pretence of an engagement at the club, he stopped
him.

"By the by," he said, "I suppose we are ostensibly
quarrelling about a painter, or something of that sort."

"Yes — anything. Zichy, for instance. Everybody saw us looking at the picture. You like it and I do not."

"Very well."

So they parted, to meet, in all probability, at dawn on the following morning, in a quiet place outside the city. Ghisleri found two friends in whose hands he placed himself, telling them that he was quite indifferent to the weapons, and only desired to meet his adversary's wishes as far as possible, since the affair was very insignificant. He remarked in an indifferent tone that, as he had once fought with Campodonico, using foils, and as the latter had not seemed satisfied on that occasion, he had no objection to pistols, if the opposite side preferred them. He wished everything to be arranged as amicably as possible, he said, and without any undue publicity. He left them at his lodging and departed to keep his engagement at the embassy. As he drove through the bitter air in an open cab, he meditated on his position, and wondered what Maddalena would say when she learned that he had been out with his old adversary. She should not know anything about the encounter until it was over, if he could keep it from her. At all events, he reflected, he had done all that a man could do to keep out of a quarrel, as he had promised her he would, and he had been driven to break a promise of a far more sacred nature than the one he had given her. If she knew the truth, too, it was for her, and for her alone, that he was to fight. He wondered whether people would say it was for Laura Arden's sake, on account of the discussion about the evil eye which had taken place at table. The suggestion annoyed him very much, but he reached his destination before he had found time to reason out the whole case, or to decide what to do. In any event it would be better if people thought that he had taken the foils in defence of an unprotected widow like Laura, than for the good name of the Contessa dell' Armi.

She was there before him, looking very lovely in a gown of palest green, half covered with old lace. The shade suited her fair hair and dazzling skin, and she looked taller in faint colours, as short women do. He found her seated in one of the smaller rooms through which he had to pass on his way to the great ball-room, and she was surrounded by four or five men of the gay set, all talking to her at once, all trying to be extremely witty, and all wishing that the others would go away. But the Contessa held her own with them, making no distinction, and keeping up the lively, empty, rattling conversation without any apparent difficulty. Pietro sat down in the circle, and made a remark from time to time, to which she generally gave a direct answer, until, little by little, she was talking with him alone, and the others began to drop away as they always did in the course of half an hour when Ghisleri appeared in Maddalena's neighbourhood. It was a thing perfectly understood, as a matter not even worth mentioning.

"Will you get me something to drink?" she said when only Spicca was left by her side.

Pietro went off towards the supper-room, which was rather distant, and as a dance was just over and the place was crowded, it was some minutes before he could get what he wanted, and go back to her with it. Spicca looked at him with an odd expression of something between amusement and sympathy as he rose and left the two together, and Ghisleri at once saw that something unusual had occurred in his absence, for Maddalena was very pale, and her hand shook violently as she took the glass he brought her.

"What is the matter?" he asked anxiously, as he sat down.

"Something very disagreeable has happened," she answered, looking round nervously.

The sofa on which they sat stood out from one side of a marble pillar, with its back to the side of the room the guests crossed who went directly to the ball-room, and facing the side by which they went from the ball-room to the rooms beyond, and to the supper-room, for there were four doors, opposite each other, two of which opened into the great hall where the dancing was going on. Maddalena was seated at the end of the sofa which was against the pillar, so that a person passing through behind her might easily not notice her presence.

"Pray tell me what it is," said Ghisleri.

"Just as you went to get me the lemonade, I heard two people talking in a low voice behind me," said Maddalena. "They must have stopped first by the door — I looked round afterwards and saw them, but I do not know either of them — some new people from one of the other embassies, or merely foreigners here on a visit. They spoke rather bad French. There was a man and a lady. They saw you cross the room and the lady asked the man who you were, and the man told her, saying that he only knew you by sight. The lady uttered an exclamation, and said that you were the one man in Rome whom she wished to see because you had been loved by — you know whom I mean — I know it hurts you to speak of her, and I understand it. The man laughed and said there had been others since, and that there was especially a certain Marquise d' Armi, as he called me, who was madly in love with you. The most amusing part of the whole thing, concluded the man, was that you were perfectly indifferent to her, as everybody knew. It was horrible, and I almost fainted. Dear old Spicca went on talking, trying to prevent me from hearing them. It was just like him."

The Contessa's lip trembled, and her eyes glittered strangely as she looked at Pietro.

"It is horrible," he said, in a low voice. He had thought that he had felt enough emotions during that day, but he was mistaken. Even now there were more in store for him. He was deeply shocked, for he guessed what she must have suffered.

"Horrible — yes! But oh — can you not tell me it is not true? Do you not see that my heart is breaking?"

"No, dearest lady," he answered tenderly, trying to

soothe her. "Not one word of it is true. How can you make yourself unhappy by thinking such a thing?"

Maddalena drew a painful breath. He spoke very kindly, but there was no ringing note of passion in his voice as there had once been. With a sudden determination that surprised him, she rose to her feet.

"Take me to the ball-room," she said hurriedly. "I shall cry if I stay here."

It was almost a relief to Ghisleri to see her accept the first man who presented himself as a partner and whirl away with him into the great hall. He stood leaning against the marble door-post, watching her as she wound her way in and out among the many moving couples. He was conscious that he might very possibly never see her again. Campodonico would of course select pistols, and meant to kill him if he could. He might succeed, though duels rarely ended fatally now-a-days. And if he did, Maddalena dell' Armi would be left to her fate. He was horror-struck when he thought of it. She might never know why he had fought, and she would perhaps believe to her last day that he had sacrificed his life for Laura Arden. He could leave a letter for her, but letters often fell into the wrong hands through faithless servants when the people who had written them were dead. Besides, would she believe his words? She had very little faith in his love for her. He sighed bitterly as he thought how right she was in that. He could see the pale, small, classic features, and the half pitiful, half scornful look of the beautiful mouth. "His last bit of comedy!" she would exclaim to herself, as she tossed his last note into the fire. And again she would be right, in a measure. In the case of risking sudden death, he said to himself that it was indeed a strange bit of comedy. He knew that he did not love her as he should. Why should he fight for her, then?

But his manliness rose up at this and smote his cynicism out of the field for a time. That little he owed Maddalena, at least — he could not do less than defend her, at whatever cost, and he knew well enough that he always would. As for his wish that she might know it, that was nothing but his own detestable vanity. For his own part, he wished with all his heart that the next morning might end his existence. He had never valued his life very highly, and of late it had been so little to his taste that he was more than ready to part with it, even violently. The future did not appall him, although, strangely enough, he was very far from being an unbeliever, and had been brought up to consider a sudden end, in mortal sin, as the most horrible and irreparable of misfortunes. To him, in his experience of himself, no imaginable suffering could be worse than the self-doubt, the self-contempt, and the self-hatred which had so often tormented him during the past years. If he were to be punished for his misdeeds with the same torture, even though it were to be never-ending, at least he should bear the pain of it alone, such as it was, without the necessity for hiding it and for going through the daily mummery of life with an indifferent face. And in that state there would be no more temptation of the kind he feared. What he had done up to the hour of death would close the chronicle of evil, and in all ages there would be no more. He was used to such refinements of cruelty as perdition could threaten him with, for he had practised them upon his own heart.

So the man "who did not care" stood watching the ball, and people envied him his successes, and his past and present happiness, and all that he had enjoyed in his three-and-thirty years of life, little dreaming of what was even then passing in his thoughts, still less that he was waiting for the message which should inform him of the place and hour fixed for encountering the man who most hated him in the world, and who had once before vainly attempted to take his life.

At the other end of the great hall the Contessa dell' Armi had paused in her waltz to take breath, and found herself next to Donna Maria Boccapaduli.

"You have not heard the news," said the latter in a low voice, bending towards Maddalena, and holding up her fan before her face. "We have all been dining at Casa San Giacinto, sixteen of us besides themselves — the two Campodonico, ourselves, Pietrasanta — ever so many of us. Ghisleri was there, next to me, and there was a discussion about the evil eye, because Pietrasanta broke a glass just as he uttered the name of the lady we do not mention — you know which — Ghisleri's friend. And then, I do not know how it was, but Ghisleri and Campodonico contradicted each other about it, because Campodonico said she was a jettatrice and Ghisleri said she was not, you know. After dinner the two went and talked in whispers at the other end of the big room, and Ghisleri looked ghastly white, and Campodonico was so angry that his eyes were like coals. A few minutes later, they both went away in a great hurry — Campodonico left his wife there. It certainly looks as though there were to be a duel to-morrow. You know how they hate each other, and how they fought long ago about that wonderful Princess Corleone who died. I can remember seeing her before I was married."

The Contessa listened to the end. She could not have grown paler than she was on that evening, but while Donna Maria was speaking the shadows deepened almost to black under her eyes, and the veins in her throat swelled and throbbed so that they hurt her. She succeeded in controlling all other outward signs of emotion, however, and when she spoke her voice was calm and quiet.

"I hardly believe that those two will fight," she said. "But, of course, they may. We shall probably know to-morrow."

Making a little sign to her partner, she began to dance with him again, and continued to waltz until the music ceased a few minutes later. She stopped near the door where Ghisleri was standing, and looked at him. He immediately came to her side, and she left the man she had been dancing with and moved away with Pietro

towards a distant room, not speaking on the way. They
sat down together in a quiet corner, and he saw that she
was very much moved and probably very angry with him.

"Will you please to tell me the truth?" she said, in a
hard voice. "I have something to ask you."

"Yes. I always do," he answered.

"Is it true that there is a quarrel between you and Don
Gianforte Campodonico?"

"Yes — it is true," replied Ghisleri, after hesitating a
few seconds.

"And that you had a discussion with him about Lady
Herbert at the San Giacinto's dinner table?"

"Yes," admitted Ghisleri, who saw that his worst fears
were about to be realised.

"Are you going to fight?" asked Maddalena, in a
metallic tone.

"Yes. We are going to fight."

"So you have already forgotten what you promised me
this afternoon. You said you would do all a man could
do to avoid a quarrel — for my sake. Six hours had not
passed before you had broken your word. That is the
sort of faith you keep with me."

Pietro Ghisleri began to think that his misfortunes
would never end. For some time he sat in silence, staring before him. Should he tell her the whole story?
Should he go over the abominable scene with Campodonico, and tell her all the atrocious insults he had
patiently borne for Bianca Corleone's sake, until Maddalena's own name had seemed to set him free from his
obligation to the dead woman? He reflected that it would
sound extremely theatrical and perhaps improbable in
her ears, for she distrusted him enough already. Besides,
if she believed him, to tell her would only be to afford
his own vanity a base satisfaction. This last view was
perhaps a false one, but with his character it was not
unnatural.

"I have kept my word," he said at last, "for I have
borne all that a man can bear to avoid this quarrel."

"I am sorry you should be able to bear so little for me," answered Maddalena, her voice as hard as ever.

"I have done my best. I am only a man after all. If you had heard what passed, you would probably now say that I am right."

"You always take shelter behind assertions of that kind. I know it is of no use to ask you to tell me the whole story, for if you were willing to tell it, you would have told it to me already. No one can conceal fact as you can and yet never be caught in a downright falsehood. Half an hour ago, when we were sitting in that other room, you knew just as well as you do now that you were to fight to-morrow, and you had not the slightest intention of telling me."

"Not the slightest. Men do not talk about such things. It is not in good taste, and not particularly honourable, in my opinion."

"Good taste and honour!" exclaimed the Contessa, scornfully. "You talk as though we were strangers! Indeed, I think we are coming to that, as fast as we can."

"I trust not."

"The phrase, again! What should you say, after all? You must say something when I put the matter plainly. It would not be in good taste, if you did not contradict me when I tell you that you do not love me. All things considered, perhaps you do not even think it honourable. You are very considerate, and I am immensely grateful. Perhaps you are thinking, too, that it would be more decent, and in better taste on my part, to let you go, now that I have discovered the truth. I am almost inclined to think so. I have seen it long, and I have been foolish to doubt my senses."

"For Heaven's sake, do not be so bitter and unjust," said Ghisleri earnestly.

"I am neither. Do you know why I have clung to you? Shall I tell you? It may hurt you, and I am bad enough to wish to hurt you to-night — to wish that you might suffer something of what I feel."

"I am ready," answered Pietro.

"Do you know why I have clung to you, I ask? I will tell you the truth. It was my last chance of respecting myself, my last hold on womanliness, on everything that a woman cares to be. And you have succeeded in taking that from me. You found me a good wife. You know what I am now — what you have made me. Remember that to-morrow morning, when you are risking your life for Lady Herbert Arden. Do you understand me? Have I hurt you?"

"Yes." Ghisleri bowed his head, and passed his hand over his forehead.

What she said was terribly, irrefutably true. The vision of true love, revived within the last few days, and delusive still that very afternoon, had vanished, and only the other, the vision of sin, remained, clear, sharp, and cruelly well-defined. He made no attempt to deny what she said, even in his own heart, for it would not be denied.

"I cannot even ask you to forgive me that," he said at last in a low tone.

"No. You cannot even ask that, for you knew what you were doing — I scarcely did. Not that I excuse myself. I was willing to risk everything, and I did, blindly, for the sake of a real love. You see what I have got. You cannot love me, but you shall not forget me. Heaven is too just. And so, good-bye!"

"I hope it may be good-bye, indeed," said Ghisleri.

"Not that — no, not that!" exclaimed Maddalena. "I wish you no evil — no harm. I had a right to say what I have said. I shall never say it again — for there will be no need. Take me back, please."

She rose to go, and her finely chiselled face was as hard as steel. In silence they went back to the supper-room, and a few moments later Ghisleri left her with Francesco Savelli and went home. On his table he found a note from his seconds, as had been arranged, naming the place and hour agreed upon for the duel, and stating that they would call for him in good time. He tossed it into the

fire which still smouldered on the hearth, as he did with
everything in the nature of notes and letters which came
to him. He never kept a scrap of writing of any sort,
except such as chanced to be connected with business
matters and the administration of his small estate. He
hesitated long as to whether he should write to Maddalena
or not, sitting for nearly half an hour at his writing-
table with a pen in his fingers and a sheet of paper before
him.

After all, what could he write? A justification of
himself in the question of fighting with Campodonico?
What difference could it make now? All had been said,
and the end had come, as he had of late known that it
must, though it had been abrupt and unexpected at the
last minute. It was all the same now whether he should
afterwards be said to have fought for Laura or for Maddalena. Besides, in real truth, if it were known, he was
fighting for neither. Gianforte's old hatred had suddenly flamed up again, and if he had spoken Maddalena's
name it was only because he found that no other means
could prevail upon the man he hated to break his solemn
vow, and because he knew that no man would bear tamely
an insult of that kind cast upon a woman he was bound
in honour to defend. But all that had been only the
result of circumstances. The quarrel was really the old
one in which they had fought so desperately, long ago.
The dead Bianca's memory still lived, and had power to
bring two brave men face to face in a death struggle.

Ghisleri rose from the table and stood before the photograph of the picture which had brought matters to the
present pass. For the thousandth time he gazed at the
wonderful likeness of her he had loved, perfect in all
points, as chance had made it under the hand of a man
who had never seen her.

"I made a promise to you once," he said, in a low
voice, "and I have kept it as well as I could. I will
make another, for your dear sake and memory. I will
not again bring unhappiness upon any woman."

Sentimental and theatrical, the world would have said. But the man who could bear to be unjustly called liar and coward rather than break his oath was able to keep such a promise if he chose. And he did.

So far as he was humanly able, too, in the world to which he belonged, he kept the first one also; for, when they bent over him as he lay upon the wet grass a few hours later, the pistol he held was loaded still. The world said that he had been shot before he had time to fire, because he was trying to aim too carefully. But Gianforte Campodonico bared his head and bent it respectfully as they carried Pietro Ghisleri away.

"There goes the bravest man I ever knew," he said to his second.

CHAPTER XIV.

THE report that Ghisleri had been killed by his old adversary in a quarrel about Laura Arden spread like wildfire through society. It was not until San Giacinto formally proclaimed that he had been to Ghisleri's lodging, and that, although shot through the right lung, he was alive and might recover, that the world knew the truth.

It was of course perfectly evident that Laura was the cause of the difference. Even San Giacinto had no other explanation to suggest, when he was appealed to, and could only say that it seemed incredible that two men should fight with pistols at a dangerously short distance, because the one said that Lady Herbert was a jettatrice, and the other denied it. If Campodonico had been less universally liked than he was, he would have become very unpopular in consequence of the duel; for, although few persons were intimate with Ghisleri, he also was a favourite with the world.

The Gerano faction was very angry with both men,

though Adele was secretly delighted. It was a scandalous thing, they said, that a duel should be fought about
a young widow, whose husband had not been buried much
more than two months. Both should have known better.
And then, Campodonico was a young married man, which
made matters far worse. Duelling was an abominable
sin, of course; but Ghisleri, at least, was alone in the
world and could risk his soul and body without the danger of bringing unhappiness on others. Gianforte's case
was different and far less pardonable.

But Casa Gerano and Casa Savelli belonged rather to
the old-fashioned part of society, though Adele and her
husband were undeniably in the gay set, and there were
many who judged the two men more leniently. The
world had certainly been saying for some time that Ghisleri went very often to see Lady Herbert, and was neglect-
ing Maddalena dell' Armi. The cruel words the Contessa
had overheard at the Embassy were but part of the current gossip, for otherwise mere strangers, like those who
had spoken, could not have already learned to repeat
them. If, then, Ghisleri was in love with Laura Arden,
it was natural enough that he should resent the story
about the evil eye. Meanwhile, poor man, no one could
tell whether he could ever recover from his dangerous
wound.

The Contessa dell' Armi was one of the very first to
know the truth. She had spent a miserable and sleepless night, and it was still very early in the morning
when she sent to Ghisleri's lodgings for news. She was
very anxious, for she knew more than most people about
the old story, and she guessed that Campodonico would
do his best to hurt Pietro. But she had no idea that
pistols were to be the weapons, and Ghisleri's reputation as a swordsman was very good. Short of an accident, she thought, nothing would be really dangerous to
him. But then, accidents sometimes happened.

The answer came back, short and decisive. He was
shot through the very middle of the right lung, he had

not fired upon his adversary, and he lay in great danger, between life and death, in the care of a surgeon and a Sister of Charity, neither of whom left his side for a moment.

Maddalena did not hesitate. She dressed herself in an old black frock she found among her things, put on a thick veil, went out alone, and drove to Pietro's lodgings. Such rash things may be done with impunity in Paris or London, but they rarely remain long concealed in a small city like Rome. He was still unconscious from weakness and loss of blood. His eyes were half closed and his face was transparently white. Maddalena stood still at the foot of the bed and looked at him, while the doctor and the nurse gazed at her in surprise. During what seemed an endless time to them she did not move. Then she beckoned to the surgeon, and led him away to the window.

"Will he live?" she asked, hardly able to pronounce the words.

"He may. There is some hope, for he is very strong. I cannot say more than that for the present."

For a few moments Maddalena was silent. She had never seen the doctor, and he evidently did not know her.

"My place should be here," she said at last. "Would an emotion be bad for him — if he were angry, perhaps?"

"Probably fatal," answered the surgeon with decision. "If he is likely to experience any emotion on seeing you, I beg you not to stay long. He may soon be fully conscious."

"He cannot know me now?" she asked anxiously.

"No. Not yet."

"Not if I went quite near to him — if I touched him?"

The doctor glanced back at the white face on the pillow.

"No," he answered. "But be quick."

Maddalena went swiftly to the bedside, and, bending down, kissed Ghisleri's forehead, gazed at him for a moment, and then turned away. She slipped a little gold bracelet formed of simple links without ornament or distinctive mark from her wrist, and put it into the Sister's hand.

"If you think he is dying, give him this, and say I came and kissed him. If he is in no danger, sell it, and give the money to some poor person. Can I trust you, my sister?"

"Yes, madame," answered the French nun quietly as she dropped the trinket into her capacious pocket.

With one glance more at Ghisleri's face, the Contessa left the room. A quarter of an hour later she was at home again. The servants supposed that she had gone to an early mass, as she sometimes did, possibly to pray for the soul of the Signor Ghisleri. The man who had gone for news of him had not failed to inform the whole household of Pietro's dangerous state, and as Pietro was a constant visitor, and was generous with his five-franc notes, considerable anxiety was felt in the lower regions for his welfare, and numerous prayers were offered for his recovery.

Maddalena sent to make inquiries several times in the course of the day, and towards evening was informed that there was more hope, but that if he got well at all it would be by a long convalescence. She herself saw no one, and no one ever knew what she suffered in those endless hours of solitude.

Laura Arden heard of the duel through her mother, who was very angry about it, as has been seen. Laura herself was greatly shocked, for at first almost every one thought that Ghisleri must die of his wound. Having been brought up in Rome, in the midst of Roman ideas, she had not the English aversion to duelling, nor, being an Anglican, had she a Catholic's horror of sudden death. She did not even yet really like Ghisleri. But she was horror-struck, though she could hardly have told why, at the thought that the strong man who had been with her when her husband died, and whom she had talked with so often since, should be taken away without warning, in the midst of his youth and strength, for a word said in her defence. Of course the Princess told her all the details of the story as she had heard them, laying particular stress upon the fact that the duel had been fought for Laura. The seconds in the affair had gravely alleged a dispute about the painter Zichy as the true cause of the quarrel, but the world had found time to make up its mind on the previous evening, and was not to be deceived by such absurd tales.

"It is not my fault, mother, if they fought about me," said Laura. "But I am dreadfully distressed. I wish I could do anything."

"The best thing is to do nothing," answered the Princess, "for nothing can do any good. The harm is done, whether it has been in any way your fault or not. To think it should all have begun in that insane superstition about the evil eye!"

"I never even knew that I was suspected of being a jettatrice. People must be mad to believe in such things. You are right, of course. What could any of us do except make inquiries? Poor man! I hope he will get over it."

"God grant he may live to be a better man," said the Princess, devoutly. She had never had a very high opinion of Ghisleri's moral worth, and late events had confirmed her in the estimate she had made. "One thing I must say, my dear," she continued. "If he recovers, as I pray he may, you must see less of him than hitherto. You cannot let people talk about you as they will talk, especially after this dreadful affair."

"I will be very careful," Laura answered. "Not that there is any danger. The poor man will be ill for weeks, at the best, and the summer will be almost here before he is out of the house. Then I shall be going away, for I do not mean to keep Herbert here during the heat."

The Princess was quite used to hearing Laura speak of the little child in that way, and she had never once referred to her husband by name since his death. She meant that the one Herbert should take the place of the other, once and for always, to be cared for and loved, and thought of at every hour of the day. She had silently planned out her life during the weeks of her recovery, and she believed that nothing could prevent her from living it as she intended. Everything should be for little Herbert, from first to last. She looked at the baby face, in which she saw so plainly the father's likeness where others could see only a pair of big brown eyes, plump cheeks, and a mouth like a flower, and she promised herself that all the happiness she would have made for the one who had been taken should be the lot of the one given to her almost on the same day. Her future seemed anything but dark to her, though its greater light had gone out. The anguish, the agonising anxiety, the first moment's joy, and at last the full pride of motherhood, had come between her and the past, deadening the terrible shock at first, and making the memory of it less keen and poignant afterwards, while not in any way dimming the bright recollection of the love that had united her to her husband. She could take pleasure now in looking forward to her boy's coming years, to the time when he should be at first a companion, then a friend, and then a protector of whom she would be proud when he stood among other men. She could think of his schooldays, and she could already feel the pain of parting from him and the joy of meeting him again, taller and stronger and braver at every return. And far away in the hazy distance before her she could see a shadowy but lovely figure, yet unknown to-day — Herbert's wife that was to be, a perfect woman, and worthy of him in all ways. It might be also that somewhere there were great deeds for Herbert to do, fame for him to achieve, glory for him to win. All this was possible, but she thought little of it. Her ambition was to know him some day to be all that his father had been in heart, and to see him all that his father should have been in outward form and stature. More than that she neither hoped nor asked for, and perhaps it was enough. And so she dreamed on, while no

one thought she was dreaming at all, for she was always
active and busy with something that concerned the child,
and her attention never wandered when it was needed.

Her mother watched her and was glad of it all. To
her, it seemed very merciful that Arden should have died
when he did, fond as she herself had been of him. She
had not believed that Laura could be permanently happy
with such a sufferer, and she had never desired the marriage, though she had done nothing to oppose it when she
saw how deeply her daughter loved the man she had
chosen. She was very much relieved when she saw how
Laura behaved in her sorrow, and realised that there was
no morbid tendency in her to dwell over-long on her
grief. One thing, which has already been mentioned,
alone showed that Laura felt very deeply, — she never
spoke of Arden, even to her mother. On this point there
seemed to be a tacit understanding between her and Donald. The faithful old servant seemed to know instinctively what she wished done. When all was over, and
while Laura was still far too ill to be consulted, he had
taken all Arden's clothes and other little effects, even to
his brushes and other dressing things, and had packed
everything in his dead master's own boxes as though for
a long journey. The boxes themselves he locked up in
a small spare room, and laid the key in the drawer of
Laura's writing-table with a label on which were written
the words, "His lordship's effects." Laura found it the
first time she came to the drawing-room, and was grateful
to the old Scotchman for what he had done. But she
could not bring herself to speak of it, even to Donald,
though he knew that she was pleased by the look she gave
him.

Of course, her manner was greatly changed from what
it had been. She never laughed now, and rarely ever
smiled, except when she held the child in her arms.
But there was nothing morbid nor brooding in her gravity.
She had accepted her lot and was determined to make the
best of it according to her light. In time she would grow

more cheerful, and by and by she would be her old self again — more womanly, perhaps, and certainly more mature, but not materially altered in character or disposition. The short months which had sufficed for what had hitherto been the chief acts of her life had not been filled with violent or conflicting emotions, and it is emotion more than anything else which changes the natures of men and women for better or for worse. The love that had been born of mingled pity and sympathy of thought had risen quickly in the peaceful, remote places of her heart, and had flowed smoothly through the sweet garden of her maidenly soul, unruffled and undeviating, until it had suddenly disappeared into the abyss of eternity. It had left no wreck and no ruin behind, no devastation and no poisonous, stagnant pools, as some loves do. The soil over which it had passed had been refreshed and made fertile by it, and would bear flowers and fruit hereafter as fragrant and as sweet as it could ever have borne; and at the last, in that one great moment of pain when she had stood at the brink and seen all she loved plunge out of sight for ever in the darkness, she had heard in her ear the tender cry of a new young life calling to her to turn back and tend it, and love it, and show it the paths that lead to such happiness as the world holds for the pure in heart.

She was calm, therefore, and not, in the ordinary sense, broken by her sorrow, — a fact which the world, in its omniscience, very soon discovered. It did not fail to say that she was well rid of her husband, and that she knew it, and was glad to be free, though she managed with considerable effort to keep up a sufficient outward semblance of mourning to satisfy the customs and fashions of polite society — just that much, and not a jot more.

But Adele Savelli said repeatedly that all this was not true, and that only a positively angelic nature like Laura's could bear such an awful bereavement so calmly. It was a strange thing, Adele added, that very good people should always seem so much better able to resign them-

selves to the decrees of Providence than their less perfect
neighbours. Of course it could not be that they were
colder and felt less than others, and consequently could
not suffer so much. Besides, Laura must have loved
Arden sincerely to marry him at all, since it appeared to
be certain that the rich uncle who was to have left him
so much money only existed in the imagination of the
gossips, and had evidently been invented by them merely
in order to make out that Laura had a secret reason for
marrying that uncle's favourite nephew. But then, people would talk, of course, and all that the relations of the
family could do was to deny such calumnious reports
consistently and at every turn.

Adele was looking very ill when the season came to an
end. She had grown thin, and her eyes had a restless,
hunted look in them which had never been there before.
Her husband noticed that she was very much overcome
when she heard the first report to the effect that Ghisleri
was killed. She seemed particularly horrified at the
statement that the original cause of the duel had been the
reputation for possessing the evil eye which Laura Arden
had so suddenly acquired, and which, as she herself had
been the very first to say, was so utterly unfounded. It
was evidently a very great relief to her to hear, later in
the day, that Pietro was not yet dead, and might even
have a chance of recovery.

No one could tell what Gianforte Campodonico thought
of the matter. He shut himself up obstinately and
awaited events. It is not probable that he felt any
remorse for what he had done, or that he would have
felt any if he had left Ghisleri dead on the field, instead
of with a bare chance of life. He had taken the vengeance he had longed for and he was glad of it, but the
impression he had of the man was not the same which he
had been accustomed to for so many years. He, who
generally reflected little, asked himself whether he could
have found the courage to bear what Ghisleri had borne
for the sake of the promise they had made together, and

which he had been the first to break. He was a brave man, too, in his way, and it would not have been safe to predict that he would fail at any given point if put to the test. But he was conscious that, in the present case, Ghisleri had played the nobler part, and he was manly enough to acknowledge the fact to himself, and to respect his adversary as he had not done before. If he stayed at home and refused to be seen in the world or even at his club immediately after the duel, it was because he would not be thought willing to glory in his victory.

But, before many days were gone by, it became apparent, so far as the world could judge, that Pietro Ghisleri would not die of the dangerous wound he had received. It would have killed most men, the surgeon said, but Ghisleri was not like other people. He, the doctor, had never seen a stronger constitution, nor one so perfectly untainted by any hereditary evil or weakness. Such blood was rare now, especially in the old families, and such strength would have been rare in any age. He had no longer any hesitation in saying that the patient had a very fair prospect of recovery, and might possibly be as healthy as ever before the end of the summer.

The Sister of Charity went about with Maddalena's bracelet in her pocket, feeling very uncomfortable about it, since she had been quite sure from the first that there was something very sinful in the whole affair. But she was quite ready to fulfil her promise if Ghisleri showed signs of departing this life, which he did not, however, either when he first regained consciousness or later. So she, on her part, said nothing, and waited for the day when she might deliver up the trinket to the Mother Superior, to be sold for the poor, as Maddalena had directed. In that, at least, there could be no harm, and she was very thankful that she was not called upon to deliver the message to Ghisleri himself, for that, she felt sure, would have been sinful, or something very like it.

The surgeon was surprised by something else in the case. As a general rule, when a man fights a desperate

duel in the very middle of the season, and especially such
a man as he knew Ghisleri to be, and is severely hurt,
he finds himself cut off from society in the midst of some
chain of events in which the whole present interest of his
life is engaged.   He is consequently disturbed in mind,
impatient of confinement, and feverishly anxious to get
back to the world, — a state of temper by no means condu-
cive to convalescence.   Ghisleri, on the contrary, seemed
to have forgotten to care for anything.   No preoccupation appeared to possess him; no desire to be back again
in the throng made him restless.   He was perfectly calm
and peaceful, always patient, and always resigned to
whatever treatment seemed necessary.   The Sister wondered much that a man of such marvellous gentleness and
resignation could have found it in him to commit mortal
sin in fighting a duel, and, perhaps, far down in her
woman's heart, she did not wonder at all at what Maddalena had done on that first morning.   The surgeon said
that Ghisleri's sweet temper had much to do with his
rapid recovery.

It need not be supposed from this that his character
had undergone any radical change, nor that he was turning, all at once, into the saint he was never intended to
be.   It was very simple.   The events of the night preceding the duel had brought his life to a crisis which,
once past, had left little behind it to disturb him.   First
in his mind was the consciousness that his love for
Maddalena dell' Armi was gone for ever, and that she
herself expected no return of it.   That alone was enough
to change his whole existence in the present, and in the
immediate future.   Then, too, he felt that he had at least
settled old scores with Campodonico and had in a measure expiated one, at least, of his past misdeeds, almost at
the cost of his life.   Morally speaking, too, he had kept
his oath to Bianca Corleone, for under the utmost provocation he had refused to fight in the old quarrel, and even
when driven to bay and forced upon new ground by Campodonico's implacable hatred, he had stood up to be

killed without so much as firing at Bianca's brother. There was a deep and real satisfaction in that, and he was perhaps too ill as yet to torture himself by stigmatising it as a bit of vanity. The world might think what it pleased. Maddalena might misjudge his motives, and Gianforte might triumph in his victory — it all made no difference to him. He was conscious that to the best of his ability he had acted according to the dictates of true honour, as he understood it; and at night he closed his eyes and fell peacefully asleep, and in the morning he opened them quietly again upon the little world of his invalid's surroundings.

He was not happy, however. What he felt, and what perhaps saved his life, was a momentary absence of responsibility, an absolute certainty that nothing more could be required of him, because, in the events in which he had played a part, that part had been acted out to the very end. He even went so far as to believe that, if he had died, it would not have made any difference to any one, except that his death might possibly have been an added satisfaction to Campodonico. He would have left no sorrowing heart behind to mourn him, nor any gap in any circle which another man could not fill up. Herbert Arden, the only friend who would have really regretted him, was already dead, and there was no one else who stood to him in any relation of acquaintance at all so close as to be called friendship. All this contributed materially to his peace of mind, though in one respect he was mistaken. There was one person who loved him still, for himself, though she knew well enough that his love for her was dead.

And it was of her, though he was mistaken about her, that he thought the most during the long hours when he lay there quietly watching the sunbeams stealing across the room when it was fine, or listening to the raindrops pattering against the windows when the weather was stormy. In her was centred the great present regret of his life, and for her sake he felt the most sincere remorse.

He asked himself, as she had asked him, what was to become of her, now that he had left her. The fact that she had been really the one to speak the word and cause the first break did not change the truth in the least. It had been his fault from the first to the last. He had not broken her heart, perhaps, because hearts are not now-a-days easily broken, if, indeed, they ever really were; but he had ruined her existence wantonly, uselessly, on the plea of a love neither pure nor lasting, and he fully realised what he had done. What chance had she ever had against him — she, young, inexperienced, trusting, wretchedly unhappy with a husband who had despised and trodden out the simple, girlish love she had offered — what chance had she against Pietro Ghisleri, the hardened, cool-headed man of the world, whose only weakness was that he sometimes believed himself sincere, as he had with her? He was not happy as he thought of it all. There had been little manliness in what he had done, and not much of the honour which he called his last shred of morality. And yet, in the world in which he had his being, few men would blame him, and none, perhaps, venture to condemn him. But that consideration did not cross his mind. He was willing to bear both condemnation and blame, and he heaped both upon himself in a plentiful measure.

Nevertheless, he was conscious of being surprised at the calmness of his own repentance, as he called it rather contemptuously, and he wished himself, as usual, quite different from what he was. And yet he had not forgotten the semi-theatrical resolution to change his life, which he had made on the night before the duel, still less had he any intention of breaking it. He had always laughed at men and women who made sudden and important resolutions under the influence of emotion, and, on the whole, he had never seen any reason for looking upon such gratuitous promises as valid, unless there had been witnesses to them, and human vanity afterwards came into play. But now, in his own case, he meant to try

the experiment. It made no difference whether he were
vain about it or not, if he succeeded, nor, if he failed,
whether he scorned his own weakness a little more than
before. No one would ever know, and since by Laura
Arden's rigid standard of right and wrong the end to be
gained belonged distinctly to the right, he would be in a
measure following her advice in regard to life in general.
Deeper down in his nature, too, there lay another thought
which he would not now evoke, lest he should himself
condemn it as sentimental. That secret promise had been
honestly intended, and had been addressed to the memory
of one who, though long dead, still had a stronger influence over him than any one now living. He hardly dared
to acknowledge the truth of this and the real meaning of
what he had done, lest, if he failed hereafter, he should
have to accuse himself of faithlessness towards the one
woman to whom he had been really true, and whom, if
she had lived, he would have loved till the end, in spite
of obstacles, in spite of mankind, in spite, he added
defiantly, of Heaven itself. All this he tried to keep out
of sight, while firmly resolving, in his own cynical way,
to try the experiment of goodness for once, and to do no
more harm in the world if he could help it.

He thought of Laura Arden, too, in his long convalescence, and her image was always pleasant to his inner
vision, as the impression she had produced on him was
soothing to recall. There were times when her holy eyes
seemed to gaze at him out of the darker corners of the
room, and he tried often to bring back her whole presence.
The pleasure such useless feats of imagination gave him
was artistic if it was anything, because he admired her
beauty and had always delighted in it. He tried to fancy
what she was doing, on certain days when he thought
more of her than usual, and to follow her life a little,
always trying in a vague way to fathom the secret of the
character that was so wonderful in his estimation. And
always, when he had been thinking of her, he came back
to the contemplation of his own immediate interests with

a renewed calm and with a peaceful sense that there
might yet be better days in store for him — possibly
days in which he should himself be better than he had
been heretofore.

How the world would have jeered, could it have suspected that Pietro Ghisleri was thinking almost seriously
of such a very commonplace subject as moral goodness,
as he lay on his back, day after day, in the quiet of his
room. How gladly would Adele Savelli have changed
places with the man who, as she thought, for the sake of
a bit of gossip she had invented out of spite, had nearly
lost his life!

CHAPTER XV.

WHEN Ghisleri was at last able to go out of the house,
his first visit was to Maddalena dell' Armi. He had
written a line to say that he was coming, and she expected
him. The meeting was a strange one, for both felt at
first the constraint of their mutual position. Ghisleri
looked at her face, which had been so hard when he had
last seen it, and he saw that it had softened. There were
no signs of suffering, however, and her expression was
almost as placid as his own. He raised her hand to his
lips and sat down opposite to her. Then the light fell
on his face and she saw how changed he was. She
remembered how he had looked when she had seen him
after he was wounded, and she saw that he was almost as
pale now as then, and that he was thin almost to emaciation.

"Are you really growing strong again?" she asked in
a tone of anxiety.

"Yes, indeed," he answered with a smile. "I feel as
though I were quite well — a little gaunt and weak, perhaps, but that will soon pass. And you — how have you
spent your time in all these weeks since I last saw you?"

"Very much as usual," replied Maddalena, and suddenly a weary look came into her eyes. "If you care to know — as long as you were really in danger I did not go out. Then I went everywhere again, and tried to amuse myself."

"Did you succeed?" asked Ghisleri, trying hard to speak cheerfully. There had been something hopeless in Maddalena's tone which shocked him and pained him.

"More or less. Why do you ask me that?"

"Because I am interested."

"Do you care for me in the least — in any way?" she asked abruptly.

"You know that I do —"

"How should I know it?"

Ghisleri did not reply at once, for the question was not easily answered. Maddalena waited in silence until he should speak.

"Perhaps you are right," he said at last. "You have no means of knowing it, and I have no means of proving it. Dearest lady, since we have both changed so much, do you not think you could believe a little in my friendship?"

"We ought to be friends — you should be my best friend."

"I mean to be, if you will let me."

A long silence followed. Maddalena sat quite still, leaning back in a corner of the sofa and looking at a picture on the opposite wall. Ghisleri sat upright on a chair at a little distance from her.

"You say that you will be my friend, if I will let you," she said slowly, after several minutes. "Even if you could imagine that I could not wish it, you ought to be my best friend just the same. If I made you suffer every hour of the day as I did on that last night, you ought to bear it, and never have one unkind thought of me. No; do not answer me yet: I have much more to say. You know that I have always told you just what I have felt, when I have told you anything about myself.

I was very unhappy when we met at that ball — or, rather, when we parted — so unhappy that I hardly knew what I said. I ought to have waited and thought before I spoke. If I could have guessed that you were to be wounded — well, it is of no use now. I am very, very fond of you. In spite of everything, if you felt the least love for me still, however little, I would say, 'Let us be as we were, as long as it can last.' As it is — "

She paused and looked at him. He knew what she meant. If there were a spark of love, she would forget everything and take him back on any terms. For a moment the old struggle was violently resumed in his heart. Ought he not, for her sake, to pretend love, and to live out his life as best he could in the letter of devotion if not in the true spirit of love? Or would not such an attempt necessarily be a failure, and bring her more and more unhappiness with each month and year? He only hesitated for an instant while she paused; then he determined to say nothing. That was really the turning-point in Pietro Ghisleri's life.

"As it is," continued Maddalena, a little unsteadily, but with a brave effort, "nothing but friendship is possible. Let it at least be a true and honest friendship which neither of us need be ashamed of. Let all the world see it. Go your way, and I will go mine, so far as the rest is concerned. If you love Lady Herbert, marry her, if she will have you, when her mourning is over."

"I do not love Lady Herbert at all," said Ghisleri with perfect truth.

"Well — if you should, or any other woman. Let the world say what it will, it cannot invent anything worse than it has said of me already. You owe me nothing — nothing but that, — to be a true friend to me always, as I will be to you as long as I live."

She put out her hand, and he took it and pressed it. As she felt his, the bright tears started to her eyes.

"What is it?" he asked tenderly, bending towards her as he spoke.

"Nothing," she answered hastily. "Your hand is so thin — how foolish of me! I suppose you will grow to be as strong as ever?"

He saw how she still loved him, in spite of all. It was not too late even now to renew the comedy, but his resolution had grown strong and unalterable in a few moments.

"You are much too good to me," he said softly. "I have not deserved it — but I will try to."

"Do not let us speak of all this any more for the present," she replied. "Since we are friends, let us talk of other things, as friends do."

It was not easy, but Ghisleri did his best, feeling that the effort must be made sooner or later and had therefore best be made at once. He kept up the conversation for nearly half an hour, and then rose to go.

"Are you not very tired?" asked Maddalena, anxiously.

"Not at all. I am much stronger than I look."

"Indeed I hope you are!" she answered, looking at him sadly. "Good-bye. Come soon again."

"Yes, I will come very soon."

Ghisleri went out and had himself driven about the city for an hour in the bright spring weather. It was all new to him now, and he looked at people and things with a sort of interest he had long forgotten to feel. A few of his acquaintances recognised him at once, and waved their hats to him if they chanced to be men, or made pretty gestures with their hands if they were women. But the greater number did not know him at first, and stared after the death-like face and the gaunt figure wrapped in a fur coat that had grown far too wide.

He was very glad that the first meeting with Maddalena was over, for he had looked forward to it with considerable anxiety. Something like what had actually been said about friendship had been inevitable, as he now saw, but he had not realised how much he was still loved, nor that Maddalena could so far humiliate herself as to

P

show that she cared for him still, and to offer a renewal of their old relations. Even now, could he have seen her pale and tear-stained face as she sat motionless in the place where he had left her, he might possibly have been weak enough to yield, strong as his determination was not to do so. But that sight was spared him, and he was glad that he had held his peace when she had paused to give him an opportunity of speaking. It was far better so. To act a miserable play with her, no matter from what so-called honourable motive of consideration, would be to make her life far more unhappy than it would ultimately be if she knew the truth. He was satisfied with what he had done, therefore, when he went back to his rooms and lay down to rest after the fatigue of his first day out. But the meeting had left a very sad and painful impression, and all that he felt of remorse and regret for what he had done was doubled now. He hated to think that by his fault she was cast upon the world, with little left to save her, "trying to amuse herself," as she had said, and he wondered at her gentleness and kindness to himself, so different from her behaviour at their last meeting. That, at least, comforted him. In a woman who could thus forgive there must be depths of goodness which would ultimately come to the surface. He remembered how often he had thought her hard, unjust, unkind, and, above all, unbelieving, in the days that succeeded the first outbursts of unreasoning love, and how, even while loving her, he had not always found it easy not to judge her harshly. She was very different now. Possibly, since she felt that she had lost her old power over him, she would be less impatient with him when she did not understand him, and when he displeased her. Come what might, treat him as she would, he owed her faithful allegiance and service — and those at least he could give. He could never atone to her, but in the changing scenes of the world he might, by devoting to her interest all the skill and tact he possessed, make her life happier and easier.

Before night he received a note from Laura Arden. She wrote that she had seen him driving, though he had not seen her pass, as he had been looking in the opposite direction. If he was able to bear the fatigue of making a call, she begged that he would come to her at any hour he chose to name, as she wished to speak to him. He answered at once that he would be at her house on the following day at three o'clock.

He knew very well what she wanted, and why she did not wait until he came of his own accord. She meant to speak to him of the duel, and her questions would be hard to answer, since she was probably in ignorance of many details of his former life, familiar enough to people of his own age. He knew, of course, that the world said he had really fought on her account, and that he could never prevail upon the world to think otherwise. But he was very anxious that Laura herself should know the truth. She might forgive him for having let people believe that she had been concerned in the matter rather than Maddalena dell' Armi, out of womanly consideration for the latter, but she would assuredly not pardon him if she continued to suppose that he had made her the subject of useless gossip.

The situation was not an easy one.

At the appointed hour he entered her drawing-room. He was almost startled by her beauty when he first saw her standing opposite to him. She had developed in every way during the many weeks since he had seen her. The perfectly calm and regular life she led had produced its inevitable good effect. She, on her part, was almost as much shocked by his looks as Maddalena had been.

"Have I not asked too much of you?" she inquired, pushing forward a comfortable chair for him, and arranging a cushion in it.

"Not at all. Thanks," he added, as he sat down, "you are very good, but pray do not imagine that I am an invalid."

"I only saw you in the street," she said, almost apologetically. "I did not realise how desperately ill you still looked. Please forgive me."

"But I should have come to-day or to-morrow in any case," protested Ghisleri. "After what has happened — yes, I think I know why you sent for me. You have heard what every one is saying. The men who came to see me before I could go out told me all about it. I knew beforehand that it would turn out as it has, though we gave our seconds another excuse, as you have probably also heard, and which, if the truth were known, was much nearer to betraying the cause of the quarrel than any one supposed. Am I right? You wished to ask me why I had the impertinence to fight a duel about you. Is that it?"   .

"I would not put it in that way," said Laura. "But I did wish to ask you why you took the matter up so violently. Please do not enter into the question now — you are not strong enough. I am very sorry indeed that I wrote to you."

"You need not be, for I am quite able to tell you all about it. I have thought the matter over, and I think you will forgive me if I tell you the whole story from beginning to end. It is a confidence, and I have not the least fear that you will betray it. If you are not willing to hear it, you will always believe that I have wantonly made you the talk of the town. It is entirely to justify myself in your eyes that I ask you to listen to what I am going to say. Some points may shock you a little. Have I your leave?"

"Yes — if you really wish to tell me for your own sake. For mine, I do not ask you to tell me anything."

"It is for my own sake. I am quite selfish. When you have heard all, you will know more or less the history of my life, of which many people know certain details."

He paused and leaned back in his deep chair, closing his eyes a moment as though he were collecting his thoughts. Laura settled herself to listen, turning in her seat so as not to face him, but so that she could look at him while he was speaking.

"I have never told any one this story," he began, "for I have never had any good reason for doing so. When I was a very young man I loved the Princess Corleone, who was, by her maiden name, Donna Bianca Campodonico, the daughter of the old Duca di Norba who died of paralysis, and own sister to Gianforte Campodonico, with whom I fought this duel. I loved that lady with all my heart to the day of her death, and being young and tactless, I showed it too much. Her brother, Gianforte, hated me in consequence, because there was talk about his sister and me — and our names were constantly coupled together. I did my best to remain on civil terms with him, but at last he insulted me openly and we fought. This first duel took place a little more than six years ago, in Naples, where Donna Bianca lived after her marriage. Campodonico did his best to kill me, and at last I ran him through the arm. On the ground, without heeding the slight wound which disabled his right arm, he demanded pistols, but the seconds on both sides refused, and declared the affair terminated. As the original challenge had come from me, his position was quite untenable. He sought occasion after that to insult me again, but I avoided him. Then the Princess fell ill. Two days before she died, she had herself carried into the drawing-room, and sent for me. Her brother was already there. She made us both promise that for her sake we would never quarrel again. We joined hands and solemnly bound ourselves, for we knew she was dying. Then I took leave of her. I never saw her again, and I shall not see her hereafter."

He paused a moment, but not a muscle of his face betrayed emotion. Laura had listened with breathless interest.

"Do not say that," she said softly.

"I lived alone for a long time," continued Ghisleri, without heeding her remark. "Then at last I came back

to the world, and did many things, mostly bad, of which
I need not speak.   I fell a little in love, now and then, and
at last somewhat more seriously with a lady of whom we
will not speak, against whose good name no slander had
ever been breathed.   Now I come to the events which
caused the duel.   People have been saying that you have
the evil eye and are a jettatrice.   The absurd tale is
repeated from mouth to mouth, and will ultimately make
society here unbearable for you.   You are enough of a
Roman to understand that.   There was a big dinner at
San Giacinto's one night, and Campodonico and I sat
opposite to each other.   He believes in this nonsense
and I do not.   Pietrasanta mentioned your name, and
accidentally broke a glass at almost the same moment.
Then a discussion arose about the existence of such a
thing as the evil eye, and Campodonico and I talked about
it across the table, while everybody listened.   We exchanged a few rather incisive remarks, but nothing more.
That was the end of the matter so far as you were concerned, and it was owing to this discussion that people
said we fought on your account."

"I see," said Laura.   "It was all a mistake, then?"

"Yes.   But I suppose Campodonico was irritated.   In
the drawing-room I lit a cigarette, and stood some time
looking at a copy of Zichy's picture of Tamara falling into
the Demon's arms.   Tamara chances to be a very striking
likeness of the Princess Corleone, and if I had reflected
that Campodonico might have also noticed the fact, I
would not have stood there looking at it as I did.   But I
forgot.   Before I knew it, he was at my elbow, evidently
very angry, for he perfectly understood why I liked the
picture.   He asked me whether I did not think that a
solemn promise such as we had made might be broken
under certain circumstances.   I said I did not think so.
He lost his temper completely, and said I was a coward.
I still refused to quarrel with him, and he grew more and
more insulting, until at last he began a sentence which I
would not let him end, to the effect that, could Donna

Bianca have been there to judge us both, she might wish the promise broken — I suppose that would have been his inference — if she could have seen that the man she had loved had fallen so low as to love the lady to whom I referred a little while ago. He named her. I answered that Donna Bianca never meant that our promise should shield the liar who slandered a good and defenceless woman, because his name chanced to be Campodonico. We told our seconds that we had quarrelled about the talent of Zichy, the painter of the picture, because no immediate and better excuse suggested itself. That is the whole story."

"It is a very strange one," said Laura, in a low voice, and looking up at his pale face. "If people only knew the truth about what they see! Tell me, Signor Ghisleri, is it a fact that you did not fire at him?"

"Yes."

"Why did you not?"

"Because — if you really care to know — I still felt bound to my promise, and I should never have forgiven myself if I had hurt him. Will you say that you understand the rest of the story, and will you forgive me if I let it be thought that the duel was about you?"

"Indeed I forgive you," Laura answered without hesitation. "You acted splendidly all through, and I would not — "

"Please do not praise me," said Ghisleri, interrupting her with word and gesture. "Whatever I did was only the consequence of former actions of mine, most of which were bad in themselves. Besides, I have told you all this by way of an apology, and I thank you very sincerely for accepting it. Let the matter end there."

"Very well. That need not prevent me from thinking what I please, need it?"

"I shall always be really grateful for any kind thought you give me."

Laura was silent for a moment. She was surprised to find that her old feeling of dislike for him had greatly diminished. She had not even noticed it when he had entered the room, for she had been at once struck by his appearance of ill-health, and her first instinct had been that of sympathy for him. And now, whatever effect his personality produced on her, she could hardly conceal her admiration of his conduct. He had told the story very simply, and she felt that he had told it truthfully, and that she was able to judge of the man from a new point of view. She could not but appreciate the courage he had shown in bearing insult, and at last, in not return-ing his adversary's fire, and he rose in her estimation because he had done these things for the sake of a woman he had really loved.

"May I ask you one question?" she inquired after the pause.

"Of course, and I will answer it if I can."

"I dare say you remember something you told me about yourself a long time ago — how you distrust yourself, and torment yourself about everything you do. Will you tell me whether you have found any fault with your own conduct in this affair, apart from everything which went before the dinner party at which you met Don Gianforte? It would interest me very much to know."

Ghisleri thought over his answer for a few seconds before he gave it.

"Except in so far as I involved your name in the affair," he said, "I do not think I reproach myself with anything very definite."

He had hardly finished speaking when the door opened, and Donald announced Don Francesco and Donna Adele Savelli. A very slight shadow passed over Laura's face, as she rose to meet her step-sister, but Ghisleri remained cold and impassive. Adele started perceptibly, as Laura had done, when she saw him, and Ghisleri was struck by the change in her own appearance. Her expression was that of a woman who is in almost constant pain, and who has grown restless under it, and fears its return at any moment. Her eyes turned uneasily, glancing about the

room in all directions, and avoiding the faces of those
present. She was pale, too, and looked altogether ill.

"I am so glad to see you, Ghisleri," she said, after she
had kissed the air somewhere in the neighbourhood of
Laura's cheek. "I had no idea you were out already,
and as we are going away to-morrow, I was afraid I might
not meet you."

"Are you going out of town so soon?" asked Ghisleri,
in some surprise.

"Yes, I am ill, and they say I must go to the country.
Do you remember when you met me in the street, and
recommended sulphonal? I took it, and it did me good
for some time. But then, all at once, I found it did not
act so well, and I lost my sleep again. I want the doctors
to give me something, but they say all those things
become a habit — chloral, you know, and morphia, and
a great many things. As if I cared! I would not mind
any habit if I could only sleep — and I see things all
night — ugh! it is horrible! Have you ever had insomnia? It is quite the most dreadful thing in the world."

She shuddered, and Ghisleri could see well enough that
the suffering to which she referred was not at all imaginary.

"No," he answered. "I have never had anything of
that kind. When I go to bed at all I sleep five or six
hours very soundly."

"How I envy you that! Even five or six hours — I,
who used to sleep nine, and always ten after a ball. And
now I very often do not close my eyes all night. The
sulphonal did me so much good. Can you not tell me of
something else?"

"The best way to get over it would be to find out what
causes it, and cure that," observed Ghisleri. "Generally,
too, a quiet and healthy life, exercise, plain food, and a
good conscience will do good." He laughed a little as he
spoke, and then he noticed that Adele was looking at him
rather strangely. He wondered idly whether her mind
were wandering in some other direction.

"Of course," he continued, "you have no idea of what produces the trouble. If you could find that out, it would be simpler."

"Yes, indeed," assented Adele, with a forced smile. "If all that is necessary were to have a good conscience and walk an hour or two every day, I should soon get well."

"I have no doubt you will in any case. Are you going to Gerano, or to your own place?"

"To Gerano. It is warmer. Castel Savello is too high for the spring. I should freeze there. It would be a charity if you would drive out and spend a day or two with us, when you are stronger. I wish you would come out and see us, Laura," she said, turning to her step-sister, to whom Francesco was talking in a low voice. "You used to like Gerano when we were girls. Do you remember dear old Don Tebaldo, who used to shed tears because you were a Protestant?"

"Indeed I do. I hear he is alive still. It is two years since I was there the last time. Francesco has been telling me all about your illness. I am so sorry. I should think you would do better to consult some good specialist. But, of course, the country can do you no harm."

"I hope not," said Adele, with sudden despondency. "I have borne enough already. I could not bear much more."

"Nobody can understand what is the matter with her," observed Francesco, and his tone showed that he did not care.

"You have let her dance too much this winter," said Laura, addressing him. "You ought to keep her from over-tiring herself."

"It is not easy to prevent Adele from doing anything she wishes to do," answered Savelli. "This winter she has insisted on going everywhere. I have warned her a hundred times, but she would not listen to me, and of course this is the result."

"When did it begin?" asked Ghisleri, who seemed

interested in Adele's mysterious illness. "When did you first lose your sleep?"

"You remember," she answered. "We were just talking of our meeting in the street, and the sulphonal. It was about that time — a little before that, of course, for I had been suffering several days when I met you."

"Ah, yes — I remember when that was," said Ghisleri, in a tone of reflection.

He joined in the conversation during a few minutes longer, and then took leave of the three. Formerly he would have gone to spend an hour or two with Maddalena, but he had no inclination to do so now. He would gladly have stayed with Laura if the Savelli couple had not come. He wished to be alone, now, and to think over what he had done. It was the first time that he had ever told the story of his love for Bianca Corleone to any one, and calm as he had seemed while telling it, he had felt a very strong emotion. He was glad to be at home again, alone with his own thoughts, and with the picture that reminded him of the dead woman. He knew that she would have forgiven him for speaking of her to-day as he had spoken, and to such a woman as Laura Arden. For in his heart he compared the two. There had been grand lines in Bianca Corleone's character, as there were in that of her passionate brother, as Ghisleri believed there must be in Laura Arden's also, and great generosities, the readiness to go to any length for the sake of real passion, the power to hate honestly, to love faithfully, and to forgive wholly — all things which Pietro missed in himself. And Laura had to-day waked the memory of that great love which had once filled his existence, and which had not ended with the life that had gone out before its day, in all its beauty and freshness. He was grateful to her for that, and he sat long in his chair after his lonely meal, thinking of her and of the other, and of poor Maddalena dell' Armi, whose very name, sounding in his imagination, sent a throb of remorse through his heart.

A pencil lay near him and he took a sheet of paper and began to write, as he often did when he was alone, scribbling verses without rhyme, and often with little meaning except in their connection with his thoughts. He was no poet.

> "A sweet, dark woman, with sad, holy eyes,
> Laid her cool hand upon my heart to-day,
> And touched the dear dead thing that's buried there.
> Her saintly magic cannot make it live,
> Nor sting once more with passionate deep thrill
> The bright torn flesh where my lost love breathed last.

> "She has no miracles for me — nor God
> Forgiveness, nor earth healing — nor death fear.
> I think I fear life more — and yet, to live
> Were easy work, could I but learn to die;
> As, if I learned to live, I should hate death.
> But I cannot hate death — not even death —
> Since that is dead which made death hateful once;
> Nor hate I anything; let all live on,
> Just and unjust, bad, good, indifferent,
> Sinner and saint, man, devil, angel, martyr —
> What are they all to me? Good night, sweet rest —
> I wish you most what I can find the least.
> We meet again soon. Have you heard the talk
> About the latest scandal of our town?
> No? Nor have I. I care less than I did
> About the men and women I have known.
> Good night — and thanks for being kind to me."

CHAPTER XVI.

DONNA ADELE SAVELLI was ill. There was no denying the fact, though her husband had ignored it as long as possible, and was very much annoyed to find that he could not continue to do so until the usual time for moving to the country arrived. As has been said already, the world attributed her ill-health to some unexpected

awakening of the family skeleton, and when the Savelli
couple suddenly retired to Gerano, it was sure that Francesco had lost money and that they had gone for economy.
But there was no lack of funds in Casa Savelli. That
ancient and excellent house had, as a family, a keen
appreciation of values great and small, and continued to
put away more of its income in safe investments than any
one knew of. Nor was there any other trouble to account
for Adele's illness, so far as any member of the household
could judge. Every one else was well, including the
children. Everybody was prosperous. It was not conceivable that Adele should have taken Herbert Arden's
death to heart in a way to endanger her own health.
She might, perhaps, feel some remorse for having spoken
of him as she had — for Savelli had discovered that something, at least, of the gossip could be traced to her — but
she could not be supposed to care so much as to fall ill.
What she suffered from was evidently some one of those
mysterious nervous diseases which, in Francesco's opinion, modern medical science had invented expressly in
order that it might deal with them. Unfortunately, the
particular man of learning who could cure Adele was not
forthcoming. The doctors who were consulted said that
something was preying on her mind, and when she assured
them that this was not the case, they shrugged their
shoulders and prescribed soothing medicines, country air,
and exercise. She particularly dreaded the night, and
could not bear to be left alone for a moment after dark.
She said she saw things; when asked what things she
saw, she seemed to draw upon her imagination. Francesco began to fear that she might go mad, though there
was no insanity in the Braccio family. The prospect was
not pleasing, and he would have greatly preferred that
she should die and leave him at liberty to marry Laura
Arden. He never dreamed that the latter would refuse
to wed the heir of all the Savelli, if he were free to ask
her hand, and in his cautious, unenterprising fashion he
loved her still, while remaining religiously faithful to

his wife — and not, on the whole, treating her unkindly. The consequence of all this was that he made her try the simple cure suggested by the doctors, and accompanied her to Gerano in the early spring.

The hereditary stronghold from which the head of the Braccio family took his principal title was a vast and gloomy fortress in the lower range of the Sabine mountains, situated in a beautiful country, and overlooking the broad Campagna that lay between it and the distant sea. The great dark walls were flanked by round towers, and were in some places ten and twelve feet thick, so that the deep embrasures of the windows were in themselves like little rooms opening off the great halls behind. The furniture was almost all old, and was well in keeping with the vaulted ceilings, the frescoed friezes, and the dark marble door-posts. Donna Adele's sleeping-chamber was as large as most of the drawing-rooms in the Palazzo Braccio, and her dressing-room was almost of the same size. To reach the hall in which she and her husband dined, it was necessary to traverse five other rooms and a vaulted passage fifty or sixty yards long, in which the steps of any one who passed echoed and rang on the stone pavement, and echoed again during some seconds afterwards in a rather uncanny fashion. The sitting-room was next to the dining-hall, and consequently also at a great distance from the bedrooms. There was more of comfort in it than elsewhere, for the walls were hung with tapestries, and there was a carpet on the floor, whereas in the other apartments there were only rugs thrown down here and there, where they were most needed; here, too, the doors had heavy curtains. But, on the whole, a more ghostly and gloomy place than the castle of Gerano could hardly be imagined, especially at dusk when the blackness deepened in the remote corners and recesses of the huge chambers, and the sculptured corbels of grey stone, high up at the spring of each arch, grew shadowy and alive with hideous grimaces in the gathering dimness.

Adele had never been subject to any fear of the supernatural, and the old place was so familiar to her from
childhood, that she had looked forward with pleasure to
seeing it again. She was attached to almost everything
connected with it, to the walls themselves, to her own
rooms, to the ugly corbels, to the lame old warder, Giacomo, and to his wife who helped him to take care of the
rooms. She was a woman quite capable of that sort of
feeling, and capable, indeed, of much more, had it fallen
in her path. She could not have hated as she did, if she
had not had some power to love also. Circumstances,
however, had developed the one far more than the other,
for her first great passion had been jealousy.

She and Francesco reached the castle in the afternoon
of the day following their visit to Laura Arden. The
weather was fine and the westering sun streamed through
the broad windows and lent everything a passing air of
life and almost of gaiety. During the first hours, Adele
felt that she must soon be better, and that she could find
some rest at last in the atmosphere which recalled her
childish days and all her peaceful girlhood.

But when the sun was low and the golden light turned to
purple and then to fainter hues, and died away into twilight, she shivered as she sat in the deep window-seat, and
she called to her husband, telling him to order the lamps.

"You used to like the dusk," he observed, as he tugged
at the old-fashioned bell-rope. "I cannot imagine what
makes you so afraid of being in the dark."

"Nor I," she said nervously. "It must be part of my
illness. Please have as much light as possible, and lamps
in the passage and in our rooms as well."

"I suppose candles will do," answered Savelli. "I do
not believe there are more than half a dozen lamps out
here. Your people always bring them when they come."

"Oh, candles, then — anything! Only let me have
plenty of light. If there were no night, I should get
well."

"Unfortunately, nature has not provided that form of

cure for invalids," said Savelli, with a laugh. "But we will do our best," he added, always willing to humour his wife in anything reasonable.

The servants' quarters were very far away, and several minutes elapsed before a man appeared, and Francesco could give the necessary orders. The gloom deepened, and Adele came from her place at the window, evidently in some sort of distress. She sat down close to her husband — almost cowering at his side. He could not see her face clearly, but he understood that she was frightened.

"I wish you would tell me what it is you see in the dark," he said, with a sort of good-natured impatience.

"Oh, please do not talk about it!" she cried. "Talk to me of something else — talk, for Heaven's sake, talk, until they bring the lamps! I sometimes think I shall go mad when there is no light."

It is not a particularly easy affair to comply, at short notice, with such a request for voluble conversation, especially when there is no extraordinary sympathy between two people, nor any close community of ideas. But it chanced that Savelli had been reading the papers he had brought with him, and he began to tell Adele the news he had read, so that he managed to keep up a fairly continuous series of sentences until the first lamp was placed on the table.

"Thank you, Carissimo," she said. "No shade!" she exclaimed quickly, as the man was about to slip one over the light.

"Do you feel better now?" inquired Francesco, with some amusement.

"Yes — much better," she answered, drawing a long breath, and seating herself by the table in the full glare of the unshaded lamp. "I only ask one thing," she continued: "Do not leave me if you can help it, and go with me when we go to our room. I am ashamed of it, but I am so nervous that I am positively afraid to be alone."

"Would it not be better to have a nurse out, to stay

with you all the time?" inquired Francesco, who had an
eye to his own liberty and comfort, and had no idea of
spending several weeks in perpetual attendance on his
wife. "And there is your maid, too. She might help."

"I have taken such a dislike to that woman that I hate
the sight of her."

"I suppose that is a part of your illness," answered
her husband philosophically.

On that first evening he scrupulously fulfilled her
wishes, and followed her closely when she went from room
to room. He was in a certain degree anxious, for her
allusion to possible madness coincided with his own pre-
conceived opinion of her case, and he dreaded such a
termination very greatly. He saw that what she said
was quite true, and that she was unaffectedly frightened
if he left her side for a moment. On the following day
he sent a messenger to the city to procure a nurse, for he
saw that he could not otherwise count on an hour's free-
dom. Being a careful man, he wished that Adele might
have been contented to be followed about by her maid
and a woman from the place, but she refused altogether
to agree to such an arrangement. In her nervous condition, she could not bear the constant presence of a person
for whom she felt an unreasoning repulsion. Moreover,
she had almost decided to send Lucia away and to get some
one more congenial in her place.

Several days passed in this way, and if she was no
better she was not worse. She drove and walked in the
spring sunshine, and felt refreshed by the clear air of
the country, but the nights were as unbearable as ever, —
endless, ghostly, full of imaginary horrors, although the
lamps burned brightly in her room till sunrise, and the
patient nurse sat by her bedside reading to herself, and
sometimes reading aloud when Adele desired it. Occasionally, and more often towards morning, snatches of
broken sleep interrupted the monotony of the long-drawn-
out suffering.

Adele had implored the doctor who had charge of her

case to give her opiates, or at least chloral; but he had felt great hope that the change to a country life would produce an immediate good effect, and had represented to her in terms almost exaggerated the danger of taking such remedies. The habit once formed, he said, soon became a slavery, and in nervous organisations like hers was very hard to break. People who took chloral often ended by taking morphia, and Donna Adele had doubtless heard enough about the consequences of employing this drug to dread it, as all sensible persons did. Adele was very far from being persuaded, but as she could not procure what she wanted without a doctor's order, which she could not obtain, she was obliged to fall back on the sulphonal which Ghisleri had recommended to her. She took it in large quantities, but it had almost ceased to produce any effect, though she attributed the little rest she got to its influence. The doctor was to come out and see her at the end of a week, unless sent for especially. Before the seven days were out, however, a crisis occurred, brought about by a slight accident, which made his presence imperatively necessary.

One evening, immediately after dinner, Adele had seated herself in a low chair by the table in the drawing-room, and had taken up a novel. For a wonder, it had interested her when she had begun it in the afternoon, and she returned to it with unwonted delight, looking forward to the prospect of losing herself in the story during a few hours before going to bed. Not far from her Savelli sat with that day's papers, gleaning the news of the day in an idle fashion, and smoking a cigarette. He rarely smoked anything else, but for some reason or other, he had, on this particular night, discovered that only a cigar would satisfy him. Many men are familiar with that craving, but the satisfaction of it rarely leads to distinct and important results. Francesco rose from his seat, laid down his paper, and went in search of what he wanted, well knowing that he could get it much faster than by a servant, and forgetting that he must leave his

wife alone for a few minutes in order to go to his dressing-room where he kept the box. As has been said, the
drawing-room was carpeted, and his step made very little
noise. Adele, intensely interested in what she was
reading, paid less attention to his movements than usual,
and indeed supposed that he had only risen to get something from another table. The heavily curtained door
which opened upon the great vaulted passage before
mentioned was behind her as she sat, and she did not
realise that Francesco was gone until she heard his echo-
ing footsteps on the stone pavement outside. Then she
started, and almost dropped her book. She held her
breath for a moment and then called him. But he
walked quickly, and was already out of hearing. Only
the booming echo reached her through the curtains,
reverberated, and died away. There was nothing to be
done but to wait, for she had not the courage to face the
dim passage alone and run after him. She clutched her
book tightly and tried to read again, pronouncing almost
aloud the words she saw. A minute or two passed, and
then she heard the echo again. Francesco was returning. No, it was not his walk. She turned very pale
as she listened. It was the step of a very lame man,
irregular and painful. The novel fell to the ground, and
she grasped the arms of her chair. It was exactly like
Arden's step; she had heard it before, in the gallery at
her father's palace, where the floor was of marble.
Nearer and nearer it came, in a sort of triple measure —
two shorts and a long, like an anapæst — and the sharp
click of the stick between. She tried to look behind her,
but her blood froze in her veins, and she could not move.
Every instant increased her agony of fear. A moment
more and Herbert Arden would be upon her. Suddenly
a second echo, that of Francesco Savelli's firm, quick
step reached her ears. Then she heard voices, and as the
curtain was lifted she recognised the tones of old Giacomo,
the lame warder, who had met her husband in the passage, and was asking for the orders to be given to the

carter who started for Rome every other night and brought back such provisions as could not be obtained in Gerano.

Adele sank back in her chair, almost fainting, in her sudden relief from her ghostly fears. Savelli talked some time with Giacomo. With a great effort at self-command, Adele took up her novel again and held it before her eyes, while her heart beat with terrible violence after having almost stood still while the fright had lasted. Then Francesco came in, with a lighted cigar between his teeth.

"Do you wish to send anything to Rome — any message?" he asked. "Nothing else, Giacomo," he said, as he saw that she shook her head.

"Good rest, Excellency," she heard Giacomo say. Then the curtain dropped, the door was closed from without, and she listened once more to the lame man's retreating footsteps — terribly like Herbert Arden's walk, though she was not frightened now.

"I asked you not to leave me alone," she said, as Savelli resumed his seat and took up the paper again.

"It was only for a minute," he answered indifferently. "I wanted a cigar. I hope you were not frightened this time."

"No. But I might have been. Another time, please ring for what you want."

Savelli, who was already deep in the local news about Rome, made an inarticulate reply intended for assent, and nothing more was said. Adele took up her book again and did her best to read, but without understanding a word as she followed the lines.

That night, in despair, she swallowed a larger dose of sulphonal than she had ever taken before. The consequence was that towards two o'clock she fell asleep and seemed more quiet than usual, as the nurse watched her. An hour passed without her waking, then another, and then the dawn stole through the panes of the deep windows, and daylight came at last. The room was quite light, and Adele was generally awake at that hour. But

this morning she slept on.   The nurse was accustomed to
take away the lamps as soon as Adele needed them no
longer, not extinguishing them in the room on account of
the disagreeable smell they made.   It chanced on this
occasion — or fate had decreed it — that one of these gave
signs of going out.   The nurse rose very softly and took
it away, moving noiselessly in her felt slippers, passing
through the open door of the dressing-room in order to
reach the corridor in which the lamps were left to be
taken and cleaned at a later hour.   She set the one she
carried upon a deal table which stood there, and tried to
put it out, so as to leave no part of the wick still smoul-
dering, lest it should smoke.   She was a very careful and
methodical woman, and took pains to be neat in doing the
smallest things.   Just now, too, she was in no hurry, for
it was broad daylight, and Adele would not be nervous if
she awoke and found herself alone.

And Adele was awake.   She opened her eyes wearily,
realised that there was no one beside her, and sat up
staring at the bright window.   Being nervous, restless,
and never at any time languid, she got up, threw a wrapper
over her, and went to the door of the dressing-room,
meaning to look at the rising sun, which was visible from
the window on the other side, the dressing-room itself
being at one of the angles of the castle, with a door leading from the corner of it into the tower.

Adele paused on the threshold, started, stared at something, turned, and uttered a piercing scream of terror.
A moment later she fell in a heap upon the floor.   She
had distinctly seen Herbert Arden's figure standing at
one of the windows, his head and hands alone concealed
by the inner shutter which, by an accident, was not wide
open, but was turned about half-way towards the panes.
He was dressed in dark blue serge, as she had often seen
him in life, with rather wide trousers almost concealing
the feet, and a round jacket.   She had even seen how the
cloth was stretched at the place where his shoulder was
most crooked, and how it hung loosely about his thin

figure below that point. He was standing close to the
window, with his back almost quite turned towards her,
apparently looking out, though the shutter hid his face.
The whole attitude was precisely as she had often noticed
it when he was alive, and chanced to be looking at something in the street — the misshapen, protruding shoulder,
the right leg bent in more than the other, not a detail was
missing as she came upon the vision suddenly in the cold
morning light.

The nurse was at her side almost instantly, bending
over her and raising her as well as she could. A moment
later the maid rushed in, — she slept on the other side of
the corridor where the nurse had left the lamp, — and then
Francesco Savelli himself, who temporarily occupied a
room next to Adele's and who appeared, robed in a wide
dressing-gown of dark brown velvet, and showing signs
of considerable anxiety. He reached the door before
which his wife had fainted and lifted her in his arms. As
he regained his upright position, his eyes naturally fell
upon the figure standing at the window. His sight was
not remarkably good, and from the fact of the shutter
being half closed the dressing-room was darker than the
sleeping-chamber. The impression he had was strong
and distinct.

"Who is that man?" he asked, staring at what he saw,
while he held Adele's unconscious form in his arms.

The nurse and the maid both started and looked round.
The latter laughed a little, involuntarily.

"It is not a man, Excellency," she said. "It is Donna
Adele's serge driving cloak. I hung it there last night
because there are not enough hooks in the dressing-room
for all her Excellency's things."

She went to the window and took the mantle, which
had been hung upon the knob of the old-fashioned bolt
by the two tapes sewn under the shoulders for the purpose. The folds of the lower part had taken the precise
shape of a man's wide trousers, and the cape, falling half
way only, hung exactly like a jacket, the fulness caused

by gathering the upper portion together at one point, giving the appearance of a hump on a man's back.

"That was what frightened her," said Savelli, as he turned away with his burden. "I do not wonder — the thing looked just as Lord Herbert did when he used to stand at the window."

Adele came to herself in a state of the utmost prostration. Her husband explained to her carefully what had happened, and tried to persuade her that she had been the victim of an optical illusion, but though she did not deny this, he could see that the occurrence had produced a very deep impression on her mind, and had perhaps had an even more serious effect on her nerves. He despatched a messenger to Rome for the doctor, and after doing all he could left her to the care of her nurse and maid and went out for a walk in the hills, glad to be free for a while from the irksome task imposed upon him when he remained at home.

While making the most desperate attempts to control herself, Adele was in a state of the wildest and most conflicting emotion. Her strength returned, indeed, in a certain measure after a few hours, but her distress seemed rather to increase than to diminish, when she was able to walk about the room and submit to being dressed. Her maid irritated her unaccountably, too, and at last, giving way to the impulse she had felt so long, she told her that she must go at the end of the month.

The maid, Lucia by name, had for some time expected that her days in Casa Savelli were numbered, for Adele had shown her dislike very plainly of late, so that the woman did not show much surprise, and accepted her dismissal respectfully and quietly, promising herself to tell tales in her next place concerning Adele's toilette which, though without the slightest foundation, would be repeated and believed all over Rome.

Later in the day Adele shut herself up in her room, at the time when the sunshine was streaming in and making everything look bright and cheerful. She stayed there a long time, and the thoughtful Lucia, watching her through the keyhole, saw with surprise that her mistress spent almost an hour upon her knees before the dark old crucifix which hung above the prayer-stool opposite to the door of the dressing-room. She noticed that Adele from time to time beat her breast, and then buried her face in her hands for many minutes. The nurse was asleep far away and Lucia was quite safe. At last Adele rose, and as though acting under an irresistible impulse sat down at a table on which she kept her own writing materials, and began to write rapidly. For a long time she kept her seat, and her hand moved quickly over the paper. Then, when she seemed to have finished, she took up the sheets as though she meant to read them over, and did in fact read a few lines. She dropped the paper suddenly, and Lucia saw the look of horror that was in her white face. She seemed to hesitate, rose, turned, and made two steps towards the crucifix, then returned, and hastily folded up the lengthy letter and slipped it into a large envelope, on which she wrote an address before she left the table a second time. When she opened the door of the dressing-room to call Lucia, the maid was quietly seated by a window with a piece of needle-work, and rose respectfully as her mistress entered.

"Send me Giacomo," said Adele, holding the letter in her hand, but as Lucia went towards the door, she stopped her. "No," she said suddenly. "Take this to him yourself; tell him to have it registered at once, and to bring me back the receipt from the post-office. Tell him to be careful, as it is very important. I am going to lie down. Come to me some time before sunset."

Lucia took the letter and went out into the corridor. Adele listened a moment, then went back into her room, bolting the door behind her, as well as turning the key in the lock. Since her fright in the morning, she instinctively barricaded herself on that side. But at present the sunshine was so bright and the place was so cheerful that her fears seemed almost groundless.

She lay down and closed her eyes.   In spite of all the
emotions of terror she had suffered on the previous evening and to-day, and although the writing of any letter so
long as the one she had just finished must necessarily be
very tiring, she felt better than she had been for a long
time, and would perhaps have fallen asleep if the doctor
had not arrived from Rome soon afterwards.

On learning all that had happened, he yielded at last
to necessity, and gave her chloral to take in small doses,
showing her how to use it.   It was evident that unless
she slept she must break down altogether before long, and
it was no longer safe to let nature have her own way.   He
had brought the medicine with him, and gave it into
Francesco's keeping, cautioning him not to let her use it
in larger quantities than he had prescribed.   After giving
various pieces of good advice he returned to the city.

Lucia gave her mistress the receipt for the registered
letter, and Adele put it away in the small jewel-case she
had brought with her to the country.   That night she
took the chloral, and fell asleep peacefully before half-
past eleven o'clock, not to awake until nearly nine on the
following morning.   She felt so much better for the one
night's rest that she went for a long walk with her husband, ate well for the first time in many weeks, and went
to bed again almost without having felt a sensation of
fear all day nor during the evening.   Once more the
chloral had the desired effect, and on the second morning
she began to imagine that she was recovering.   The world
looked bright and cheerful, the swallows wheeled and
darted before her windows, and the thrushes and black-
birds sang far down among the fruit-trees.   Even Francesco was less tiresome and unsympathetic than usual.
She was in such a good humour that she almost repented
of having dismissed Lucia.

Then the blow came.   The post brought her a letter
addressed in a small, even handwriting, very plain and
entirely without flourish or ornament — such a hand as
learned men and theologians often write.   The contents
read as follows:

"Most Excellent Princess, I have to inform you that I have just received, registered, and evidently addressed by your most excellent hand, an envelope bearing the Gerano postmark, but containing only four blank sheets of ordinary writing paper. As I cannot suppose that your Excellency has designed to make me the object of a jest, and as it is to be feared that the blank paper has been substituted for a writing of importance, by some malicious person, I have immediately informed your Excellency of what has occurred. Awaiting any instruction or enlightenment with regard to this subject which it may please you, most Excellent Princess, to communicate, I write myself

"Your Excellency's most humble, obedient servant,

"Bonaventura, R.R. P.P.O. Min."

Now Padre Bonaventura of the Minor Order of St. Francis was Adele's confessor in Rome. After the long struggle which Lucia had watched through the door, Adele's conscience had got the upper hand, aided by the belief that in following its dictates she would be doing the best she could towards recovering her peace of mind. Not being willing to go to the parish priest of Gerano, who had known her and all her family from her childhood, and who was by no means a man able to give very wise advice in difficult cases, and being, moreover, afraid of rousing her husband's suspicions if she insisted upon going to Rome merely to confess, she had written out a most careful confession of those sins of which she accused herself, and, as is allowable in extreme cases, had sent it by post to Padre Bonaventura.

The news that such a document had never reached its destination would have been enough to disturb most people.

CHAPTER XVII.

Laura Arden's plans for the summer were not by any means settled, but she was anxious to leave Rome soon, both because travelling in the heat would be bad for little Herbert, and because she wished to quit the rather expensive apartment in which she had continued to live after her husband's death. A far smaller and less pretentious dwelling would be amply sufficient for her next winter, and in the meantime she intended to go to some quiet town either in Switzerland or by the seaside, and to keep as much alone as possible. Her mother might be willing to spend a month or two with her, and Laura would be very glad of her company, but there was no one else whose society she desired. She could, of course, go to England and stay at her brother-in-law's house in solemn and solitary state, but she feared the long journey for her child, and she cared little for the sort of existence she must lead in the magnificent country-seat, in the absence of the Lulworths themselves. It would be pleasant to lead a very simple and quiet life somewhere out of the world, and as far as possible from the scene of all her sufferings. If Adele and Francesco had not appeared while Ghisleri was making his first visit, she would probably have asked his advice. He had been almost everywhere, and being himself fond of solitude, would in all likelihood have told her of some beautiful and secluded spot where she could live in the way she desired. But in the presence of her step-sister she had not cared to speak on the subject.

After they had left her she thought a long time of Ghisleri and his story, and, for the first time in her life, she wished she might see him again before long. He had shown her a side of himself which she had neither seen nor guessed at before, and she began to understand, dimly at first and then more clearly, the strong liking her husband had always shown for him. He was capable of deep and earnest beliefs and of high and generous impulses, in spite of his contempt for himself and of the irregular life he led. His present existence, so far as she knew anything of it, she condemned as unworthy. She was not, however, a woman so easily shocked at the spectacle of evil in the lives of others as might have been expected. There was a great deal of sound good sense in the composition of her character, and she had seen enough of the world to have learnt that perfection is a word used to define what is a little better than the average. What she had disliked in Ghisleri from her first acquaintance with him was not connected with his reputation, of which, at that time, she had known very little. Besides, though people called him fast and wild and more or less heartless, he was liked, on the whole, as much as any unmarried man in society. He was known to be honourable, courageous, and very discreet, and the latter quality almost invariably brings its reward in the end. That he should have been entangled in more than one love affair was only what was to be expected of such a man, at two or three and thirty years of age, and no one really considered him any the worse on that account, while the great majority of women thought him vastly more interesting for that very reason. Laura was not, perhaps, so entirely different from the rest of her sex as Ghisleri was fond of believing. Her education had not been that of young Roman girls, it is true, and the singular circumstances of her short married life had not developed her character in the same direction as theirs generally was by matrimony. But in real womanliness she was as much a woman as any of them, liable to the same influences and to the same class of enthusiasms. Because she had loved and married Herbert Arden, it did not follow that she could not and did not admire all that was brave and generous and strong, independently of moral weakness and faults.

Arden himself, indeed, though he had excited her pity by his physical defects, had commanded her respect by the manly courage he showed under all his sufferings. She had been able to forget his deformity in the superior gifts of intelligence and heart which had unquestionably been his, and, after all, she had loved him most because she had felt that but for an accident he would have been pre-eminently a manly man. Cripple as he was, she had always known that she could rely on him, and her instinct had always told her that he could protect her.

But she had never trusted Ghisleri. He had the misfortune to show his worst side to most people, and he had shown it to her. She had seen more than once that he was ready to undertake and carry out almost anything for his friend's sake, and she had been honestly grateful to him for all he had done. But she had not been able, until now, to shake off that feeling of distrust and timid dislike she had always felt in his presence. She had, indeed, succeeded tolerably well in hiding it from him, but it had always made her cold in conversation and somewhat formal in manner, and he, being outwardly a rather formal and cold man had, so to say, put himself in harmony with her key. For the first time in their acquaintance, and under pressure of what he considered necessity, he had suddenly unbent, and had told her the principal story of his life with a frankness and simplicity that had charmed her. From that hour she judged him differently. After that first visit, he went often to see her, and on each occasion he felt drawn more closely to her than before.

"You are very much changed," he said to her one day. "Do you mind my saying it?"

"Not in the least," Laura answered, with a smile. "But in what way am I different?"

"In one great thing, I think. You used to be very imposingly calm with me. You never seemed quite willing to speak freely about anything. Now, it is almost always you who make me talk by making me feel that you will talk yourself. That is not very clearly put, is it? I do not know whether you ever disliked me — if you did, you never showed it. But I really begin to think that you almost like me. Is there any truth in that?"

"Yes — a great deal." She smiled again. "More truth than you guess — for I do not mind saying it since it is all over. I did not like you, and I used to try and hide it. But I like you now, and I am quite willing that you should know it."

"That is good of you — good as everything you do is.

But I would really like to know why you have changed your mind. May I?"

"Because I have found out that you are not what I took you for."

"Most discoveries of that kind are disappointments," observed Ghisleri, with a dry laugh.

"That is just the sort of remark I used to dislike you for," said Laura. "The world is not all bad, and you know it. Yet out of ten observations you make, nine, at least, would lead one to believe that you think it is."

"Excepting yourself, we are all as bad as we can be. What is the use of denying it?"

"We are not all bad, and I do not choose to be made an exception of. I am just like other people, or I should be if I were placed as they are. I not only am sure that you are not a bad man, but I am quite convinced that in some ways you are a very good one."

"What an odd mistake!"

"Why do you persistently try to make yourself out worse than you are, and to show your worst side to the world?"

"I suppose that is the side most apparent to myself," answered Ghisleri. "I cannot help seeing it."

"Because you are not Launcelot, you take yourself for Cæsar Borgia —"

"That would be flattering myself too much. Borgia was by far the more intelligent of the two. Say Thersites."

"I know nothing about Thersites."

"Then say Judas. There seems to be very little difference of opinion as to that personage's moral obliquity," Ghisleri laughed.

"Very well," said Laura, gravely. "I suppose you have no doubt, then, that Judas would have acted as you did in your affair with Don Gianforte. He would, of course, have submitted to insult rather than break a promise, and would have allowed —"

"Will you please stop, Lady Herbert?" Ghisleri fixed his blue eyes on her.

"No, I will not," answered Laura, with decision. "What I like about you is precisely what you try the most to hide, and I mean to see it and to make you see it, if possible. You would be much happier if you could. I suppose that if the majority of people could hear us talking now, they would think our conversation utterly absurd. They would say that you were posing, in order to make yourself interesting, and that I was enough attracted by you to be deceived by the comedy. Is not that the way the world would look at it?"

"Probably," assented Ghisleri. "Perhaps I am really posing. I do not pretend to know."

"I am willing to believe that you are not, if you will let me, and I would much rather. In the first place, you are, at all events, not any worse than most men one knows. That is evident enough from your actions. Secondly, — you see I am arguing the case like a lawyer, — if you had not a high ideal of what you wish to be, you would not have such a poor opinion of what you are. Is that clear?"

"If there were no right, there could not possibly be any wrong. But black would be black, even if you could only compare it with blue, green, and yellow, instead of with white."

"I am not talking of chromolithographs," said Laura. "What I say is simple enough. If you did not wish to be good, and know what good means, and if you had not a certain amount of goodness in you, you would not think yourself so bad. And you are unhappy, as you have told me before now, because you think all your motives are insincere, or vain, or defective in some way. I suppose you wish to be happy, and if you do, you must learn to find some satisfaction in having done your best. I have said precisely what I mean, and you must not pretend to misunderstand me."

"Think yourself good, and you will be happy," observed Ghisleri. "That is the modern form of the proverb."

"Of course it is, and the better reason you really have

for thinking yourself good, the more real and lasting your happiness will be."

Ghisleri laughed to himself, and at himself, as he went away, for being so much impressed as he was by what Laura said. But he could not deny that the impression had been made and remained for some time after he had left her. There was a healthy common-sense about her mind which was beginning to act upon the tortuous and often morbid complications of his own. She seemed to know the straight paths and the short cuts to simple goodness, and never to have guessed at the labyrinthine ways by which he seemed to himself to be always trying to escape from the bugbear sent to pursue him by the demon of self-mistrust. He laughed at himself, for he realised how utterly impossible it would always be for him to think as she did, or to look upon the world as she saw it. There had been a time when he had thought more plainly, when a woman had exerted a strong influence over him, and when a few good things and a few bad ones had made up the sum of his life. But she was dead, and he had changed. Worse than that, he had fallen. As he sat in his room and glanced from time to time at the only likeness he had of Bianca Corleone, he thought of Beatrice's reproach to Dante in the thirty-first canto of the "Purgatory":

> "And yet, because thou'rt shamed of me in all
>   Thy sin, and that in later days to come
>   Thou mayst be brave, hearing the Siren's voice
>   Sow deep the seed of tears and hear me speak.
>   So shalt thou know how thou should'st have been moved
>   By my dead body in ways opposite.
>   Nor art nor nature had the power to tempt thee
>   With such delight as that fair body could
>   In which I lived — which now is scattered earth —
>   And if the highest joy was lost to thee
>   By my young death, what mortal living thing
>   Should have had strength to drag thee down with it?"

As he repeated the last words he started for they reminded him with painful force of Gianforte Campodonico's insulting speech, and he detested himself for even allowing the thought to cross his mind — for allowing himself to repeat Beatrice's words up to that point. It was he who had dragged down Maddalena dell' Armi to his level, not she who had made him sink to hers. And yet Campodonico had said almost the same thing as Beatrice, and certainly without knowing it. In his heart he knew that Bianca might have reproached him so, but then, deeper still, he knew that the reproach, from her lips, would have fallen on himself alone, and would never have been meant for Maddalena.

Ghisleri fell to thinking over his own life and the lives of others, in one of those black moods which sometimes seized him and in which he believed in no one's motives, from his own upward. In the course of his lonely and bitter meditations, he came across an idea which at first seemed wild and improbable enough, but which, little by little, took shape as he concentrated his attention upon it, and at last chased every other memory away. He was not naturally an over-suspicious man, but when his suspicions were once roused he was apt to go far in pursuit of the truth, if the matter interested him. He rose and got a book from the shelves which lined one side of the wall, and began to turn over the pages rapidly, until he stopped at the place he was looking for. He read three or four pages very carefully twice over and returned the volume to its place. Then he sat down to think, and did not move for another quarter of an hour. At the end of that time he called his servant, a quiet, hard-working fellow from the Abbruzzi, who rejoiced in the name of Bonifazio.

"Do you happen to know," he asked, "if there was much scarlet fever in the city last winter? I have always wondered how poor Lord Herbert caught it."

Bonifazio had known Lord Herbert for years, just as Donald had known Ghisleri, for the two friends had often made short journeys together, taking their servants with them. The Italian thought a long time before he gave an answer.

"No, Signore. I do not remember hearing that there were many cases. But then, I am not in the way of knowing. It may have been."

"You are a very discreet man, Bonifazio," said Ghisleri. "Lord Herbert fell ill on the day after he had dined in Casa Savelli. Do you think you could find out for me whether any one of the servants had the scarlet fever at that time?"

"Perhaps, signore. I will try. I know Giuseppe, the butler, who is a very good person, but who is not fond of talking. When there is such an illness they either send the servants to the hospital, in the Roman houses, or else they put them in an attic and try not to let any one know. For the rest, I will do what I can. You say well, Signore, for it is possible that the blessed soul of the Milord caught the fever at the dinner in Casa Savelli."

"That is what I think," said Ghisleri. And he thought a good deal more also, which he did not communicate to his man.

Bonifazio, as his master said, was discreet. He was also very patient and very uncommunicative, as the men of the Abbruzzi often are. They make the best servants when they can be got, for, in addition to the good qualities most of them possess in a greater or less degree, they are almost always physically very strong men, though rarely above middle height, and often extremely pale. Ghisleri knew that so soon as Bonifazio had anything to tell, he would tell it without further question or reminder.

Several days passed, during which Ghisleri, who gained strength rapidly, began to resume his former mode of life, went to the club, saw his friends, and made a few visits. He went more than once to Maddalena's house and stayed some time with her when he found her alone. Little by little he fancied that her look was changing and growing more indifferent. He was glad of it. He wished that he might be to her exactly what she was to him. That, indeed, could never be, but he wished it were possible. He knew that when she ceased to love him altogether, she could never feel friendly devotion, gratitude, or respect for him, and he felt all three for her in a far greater degree than she could imagine. On the whole, during that time their relations were peaceable, and altogether undisturbed by the frequent differences that had so often nearly estranged them from one another in earlier days. There was, of course, an air of constraint about their meetings, more evident in Maddalena's manner than in Ghisleri's, and the latter hardly hoped that this could ever quite wear off and leave at last a sincere and true friendship behind it. That was, indeed, the best that could be hoped for either of them, and he had no right to expect the best, nor anything approaching to it.

One evening as he was dressing for dinner, Bonifazio gave him the news he desired. It had not been easy to extract any communication on the subject from old Giuseppe, the Savelli's butler, but such as he had at last given was clear, concise, and to the point. There had been a case of scarlet fever in the house. Donna Adele's maid had taken it, and was just convalescent at the time when the Ardens dined with Adele and her husband. The woman's name was Lucia, and on falling ill she had been at once removed to a distant room in the upper part of the palace. The case had been rather a severe one, Giuseppe believed, and it was only within the last few weeks that Lucia seemed to have regained her strength. She was at present at Gerano with her mistress, but had written to the wife of the Savelli's porter saying that she had been dismissed, and was to leave at the end of the month, and asking for assistance in finding a new place. Ghisleri was satisfied for the present. It was quite clear that Arden must have caught the fever that killed him so suddenly in Casa Savelli. Whether Donna Adele had in any way communicated the contagion was another matter, and not easily decided. Her inexplicable nervousness, beginning about the time that Arden died, might be accounted for on the ground that she was aware of

having been the unintentional cause of his illness, and felt that by a little precaution she might have averted the catastrophe. The idea was constantly present in Ghisleri's mind, but it lacked detail and clearness, and constituted at most a rather strong suspicion. Of course it was quite possible, and, considering Adele's character, more than likely, that she had never been near the maid during her illness. If she had never had the scarlet fever herself, it was quite certain. But that was a point easily settled, and was a very important one.

On the following day, Ghisleri called at the Palazzo Braccio. The Princess received him, as she always did, without any signs of satisfaction, but without marked coldness. To her he was always "that wild Ghisleri," and she thoroughly disapproved of him, wishing that he would not visit her daughter so often. He was quite aware of the feeling she entertained towards him, and was always especially careful in his conversation with her. In spite of her long residence in Rome, as a Roman, and among Romans, she had remained altogether English in nature. Laura, English on both sides by her birth, had far less of prejudice than her mother, and was altogether more of a cosmopolitan in every way. On the present occasion, Ghisleri led the conversation so as to speak of her. He began by asking the Princess where she herself meant to spend the summer, and whether she intended to be with her daughter.

"I hope to be with her a great part of the time," she answered. "I do not like to think of her as travelling about the world alone. Indeed, I do not at all approve of her living without a companion, as she insists upon doing. She is far too young, and people are far too ready to talk about her."

"She has such wonderful dignity," answered Ghisleri, "that she could do with impunity what most women could not do at all. Besides, her mourning protects her for the present, and her child. She is looking wonderfully well —do you not think so?"

"Yes. When one thinks of all she has suffered, it is amazing. But she was always strong."

"I should suppose so. Any one else would have caught the scarlet fever."

"As for that," said the Princess, unsuspiciously, "people rarely have it twice."

"She has had it, then."

"Oh, yes. Both the girls had it at the same time, when they were little things. Let me see — Laura must have been six years old then. They had it rather badly, and I remember being terribly anxious about them."

"I see," answered Ghisleri, carelessly. "That accounts for it. But to go back to what we were speaking of, I wonder that Lady Herbert does not spend the summer with you at Gerano, if you go there as usual."

"I do not think she will consent to that," said the Princess, rather coldly. "She says she prefers the north for the baby. It is quite true that it is often very hot at Gerano."

"Donna Adele was good enough to ask me to go out and spend a day or two while she is there. It must be very pleasant just now, in the spring weather."

"Why do you not go?" asked the Princess, with more warmth, for she preferred that Ghisleri should be where he could not see Laura every day, as she believed he now did. "You would be doing them both a kindness. Poor Adele was obliged to go to the country against her will — she is in such a terribly nervous state. I really do not know what to make of it."

"What news have you of her?" inquired Ghisleri, in a tone of polite solicitude. "Is she at all better?"

"She was better after the first few days. Then it appears that she had a fright — I do not quite understand how it was from what Francesco wrote to my husband — but it seems to have been one of those odd accidents — optical illusions, I suppose — which sometimes terrify people."

"How very unfortunate! What did she fancy she saw?"

"It was absurd, of course!" answered the Princess, who had no special reason for being reticent on the subject. "It seems that there was a blue cloak of hers hanging somewhere in her dressing-room, — at a window, I believe, — and she went in suddenly very early in the morning before it was quite broad daylight, and took the cloak for a man. In fact she thought it was poor dear Arden. You know he always used to wear blue serge clothes. Francesco saw it himself afterwards and says that it was extraordinarily like. But I cannot understand how any one in their senses could be deceived in that way. Adele is dreadfully overwrought and imaginative. She has danced too much this winter, I suppose."

When Ghisleri went away he was almost quite persuaded that Adele was conscious of having communicated the fever to Arden. Of course, it might all be mere coincidence, but to him the evidence seemed strong. He wrote a note to Adele, asking whether he might avail himself of her invitation, and spend a day at Gerano. Her answer came by return of post, begging him to come at once, and to stay as long as possible. The handwriting was so illegible that he had some difficulty in reading it. To judge from that, at least, Adele was no better.

Before leaving Rome, he thought it best to inform Laura of his intended visit. He had never spoken of her step-sister in a way to make her suppose that he disliked her, but Laura knew very well what part he had played at the time when Adele was spreading slanderous reports, for her mother had repeated the story precisely as the Prince had told it to her. Ghisleri, of course, was not aware of this, for Arden had not mentioned the matter to him, unless his reference to the enemies he and Laura had in Rome, during the last conversation he had with his friend, could be taken as implying that Ghisleri knew as much as he himself. But in any case, he was sure that Laura would be surprised at his going to Gerano, even for a day, and it was better to warn her beforehand, and if possible give her some reasonable explanation of his conduct. He chose to refer his visit at once to motives of curiosity, together with a natural desire to breathe the purer air of the country, now that he was able to make the short journey without fatigue or danger.

"I have never been to Gerano," he added. "It is said to be a wonderful place — one of the finest mediæval castles in this part of the world. I really wish to see it — they say the air is good — and since Donna Adele is so kind as to ask me, I shall go."

"You would see it better if you went when my mother and step-father are there. He would show you every-thing and give you all sorts of historical details which Adele has forgotten and which Francesco never knew."

"No doubt, but there is one objection," answered Ghis-leri. "They have never asked me. I am not a favourite with the Princess. I am sure you know that."

"She thinks you are very wild," said Laura, with a smile. "She disapproves of you on moral grounds — not at all in the way I used to — and still do, sometimes," she added, incautiously.

"Still?"

"Oh, it is very foolish! Do not talk about it. When are you going out?"

Laura had undeniably felt a sudden return of her old distrust in him, when she had heard of the visit. It was natural enough that she should, considering what she knew. She suspected some new and tortuous develop-ment of his character, and would have instinctively drawn back from the intimacy she felt was growing up between him and herself, had she not by experience found out that she might be quite wrong about him after all. She tried, at the present juncture, to shake off the sensation which was now far more distasteful to her than it had formerly been, in proportion as she had fancied that she under-stood him better. But she could not altogether succeed. It was too strange, in her opinion, that he should will-ingly be Adele's guest, and put himself under even a slight obligation to her. It showed, she thought, how individual views could differ in regard to friendship. She was even rather surprised to find that she was asking herself whether, if Gianforte and Christina Campodonico possessed a habitable castle and invited her to stop with them, she would accept, considering that Gianforte had almost killed her husband's best friend. She unhesitatingly decided that she would not, and resented Ghisleri's willingness to receive hospitality from one who, as he well knew, had foully slandered both Arden and herself. Her doubts were certainly justifiable to a certain extent. But there was no immediate probability that they would be cleared away for the present. Ghisleri understood her perfectly, and wondered whether he were not risking too much in endangering a friendship so precious to him for the sake of following out a suspicion which might, in the end, prove to have been altogether without foundation. On the other hand, his natural obstinacy of purpose when once called into play was such as not to leave the smallest hesitation in his mind between doing what he had determined to do, or not doing it, when he had once made up his mind, irrespective of consequences. Having lost sight of the virtue of constancy, he clung to a vicious obstinacy as a substitute.

CHAPTER XVIII.

When Adele had read Padre Bonaventura's letter twice over and had realised its meaning, she behaved like a person stunned by an actual blow. She sank into the nearest chair, utterly overcome. She had barely the presence of mind to tear up the sheet of paper into minute shreds, which she gathered all in one hand, until she could find strength to scatter them out of the window. The position was a terrible one indeed, and for a long time she was unable to think connectedly about it, or of anything else. But for the two nights of sound sleep she had got by taking the chloral, she must inevitably have broken down. As it was, her strong constitution had asserted itself so soon as she had been able to rest, and she was better able to meet this new and real trouble than she had been to face the imaginary horror of Herbert Arden's presence in her dressing-room. But even so, half an hour elapsed before she was able to rise from her seat. She tossed the scraps of paper out of the window and watched them as the wind chased them in all directions, upwards and downwards, upon the castle wall. Then, all at once, she began to think, and her brain seemed to act with an accuracy and directness it had never had before.

Either the letter had been opened in the house or at the post-office. It could not have been opened in Rome, or at least, the probabilities were enormously against such an hypothesis. It was scarcely more like that the man at the Gerano post-office should have ventured to tamper with a sealed envelope coming from the castle, and for which he had given a receipt before taking charge of it. He could not have the smallest interest in reading Donna Adele's correspondence, and he had everything to lose if he were caught. He would certainly not have supposed that she or her husband, having but lately left the city, were sending back a sum of money in notes large enough to make it worth his while to incur such a risk. In other words, the theft had been committed in the house, and no one but Lucia could have been the thief. Lucia had been summarily dismissed; Lucia was the only servant in the establishment who had serious cause for discontent; Lucia had guessed from the address that the letter contained something at least of the nature of a confession, and had resolved to hold her mistress in her power. Moreover, it was possible — barely possible — that Lucia knew something else. In any case, she had read every word Adele had written with her own hand, and Adele knew very well why the woman had not returned the sheets to the envelope after mastering their contents. She was utterly, hopelessly, and entirely in Lucia's power. The maid would go from her to a new situation, and wherever she might be would always be able to control Donna Adele's life by merely threatening to betray what she knew to the person or persons concerned.

Adele felt that her courage was almost failing her in this extremity, at a time when she needed more than she had ever possessed. And yet it was necessary to act promptly, for the maid might even now be engaging herself with some one else. Come what might, she must never leave Casa Savelli, if it cost Adele all the money she could beg of her husband or borrow of her father to keep the woman with her. First of all, however, she must regain some sort of composure, lest Lucia should suspect that the post had brought her news of the loss of the document. She looked at herself in the glass and scrutinised every feature attentively. She was very pale, but otherwise was looking better than two days earlier. Any kind of stimulant, as she knew, sent the blood to her face in a few minutes, and she saw that what she needed was a little colour. A teaspoonful of Benedictine cordial, of which she had a small flask in her dressing-case, was enough to produce the desired effect. The doctor had formerly recommended her to take it before going to sleep, but she did not like such things, and the flask was almost full. She saw in the mirror that the result was perfectly satisfactory, and when she at last met her husband he remarked that her appearance was very much improved.

"I feel so much better!" she exclaimed, knowing that she was speaking the first words of a comedy which would in all probability have to be played during the rest of her life. "I always said that if they would only give me something to make me sleep I should get well at once."

She walked again on that day, and by an almost superhuman effort kept up appearances until bedtime, even succeeding in eating a moderately abundant dinner. That night she told Lucia that, on the whole, she would prefer to keep her, that she had always been more than satisfied with her services, and that if she had suddenly felt an aversion to her, it was the result of the extreme nervousness she had suffered of late. Now that she could sleep, she realised how unkind she had been. Lucia humbly thanked her, and said that she hoped to live and die in the service of the most excellent Casa Savelli. Thereupon Adele thanked her too, said very sweetly that she was a good girl and would some day be rewarded by finding a good husband, and ended by giving her five francs. She reflected that to give her more might look like the beginning of a course of bribery, and that to give nothing might be construed as proceeding from the fear of seeming to bribe.

The second day could not be harder than the first, she said to herself, as she swallowed her chloral and laid her head upon the pillow, to be read to sleep by the nurse. She slept, indeed, that night, but not so well as before, and she awoke twice, each time with a start, and with the impression that Lucia was reciting the contents of the lost letter to Laura Arden and a whole roomful of the latter's friends.

Under the circumstances, she behaved with a courage and determination admirable in themselves. Few women could have borne the constant strain upon the faculties at all, still fewer after such illness as she had suffered. But she was really very strong, though everything which affected her feelings and thoughts reacted upon her physical nature as such things never can in less nervously organised constitutions. She bore the excruciating anxiety about the lost confession better than the shadowy fear of the supernatural which still haunted her in the hours of the night. On the third day she begged her husband to increase the dose of chloral by a very small quantity, saying that if only she could sleep well for a whole week she would then be so much better as to be able to give it up altogether. Savelli hesitated, and at last consented. Since she had seemed so much more quiet he dreaded a return of her former state, for he was a man who loved his ease and hated everything which disturbed it.

The doctor had particularly cautioned him to keep the chloral put away in a safe place, warning Francesco that the majority of persons who took it soon began to feel a craving for it in larger quantities, which must be checked to avoid the risk of considerable damage to the health in the event of its becoming a habit. It was, after all, only a palliative, he said, and could never be expected to work a cure on the nerves except as an indirect means to a good result. Francesco kept the bottle in his dressing-bag, which remained in his own room and was fitted with a patent lock. He yielded to Adele's request on the first occasion, and she went with him as he took the glass back to strengthen the dose. "Why do you keep it locked up?" she said. "Do you suppose I would go and take it without consulting you?"

"The doctor told me to be careful of it," he answered. "The servants might try a dose of it out of curiosity." He took what he considered necessary and locked the bag again, returning the key to his pocket.

Two or three days passed in this way. Adele began to feel that she longed for the night and the soothing influence of the chloral, as she had formerly longed for daylight to end the misery of the dark hours. The days were now made almost intolerable for her by the certainty that her maid knew her secret, and by the necessity for treating the woman with consideration. Yet she could do nothing, and she knew that she never could do anything to lessen her own anxiety, as long as she lived. She was much alone, too, during the day. She walked or drove with her husband during two or three hours in the afternoon, but the rest of the time hung idly on her hands. It is true that his society was not very congenial, and under ordinary conditions she would rather have been left alone than have been obliged to talk with him. At present, however, she thought less when she was with him, and that was a gain not to be despised. She had quite forgotten that she had asked Ghisleri to come out and spend a day or two, when his note came, reminding her of the invitation, and asking if he still might accept it. Francesco liked him, as most men did, and was glad that any one should appear to vary the monotony of the dull country life with a little city talk. He bade her write to Pietro to come and stay as long as he pleased, if she herself cared to have him. She concealed her satisfaction well enough to make Francesco suppose that she wished the guest to come for his sake rather than her own.

Ghisleri started early, taking his servant with him, and reached Gerano in time for the midday breakfast. Francesco Savelli received him with considerable enthusiasm, and Adele's habitually rather forced smile became more natural. Both felt in different ways that the presence of a third person was a relief, and would have been delighted to receive a far less agreeable man than their present guest. They overwhelmed him with questions about Rome and their friends.

"Of course you have seen everybody and heard everything, now that you are so much better," said Adele, as they sat down to breakfast in the vaulted dining-room. "You must tell us everything you know. We are buried alive out here, and only know a little of what happens through the papers. How are they all? Have you seen Laura again, and how is the baby? My step-mother writes that she is going to spend the summer with them in some place or places unknown. I never thought of her as a grandmother when my own children were born — of course she is not my mother, but it used to seem just the same. What is Bompierre doing? And Maria Boccapaduli? I am dying to hear all about it."

Ghisleri laughed at the multitude of questions which followed each other almost without a breathing-space between them.

"Donna Maria would have sent you her love if she had known that I was coming to Gerano," he answered. "As for Bompierre, he is an inscrutable mixture of devotion and fickleness. He attaches himself to the new without detaching himself from the old. He worships both the earthly and the Olympian Venus. He is a good fellow, little Bompierre, and I like him, but it is impossible for any man to adore women at the rate of six at a time. I begin to think that he must be a very deep character.".

"That is the last thing I should say of him," observed Savelli, who was deficient in the sense of humour.

"How literal you are, Francesco," laughed his wife. "And yourself, Ghisleri — tell us about yourself. Are you quite well again? You still look dreadfully thin, but you look better than when I saw you last. What does your doctor say?"

"He says that if I do not happen to catch cold, or have a choking fit, or a cough, or any of fifty things he names, and if I do not chance to get shot in the same place again, in the course of a year or two I may be as good a man as ever. It appears that I have a good constitution. I always supposed so, because I never had anything the matter with me, so far as I knew."

"No one will ever forgive Gianforte!" exclaimed Adele. "If you had died, he would have had to go away for ever. Everybody says he was utterly in the wrong."

"The matter is settled," said Ghisleri, "and I do not think either of us need have anything to say about the other's conduct in the affair. I suppose you have heard that the ministry has fallen," he continued, turning to Savelli. "Yesterday afternoon — the old story, of course — finance."

"For Heaven's sake do not begin to talk politics at this hour," protested Adele. "To-night, when I am asleep, you can smoke all the cigars in the house, and reconstitute a dozen ministries if you like. I want to hear all about my friends. You have not told me half enough yet."

"Where shall I begin? Ah, by the bye, there is an engagement, I hear. I have not left cards because it is not official. Pietrasanta and Donna Guendalina Frangipani — rather an odd match, is it not?"

"Pietrasanta!" exclaimed Adele. "Who would have thought that! And Guendalina, of all people! But they will starve, my dear Ghisleri; they will positively not have twenty thousand francs a year between them."

"No," said Savelli, "you are quite right, my dear — twelve — seventeen — eighteen thousand five hundred, almost exactly."

Savelli was intimately acquainted with the affairs of his friends, and both parties were related to him in the present case. He prided himself upon his extreme exactness about all questions of money.

So they talked and gossiped throughout the meal. Ghisleri knew just what sort of news most amused his hostess, and as usual he succeeded in telling her the truth about things and people without saying anything spiteful of any one. He had resolved, too, that he would make himself especially agreeable to the couple in their voluntary exile. He had come with a set purpose, and he meant to execute it if possible. As he was evidently not yet strong, Savelli proposed that they should drive instead of walking. Ghisleri acceded readily, though he would have preferred to stay at home after having travelled nearly thirty miles in a jolting carriage during the morning. The sensation of physical fatigue which he constantly experienced since he had been wounded was new to him and not at all pleasant.

Nothing of any importance occurred during the afternoon. The conversation continued in much the same way as it had begun at breakfast, interspersed with remarks about agriculture and the probabilities of crops. Savelli understood the financial side of farming better than Ghisleri, but the latter had a much more practical acquaintance with the capabilities of different sorts of land.

After they had returned to the castle, Francesco left Ghisleri with his wife in the drawing-room, and went off to his own quarters to talk with the steward of the estate. Tea was brought, but Pietro noticed that Adele did not take any.

"I suppose you are afraid that it would keep you awake at night," he remarked. "How is your insomnia? Do you sleep at all?"

"I am getting quite well again," Adele answered. "You know I always told you that I needed something really strong to make me sleep. The doctor has given me chloral, and I never wake up before eight or nine o'clock. It is a wonderful medicine."

"Insomnia is one of the most unaccountable things," said Ghisleri, in a meditative tone. "I knew a man in Constantinople who told me that at one time he never slept at all. For three months he literally could not lose consciousness for a moment. I believe he suffered horribly. But then, he had something on his mind at the time which accounted for it to a certain extent."

"I suppose he had lost money or something of that kind," conjectured Adele, stirring two lumps of sugar in a glass of water.

"No, it was much worse than that. He had accidentally killed his most intimate friend on a shooting expedition in the Belgrad forest."

Ghisleri heard the spoon rattle sharply against the glass, as Adele's hand shook, and he saw that she bent down her head quickly, pretending to watch the lumps of sugar as they slowly dissolved.

"How terrible!" she exclaimed, in a low voice.

"Yes," answered Ghisleri, in the same indifferent tone. "But if you will believe it, he had the courage to refuse chloral, or any sort of sleeping-draught, though he often sat up reading all night. He had been told, you see, that the habit of such things was much more dangerous than insomnia itself, and he was ultimately cured by taking a great deal of exercise. He had an extraordinary force of will. I believe he has never felt any bad effect from what he endured. You know one can get used to anything. Look at the people who starve in public for forty days and do not die."

"We shall see Pietrasanta and his wife doing that for the next forty years," said Adele, with a tolerably natural laugh. "They ought to go into training as soon as possible if they mean to be happy. They say nothing spoils the temper like hunger. Were you ever near being starved to death on any of your travels, Ghisleri?"

"No; I never got further than being obliged to live on nothing but beans and bad water for nine days. That was quite far enough, though. I got thin, and I have never eaten beans since."

"I do not wonder. Fancy eating beans for nearly a fortnight. I should have died. And where was it? Were you imprisoned for a spy in South America? One never knows what may or may not have happened to you — you are such an unaccountable man!"

"That never happened to me. It was at sea. I took it into my head to go to Sardinia in a small vessel that was sailing from Amalfi with a cargo of beans to bring back Sardinian wine. We were becalmed, and got short of provisions, so that we fell back on the beans. They kept us alive, but I would rather not try it again."

"What endless adventures you have had! How tame this society life of ours must seem to you after what you have been accustomed to! How can you endure it?"

"It is never very hard to put up with what one likes," answered Ghisleri, "nor even to endure what one dislikes for the sake of somebody to whom one is attached."

"If any one else said that, it would sound like a platitude. But with you, it is quite different. One feels that you mean all you say."

Adele was evidently determined to be complimentary, and even more than complimentary, to-day. She was never cold or at all unfriendly with Ghisleri, whom she liked and admired, and whom she always hoped to see ultimately established as a permanent member of her own immediate circle, but he did not remember that she had ever talked exactly as she was talking now, and he attributed her manner to her nervousness. He laughed carelessly at her last remark.

"I am not used to such good treatment," he said, "though I never can understand why people take the trouble to doubt one's word. It is so much easier to believe everything — so much less trouble."

"I should not have thought that you were a very credulous person," answered Adele. "You have had too much experience for that."

"Experience does not always mean disillusionment. One may find out that there are honest people as well as dishonest in the world."

If Laura Arden had been present she would have been more than ever inclined to distrust Ghisleri just then. She would have wondered what possessed him to make him say things so very different from those he generally said to her. As a matter of fact, he wished Adele to trust him, for especial reasons, and he knew her well enough to judge how his speeches would affect her. She had betrayed herself to him a few minutes earlier and he desired to efface the impression in her mind before leading her into another trap.

"Do you think the world is such a very good place?" she asked. "Have you found it so?"

"It is often very unjustly abused by those who live in it — as they are themselves by their friends. Belief on the one side must mean disbelief on the other."

This time Adele gave no sign of being touched by the thrust. She was too much accustomed to whatever sensations she experienced when accidental or intentional reference was made to her astonishing talent for gossip.

"As for that," she said quite naturally, "every one talks about every one else, and some things are true just as some are not. If we did not talk of people how should we make conversation? It would be quite impossible, I am sure!"

"Oh, of course. But if there is to be that sort of conversation, it can always take the form of a discussion, and one can put oneself on the right side from the beginning just as easily as not. It saves so much trouble afterwards. The person who is always on the wrong side is generally the one about whom the others are talking. If we could hear a tenth of what is said about ourselves I fancy we should be very uncomfortable."

"Yes, indeed. Even our servants — think how they must abuse us!"

"No doubt. But they have a practical advantage over us in that way. When they really know anything particularly scandalous about us they can convert it into ready money."

Ghisleri had not the least intention of conveying any hidden meaning by his words, for he was of course completely ignorant of the occurrence which had disturbed Adele's whole life more than any other hitherto. But he noticed that she again bent over her glass and looked into it, though the sugar was by this time quite dissolved. Her hand shook a little as she moved the spoon about in the sweetened water. Then she drank a little, and drew a long breath.

"That is always a most disagreeable position," she said boldly. "We were talking about it the other day. I wish you had been there. Gouache was telling a foreigner — Prince Durakoff, I think it was — the old story of how Prince Montevarchi was murdered by his own librarian because he would not pay the man a sum of money in the way of blackmail. You know it, of course. The two families, the Montevarchi and the Saracinesca, kept it very quiet and no one ever knew all the details. Some people say that San Giacinto killed the librarian, and some say that the librarian killed himself. That is no matter. What would you have done? That is the question. Would you have paid the money in the hope of silencing the man? Or would you have refused as the old Prince did? Gouache said that it was always a mistake to yield, and that Montevarchi did quite right."

Ghisleri considered the matter a few moments before he gave an answer.   He was almost sure by this time that she actually found herself in some such position as she described, and that she really needed advice.   It was characteristic of the man who had been trying to make her betray herself and had succeeded beyond his expectation, that he was unwilling to give her such counsel as might lead to her own destruction.   In his complicated code, that would have savoured of treachery.   He suddenly withdrew into himself as it were, and tried to look at the matter objectively, as an outsider.

"It is a most difficult question to answer," he said at last.   "I have often heard it discussed.   If you care for my own personal opinion, I will give it to you.   It seems to me that in such cases one should be guided by circumstances as they arise, but that one can follow very safely a sort of general rule.   If the blackmailer, as I call the person in possession of the secret, has any positive proof, such as a written document, or any other object of the kind, without which he or she could not prove the accusation, and if the accusation is really of a serious nature, then I think it would be wiser to buy the thing, whatever it is, at any price, and destroy it at once.   But if, as in most of such affairs, the secret is merely one of words which the blackmailers may speak or not at will, and at any time, I believe it is a mistake to bribe him or her, because the demand for hush-money can be renewed indefinitely so long as the person concerned lives, or has any money left with which to pay."

Adele had listened with the greatest attention throughout, and the direct good sense of his answer disarmed any suspicion she might have entertained in regard to the remark which had led to her asking his advice.   She reasoned naturally enough that if he knew anything of her position, and had come to Gerano to gather information, he would have suggested some course of action which would throw the advantage into his own hands.   But she did not know the man.   Moreover, in her extreme fear of discovery, she had for a moment been willing to admit that he might know far more than was in any way possible, if he knew anything at all; whereas in truth he was but making the most vague guesses at the actual facts. It was startling to realise how nearly she had taken him for an enemy, after inviting him as a friend, and in perfectly good faith, but as she thought over the conversation she saw how naturally the remarks which had frightened her had presented themselves. There was her own insomnia — he had an instance of a man who had suffered in the same way. A remark about unjust abuse of other people — that was quite natural, and meant nothing. Blackmail extorted by servants — she had herself led directly to it, by speculating upon what servants said of their masters. It was all very natural. She made up her mind that she had been wrong in mistrusting his sincerity. Besides, she liked him, and her judgment instinctively inclined to favour him.

"I think you are quite right," she said, after a few moments' thought. "I never heard it put so directly before, and your view seems to be the only sensible one. If the secret can be kept by buying an object and destroying it, then buy it. If not, deny it boldly, and refuse to pay. Yes, that is the wisest solution I have ever heard offered."

Ghisleri saw that he had produced a good effect and was well-satisfied. He turned back to a former point in order to change the subject of the conversation.

"That old story of the Montevarchi has interested me," he said. "I wish I knew it all. Without being at all of an historical genius, I am fond of all sorts of family histories. Lady Herbert was saying yesterday that there are many strange legends and stories connected with this old place, and that your father knows them all. You must know a great deal about Gerano yourself, I should think."

"Oh, of course I do," answered Adele, with alacrity. "I will show you all over the castle to-morrow morning.

It is an enormous building, and bigger than you would ever suppose from the outside. I will show you where they used to cut off heads — it is delightful! The head fell through a hole in the floor into a heap of sawdust, they say. And then there is another place, where they threw criminals out of the window, with four seats in it, two for the executioners, one for the confessor, and one in the middle for the condemned man. They did those things so coolly and systematically in those good old days. You shall see it all; there are the dungeons, and the trap-doors through which people were made to tumble into them; there is every sort of appliance — belonging to family life in the middle ages."

"I shall be very glad to see it all if you will be my guide," said Ghisleri.

They continued to talk upon indifferent subjects. At dinner Pietro took much pains to be agreeable, and succeeded admirably, for he was well able to converse pleasantly when he chose. Though extremely tired, he sat up till nearly midnight talking politics with Savelli, as Adele had foreseen, and when he was at last shown to his distant room by Bonifazio, who had spent most of his day in studying the topography of the castle, he was very nearly exhausted.

* * *

CHAPTER XIX.

PIETRO GHISLERI slept soundly that night. Of late, indeed, he had become less restless than he had formerly been, and he attributed the change to the weakness which was the consequence of his wound. There were probably other causes at work at that time of which he was hardly conscious himself, but which ultimately produced a change in him, and in his way of looking at the world.

He stood at his open window early in the morning, and gazed out at the fresh, bright country. The delicate hand of spring had already touched the world with colour, and the breath of the coming warmth had waked the life in all those things which die yearly, and are yearly raised again. Ghisleri felt the morning sun upon his thin, pale face, and he realised that he also had been very near to death during the dark months, and he remembered how he had wished that he might be not near only to dying, but dead altogether, never to take up again the play that had grown so wearisome and empty in his eyes.

But now a change had come. For the first time in years, he knew that if the choice were suddenly offered him at the present moment he would choose to live out all the days allotted to him, and would wish that they might be many rather than few. There was, indeed, a dark spot on the page last turned, of which he could never efface the memory, nor, in his own estimation, outlive the shame. In his day-dreams Maddalena dell' Armi's coldly perfect face was often before him with an expression upon it which he feared to see, knowing too well why it was there — and out of a deeper depth of memory dead Bianca Corleone's eyes looked at him with reproach and sometimes with scorn. There was much pain in store for him yet, of the kind at which the world never guessed, nor ever could. But he would not try to escape from it. He would not again so act or think as to call himself coward in his own heart's tribunal.

He looked out at the distant hills, and down at the broad battlements and massive outworks of the ancient fortress, and fell to thinking rather idly about the people who had lived, and fought, and quarrelled, and slain each other, within and around those enormous walls, and then he thought all at once of Adele Savelli, and of his suspicions regarding her. He was in a particularly charitable frame of mind on that morning, and he suddenly felt that what he had almost believed on the previous night was utterly beyond the bounds of probability. It seemed to him that he had no manner of right to accuse any one of the crime he had imputed to her, on the most shadowy grounds, and absolutely without proof, unless the coincidence of her uneasy behaviour, with certain vague remarks of his own, could be taken as evidence. He sat down to think it all over, drinking his coffee by the open window, and enjoying the sunshine and the sweet morning air. The whole world looked so good and innocent and fresh as he gazed out upon it, that the possibilities of evil seemed to shrink away into nothing.

But as he systematically reviewed the events of the past months, his suspicion returned almost with the force of conviction. The coincidences were too numerous to be attributed to chance alone. Adele's distress of mind was too evident to be denied. Altogether there was no escaping from the conclusion that willingly or unwillingly she had been consciously instrumental in bringing about Arden's illness and death. Her questions about the wisest course to pursue in cases of blackmail, pointed to the probability if not the certainty that some third person was acquainted with what had happened, and this person was in all likelihood the maid Lucia. So far his reasoning took him quickly and plausibly enough, but no further. How the scarlet fever had been communicated from Lucia to Herbert Arden was more than Ghisleri could guess, but if Adele was really in the serving woman's power, it must have been done in such a way as to make what had happened quite clear to the latter. After thinking over all the possibilities, and vainly attempting to solve the hard problem, Ghisleri found himself as much at sea as ever, and was driven to acknowledge that he must trust to chance for obtaining any further evidence in the matter.

Meanwhile Adele had determined to follow his advice. Her anxiety was becoming unbearable, and she felt that she could not endure such suspense much longer. To accuse Lucia directly of having opened the letter and committed the theft would be rash and dangerous. There was a bare possibility that some one else might have done the deed. She must in any case be cautious.

"Lucia," she said that morning, while the woman was doing her hair, "do you remember that some days ago I gave you a letter to be registered, and that you brought back the receipt for it from the post-office?"

"Yes, Excellency, I remember very well." Lucia had been expecting for a long time that her mistress would question her and she was quite prepared. She had good nerves, and the certainty that the great lady was altogether in her power made her cool and collected.

"A very extraordinary thing happened to that letter," said Adele, looking up at her own face in the glass, to give herself courage. "It was rather important. I had written to Padre Bonaventura, asking spiritual guidance, and I particularly desired an answer. But he wrote to me by return of post, saying that when he opened the envelope he found only four sheets of blank paper without a word written on them. You see somebody must have thought there was money in the letter."

"They are such thieves at the post-office!" exclaimed Lucia. "But this is a terrible affair, Excellency! What is to be done? The post-master must be sent to the galleys immediately!"

In Lucia's conception of the law such a summary course seemed quite practicable.

"I am afraid that would be very unjust, and could do no good at all," said Adele. "I am quite sure that the post-master would not have dared to open a letter already registered, and for which he had given a receipt. As for any one in the house having done it, I cannot believe it either. I gave it into your hands myself and you brought me back the stamped bit of paper — it is there in my jewel case. I only wish you to find out for me, very quietly and without exciting suspicion, who took that letter to the post. If I could get it back I would give the person who brought it to me a handsome reward. You understand, Lucia, how disagreeable it is to feel that a letter concerning one's most sacred feelings is lost, and has perhaps been read by more than one person."

"I cannot imagine anything more dreadful! But be easy, Excellency. I will do all I can, and none of the servants shall suspect that I am questioning them."

"I shall be very much obliged to you, Lucia," said Adele. "Very much obliged," she repeated, with some emphasis.

"It is only my duty to serve your Excellency, who has always been so good to me," answered Lucia, humbly.

Adele knew that there was nothing more to be said for the present, and she congratulated herself on having been diplomatic in her way of offering the bribe. Lucia would now in all likelihood take some time to decide, but for the present she would certainly not part with the precious document. Adele felt sure that it had neither been destroyed nor sent out of the castle. Lucia probably kept it concealed in a safe corner of her own room, under lock and key, and to attempt to get possession of it by force would be out of the question. As in most Italian houses, the servants all locked their own rooms and carried the keys about with them. Lucia, of course, did like the rest.

But Lucia, on her side, distrusted her mistress. Knowing what she now knew of Adele, she believed her capable of almost anything, including the picking of a lock and the skilful abstraction of the letter from its secret hiding-place. As soon as she was at liberty she went and got the paper and concealed it in her bosom, intending to keep it there until she could select some safe spot in a remote part of the castle, where she might put it away in greater safety. To carry it about with her until Adele took her back to Rome would be rash, she thought. Adele might suspect where it was at any moment, and force her to give it up. Or it might be lost, which would be even worse.

Adele herself felt singularly relieved. She had very little doubt but that Lucia would come to terms. She might, indeed, ask a very large sum, and it might be very inconvenient to be obliged to find it at short notice. But the sole heiress to an enormous estate would certainly be able to get money in some way or other. In the meantime Lucia would not offer it to any one else, since of all people her mistress would be willing to make the greatest sacrifice to obtain possession of it. On the whole, therefore, Adele's anxiety diminished on that day, and she seemed better when she met her husband and Ghisleri in the great court-yard where they were sunning themselves and continuing their talk about politics.

"I promised that I would show you the castle," she said to Pietro. "Would it amuse you to go with me now? Francesco does not care to come, of course, and he always has his business with the steward to attend to before breakfast."

Pietro expressed his readiness to follow her from the deepest dungeon to the topmost turret of the castle.

"Have you slept well?" he asked, as they moved away together. "You are looking much better this morning."

"Yes. I feel better," she answered. "Do you know I think your coming has had something to do with it. You have cheered us with your talk and your news. We were fast falling into the vegetable stage, Francesco and I."

Ghisleri smiled, partly out of politeness and partly at his own thoughts.

"I am glad to have been of any use," he said. "I will do my best to be amusing as long as you will have me."

"You need not take it as such an enormous compliment," Adele laughed. "Of course, you are very agreeable, — at least, you can be when you choose, — but the great thing is to have somebody, anybody one knows and likes a little, in this dreary place. Shall we begin at the top or the bottom? The prisons or the towers? Which shall it be?"

"If there is a choice, let us begin in the lower regions," answered Ghisleri. "Do you like me a little, Donna Adele?" he asked, as she led the way along the curved and smoothly paved descent which led downwards to the subterranean part of the fortress.

She laughed lightly, and glanced at him. She had always wished to make a conquest of Pietro Ghisleri, but she had found few opportunities of being alone with him, for he had never been among the assiduous at her shrine. She knew also how much he admired Laura Arden, and she suspected him of being incipiently in love. It would be delightful to detach him from that allegiance.

"Yes," she said, "I like you a little. Did you expect me to like you very much? You have never done anything to deserve it."

"I wish I could," answered Ghisleri, with complete insincerity. "But I am afraid I should never get so far as that."

"Why not?"

"When a woman loves her husband —" He did not finish the sentence, for it seemed unnecessary.

"I do not want you to make love to me," Adele answered, "though I believe you know how to do it to perfection. It is often a very long way from liking very much to loving a very little. This is the place where old Gianluca kept his brother Paolo in prison for eighteen years. Then Gianluca died suddenly one fine morning, and Paolo was let out by the soldiers and immediately threw Gianluca's wife out of the window of the east tower, and cut off the heads of his two sons on the same afternoon. I will show you where that was done when we go up stairs. Paolo was an extremely energetic person."

"Decidedly so, I should say," assented Ghisleri. "You are all descended from him, I suppose."

"Yes, he took care that we should be, by killing all the other branches of the family. Those hollows in the stone are supposed to have been made by his footsteps. Think what a walk! It lasted eighteen years. But it is an airy place and not damp. Those windows were there then, they say. Do you see that deep channel in the wall? It leads straight up through the castle to the floor of the little passage between the old guard-room

and one of the towers. There used to be a trap-door—
it was still there when I was a little girl, but my father
has had a slab of stone put down instead. They used to
entice their dearest and most familiar enemies up there,
and just as the man set foot on the board a soldier in the
tower pulled a bolt in the wall and the trap-door fell. It
is two hundred feet, they say. It was so cleverly managed! They say that the last person who came to grief
there was a Monsignor Boccapaduli in the year sixteen
hundred and something, but no one ever knew what had
become of him until the next generation."

Familiar from her childhood with every corner of the
vast building, she led Ghisleri through one portion after
another, telling such of the tales of horror as she remembered. Little by little they worked their way to the
upper regions. In the guard-room, a vast hall which
would have made a good-sized church, she showed him the
great slab of stone the Prince had substituted for the
wooden trap-door of former days, and which had merely
been placed over the yawning chasm without plaster or
cement, its own weight being enough to keep it in position.
They passed over it and ascended the stairs in the tower,
emerging at last into the bright sunshine upon one of the
highest battlements. They sat down side by side on a
stone bench.

"It is pleasanter here," said Adele. "There is a sort
of attraction about those dreadful old places down below,
because one never quite realises all the things that happened there, and it is rather like an old-fashioned novel,
all full of murder and sudden death. But the sunshine
is much nicer, is it not? Shall we stay up here till it is
time for breakfast?"

"By all means. It is a delightful place for a good
talk." Ghisleri was tired, and glad to sit down.

"Then you must talk to me," continued his companion. "Between the stairs and playing guide, I have no
voice left. What will you talk about? Tell me all
about your own castle. They say it is very interesting.
I wish I could see it!"

"After Geráno it would seem very tame to you. It is mostly in ruins, and what there is left of it is very much the worse for wear. I would not advise you to take the trouble to stop, even if you should ever pass near it."

"That is a way you have of depreciating everything connected with yourself," said Adele. "Why do you do it?"

"Do I?" asked Ghisleri, carelessly. "I suppose I have the idea that it is better to let people be agreeably surprised, if there is to be any surprise at all. When you have heard that a man is insufferable, if he turns out barely tolerable you think him nice."

"Then it is mere pose on your part, with the deliberate intention of producing an effect?"

"Probably — mere pose." Ghisleri laughed; he looked at the woman at his side and wondered whether he could ever find out the truth about Arden's death, and the connexion with it which, as he believed, she must have had.

She, on her part, did not even guess that he suspected her. The thought had crossed her mind on the previous afternoon, but she had very soon dismissed it. She found relief and change from the monotonous suffering of the past days in talking to him, and she tried to enjoy what she could without allowing her mind to wander back to its chief preoccupation. Ghisleri was very careful not to rouse her suspicion by any accidental reference to what filled his thoughts as much as it did her own, and they spent more than half an hour in aimless and more or less amusing conversation.

Gerano did not offer any very great variety of amusement. After breakfast, there was the usual interval for smoking and coffee, and after that the usual drive of two or three hours in the hills. Then, tea and small talk, the dressing hour, the arrival of the post with the morning papers from Rome, dinner, more smoking, and more conversation, and bed-time was reached. It was not gay, and when he retired for the night Ghisleri was beginning to wonder how long he could endure the ordeal with equanimity. He was not generally a man very easily bored, and the reasons which had brought him to Gerano were strong enough in themselves to make him ready to sacrifice a good deal, but he realised that he was not making any advance in the direction of discovering the secret. He had learned more in the first few hours of his stay than he had learned since, and so far as he could see, he was not likely to find out anything more. He had noticed, too, the improvement in Adele's appearance on that day. It was possible that she had already acted upon the general advice he had given her, and that she had insured the silence of the person she dreaded, if any such person existed. But it was equally possible that no one knew what she had done, and that she had not meant anything by the question.

The third day passed like the second, and the fourth began without promising any change. Adele appeared as usual at eleven o'clock and spent an hour with Ghisleri. They were becoming more intimate by this time than they had ever been before during their long acquaintance, and Adele flattered herself that she had made an impression. Ghisleri would not forget the hospitality she had offered him, and next year would be more often seen in the circle of her admirers. She even imagined that he might fall into a sort of mild and harmless flirtation, if she knew how to manage him.

A little before the hour for breakfast she went to her room. Lucia was there, as usual, waiting in case she should be needed. As she retouched Adele's hair, and gave a final twist with the curling tongs to the ringlets at the back of her mistress's neck, she began to speak in a low voice and in a somewhat hurried manner.

"I have found out who took the letter, Excellency," she said. "It is in a safe place and no one else has seen it. The person will give it to me at once if the reward is large enough."

Adele's eyes sparkled, and a little colour rose in her cheeks. Lucia watched the reflection of her face in the mirror.

"How much does she ask?" she inquired, without hesitation, and with a certain business-like sharpness in her tone.

There was a moment's pause, as Lucia withdrew the tongs from the little curl.

"She asks five thousand francs," she said, in some trepidation, for she had hardly ever in her life even spoken of so large a sum.

"That is a great deal," answered Adele, pretending to be surprised, while doing her best to conceal her satisfaction. "I have not so much money out here; indeed, Don Francesco has not either. She must wait until we go to Rome."

"A year, if your Excellency pleases," said the maid, blowing scent upon a transparent handkerchief from an atomizer.

"In the meanwhile I should like to have the letter. I suppose she would accept my promise — written, if she requires it?"

"Of course she would, and she would give me the papers at once — or instead of a promise, I have no doubt she would be perfectly satisfied with a bit of jewelry as a pledge."

"That would be simpler," said Adele, coldly. She could not but be astonished at the woman's cool effrontery, though it was impossible to refuse anything she asked. "I will give you a diamond for her to keep as a pledge," she added, "but I want the letter this afternoon."

"Yes, Excellency."

During the midday meal Adele was by turns absent and then very gay. She seemed restless and uneasy during the coffee and cigarette stage of the afternoon. Ghisleri watched her with curiosity. Fully half an hour earlier than usual she went to her room to get ready for the regulation drive.

Lucia was waiting for her, pale as death and evidently in a state of the greatest agitation. Without a word Adele unlocked her jewel case, took out a little morocco covered box, opened it, and glanced at a pair of diamond ear-rings it contained, shut it again and held it out to Lucia. To her surprise the woman drew back, clearly in great terror, and trying to get behind the long toilet table as though in fear of bodily harm.

"What is the matter?" asked Adele, in surprise. "Where is the letter? Why do you not give it to me?"

"A great misfortune has happened," gasped Lucia, hardly able to speak. "I cannot get it from the person."

"What!" Adele's voice rang through the room. "Do you want more money now? What is this comedy?"

"The letter is not there — I — she does not know where it is. It is lost — Excellency — "

"Lost? Where did you hide it?"

Lucia was almost too frightened by this time to tell connectedly what had happened, but Adele understood before long that the maid had looked about for a safe place in which to hide the precious document, and had at last decided to slip it under the great slab of stone which has been already mentioned as covering the opening of the oubliette between the guard-room and the tower. Lucia had found that on one side, owing to the irregularity of the old pavement, there was room to lay the folded papers, and that she could just slip her hand in so as to withdraw them again. She was, of course, quite ignorant that the stone covered a well of which the shaft penetrated to the lowest foundation of the castle, and that one touch of her hand, or a gust of wind, was enough to send the light sheets over the edge close to which she had unwittingly placed them. Adele still pretended to be angry, but she drew a long breath of relief. She knew the exact spot at which to look for what she wanted. She locked up her diamonds again, scolding Lucia for her carelessness all the time, and doing her best to be very severe. Lucia bore all that was said to her very meekly, for she had expected far worse. In her opinion some one had accidentally discovered the letter, and taken it, and would make capital out of it as she had meant to

T

do. Her disappointment was as great, as the sum of five thousand francs had seemed to her enormous, but her fear soon vanished when she saw that Adele had no intention of doing her any bodily injury, nor, apparently, of dismissing her again. That the papers were really gone from the place of concealment she knew beyond a doubt. She had lit a taper in her effort to find them, and had thrust it under the slab, bending low and looking into the crevice. Nothing white of any sort had been visible.

Adele dressed herself for going out and left the room. But instead of joining her husband and Ghisleri at once, she turned out of the main passage by the cross corridor which led to the court-yard, went out and walked quickly down the inclined road by which she had led Ghisleri to Paolo Braccio's dungeon. There, where the shaft of the oubliette came down, she was quite sure of finding the little package of sheets which meant so much to her and which had almost meant a fortune to Lucia. She crossed the worn pavement rapidly. There was plenty of light from the grated windows high up under the vault, and she could have seen the paper almost as soon as she entered the place. She stopped short as she reached the foot of the channel in the wall. There was nothing there. She stared up into the blackness above in the hope of seeing a white thing caught and sticking to the stones, but she could not distinguish the faintest reflection of anything. Yet she was convinced that the thing must have fallen all the way. The shaft, as she well knew, was quite perpendicular and the masonry compact and well finished. The object of those who had built it had been precisely to prevent the possibility of the victim catching on a projection of any sort while falling.

Adele turned pale and leaned against the wall, breathing hard. If Lucia had acted differently she might have been suspected of having told a falsehood, and of keeping the letter back in order to extort a larger sum for it at some future time. But Lucia had evidently been frightened. Moreover, the woman was undoubtedly ignorant of the existence of the well under the stone, or, she would never have been so foolish as to choose such a place for hiding anything so valuable, and it was clear that she had no idea of the manner in which the package had disappeared. That it must have reached the bottom, Adele was quite sure. In that case some one had been in the dungeon before her and had picked it up, but who the some one might be she had no means of conjecturing.

She hardly knew how she reached the court-yard again. It cost her a superhuman effort to walk. In the passage she met her husband.

"What is the matter?" he asked, as soon as he saw her face.

"I feel very ill — I wanted to breathe the air." She seemed to be gasping for breath.

Francesco drew her arm through his and walked with her to her room. She was clearly not in a state in which she could think of going out.

Savelli went back and explained to Ghisleri, who, if anything, was glad to escape from the monotonous drive. He got a book and shut himself up in his room to read. That evening Savelli told him that Adele was worse, and was in a state of indescribable nervous agitation. It was clearly his duty to go away, if Adele were about to be seriously ill, and he told Bonifazio to pack his things that night. If matters did not improve, he would leave on the following morning.

Though Francesco was not much affected by his wife's sufferings, the dinner was anything but brilliant, for he anticipated a renewal of all the annoyance of the first few days. Moreover, if Adele was liable to sudden relapses of this kind at any moment, and without the smallest reason or warning, his life would, before long, be made a burden to him. As the husband of a permanent invalid he could hope for very little liberty or amusement. A wife may go into the world without her husband, because he is supposed to be occupied with more important affairs, but a husband who frequents parties when his wife is constantly suffering, is considered heartless in the extreme. That, at least, is society's view of the mutual obligation, and if it is not the just one, it is at least founded upon the theory of woman's convenience, as most of society's views are.

Francesco was easily prevailed upon to give Adele an increased dose of chloral, in the hope that she might sleep, and consequently give him less trouble on the next day. But in this conclusion he was mistaken. She awoke in great pain, suffering, she said, from a violent headache, and so nervous that her hand trembled violently and she was hardly able to lift a cup to her lips when the nurse brought her tea. Savelli did not attempt to keep Ghisleri when the latter announced his intention of returning to town, though he pressed him to come out again, as soon as Adele should be better. The man who drove Pietro back was instructed to bring the doctor out to Gerano, with fresh horses, and especially not to forget five hundred cigarettes which Francesco wanted for himself.

Ghisleri left many messages for Adele, and departed with Bonifazio, very little wiser than when he had arrived, but considerably more curious.

CHAPTER XX.

It was a relief to be with Laura Arden again for an hour on the day after his return, as Ghisleri felt when he was installed beside her in the chair which had come to be regarded as his. She received him just as usual, and he saw at once that if she had at all resented his visit to Adele, she was not by any means inclined to let him know it. There was a freshness and purity in the atmosphere that surrounded her which especially appealed to him after his visit to Gerano. Whatever she said she meant, and if she meant anything she took no trouble to hide it. He compared her face with her step-sister's, and the jaded, prematurely world-worn look of the one threw the calm beauty of the other into strong relief. He felt no pity for Adele. What she was, she had made herself, and if she suffered, it was as the direct and inevitable consequence of the life she had led and of the things she had done. So, at least, it seemed to him, and if he could have known the whole truth at that time, he would have seen how right he was. The ruthless logic of cause and effect had got Adele into its will and was slowly grinding her whole existence to dust.

"It is strange," he said to Laura, "that you and your step-sister should be so unlike in every way. It is true that you are not related, but you were brought up in the same house, by the same people, and yet I do not believe you have a single idea in common."

"No," answered Laura, "we have not. We do not like the same persons, nor the same things, nor the same thoughts. We were made to be enemies — and I suppose we are."

It was the first time she had ever said so much to him, and even now there was no rancour in her tone.

"If all enemies were like you, at least, this would be a very peaceful world."

"You do not know me," answered Laura, with a smile. "I have a bad temper. I could tell you something about it. I once felt as though I would like to strangle a certain person, and as though I could do it. Do not imagine that I am all saint and no sinner."

"I like to imagine all sorts of nice things about you," said Ghisleri. "But I could never make them nice enough."

"That is just it. It would need an enormous imagination."

"But I am not sure that I should like to think of you as being on very good terms with Donna Adele, and I am almost glad to hear you admit that you are enemies. There is a satisfaction in knowing that you are human, as well as in believing you to be good."

"How is Adele?" Laura asked.

"The last I heard was that she was much worse. She behaves in the most unaccountable way. She has the look of a woman in some very great mental distress — pursued and haunted by something very painful from which she cannot escape."

".I had the same feeling about her the last time I saw her. I know that look very well. I have seen it in your face, sometimes, as well as in hers."

"In mine?" Ghisleri looked keenly at her, as though to ascertain whether she meant more than she said, for the first time in his acquaintance with her. "When did I ever show you that I was in trouble?" he asked.

"That was some time ago. You have changed since your illness. You used to look harassed sometimes, like a man who has a wound in the heart. Perhaps it is only something which depends on the way your eyes are made. The first time I ever noticed it was — yes, I remember very well — it was more than a year ago, that night when you spoke your poem in the Shrove Tuesday masquerade. It was not when you were talking to me. You looked perfectly diabolical then. It was later. I saw you standing alone in a doorway after a dance."

"What a memory you have! I was probably in a bad humour. I generally am, even now."

"Why do you say even now?" asked Laura, watching his face.

"Oh, I hardly know," he answered. "All sorts of things have happened to me since then, to simplify my existence. At that time it was very particularly complicated."

"And how have you simplified it?" She put the question innocently enough, and quite thoughtlessly, not even guessing at the truth.

"It has been simplified for me. It came near being simplified into being no existence at all. A few inches made the difference."

"Yes," said Laura, thoughtfully, "the greatest of all differences to you."

"And none at all to any one else," added Ghisleri, with a dry laugh.

She turned her great dark eyes upon him. The lids drooped a little as she scrutinised his face somewhat coldly, but with an odd interest.

"I suppose that might be quite true," she said at last. "Perhaps it is. But I do not like you any the better for saying it in that way."

Ghisleri was silent, but he met her gaze quietly and without flinching, until she looked away. She sighed a little as she took up a bit of embroidery she was doing for some garment of little Herbert's.

"Why do you sigh?" he asked, not expecting that she would answer the question.

"For some one," she said simply, and she began to make a few stitches.

He knew that she was thinking of Maddalena dell' Armi, and his heart smote him.

"I was wrong to say it," he answered, in a more gentle tone. "There was perhaps one exception to the rule."

Ghisleri grew even more careful of his speech after that. But he did not see Laura often before she went away northward for the summer. The spring was going fast, and the time was coming when Rome would be its quiet old-fashioned self again for those few who loved it well enough to face the heat of July and August. Almost every one was thinking of going away. The Prince and Princess of Gerano were going out to the castle earlier than usual, for the news of Adele grew steadily worse. Francesco now had the doctor out regularly three times a week, and was forced to lead an existence he detested. His wife was by this time quite unable to get rest without taking very large quantities of chloral, and at times her sufferings were such that it seemed almost advisable to give her morphia. Every one, however, who brought intelligence from Gerano agreed in saying that she did her best to keep up, and seemed to dread the idea of an illness which might keep her permanently in her room.

Whenever she felt able she insisted on driving out and on going through the regular round of monotonous country occupations. Her father and step-mother therefore determined to go out and help Francesco to take care of her, and make her existence as bearable as possible. Amongst all her friends she was spoken of with the utmost compassion, and no one ever suggested that her illness could proceed from any such cause as Ghisleri believed to be at the root of it.

A few days before Laura Arden was to go away Donald came to Pietro's room in the morning, with a very grave face. Lady Herbert, he said, thought that Ghisleri would understand why she did not write, but sent Donald in person with a verbal message. She was going away, and was about to give up the apartment in which she had spent the winter, without any intention of taking it again in the following year. There were certain things that had belonged to Lord Herbert — Lady Herbert had no home and did not like to send them to Lord Lulworth — would Ghisleri take charge of them in her absence? Pietro, of course, assented, and two hours later Donald arrived with a large carriage load of boxes. Ghisleri looked on with a very unpleasant sensation in his throat as his old friend's effects were brought up stairs and deposited in a room where he kept such things of his own. When they were all piled together in a corner, he took an old green curtain and covered them with it, spreading it carefully over them with his own hands. Then he locked the door and went away. Some men and women when they die seem to leave something of life behind them, which the mere sight of anything that has belonged to them has power to recall most vividly to the perceptions of those who have known them and loved them. Ghisleri understood Laura Arden's feeling about her husband's belongings. He knew, or thought he knew, that from the moment her child had been given to her, she had desired that no material object should revive the sorrow she had felt so deeply. The memory she cherished was wholly spiritual, and upon its remaining so her peace of mind largely depended. The one Herbert was to live in the other — and there must not be two. Not every one, perhaps, would have understood her so readily.

The day came for bidding her good-bye. It was with a somewhat heavy heart that he went up the stairs of her house for the last time. Much of the little happiness he had known during the past months was associated with the place and with her, and not a little of the sorrow as well. The drawing-room was bare, and had lost the comfortable, inhabited look which even a furnished lodging takes from all the little objects a woman brings to it, and which she alone knows how to dispose and arrange as though they were in constant use, thereby at once producing the impression that the habitation she has chosen has been lived in long.

Once more Ghisleri sat in the familiar chair near the open window, and once more Laura took her place in the corner of the great sofa.

"I have come to say good-bye," he began. "You are still decided to go to-morrow, I suppose."

"Yes. I have not changed my plans. Please do not come to the station to see me off, nor send flowers, nor do any of the things which are generally done. I would rather not see any one I know after leaving this house."

"May I write to you?" asked Ghisleri.

"Of course. Why not?"

"I do not know, I am sure. I thought it better to ask you. Some women hate correspondence except with their nearest and dearest. I will give you the news of Rome during the wild gaiety of July and August."

"Are you not going away at all?" asked Laura, in some surprise. "You ought to; it will do you good."

"I hardly know. I like to be alone in summer. It gives one time to think. One has a chance of leading a sensible life when nobody is here to see. The days pass pleasantly — plenty of reading, a diet of watermelon and sherbet, and a little repentance — it is magnificent treatment for the liver."

Laura looked at him and then laughed very softly.

"You seem amused," said Ghisleri, gravely. "What I say is quite true — the result of long experience."

"I was not laughing at what you said, but at the idea that you should still think it worth while to make such speeches to me."

"If I can make you laugh at all it is worth while."

"At all events, it is good of you to say so. Which of the three subjects do you mean to take for your letters to me — your reading, your food, or your repentance?"

"The food would be the simplest and safest topic. You can read for yourself what you please. Repentance, when it is not a habit, is rarely well done. But one can say the most charming things about strawberries, peaches, and figs, without ever offending any one's taste."

"I think you grow worse as you grow older," said Laura, still smiling. "But if you would take your programme seriously, it would not be a bad thing, I fancy. Seriously, however, you ought to get away from Rome."

"I should be tempted to go and stay a week near you, if I went away at all," said Ghisleri.

Laura did not answer at once. She glanced at him with a vague suspicion in her eyes which disappeared almost instantly, and then took two or three stitches in her embroidery before she spoke.

"I would rather you should not do that," she said at last. "I may as well tell you what I think about it. To me, and to you, it seems thoroughly absurd that you should not see me whenever we choose to meet. There are many reasons why I should look upon you as a friend, and why you should come more often than any other man I know. But the world thinks differently. My mother has spoken to me about it more than once, and in one way she is right. You know what a place this is, and how every one talks about everybody. Unfortunately, I believe that you are one of the men about whose private affairs society is most busy. I cannot help it now. I have no right to say anything about your life, past or present, but you have told me enough about yourself to make me understand why there is always gossip about you, and why there always will be. Then, too, you will never make people believe that you did not fight that duel about me, for you cannot tell any one what you told me. The consequence is, that you and I look at it all from one point of view, and the world sees it from quite another. I think it is better to say all this once, and to be done with it. As we shall not meet for several months, people will forget to talk. Am I right to speak to you?"

"Perfectly right," answered Ghisleri. An expression of pain had settled on his lean face while she had been talking, and did not disappear at once. Laura saw it and was silent for a moment.

"I am sorry if I have hurt you," she said presently. "Perhaps I was wrong."

"No, you were quite right," Ghisleri replied. "You would have been very wrong indeed not to tell me. If you did not, who would? But I had no suspicion of all this. I believed that for once they might let me alone, considering what you are — and what I am. The contrast might protect you in the eyes of some persons. Lady Herbert Arden — and Pietro Ghisleri."

He pronounced his own name with the utmost bitterness.

"Please do not speak of yourself in that way," said Laura, with something like entreaty in her voice.

"It is true enough," he answered. "An intelligent being might understand that I could be useful to you, but not that you — " He stopped short, and his tone changed. "I am talking nonsense," he said briefly, by way of explaining the truth.

"I think you are, in a way," said Laura, quietly. "It is your old habit of exaggeration. You make me an impossible creature between an archangel and the good mamma in children's story books, and you refer to yourself as to a satanic monster whom no honest woman could call her friend. You are quite right. It is sheer nonsense. If you stay in Rome to repent, as you suggest in fun, do it in earnest. I am not talking of your sins, which are not half so bad as you pretend, but of this silly view you insist upon taking of your own life. If you must think perpetually of yourself, judge yourself by some reasonable standard. You live in the world and you have no right to expect to find that you are a saint. If that is what you wish, take vows, turn monk, and starve yourself up to heaven if you can. And if you chance to think of me, do not set me on a pedestal, and build a church over me, and pray at me. I do not like that sort of thing — it is all unnatural and absurd. I am a woman and nothing else, better than some by force of circumstances, and not so good as some others, perhaps for the same reason. All the rest that you imagine is sentimental trash, and not worth the time it takes you to think it. You will not be wasting your summer if you can get rid of it all by the time we meet in the autumn."

For once in his life, Ghisleri was taken by surprise. He had not had any idea that Laura could express herself so strongly on any point, still less that she could talk so plainly about himself. He was far too manly, however, not to be pleased, and his expression changed as he listened to her. She smiled as she finished, and began to make stitches again.

"No one ever gave me so much good advice in so short a time," he said, with a laugh. "You have a wonderful power of condensing your meaning. Do you often talk in that way?"

"Not often. I think I never did before. Do you not think there is some sense in what I say?"

"Indeed, I begin to believe that there is a great deal," Ghisleri answered. "At all events, I shall not forget it. Perhaps you will find me partially reformed when you come back. You must promise to tell me."

"It will take me some time to find out. But if I succeed I will tell you."

His mood had changed for the better, and he talked of

Laura's plans during nearly half an hour. At last he rose to go.

"Good-bye," he said, rather abruptly.

She looked up quietly as she took his hand, and pressed it without affectation.

"Good-bye. I wish you a very pleasant summer — and — since we are parting — I thank you with all my heart for the many kind and friendly things you have done for me."

"I have done nothing. Good-bye, again."

He turned and she stood looking at his retreating figure until he had disappeared through the door.

"I believe there is more good in that man than any one knows," she said to herself. Then she also left the room and went to see whether little Herbert were awake, and to busy herself with the last arrangements for his comfort during the journey.

Ghisleri knew that another parting was before him in the near future. As usual, Maddalena dell' Armi was going to spend a considerable part of the summer with her father in Tuscany. He went to see her tolerably often, and their relations had of late been to all appearances friendly and undisturbed. But he doubted whether the final interview before they separated for several months could pass off without some painful incident. He knew Maddalena's character well, and if he did not know his own, it was not for want of study. He almost wished that he might, on that day, choose to call at a time when some other person was present, for then, of course, there could be no show of emotion on either side, nor any words which could lead to such weakness. He went twice to the house during the week which intervened between Laura Arden's departure and the day fixed for Maddalena's, saying each time that he would come again, a promise to which the Contessa seemed indifferent enough. She would always be glad to see as much of him as possible, she said. The last day came. She was to leave for Florence on the following morning. Ghisleri rang, was admitted, and found her alone.

"I knew you would come," she said, "though it is so late."

"Of course. Did I not say so? I suppose you are still decided to go to-morrow."

He was conscious that he was saying the very same indifferent words which he had said a few days earlier to Laura, and Maddalena answered him almost as Laura had done.

"Yes. Of course you must not come to the station. That is understood, is it not?"

"Since you wish it, I will certainly not come. So we are saying good-bye until next season," he continued, breaking the ice as it were, since he felt it must be broken. "I will try and not be emotional, and I ask you to believe — this once — that I am in earnest. I have something to say to you. May I? Will you listen to me? You and I cannot part with two words and a nod of the head, like common acquaintances."

"I will hear all you care to say," answered Maddalena, simply. "And I will try to believe you."

He looked at the pale face and the small, perfect features before he spoke, to see if they were as hard as they often were. But for the moment the expression was softened. The evening glow played softly upon the bright hair, and threw a deep, warm light into the violet eyes, as she turned towards him.

"What is it?" she asked, as he seemed to hesitate. "Has anything happened? Are you going to be married?"

The question shocked him in a way he could not explain.

"No. I am not thinking of marrying. We have been a great deal to each other, for a long time. But for my fault — and it is, of course, my fault — we might be as much in one another's lives as ever. We used to meet in the summer, but that will not happen this year. When you come back, we may both be changed more than we think it possible to change at present."

"In what way?"

"I do not know. Perhaps, when we meet again, we

shall feel that we are really and truly devoted friends. Perhaps you may hate me altogether —"

"And you me."

"No, that is not possible. I am not very sure of myself as a rule. But that, at least, I know."

"I hope you are right. If you are not my friend, who should be? So you think I hate you. You are very wrong. I am still very fond of you. I told you so the other day. You should believe me. Remember, when it all ended, it was you who had changed — not I. I am not reproaching you. I might say that you should have known yourself better than to think that you could be faithful; but you might tell me — and it would be quite as just — that I, a woman, knew what I was doing and had been taught to look upon my deeds as you never could. But it was you who changed. If you had loved me, I should have loved you still. Little things showed me long ago that your love was waning. It was never what it was in those first days. And now I have changed, too. I love what was once, but if I could have your love now as it was at its strongest and best, I would not ask for it. Why should I? I could never trust it again, and anything is better than that doubt. And I want no consolation."

"Indeed, I should have very little to offer you, worth your accepting," said Pietro, in a low voice.

"If I needed any, the best you could give me would be what I ask, — not as consolation at all, but as something I still believe worth having from you, — and that is your honest friendship."

Ghisleri was moved in spite of himself. His face grew paler and the shadows showed beneath his eyes where Maddalena had so often seen them.

"You are too kind — too good," he said, in an unsteady tone.

The last time he had said almost the same words had been when he made his first visit to her after his long illness. Then she had been touched, far more than he.

She looked at him for a few moments and saw that he felt very strongly.

"Do not distress yourself," she said gently. "Pray do not — it hurts me, too. I mean what I say. I do not believe you can be faithful in love now — to any one. You gave all you had to give long ago. But I have watched you since we became what we are now, and I will do you justice. I do not know any man who can be a more true and devoted friend. You see, I meant what I said."

"If it is true — if I can be a friend to any one, I will be one to you. But that is not what I would have, if I could choose."

"What would you have, then?"

"What is impossible. That is what one would always like. Let us not talk of it. It does no good to wish for what is beyond wishing. I thank you for what you have said — dear. I shall not forget it. Few women could be so good as you are to me. You would have the right to be very different if you chose."

"No, I should not. There are reasons — well, as you say, let us not talk about it. We have made up our minds to meet and part as we should — kindly always, lovingly as friends love, truthfully now, since there is nothing left for us to distrust."

She had never spoken to him in this way in all the meetings that had followed his recovery. He wondered if there had been any real change in her nature, or whether this were not at last the assertion of her natural self. She spoke so seriously and quietly that he could not doubt her.

"I have seen that you can act in that way," she continued presently. "You have done more for the sake of the mere memory of your friend than many men would do for love itself."

"Not so much as I would do for the memory of love," said Ghisleri, turning his face away.

"Was it so sweet as that?" she asked.

"Yes."

"And yet you have loved better and longer in other days."

"As I was a better man," he said, finding no other answer, for he knew it was true.

Maddalena sighed. Perhaps she had hoped that this last time he would say what he had never said — that he had loved her better than Bianca Corleone.

"You must have been different then." She spoke a little coldly, in spite of herself. A moment later she smiled. "How foolish it is of me to think of making comparisons, now that it is all over," she said. "So you are not coming to Tuscany this summer, and I shall not see you till next autumn. Why do you not come?"

"I want to be alone a long time," answered Ghisleri. "It is much better. I am bad company, and besides, I am not strong enough to wander about the world yet. I need a long rest."

"It seems so strange to think of you as not being strong."

"Yes — I who used to be so proud of my strength. I believe that was my greatest vanity when I was very young."

"How full of contradictions you are!" Maddalena exclaimed, as she had often done before.

Ghisleri said nothing, for he knew it better than she could. It was growing late, for the sun had gone down and the twilight deepened in the room. He rose to go, and took her hand as she stood up beside him.

"Good-bye," he said, almost in a whisper. "May God forgive me, and bless you — always."

"Good-bye — dear."

He went out. It had been a strange meeting, and the parting was stranger still. Very often,' throughout the long summer months which followed, Ghisleri thought of it, recalling every word and gesture of the woman who had loved him so deeply, and for whom he had nothing left but the poor friendship she was so ready to accept. But that at least he could give her, kindly, lovingly, and

U

truthfully, as she herself had said, and he was grateful to her for asking it of him, though no kindness of hers could heal the wound he had given himself in injuring her. He thought less harshly of the world for half a year or so after that day, and began to believe that it might not be so abominable a place as he had sometimes been inclined to think it.

He wrote to Maddalena from time to time, short letters, which said little, but which she was glad to receive and which she often answered in the same strain, with a small chronicle of small doings made to bear the weight of a sweeping comment now and then. Little enough of interest there was in any of those epistles, but there was a general tone in them which assured each that the other had not forgotten that last meeting.

Ghisleri did not write to Laura, though he could hardly have told why, especially as he had spoken of doing so. Possibly he felt that she would not understand him through a letter as she did when they were face to face, and he feared to make a bad impression.

Of Adele Savelli he had news often, through people who were in intimate correspondence with her and with her step-mother, who spent the greater part of the summer at Gerano. From all accounts she had begun to improve with the warm weather, and though she still looked ill and greatly changed from her former self, she was said to be very much better. It was commonly reported that morphia had saved her, and it was whispered that she was a slave to it in consequence. Ghisleri cared very little. He had almost given up the idea that she had been concerned in bringing on Arden's illness, and even if he sometimes still thought she had been, he saw the impossibility of going any further than he had gone already in the attempt to discover the truth.

CHAPTER XXI.

BEFORE attempting to chronicle the events which were the ultimate consequences of those already described, it will be necessary to explain how it was that very little worth recording occurred during nearly three years after the day on which Pietro Ghisleri said good-bye to the Contessa dell' Armi, when she was going to make her customary visit to her father.

In the natural course of things, every one returned in the following autumn, in more or less lively expectation of the season to come. Laura Arden expected nothing of it, in the way of amusement, nor did she look forward to anything of the sort in her life as possible for many seasons to come.

Maddalena dell' Armi, on the other hand, expected much, and was, on the whole, disappointed. Ghisleri had grown indifferent to such a degree as to be almost unrecognizable to his friends. He went out very little, and was said to be busy with some speculation in which he was ruining himself, but of which, as a matter of fact, he had never even heard. Adele Savelli went everywhere, thin, nervous, and careworn, and apparently driven to death by the necessity for excitement. There were people who said she was going mad, and others who said she lived on morphia and that it must ultimately kill her. The division of opinions concerning the nature of her malady still existed, and the wildest stories were sent adrift at a venture down the dangerous rapids of conversation. Donna Adele had quarrelled about Laura with her father, who had disinherited her as far as he was able, and she led a life of daily torment in Casa Savelli in consequence. That was one of the tales. Then it was stated that Francesco's passion for Laura Arden had suddenly developed to heroic proportions, and that his wife was eating her heart out. Thirdly, there was a party which asserted confidently that Adele herself was in love with Pietro Ghisleri, who did not even take the trouble to go and see her more than once or twice a month. The only point upon which opinion was unanimous was Laura Arden's personal and undivided responsibility for all the evil that happened to Adele Savelli. In the first year, so long as Laura never went into the world, the reputation society had given her harmed her very little, and but for the extremely thoughtful kindness of one or two communicative friends, she might have remained in ignorance of it altogether. As it was, she was indifferent, except when she was amused by the still current accusation of possessing the evil eye.

That Laura was an undoubted and dangerous jettatrice was now commonly accepted as a matter of fact. Since Ghisleri and Campodonico had fought, the men had been circumspect in their remarks, but there were few who did not make the sign when they saw her go by. If anything had been needed to prove the fact, there was the issue of the duel. The man who had taken Laura's side had nearly lost his life, though he had fought several times previously without ever receiving any serious hurt. That was proof positive. Adele's illness, too, dated almost from the day of her reconciliation with Laura, and seemed likely to end fatally. Then, almost at the same time, the Contessa had broken with Ghisleri in the most heartless way, as the world said. For the world knew something about that, too, and could have told the whole story most exactly as it had never happened, and detailed several conversations accurately which had never taken place. Poor Ghisleri! The world pitied him sincerely, and hated Laura Arden for being the evil-eyed cause of all his misfortunes. How could he still go to see her, knowing, as he must, how dangerous it was? Had she not almost killed him and Adele, as well as quite killing her husband? People who touched Laura Arden's hand would do well to shut themselves up and lie safe at home for four and twenty hours, until the power of the jettatura was past. Those black eyes of hers meant no good to any one, in spite of her inspired, nun-like looks.

All these things were said, repeated, affirmed, denied, discussed, and said again in the perpetual vicious circle of gossip, while the persons most concerned lived their own lives almost altogether undisturbed by the reports affecting them. No one refused to bow to Laura Arden in the street, although she was supposed to have the power of bringing murder, pestilence, and sudden death on those who went too near her. Nobody ventured to condole with Adele Savelli upon her husband's flighty conduct, still less upon the supposed loss to her of half the Gerano estate. Nor did any one express to Ghisleri anything like sympathy for having been so abominably treated by the Contessa. Such frankness would have been reprehensible and tactless in the extreme.

Adele Savelli's existence was in reality far more wretched than any one could have supposed at that time, and it was destined to be made yet more miserable before a second year had elapsed.

In the spring of the year following that described in the last chapter, the Contessa dell' Armi surprised Ghisleri with a very startling piece of news. They were talking together in the grand stand at one of the May races.

"You know I always tell you everything I hear that seems to be of any importance," she said. "We generally know what to believe. I heard a story last night which is so very odd that there may be some truth in it. As it may be nothing but a bit of mischief, I will not name the person who told me. It is said that more than a year ago, when Adele Savelli thought she was dying out at Gerano, she did not wish to confess to the parish priest, whom she had known all her life, and so she wrote out a general confession and sent it to a priest here in Rome. Is that possible, do you think?"

"Such things have been done," answered Ghisleri. "I do not know what the rule is about them, but the case is possible."

"I was not sure. Now they say that this confession of Adele's never reached its destination, and that a copy of it, if not the original, is in circulation in society, passing quietly from hand to hand. That is a strange story, is it not?"

"A very strange story." Pietro's face was grave, for he remembered many circumstances which this tale might explain. "And what is the confession said to contain?" he asked, after a pause.

"Some extraordinary revelations about Adele's social career; it is even hinted that there is something which might bring very serious consequences upon her if it were known, though what it is no one can find out. That is what I heard, and I thought it worth while to tell you. I think, so far as I am concerned, that I shall deny it. It looks improbable enough, on the face of it. One need not ·say that its very improbability makes one think it cannot be all an invention."

"No. I think you are wise — and charitable as well. If there is any truth in it, Donna Adele will have another illness when it reaches her ears. I suppose people have not failed to say that it was Lady Herbert who had the confession stolen through a servant."

"Strange to say, no one has said that yet, but they will," added Maddalena, with conviction. "Here comes Savelli — take care! Will you put fifty francs for me on the next race? Here is the note."

There was no exaggeration in the Contessa's account. The story was actually in circulation, if the lost confession was not. Unlike the majority of such tales, however, this one was not openly repeated or commented upon where more than two people were present. It disappeared and reappeared in unexpected places like the river Alpheus of old, but its shape was not materially changed. It was told in whispers and under terrible oaths of secrecy, and occasionally — very rarely, indeed — the mere word "Confession," spoken in casual conversation, made people smile and look at each other. There was not even a scandalous little paragraph in any of the daily papers, referring to it. For there are moments when society can keep its secrets, strangely communicative as it is at other times. The houses of Savelli and Gerano were too important and, in a way, too powerful still, to be carelessly attacked. Indeed, society very much preferred that neither the one nor the other should be attacked at all, and behaved so carefully in this one instance, that it was very long before any one discovered that a few weeks before the rumour had been set afloat Francesco Savelli had himself summarily dismissed Adele's maid for the really serious offence of helping her mistress to procure more morphia than the doctor's orders allowed. It was longer still before any one knew that the maid's name was Lucia, and that she had immediately found a situation with Donna Maria Boccapaduli. What was never known to the public at all was that when Savelli sent her out of the house, Lucia had threatened to make certain revelations injurious to the family if he persisted, but that Francesco had not paid the slightest attention to the menace, nor even spoken of it to his wife. He was selfish, cold, and was very far from admirable as a man, but he had been brought up in good traditions, and had the instincts of a gentleman when his own comfort was not endangered by them.

All Ghisleri's suspicions revived at the news Maddalena gave him. Again he took down the medical work he had consulted on the evening when the idea that Adele was in some way guilty of Arden's death had first flashed across his mind, more than a year previously. Again he read the chapter on scarlet fever carefully from beginning to end, and sat down to think over the possibilities in such a case, and once more, after several days of serious consideration, he grew sceptical, and abandoned the attempt to fathom the mystery, if mystery there were. He knew that even without that, Adele might have written many things to her confessor in confidence which, if repeated openly in the world, would do her terrible harm.

He was quite sure that all the infamous slanders on Laura and her husband could ultimately be traced to Adele alone, and it was possible that the stolen document contained a full account of them, though how any sane person could be rash enough to trust such a statement to the post was beyond Ghisleri's comprehension. He did not know that Adele had hardly been responsible for her actions on that day and on many succeeding ones. He had seen, while at Gerano, that she was far from well, but she had been apparently in full possession of her senses. That she should have entrusted to paper the confession that she had wilfully and successfully attempted to make Herbert Arden catch the scarlet fever in her own house, he could not believe, though he thought it possible that the crime might have actually been committed.

He saw strong reasons for thinking that the confession had either been destroyed, or had never really been shown, but that some third person had known something of its contents and had perhaps betrayed the knowledge in a fit of anger. The Contessa dell' Armi could never tell him anything further than she had communicated at the races, and she, as he knew, was intimate with many who would be acquainted with all the current gossip. Strange to say, the story neither developed nor changed; and contrary to his expectations and to Maddalena's own, no one ever suggested that Lady Herbert Arden had been instrumental in causing the confession to be stolen. The men did not talk about the story at all, or, at least, no one ever hinted at it when Ghisleri was present.

Laura saw him often during that winter, though not so regularly as in the first months which had succeeded her husband's death. It was evident to Pietro that the Princess was seriously disturbed by his frequent visits to her daughter, and he willingly restricted them rather than give offence to the elderly lady. As was to be expected, he gradually became more intimate with Laura as time went on. There were strong bonds of friendship between them, and the elements of a deep sympathy.

On more than one occasion each had spoken to the other the whole thoughts of the moment, as people like themselves rarely speak to more than one or two persons who come into their lives. Ghisleri felt that Laura was taking the place of everything in his existence for which he had formerly cared, and the thought of love for any woman had never been so far from him as during that year and the following summer. He began to take a pleasure in small things that concerned her, which he had rarely found in the great emotions of his former life. Occasionally, when he was in a bad temper, he sneered at himself and said that he was growing old, and was only fit to be the guardian of distressed widows and fatherless children. But in spite of such moments, he was sometimes conscious of something not unlike happiness, and he was, on the whole, far more cheerful and less discontented with himself than he had formerly been.

"It is the calm before the storm," he said to Laura one day, with a laugh. "Something appalling is going to happen to me before long."

"I do not believe it," she answered, confidently. "You have lived such an existence of excitement for so many years, that you cannot understand what peace means now that you have tried it. Of course if you go in search of emotions again, you will find them. They grow on every bush, and are as cheap as blackberries."

Laura laughed a little, too, as she made the reply. She thought much of Ghisleri now, and she could hardly realise what her life would be without him. Little Herbert first, then her mother, then Pietro — so the three stood in their respective order when she thought of her rather lonely position in the world. For she was very lonely, even when Arden had been dead eighteen months or more. Her old acquaintances rarely came to see her, and when they did there was a constraint in their manner which told of fear, or dislike, or both. The idle tale of the evil eye which she had so heartily despised once upon a time had done its work. In the following year, when,

in the natural course of events, she would have gone out occasionally in a very quiet way, she found herself almost cut off from society.

Even then she did not care so much as might have been expected. But her mother was in despair. She and the Prince constantly had Laura to dine with them, and always asked at the same time two or three friends with whom she had formerly been more or less intimate. But when it became known that "to dine quite informally" meant that the person invited was to meet Laura Arden, it became very hard to find evenings when any one chanced to be free to accept an invitation to the Palazzo Braccio. Incredible as it may seem, Laura was almost ostracised. No one who has not seen the social ruin which such a reputation as hers brings with it, could believe how complete it can be. Ghisleri ground his teeth in impotent anger against the stupid and cruel superstition which possessed his fellow-citizens, and which in a year or two would inevitably drive Laura to leave Rome, as it had driven others before then. He could do nothing, for the thing was never mentioned before him, and moreover he would be far more careful now than he had ever been not to be drawn into a quarrel on Laura's account.

For he was well aware that his position towards her was anomalous and might very easily be misunderstood in a society where almost all were prejudiced against her. He supposed that the world expected him to marry her when a little more time had passed, and he knew that nothing was further from his thoughts. It was at this time, just two years after Herbert Arden's death, that he began to torment himself, perhaps with better reason than in former days. Knowing as he did what might be said, and what in all likelihood was said about his friendship for Laura, the advisability of discontinuing his visits almost altogether presented itself for consideration, and would not be summarily annihilated by any specious argument. It had formerly seemed to him treacherous even to think of loving Arden's wife, though the thought had rarely crossed his mind even as the wildest hypothesis until some time after his friend had been dead and buried. It now seemed as impossible as ever to love her, but he was obliged by the commonest of common sense considerations to admit that such an affection would not imply the smallest breach of faith to Arden's memory. She was a widow, and any man who knew her had a right to love her and to ask her hand if he so pleased. That right, then, was his also, if ever he should need to avail himself of it. But it was precisely because he did not love Laura Arden that the doubt as to his own conduct arose. As he had no intention of asking her to marry him, could he and should he put her in such a position as to favour speculation in regard to her? Unquestionably he should not. But in that case, what was he to do? The old, ignoble, worldly instinct told him to create a diversion by causing gossip in other directions, where scandal would be easily manufactured, and then to procure himself the liberty of doing what he pleased behind the world's back, so to say. But to his credit it must be admitted that he did not entertain the idea for a moment. It disgusted him and he sought for a solution elsewhere, trying, in his imagination, every conceivable expedient by which he fancied that he might enjoy Laura's society without compromising her in any way. In such cases, however, it is hard to find a stratagem which shall at once satisfy the exigencies of the situation, and an honest man's conscience and sense of honour. He had long given up the custom of going to see Laura every other day, and when she was at her mother's house he was rarely invited, on account of the Princess's prejudice against him, and which no good conduct on his part seemed capable of destroying. To give up seeing Laura altogether was a sacrifice so great that he did not feel strong enough to make it; nor, perhaps, would Laura herself have understood it. Yet, unless he kept away from her for a long time, he knew that the all-wise world would continue to say that he saw her every day. The more he thought about it, the harder he found it to come to any decision. Considering the terms on which he now saw her, and that in former times they had more than once spoken of the same matter, he at last reluctantly resolved to lay the question before her, and to let her decide what he should do. He hated to ask advice of any one, and he detested even the appearance of shifting responsibility upon another. But he could see no other way.

Laura found it as hard to come to a determination as he had. During the last six months he had become almost a necessary part of her life, and she would have turned to him as naturally as he now turned to her for counsel in any difficult situation. Her own character was too simple and straightforward to demand the elaborate explanations of the nature of friendship, which he required of himself; but when he put the difficulty before her she saw it plainly enough.

"For myself, I am perfectly indifferent," she said at last. "I do not see why I should sacrifice anything because there are people bad enough to imagine evil where there is none. You and I need no justification of our friendship, and as I cannot see that I, at least, am much in debt to the world, it is not clear to me why I should care what it says. But I have to consider my mother."

"And yourself, in spite of what you say," answered Ghisleri. "You yourself are first — your mother next."

"Of course you, as a man, look at it in that light. But if it were not for my mother, do not imagine that I should take any notice of what people choose to say. They have said such vile things of me already that they can hardly invent anything worse. If it were perfectly indifferent to you, I do not say but that I might prefer to be careful."

"If what were indifferent?" asked Ghisleri, who did not understand the rather enigmatic speech.

"If you were quite an indifferent person to me — which you are not."

Her eyes met his frankly, and she smiled as she spoke. There was not a trace of timidity or shyness in the speech. She had no reason whatever for concealing the fact that she liked him. But he, on his part, experienced an odd sensation, the meaning of which was by no means clear to him. He could not have told whether it partook more of satisfaction or of disappointment, but it was a distinct emotion of a kind which he had never expected to feel in her presence.

"I am glad you like me," he said. "I should be very unhappy if you did not. I value your friendship more than anything in the world."

"You have earned it if ever a man did," she answered.

"It is enough that I have it. I do not know how I have deserved anything half so precious."

"I know more of what you have done for me than you suppose," said Laura. "Never mind that. The facts are simple enough. We are good friends; we depend, for a certain amount of happiness, upon seeing one another often; because the world does not understand, it expects us to sacrifice our inclinations. For my part, I refuse. There is only one person to be consulted — my mother, who is dearer to me than any friend can be. I will speak to her and make her see the truth. In the mean time do nothing, and forget all this absurd complication. It is only the unreal shadow of an artificial morality which has no foundation nor true existence whatever. You know that better than I."

Ghisleri laughed.

"When you choose to express yourself strongly, you do not lack force," he said. "In the old days I used to fancy that if you spoke out plainly, your sentiments would take the form of a prayer, or a hymn, or something of that sort."

"I am much more human than you think me," Laura answered. "I told you so once, and you would not believe me."

Laura therefore took the matter into her own hands,

and spoke to her mother about it. But the Princess was not easily persuaded, and when the summer came the two were still at variance. A woman like Laura's mother is hard to move when she has allowed a prejudice to take firm root in her mind, and becomes altogether obstinate when that prejudice is tolerably well founded. It was an unquestionable fact that Ghisleri had always been considered a dangerous and rather fast man, whose acquaintance did not improve a woman's reputation, and the Princess of Gerano had no means of understanding his real character. It was a constant wonder to her that Laura should like him. The excellent lady never at all realised that the blood of poor Jack Carlyon was in his daughter's veins, and that, sooner or later, it might make itself felt and produce rather unexpected results. Carlyon's chief characteristic had been his recklessness of consequences. If the Princess had remembered that, she would have understood better why Laura had married Herbert Arden in spite of his deformities, and why she made an intimate friend of Pietro Ghisleri in spite of his reputation. But Laura had never shown any subversive tendencies in childhood or early youth, and her fearless truthfulness, her rather melancholy and meditative nature when a young girl, and her really charitable heart had combined with her pale beauty and saintly eyes to make her mother suppose her infinitely more submissive, obedient, and nun-like than she actually was. After long and patient discussion Laura turned rather suddenly.

"I am not a child, mother," she said. "I know Signor Ghisleri very much better than you, and better than most people can. I know enough of his past life to understand that, although he has done many foolish things and some cruel ones, he is not what I call a bad man, and he has changed very much for the better during the last two years. I will not give up his friendship for the sake of pleasing a set of people who do not even pretend to like me."

"Laura, Laura, take care! You are falling in love with that man, and he is not fit to be your husband."

"In love?" Laura's deep eyes flashed angrily, for the first time in her mother's recollection of her. "You do not know what you are saying, mother."

The Princess sighed, and turned her face away. She attributed the extraordinary change in her daughter to Ghisleri's bad influence, and her prejudice against him increased accordingly. She could not see that the girl had developed in the course of years into a fully grown woman whose character had not turned out to be what she had expected.

And Laura was very angry at the suggestion that she could possibly love Ghisleri — quite unjustifiably so, her mother considered. But here, again, the elder woman did the younger an injustice. Love was very far from Laura's thoughts just then, though her friendship for Pietro was assuming an importance it had not had before.

She did not speak again for some minutes, and when she did, she spoke quietly and without any show of anger. Her tone was not hard, nor was anything she said either cutting or defiant, but the Princess felt that there was to be no appeal from the verdict.

"Dearest mother," she said, "I never did anything and I never will do anything with the intention of displeasing or hurting you. But I have my own life to lead, and my own responsibilities to bear, in my own way. There are some things in which I must judge for myself, and one of them is in the matter of choosing my friends."

"If you had chosen any one but that wild Ghisleri!" sighed the Princess.

"A man who knew him better than either you or I can, loved him dearly, and when he was dying bade him take care of me. The promise then made has been faithfully kept. I will not shut my door to my husband's old friend, who has become mine, merely because the world is what it is — a liar, an evil speaker, and a slanderer."

Laura was a little pale, and the lids drooped over her eyes as though to hide something she would not show.

It was the first time she had ever spoken of Herbert Arden since her child had been born.

If the world had been aware that the matter of her intimacy with Ghisleri had been under discussion, it would have been much delighted by her decision. It would really have been too unkind of Laura to deprive it of a subject of conversation full of never-flagging interest. For not a day passed without a reference to Pietro's devotion to her, and the reference was rarely made without a dash of spite and a little flavouring of social venom. Laura was not to be forgiven for having made Ghisleri prefer her company to that of a score of other women, all, in their own estimation, as good-looking as she, and infinitely more agreeable.

Ghisleri himself accepted the situation, since Laura wished him to do so, though he was constantly uneasy about his own position. It seemed to him that if there were the slightest danger of giving colour to any serious slander on her name it must be his duty to disobey her and altogether discontinue his visits. And he knew also that he would naturally be the last person to hear what was common gossip. The season, however, passed on quietly enough until Lent began, bringing the period of mortification and fasting during which society uses its legs less and its tongues more. This, it may be here again said for the sake of clearness, was the Lenten season of the second year after Arden's death, and after the final break between Ghisleri and Maddalena dell' Armi.

At that time several events occurred which it is necessary to chronicle in greater detail, for the better understanding of this history, and for the more complete refutation of the story which passed commonly current for some time afterwards, and which very nearly brought about the most irreparable consequences.

CHAPTER XXII.

DURING nearly a year a large number of persons had been acquainted with the story of Adele's written confession, but, as has been shown, the matter was considered so serious as to deserve secrecy — the highest social honour which can be conferred on truth. It had never reached the ears of any member of the Savelli or of the Gerano families, and but for Maddalena dell' Armi, Ghisleri himself would never have heard it.

Although Adele was suffering the dire results of her evil deeds in the shape of almost incurable morphinism, the principal cause of her first fears and consequent illness no longer troubled her as it had once done. She now believed that the confession had, after all, caught upon some projection or in some crevice of the masonry in the shaft of the oubliette at Gerano, and that it would never be heard of again. It was incredible, she thought, that if any person had found it and read it, he or she should not attempt to extort a large sum of money for it. But no one appeared to demand anything. That was sufficient proof that no one possessed the document, and it must therefore have remained safely where it had fallen. Her one and only fear was lest something should happen to that part of the castle which might make repairs necessary, and possibly lead to the discovery of the letter. But that was improbable in the extreme. The massive walls had stood as they were during nearly four centuries, and did not show any signs of weakness. As for Lucia, if she ever betrayed the secret, or hinted to her present mistress that there was a secret to betray, and if any story got afloat by her agency, Adele could deny it, and her position was strong enough in the world to force most people to accept her denial. She almost laughed at the idea. The principal statement contained in the confession would seem almost grotesque in its improba-

x

bility. She knew very well that if she ever heard such an action imputed to her worst enemy she would not believe it; she would not even take the trouble to repeat it, because nothing was more foolish than to get the reputation of telling incredible tales. She was quite sure of this, for when she mentally tried the position she found that she could not have given credence to such a legend even if any one had accused Laura Arden of having done the deed. And as she hated Laura with a whole-hearted hatred that did not hesitate at trifles, she considered the argument to be conclusive.

Her hatred grew as the fatal effects of the morphia began to unsettle her brain and disturb the strong power of self-control which had borne her through so many dangers. The necessity for keeping up an outward show of good relations with her step-sister on pain of the severest financial punishment if she angered her father, irritated her extremely. She was well aware that, in spite of the reconciliation and of her own behaviour, the world still chose to believe most of the things she had formerly said of Laura, and that the latter's position was anything but enviable. Nevertheless, Laura seemed to survive very well, and in Adele's opinion had obtained far more than her share of good things. That she had really suffered terribly, in her own way, by the death of her husband, none knew better than Adele, and that, at least, was a satisfaction. But in other ways she was singularly fortunate. Her little boy was as sturdy and strong and sound as any mother could have wished; for deformity which is the result of accident is not inherited. Moreover, there seemed to be little doubt but that the uncle from whom Arden had expected a large fortune would now leave his money to little Herbert. Laura was, of course, decidedly poor at present, judging from Adele's point of view, but in the life she led she needed very little money, and what she had sufficed for her wants. She was evidently quite contented. Then, as though the rest were not enough, she had what Adele called a monopoly of Pietro

Ghisleri, who acted as though he intended to marry her, and whom she received as though she meant to accept him. As Laura Arden, society could treat her as it pleased, but as Ghisleri's wife, society would not only open its arms to her, but would in all likelihood espouse her cause in any future difference or difficulty. Ghisleri would know how to assure her position, and would have no difficulty in making her respected, for he was a most particularly unpleasant person to quarrel with and it was not every one who had Campodonico's luck. Of course, there might yet be time to prevent the marriage, and Adele rashly resolved that if that were possible she would accomplish it.

Of late she had begun to include Ghisleri in her hatred of Laura, having finally given up the attempt to attract him into her immediate circle. He was always the same with her, and never, in the course of years, had seemed willing to advance beyond the limits of ordinary and friendly acquaintance, though she had often tried to draw him further. The ordinary methods failed with him. He could not be tempted into making confidences, which step is one of the first and perhaps the most important in the ordinary, business-like flirtation. He was apparently indifferent to praise as he was to blame, except from one or two persons. He never had an enemy, to ruin whom he needed a woman's help — a short method of reaching intimacy which is not to be despised in dealing with refined bad people. Least of all, was he a man who could be led to compromise himself in a woman's eyes in such a way as to consider it his duty to make love to her. Adele had tried all these approved ways of beginning a serious flirtation with Pietro, but had failed each time, and it enraged her to see that Laura could keep him without any stratagem at all, by sheer force of attraction. For she had no belief at all in their platonic friendship. One or the other, or both, must be in love, for the very simple and well-known reason that a permanent close friendship between man and woman within certain limits of age was an utter impossibility. Laura was perhaps too foolish to realise the fact, but Ghisleri was certainly not the man to forget it. She disliked him because she had not been able to attract him herself, and she hated him for being attracted by Laura.

She now made up her mind that unless she could ruin him in Laura's estimation, the marriage could not be prevented, and she began to revolve the chances for accomplishing her purpose. Her intelligence was not what it had been, for it was subject now to fits of abnormal activity and to a subsequent reaction, in which she was not always perfectly well aware of what was going on around her. In the one state she was rash, over-excited, nervous; in the other she was dull and apathetic, and lost herself in hazy dreams of a rather disconnected character. The consequence was that she found it very hard to hit upon any consecutive plan which presented even the faintest hope of success. Several times she was on the point of doing something very foolish, when she had almost lost control of herself, and she was only saved by the long habit of worldly tact which would probably survive all her other faculties if they were wrecked by the habit which was killing her. But she grew distrustful of herself and of her powers, and a new suffering was added to the many she already had to bear, as she gradually became conscious of the terrible change in herself. She tried to find out all she could about Pietro Ghisleri. At that time all Rome was going mad about making money by speculation, and all sorts of dishonest transactions necessarily went on under cover of greater ones honest in themselves. Adele did her best to ascertain whether Ghisleri were connected with any of them, or with any affair whatever of a nature which could be criticised. But she failed altogether. He looked on at the general rush for money with perfect indifference, and was quite content with the little he already possessed. It struck Adele that a card scandal would do him as much harm as anything, and she made inquiries as to his fondness for play, but was informed that he rarely played at all, and generally lost a little if he did.

He was hard to catch. So far as she could learn, he had changed his mode of life very considerably during the past two years. It was quite certain that he had definitely broken with Maddalena dell' Armi, though no one was really sure of the exact date at which the rupture had taken place. They were both clever people who kept their secrets to themselves on the simple plan that, if a thing is not to be known, it should not be told. Laura was the only other woman whom he visited regularly, and his doings were far too well known to make it possible to float a scandal about him in connexion with some one else, which should reach Laura's ears. Besides, Laura would not care. She was quite capable of not taking the slightest notice, just as in former times she had not cared whether he saw Maddalena every day or not. All she wanted, thought Adele, was that Ghisleri should be at her feet — and there he was.

At last she hit upon the rather wild plan of asking Ghisleri himself what she had better do. There was something diabolical in the idea of taking his own advice in order to ruin him, which appealed to her in the present state of her brain and nerves. They often met in society, and she caught sight of him that very night at a Lenten party in Casa Montevarchi — one of the last ever given in that house, by the by, for the family was ruined soon afterwards. She followed him in the crowd and touched his shoulder with her fan.

"Will you give me your arm?" she asked. "Thanks. I want to sit down somewhere. There is a sofa over there."

"You still come to these talking matches, I see," said Ghisleri, as they sat down. "It must be for the sake of saying something interesting, for it can certainly not be in the hope of hearing anything of the kind."

"You can still make sharp speeches," laughed Adele. "I thought my step-sister had converted you, and that you were turning into a sort of Saint Propriety."

"Oh, you thought so," said Pietro, coolly. "Well, you see you were mistaken. There is as little of propriety about me as usual, or of saintship either."

He looked at the worn and dilapidated features of the woman beside him, at her hollow cheeks and lustreless eyes, and he almost pitied her. He wondered how she had the courage to keep up the comedy and to face the world as she did, night after night, old before her youth was half over, ugly when she had been pretty but two years earlier, weary always, and haunted by the shadow of the poison to which she was a slave.

"You need not be angry," she answered. "I did not mean anything disagreeable. I wish you would say more sharp things, it is refreshing to hear a man talk after listening to a pack of little boys."

"Why do you listen to them?"

"They amuse me for five minutes, and when I have tolerated them as long as that I cannot get rid of them. Then I begin to long for a little serious talk with a man like you — a man one can ask a question of with the hope of getting a reasonable answer."

"You are very good to put it in that way," said Ghisleri. "Have you any particular question to ask me now? I will be as intensely reasonable as I can in my reply, on condition that it is a thing of which I know nothing whatever."

"What an extraordinary restriction!" exclaimed Adele.

"Not at all. If I should know anything about the matter in hand it would be sure to be so little that it would confuse me and hamper the free working of my imagination, which might otherwise produce interesting and even startling effects. You may have heard that a little knowledge is dangerous. That is the meaning of the proverb."

"I knew I should get something original from you. You always say something which no one else would."

"And you always discover in me some new and beautiful quality which had escaped my notice," answered

Ghisleri. "Is it with a view to getting some particular sort of answer to the question you meditate, that you flatter me so nicely before asking it?"

"Of course," laughed Adele. "What did you expect? But I do not think you would answer the question at all. You would give me a dissertation on something else and then go away and leave me to be torn to pieces by the little boys again."

"What an awful death!" laughed Ghisleri. "I will not leave you. I will protect you against whole legions of little boys."

"You look as if you could. You are quite as strong as ever now, are you not? You never feel any pain from your wound?"

"Never," answered Pietro, indifferently. "Was that the grave question to which you wanted a serious and well-considered reply?"

"Do not be absurd!" cried Adele, with a laugh. "One has to make civil inquiries of that kind sometimes. It is a social duty. Even if I hated you I should ask if you were well."

"Of course. The old-fashioned poisoners in the middle ages did that. It was of no use to waste expensive poison on a man who was ill and might die without it. They practised economy."

"What a horrible idea!" exclaimed Adele, shuddering.

"Horrible ideas were the fashion then," pursued Ghisleri. "I have thought a great deal about those times since you showed me those interesting places at Gerano, nearly two years ago. The modern publisher of primers would have made his fortune under the Borgia domination. Fancy the titles: 'Every man his own executioner, a practical guide for headsmen, torturers and poisoners, by a member of the profession (diploma) with notes, diagrams, and a special table of measurements and instructions for using the patent German rack, etc.' Does not that sound wildly interesting? They would have had it on the drawing-room table in every castle. It would have been a splendid book for hawkers.   Gerano made me think of it."

Adele laughed in rather a forced way, and her eyes moved uneasily, glancing quickly in one direction and another.

"You would have been a dreadful person in those times, I am quite sure," she said.   "You would have been a monster of cruelty."

"Of course I should.   So should we all.   But we manage those little things so easily now, and so much more tastefully."

"Exactly," said Adele, who saw her chance and an opportunity of turning the conversation at the same time. "I would like your views upon modern social warfare. If you wished to ruin your enemy, how would you go about it?"

"A man or a woman?" asked Ghisleri, calmly.

"Oh, both.   A man first.   It is always harder to injure a man than a woman, is it not?"

"So they say.   Do you wish to kill the man or to ruin him altogether, or only to injure him in the eyes of the world?"

"Take the three in the other order," suggested Adele. "A mere injury first — and the rest afterwards."

"Very well.   I have something very neat in the killing line — to use the shopkeeper style.   I will keep it to the end.   Let me see.   You wish to do a man a great injury — enough, say, to make a woman who loves him turn upon him.   Is that it?"

"Yes, that would do very well," said Adele, as though she were discussing the fashion of a new frock.

"If you happen to be a good hand at forgery," answered Ghisleri, with perfect equanimity, "write a number of letters purporting to be from him to another woman. Put anything you like into them, take them to the woman who loves him, and ask a large sum for them.   She will probably pay it and leave him.   You will accomplish your object and earn money at the same time.   If you cannot forge his handwriting, forge that of an imaginary woman — that is easy enough — and follow the same course as before. It is almost sure to succeed."

"What a surpassingly diabolical scheme!" exclaimed Adele, with a laugh.

"Yes, I flatter myself it is not bad. Of course you can make the matter public if only you are sure of the forgery being good, or of an imaginary woman being forthcoming at the right moment. But, on the whole, the finest way of ruining a man before the world is to steal his money. No reputation can stand poverty and slander at the same time."

"But it is not always easy to steal a man's money," objected Adele.

"Oh, yes, unless a man is very rich. Bring a suit against his title, and if he fights it, the lawyers will eat up all he has. Then you can play the magnanimous part and say that you give up the suit out of pity for him. That is very pretty, too. But the prettiest of all is the new way of killing people, because nobody can possibly find you out."

"What do you make them die of?" asked Adele nervously.

"Cholera — typhus — fever, almost anything you please. It is a convenient way because the epidemic of the day is generally the most ready to hand. What did you say? I beg your pardon, I thought you spoke. Yes, it is delightful, and in most cases I believe it is almost sure to succeed. I dined with Gouache last night, and Professor Wüsterschinder, the great German authority on cutting up live rabbits, you know, was there. A charming man — speaks French like a human being, and understands Italian well. I liked him very much. The conversation turned upon murder. You know Gouache has a taste for horrors, being the gentlest and kindest of men. The professor told a long story of a doctor who murdered the father, mother, and aunt of a girl whom none of the three would let him marry. He did it in the course of medical treatment, with three different vegetable poisons — masterly, the professor said. There was an inquiry and they dug everybody up again, and all that sort of thing, but no one could positively prove anything and the doctor married the girl after all."

"You seem full of horrors this evening," said Adele, moving one shoulder in a restless, jerking way which was becoming a habit.

"I always am," answered Ghisleri, turning his cold blue eyes on her. "I know the most horrible things and am always just on the point of saying them."

"Please do not!" exclaimed Adele, shrinking away from him into the corner of the sofa, almost in physical fear of him now.

"I was telling you about the cholera trick, or I was going to tell you. The other story was only the prelude. After giving it to us with a number of details I have forgotten, Professor Wüsterschinder launched out about the wonders of science, as those men always do, and positively made me uncomfortable with the numbers of unfortunate rabbits and puppies he cut to shreds in his conversation. Then he came to the point and began to explain how easy it is to murder people by natural means like typhus. It is done by taking the — good Heavens, Donna Adele, what is the matter!"

Adele had uttered a short, low cry, and her face had turned very white. Her lips were contorted in an expression of anguish such as Pietro had never seen, and her fingers were twisting together as though they would break.

"Can I do anything?" he asked, anxiously. He feared she was going to be seized by some kind of convulsion, but the woman's strong will helped her even then.

"Hold my fan before my arm," she managed to say, and she felt for something in her pocket with her right hand.

In a moment she produced a tiny syringe with a point like a needle, and a little bottle. With incredible quickness and skill she filled the syringe, pricked the skin on her left arm, and ran the point into it, and then pressed the tiny piston slowly till it would go no further. In little more than one minute she had put everything into her pocket again, and taking her fan from Ghisleri's hand, leaned back in the corner of the sofa, with a sigh of relief.

"I am afraid I made you nervous," he said, in a tone of apology.

"Not at all," she answered. "I had forgotten to take my morphia before coming — that was all. I suffer terribly with pains in my head when I do not take it."

"And is the pain gone already?" asked Ghisleri, in some surprise, and wondering how she would answer.

"Oh, no! But it will be gone very soon. I am quieter when I know I have taken the morphia. Of course," she said, with a forced laugh, "you must not suppose that I take it often, not even every day. I believe it is very bad in large quantities."

"Of course." Ghisleri could hardly help smiling at the poor attempt to disclaim any slavery to the fatal drug, contradicting, as it did, what she had said but a moment before.

For the third time since Arden's death the conviction came upon him that Adele had been the responsible cause of it, and this time it was destined to be permanent. The theory of coincidence was exhausted, and he abandoned it. The stories he had told her about Professor Wüsterschinder, the great German authority, were quite true, and Ghisleri's eyes had been opened on the previous evening to the possibilities of evil disclosed by modern science. He was not yet sure of what Adele had done, but he was convinced that the general nature of the process she had employed to communicate the fever to Arden was similar to those which the professor had described, and that she must, in all probability, have got the necessary information from a scientific book or article on the subject, which she had either procured expressly, or which had perhaps fallen under her eyes by chance.

She, on her part, had been desperately frightened, as she had good cause to be, for it was almost inconceivable to her that he could have accidentally gone so near the mark as he was going when her cry had stopped him. She felt that if he had pronounced the next half a dozen words, she must have gone mad there and then in the drawing-room where she sat, and she had instinctively prevented him proceeding any further. Then in the convulsion of terror she felt, she had resorted to her sole comforter, the morphia, and it had not played her false. In a short time its influence was at work and indeed the mere act of taking it was in itself soothing in the extreme. She felt herself growing calm again and more able to face the new difficulties and terrors that had arisen in her path. And they were many. She had no doubt now that Ghisleri had either read the lost confession or had spoken with some one who had. It was appalling to think that in that very room there might be a score of persons who knew what that letter contained as well as he. The morphia helped her wonderfully. But it was clear that Ghisleri had her in his power. An idea flashed across her mind. It was so simple that she wondered how she had not thought of it before. The letter had really fallen to the bottom of the shaft. Ghisleri, interested perhaps in the story of Paolo Braccio, had strolled down to the dungeon again by himself and had seen the paper lying there. In that case he alone knew of its existence or of its contents, besides herself and Lucia. The thought was so agreeable, compared with the alternative of supposing that all society knew the details of her evil deeds, that she clung to it. Then she looked at the man who, as she supposed, had power to dispose of her existence at his pleasure, and she wondered whether he had a price. All men had, she had heard. But as it seemed to her now, this particular man would not be like the generality, or else the price he would set on her letter would be of

the kind which she could not possibly pay, because she
would never be able to obtain for him what he might
want. The feeling she had known in the first months of
her torment returned upon her now, and very strongly —
the awful feeling of degradation compared even with the
worst of the people she knew. In her eyes, Ghisleri,
with all his misdeeds, seemed a being of superior purity
and goodness. He had never done what she had done,
nor anything approaching to it in the most distant way.
He had faced men in fair fight, and hurt them, and been
almost mortally hurt himself, but he had never stabbed
an enemy in the back nor dealt a blow in the dark. He
had loved more than one woman, and had been loved in
return, but no one had ever hinted that a woman's confidence had passed his lips, nor that he had ever spoken
lightly of any woman's good name. If he had done evil,
he had done it fairly, defiantly, above board, and in the
light of day. Adele envied him with all her heart as he
sat there beside her, confident in his own honourable reputation — as honour is reckoned in the world — and free to
go and to come and to do what seemed good in his own
eyes without a second thought of the consequences or the
least fear of betraying himself. There was not at that
moment one person in the room with whom she would
not have been only too glad to exchange places, station,
fortune, name, reputation — everything. And she fancied Ghisleri knew it, as indeed he almost did, and she
feared to meet his eyes.

The silence had lasted so long that it was fast becoming
awkward. It was rarely indeed that Ghisleri forgot the
social duty of destroying silence ruthlessly the moment
it appears, with any weapon which comes to hand, from
a feather to a bombshell. But on the present occasion
his thoughts were so many and so complex as to fill his
mind completely for a few minutes, so that all outward
considerations sank into insignificance. The effort was
made at last by Adele, the one of the two who had by
far the most at stake in playing her part.

"Are you aware," she began, with an attempt at play-
fulness which was almost weird, "that you have not
spoken a single word during the last quarter of an hour?
Have you quite forgotten my existence? My dear friend,
you are growing almost rude in your old age!"

"Good manners were never anything but an affectation
with me," answered Ghisleri. "But you are quite right.
There are little conventions of that sort which must be
respected if society is to keep together and hold up its
head — though why it should not lay down that same head
and let itself go to pieces is beyond my comprehension.
Present company is always excepted, you know — so you
and I would survive as glorious and immortal relics of a
by-gone civilisation."

He hardly knew what he was saying, but he let the
words run on with the easy habit of talking and saying
nothing which sometimes saves critical situations for
those who possess it and which can be acquired by almost
any one who is not shy. The first step in studying that
useful accomplishment is to talk when everybody else is
talking, and not to pay the slightest attention to the
sounds which pass one's lips. Any noise will do, bad or
good — as the bearer of the good news to Aix put it —
only, if possible, from the first let the noise take the shape
of words. As every one else is talking, no one will hear
you. Some of Mother Goose's rhymes are excellent for
such practice, but those who prefer to recite the Eton
grammar will obtain a result quite as satisfactory in the
end. No one listens, and it makes no difference. You
will then get a reputation for joining cheerfully in the
talk of the day. But if you sit looking at your plate
because you have nothing to say, the givers of dinner
parties will curse you in their hearts, and will rarely ask
you to eat their food, which treatment, though it will
ultimately prolong your life, will not contribute to your
social success. Gradually, if you practise the system
assiduously, you will be able to walk alone, so to say.
By attraction, your unconscious phrases will become

exactly like those of your neighbours. You will then only need to open your mouth, stretch the vocal chords, and supply the necessary breath, and admirably constructed inanities will roll out, even when everybody is listening, and while you are gaining time to select in your mind a sufficiently cutting epithet with which to adorn your friend Smith Tompkins's name when it is mentioned, or while you are nicely calculating the exact amount of money you can ask the said Smith Tompkins to lend you the next time you have lost at baccarat.

CHAPTER XXIII.

THE state of certainty in regard to Adele's doings, at which Ghisleri had now arrived, seemed to make any action in the matter useless if not practically impossible. He ascertained without difficulty the law concerning such attempts to do bodily injury as he was quite sure she had made. The crime was homicide when the attempt led to fatal results. There was no doubt of that. On the other hand, even if it should seem advisable to bring Adele to justice, and to involve both the Savelli and Gerano families in an affair which would socially ruin them for at least one whole generation, in case Adele were convicted, yet the positive proofs would be very hard to produce, and the ultimate good to be gained would be infinitesimally small compared with the injury done to innocent persons. The best course was to maintain the most absolute secrecy and to discourage as far as possible any allusions others might make to the mystery of the lost letter. Ghisleri, too, understood human nature far too well to suppose that Adele had in the first instance desired or expected to kill Herbert Arden. She had most probably only meant to cause Laura the greatest possible anxiety and trouble by bringing a dangerous illness upon her husband. Scarlet fever, as is well known, is not often fatal to adults in Italy, and such cases as Arden's in which death ensues within eight and forty hours, are so rare as to be phenomenal in any part of the world. But Ghisleri had found them described in the book he chanced to possess, under the head of "rudimentary cases ending fatally"—and it was there stated that they were the consequence of "a very violent infection." Adele, in practising some one of the methods of fever-poisoning which the great professor had described so vividly at Gouache's, had of course not known exactly what result she was about to produce. She had assuredly not foreseen that Arden would die, and had very probably not even believed that he would really take the fever at all. As for the wish to do harm, Pietro explained that naturally enough. He knew that the dinner of reconciliation must have been brought about by the Prince of Gerano, and he guessed that in the interview between the father and the daughter Adele had been deeply humiliated by being forced to yield and by the necessity of openly retracting what she had said of Arden and Laura. In a woman whose impulses were naturally bad, and whose mind had never been very well balanced, it was not very hard to explain how the idea had presented itself, if chance had at that moment thrown the necessary information into her way. The whole story was now sufficiently connected from first to last, and Ghisleri, as he thought over it, saw how all the details he remembered confirmed the theory. He recollected the doctor's remarks about the case, and how surprised he had been by its extraordinary violence. He recalled vividly all that he had heard of Adele's behaviour immediately after the dinner party, and his own impression of her appearance when he had met her in the street and had recommended her a soporific, was extremely distinct, as well as her behaviour whenever, in the course of the past two years, he had said anything intentionally, or not, which she could construe as referring to her crime. The chain was complete from the beginning to the end and her present dangerous state was the direct consequence of the very first slander she had cast on Laura Arden.

What Ghisleri felt when he was fully persuaded that Adele Savelli had brought about the death of his best friend, is not easily described. In natures like his, the desire for vengeance is very strong — strongest when most justified. The instinct which demands life for life is always present somewhere in the natural human heart and, on the whole, the great body of human opinion has in most ages approved it and given it shape in law — or sanction, where laws have been or still are rudimentary. Ghisleri was not therefore either unusually cruel or blood-thirsty in wishing that Adele might expiate her crime to the full. But in this case, even if capital punishment had not been abolished in Italy, the law would not have applied it, and personal revenge without the law's assistance being out of the question in the nineteenth century, Pietro could hardly have invented a worse fate than actually awaited his friend's murderess. There was a grand logic, as it seemed to him, in the implacable retribution which was pursuing and must before long overtake Adele Savelli. He could enjoy the whole satisfaction of the most complete vengeance without so much as raising a finger to hasten it. That was the first result of his cogitations, and he was very well pleased with it. He bought books containing accounts of morphinism and calmly tried to calculate how long Adele had to live, what precise phenomena her end would exhibit, and to decide whether she would lose her mind altogether before the physical consumption of the tissues destroyed her body.

But before long he became disgusted with himself, for he was not cruel by nature, though capable of doing very cruel things under the influence of passion. It was probably not from any inherent nobility of character, but rather out of the commonest pity combined with a rather uncommon though material refinement of taste, that he at

Y

last turned from his study and contemplation of Adele's sufferings and resolutely put her and them out of his mind.

"Heaven can do with her what it pleases. I will think no more about it," he said to himself one day, and the saying was profoundly characteristic of the man.

He had never been an unbeliever since the last years of his boyhood, when, like many boys in our times, he had already fancied himself a man, and had thought it manly to believe in nothing. But such a state of mind was not really natural to him, nor even possible for any length of time. Of his intimate convictions he never spoke, for they concerned no one, and no one had a right to judge him. But that he really had certain convictions no one who knew him well could doubt, and on certain occasions they undeniably guided his actions.

Laura Arden had not heard even the faintest hint about the lost letter, and it became one of Ghisleri's principal occupations to keep the story from her. She was, of course, not in the way of hearing it unless some unusually indiscreet person should take pains to acquaint her with it; but such people are unfortunately not uncommon, and Pietro knew that at any moment Laura might hear something which would make her look at her husband's death in a new light. The shock would be terrible, he knew, and he did not like to think of it. He little suspected that when the story reached her ears it would be so distorted as to convey a very different meaning to her, nor did he guess the part he himself was to play in what followed.

A month and more passed away without any incident of importance. He saw Laura constantly and met Adele occasionally in society. The latter always greeted him with a great affectation of cordiality, but evidently avoided conversing with him alone. Her expression when she looked at him was invariably smiling, but the eyes which had grown so strange under the daily influence of the poison had something in them on the rare occasions when they met his that might have warned him had he suspected danger. But he anticipated nothing of that sort for himself. He supposed rather that she felt herself to be in his power and feared him, so that she would carefully avoid doing anything which might provoke him. But in this he was very much mistaken. He neither knew that she believed her lost letter to be in a safe place, where no one could find it and where it must ultimately turn to dust, nor realised how far her mind was already unbalanced. Still less did he understand all the causes for which she so sincerely hated him. Even had he felt that she was an active adversary, he would have undervalued her power to do him harm.

Adele meditated her last stroke a long time. Though Ghisleri had frightened her terribly during the conversation she had herself asked for on that memorable evening in Casa Montevarchi, he had also suggested the very idea of which she had long been in search. She turned it over, twisted it, so to say, into every possible shape, and at last reached a definite plan. There was already something of madness in the scheme she ultimately adopted, and which she carried out with an ingenuity and secrecy almost beyond belief.

Laura Arden was surprised one morning by receiving a letter addressed to her in an unknown handwriting, which she at once judged to be that of a woman, though it was small, cramped, and irregular.

"Madam," the letter began, "I apply to your well-known charitable heart in the greatest conceivable distress. My husband, who was for a long time in the service of one of the noblest Roman families as a clerk in the steward's office, lost his position in the ruin which has lately overtaken that most excellent house. He walks the streets from sunrise to sunset in search of employment, and returns at night to contemplate the spectacle of misery afforded him by his starving family. Misery is upon us, and there is no bread, nor even the commonest food, such as day labourers eat, with which to quiet the piteous cries of our children."

There followed much more to the same effect. The style was quite that of a woman of the class to which the writer claimed to belong, and the appeal for help, though couched in rather flowery language, had a ring of truth in it which touched Laura's heart. It had, indeed, been copied, with a few alterations, from a genuine letter which Adele Savelli had chanced to receive. The concluding sentences stated that the applicant, who had never known poverty before was ashamed, for her husband's sake, to give the name which had so long been respectable. If Lady Herbert Arden was moved to pity and would give anything — the very smallest charity — would she put it into an envelope and send it to 'Maria B.' addressed to the general post-office?"

Laura hesitated a moment, and then slipped a five franc note with her card into an envelope and addressed it as requested in the letter. On the next day but one she received a second, full of gratitude, and expressing the most humble and sincere thanks for the money, but not asking for anything more. This also was copied from a genuine communication, and the style was unmistakably the same. Adele had answered the first by sending a larger sum than Laura had given, in order that the reply might be relatively effusive.

A week passed, and Laura heard no more from Maria B., and had almost forgotten the incident when a third letter came, imploring further assistance. Laura was far from rich, and gave all she could in the way of charity to such poor people as she considered to have an especial claim upon her consideration. On this occasion, therefore, she made no reply. This was exactly what Adele expected, and suited her plan admirably. After a sufficient time had elapsed to make it quite plain that Laura did not intend to answer the second appeal, another communication came through the post.

The tone this time, was, if possible, more humble and piteous than before. After enumerating and discanting upon the horrible sufferings the family underwent, and declaring that unless some charitable Christian would give assistance in some shape, even were it but a loaf of bread, the whole household must inevitably perish, and after adding that father, mother, and all four children — the latter of tender age — expected to be turned into the street by a hard-hearted landlord, Maria B. made a distinct proposition. Contemptible as it must appear in the eyes of a great and rich English lady to take advantage of having discovered a secret in order to beg a charity, necessity knows no law. The ex-clerk was in possession of certain letters written by a near connexion of Lady Herbert's to a person with whom the latter was intimately acquainted, and whom, it was commonly reported, she was about to marry. These letters, five in number, referred to a transaction of a very peculiar nature, which it would be advisable not to make public, for the sake of the persons concerned. It was very far from Maria B.'s thoughts to degrade herself by setting a price upon the documents. If Lady Herbert cared to possess them they should be hers, and any small reward she might be willing to give would be humbly and thankfully accepted. In order that she might judge of the nature of the letters in question, Maria B. enclosed a copy of the one last written before the transaction alluded to had been concluded. Lady Herbert would be able to understand the names from the initials used by the copyist.

Laura, even then, did not suspect in the least what she was about to find. She unfolded the separate sheet which had dropped from the letter when she had opened it, and began to read with an expression of curiosity and some amusement.

"MY DEAR G. : — Of course I understand your position perfectly and I have known you long enough to be sure that you will take every advantage of it, short of doing me an open injury, which would hardly be for your own good. I know perfectly well, also, where you found the paper at Gerano, for I went to the spot myself to look for it, and it was gone. You had been there before me — by chance, no doubt, since you could not possibly guess that there was anything there worth finding. It is quite clear that if you really circulate that letter among our mutual friends, you will subject me to the ridicule of all Rome and to an amount of humiliation which I am not prepared to endure. You see I am quite willing to come to terms. But I think your demand is really out of all proportion to the circumstances. A hundred thousand francs for a miserable scrap of paper! Absurd, my friend. You are not the accomplished scoundrel I took you for if you suppose that I will pay that. Fifty thousand is the most I can possibly offer you. If you are satisfied with that, wear a gardenia in your coat to-night at the Frangipani dance. As for my behaviour in public, you need not warn me. I can keep my countenance almost as well as you. A. S."

The letter dropped from Laura's hands before she had read to the end. An instant later she took it up again and tore it to the smallest shreds. She had heard of cases of blackmail, but never of anything so infamous as this. She did not hesitate long, but wrote within the hour a few lines to Maria B. in which she warned the latter not to dare to proceed with her abominable fraud, and rather rashly threatened her with the law if she attempted anything further of the same kind. As for speaking to Ghisleri about it, the idea never crossed her thoughts.

Again three days passed. Then, one morning, the post brought a large and rather bulky letter, registered and addressed in a round, ornate, clerk's hand. Adele had got the address written at the post-office on pretence that her own handwriting was not legible enough. Laura supposed that the missive contained a business communication from her banker, and opened it without the least suspicion. It contained three greyish-blue envelopes of the paper now very commonly used for daily correspondence. All three were opened in a peculiar way, and precisely as Laura had more than once seen Ghisleri open a letter in her presence. He had a habit of tearing off a very thin strip along one edge, with so much neatness as almost to give the paper the appearance of having been cut with a sharp instrument. All three were addressed to him, moreover, in Adele Savelli's handwriting, without any attempt at disguise. Laura held them in her hand, turned them over, and saw the tiny prince's coronet over a single initial which Adele had used for years. There was no mistaking the authenticity of everything about the envelopes. Laura's heart stood still. There was no word of explanation from her former correspondent, but Laura recollected that the latter had said that the letters were five in number, whereas these were only three. It was clear that the remaining two had been kept back as a tacit threat in case the request for money were not complied with. Laura's first impulse was to treat them as she had treated the copy Maria B. had at first sent her, and to tear them into minute shreds, without so much as glancing at the contents. But a moment's reflection made her change her mind. She slipped them all back into the large envelope and locked them up in the drawer of her writing-table, putting the key into her pocket. Then she wrote a note to Ghisleri, asking him to come and see her as soon as possible, and despatched Donald with it immediately.

She sat down to wait, strangely affected by what had happened. It is hardly to be wondered at, if the whole thing seemed inexplicable. Even at first she could not suspect Pietro Ghisleri. She would hardly have believed him capable of such an action as he was accused of had she seen him write the letters to which these of Adele were supposed to be answers. And yet those answers were there in the drawer, within reach of her hand. She had not the slightest doubt but that the original of which she had already seen a copy was amongst them. She could take it out and read it if she pleased. It was damning evidence — but she would not have believed in Ghisleri's guilt for twice as much proof as that. The one thing she was forced to admit was that Adele had really written the letters, though when, or for what purpose, or in what connexion, she could not guess. The whole thing might turn out to be some Carnival jest carried on by correspondence, and of which she had never heard. That was the only explanation she could find, as she waited for Pietro Ghisleri. He came within the hour.

"Has anything happened?" he asked, as he took her hand. "I thought there was something anxious about your note."

"Something very strange has happened," she answered, looking into his bright blue eyes, and acknowledging for the hundredth time that she would believe him in spite of any testimony to the contrary. "Sit down," she said. "I have something to give you which seems to belong to you. I will tell you the story afterwards."

She opened the drawer again and handed him the envelope. He looked at it in surprise.

"Am I to read what is inside?" he asked.

"See for yourself."

He took out the letters and looked at them as he had first looked at the outer address. Then, realising that they were addressed to himself, his expression changed. He recollected Adele's handwriting though she had rarely written to him anything more than an invitation, and he knew the paper on which she wrote. But where or when he had received these particular ones, or how they had got into Laura's hands, was a mystery.

"What are they?" he asked. "Are they old invitations? Why have they been sent to you?"

"I believe them to be forgeries," said Laura, "or else that they refer to some standing jest you and she once may have kept up for a time. I have not read them, but I have read a copy of one of them which was sent me, and I know what they are about. I will tell you the whole story afterwards. See for yourself, as I said before."

Ghisleri drew out the first sheet.

"If they are forgeries, they are very cleverly done," he said, with a laugh. "The person has even imitated my way of opening a letter."

His face grew very grave, as Laura watched it while he was reading, and his brow knit together angrily. He read the second and the third, and she could see his anger rising visibly in his eyes as he silently looked at her each time he had finished one of them. When he had reached the end of the last he did not speak for some moments.

"Did you say that you knew what these letters were about?" he asked at length, in a steady, cold voice.

"I think so. I read a copy of one of them almost without knowing what I was doing. Adele pretends that you are trying to get money from her for a letter of hers you found at Gerano."

"Yes, that is what they are about. It is her doing, but it is my fault."

"Your fault!" exclaimed Laura. "But surely there never even was such a letter as she refers to. Do you understand at all?"

"Yes, I understand much too well. She has done this for a distinct purpose. Tell me in the first place one thing. Do you still trust me in the face of such evidence as this?"

"I trust you as much as ever," answered Laura.

"Thank you," he said simply, and he looked into her deep eyes a moment before he continued. "There are two stories to tell, yours and mine. Tell yours first. Tell me how you came by the copy you speak of. Who sent it to you, and when?"

As briefly as she could, Laura gave him all the details she could remember from the day she had received the first request for help from Maria B. It was painful to her to repeat what she could of the substance of the copy sent her, but she went through with it to the end.

"That letter is not among these," said Ghisleri, thoughtfully. "It is one of the two which have been kept back for future use. Now let me tell you what I can remember. Do not be surprised that I should never have told you the story before. Since you can trust me in such a matter as this, you will believe me when I say that there was a good reason for not telling you."

He gave a concise account of the conversation which had taken place between himself and Adele at the Montevarchi's party, omitting only what referred to his own suspicions concerning the manner of Arden's death. If possible, he meant always to conceal that side of the question from Laura. But it was necessary to tell her something about the document constantly mentioned in the letters.

"There is a story in circulation," he said, "to the effect that when Donna Adele was ill at Gerano nearly two years ago, she was unwilling to confess to the parish priest, and wrote a confession to be sent to her confessor in Rome. A servant stole it, says the story, and it is supposed to be in existence, passing from hand to hand in society. It is quite possible that she believes that I bought it of the thief. But I doubt even that. She has most probably regained possession of it before attempting this stroke. And this is almost what I suggested to her in a general way, and laughing, as one way of ruining a man. I remember my own words — an injury that would make a woman who loves a man turn upon him. Substitute friendship for love, and the case is almost identical."

"Yes," Laura answered thoughtfully. "Substitute friendship for love." She hardly knew why she repeated the words, and a moment later a faint colour rose in her cheeks.

"She has done this thing, therefore, with the deliberate intention of ruining me in your eyes," said Ghisleri.

"And she has utterly failed to do so, or even to change my opinion of you a little. But it is very well done. There are people who would have been deceived. The idea of forging — it is not forging — of writing imaginary letters to you herself is masterly."

"I do not think she is quite sane. The morphia she takes is beginning to affect her brain. She does not always know what she is doing."

"You take far too merciful and charitable a view," answered Laura, with some scorn.

"No, on the contrary, if she were quite what she used to be, she would be more dangerous — she would not make mistakes. Two or three years ago she would not have gratuitously thrown herself into danger as she has now. She would not have made such a failure as this."

"And what a failure it is! Do you know? It was very puzzling at first. To know positively that you never could have received those letters, and yet to see that they are still in existence, addressed to you, and opened in your peculiar way. I felt as though I were in a dream."

"I wonder you did not feel inclined to believe me guilty. The evidence was almost as strong as it could be. In your position I should have hesitated."

"Would you have believed such a thing of me, if it had been just as it is, only if the letters had gone to you instead of to me?" asked Laura.

"Certainly not!" exclaimed Ghisleri, with strong emphasis. "That would be quite another matter."

"I do not see that it would. You would have been exactly in my position, as you hinted a moment ago."

"I was not thinking of you. The day I do not believe in you I shall not believe in God. You are the last thing I have left to believe in — and the best, my dear friend."

He was very much in earnest, as Laura knew from the tone of his voice. But she would not look at him just then, because she felt that he was looking at her, and she preferred that their eyes should not meet.

"Will you do anything about this?" she asked, after a pause, and not referring to what he had last said. "Will you destroy those vile things?"

"Since they are addressed to me, I suppose I have a right to do so," answered Ghisleri, and he began slowly to tear up the sheets of the first letter.

"There can be no doubt about their being genuine?" asked Laura, with sudden emotion.

"Not at all, I should say. But you are the best judge of that. You should know her handwriting better than I. If you like," he added, with a short laugh, "I will go and show them to her and ask her if she wrote them. Shall I?"

"Oh, no! Do not do that!" exclaimed Laura, who knew that he was quite capable of following such a course as he suggested.

There was apparently nothing to be done. Laura believed that any attempt to make use of the two remaining letters would be as abortive as the first, and there could certainly be no use in keeping those which had been sent. On the contrary, it was possible that if they were preserved, chance might throw them into hands in which they might become far more dangerous than they were.

"Shall I write to Maria B., whoever she is?" asked Laura.

"You might send her another five francs," answered Ghisleri, grimly. "It would show her how much you value the documents she has for sale."

"I will," said Laura, with a laugh. "How furious she will be! Of course it is Adele who gets these things."

"Of course. Five francs is quite enough."

And Laura, little knowing or guessing how it would be used against her, sent a five-franc note with her card in an envelope and addressed it. On the card she had written in pencil, "For Maria B., with best thanks."

"There is one other thing I would like to do," she said. "But I do not know whether you would approve. It would give me such satisfaction — you know I am only a woman, after all."

"What is that?" asked Ghisleri, "and why should you need my approval?"

"Only this. To-morrow, and perhaps the next day, when she is quite sure I must have received those letters, I would like to drive with you in an open carriage where we should be sure to meet Adele. I would give anything to see her face."

Ghisleri laughed. The womanly side of Laura's nature was becoming more apparent of late, and its manifestations pleased and surprised him. He thought Laura would hardly have seemed human if she had not wished to let Adele see how completely the attempt had failed which she had so ingeniously planned and carried out.

"If anything would make the town talk, that would," he answered. "The only way to manage it would be to get the Princess to go with you and then take me as—" He stopped short, rather awkwardly.

"I should rather go without her," said Laura, turning her face away to hide her amusement at the slip of the tongue of which he had been guilty.

In Rome, for Ghisleri to be seen driving with the Princess of Gerano and her daughter would have been almost equivalent to announcing his engagement to Laura.

CHAPTER XXIV.

ADELE had not anticipated such complete failure in the first instance. The five-franc note with Laura Arden's card told her plainly enough what her step-sister thought of the matter, but she had no means of finding out whether Ghisleri had been informed of what she had done or not, and her efforts to extract information from him when she met him were not successful. His tone and his manner towards her were precisely the same as formerly, and he was as ready as ever to enter into desultory conversation with her; but if she ventured to lead the talk in such a direction as to find out what she wanted to know, he instantly met her with a counter-allusion to her doings which frightened her and silenced her effectually. So the months passed in a sort of petty skirmishing which led to no positive result, and she secretly planned some further step which should complete those she had already taken, reverse Laura's judgment, and completely ruin Pietro Ghisleri with her and before the world. The uneasy workings of her unsettled brain grew more and more tortuous every day, until at last she felt unable to reason the question out without the help of some experienced person. She felt quite sure that there must be some way out of all her difficulties, by a short cut to victory, and that a clever man, a good lawyer, for instance, if he could be deceived into believing the story she had concocted, would know how to make use of it against her enemies. The difficulty was two-fold. In the first place she must put together such a body of evidence as no experienced advocate could refuse as ground for an action at law, and, secondly, she must find the said advocate and explain the whole matter to him from her own point of view. The action would be brought in self-defence against Pietro Ghisleri, who would be accused of having systematically attempted to levy blackmail. That was the crude form in which the idea suggested itself to Adele when she set to work.

Her conviction now was that Pietro was only partially aware of the substance of the lost confession, and that the letter containing it was still at Gerano. This being the case, she could freely speak of it to her lawyer and describe the contents in any way she pleased, so as to turn the existence of the document to her own advantage. In the letters she had sent Laura and in the other two which she kept by her for future use, she had been careful never to say anything conclusive. Maria B. had indeed spoken of the transaction as being ended, but that could be interpreted as the unfounded supposition of a person not fully acquainted with the facts, and desirous of making money out of them as far as possible. The hardest thing would probably be to produce the woman who was supposed to have written to Laura, in case she should be needed. Money well bestowed, however, would do much towards stimulating the memory of some indigent and unscrupulous person, and the part to be played would, after all, be a small and insignificant one. On the other hand, the weak point in the case would be that Adele, while able to produce an unlimited number of her own letters to Ghisleri, would not have a single line of his writing to show. She could, indeed, fall back upon her own natural sense of caution, and declare that she had destroyed all he had written, in the mistaken belief that it would be safer to do so, and her lawyer could taunt his opponent with his folly in not doing likewise; but that would, after all, be rather a poor expedient. Or it might be pretended that Pietro had invariably written to her in a feigned handwriting signing himself, perhaps, with a single initial, as a precaution in case his letters should fall into the wrong hands. In that case she could produce whatever she chose. The best possible plan would be to extract one or two short notes from him upon which an ambiguous construction might be put by the lawyers. All this, Adele reflected, would need considerable time, and several months must elapse before she could expect to be ready. Her mind, too, worked spasmodically, and she was subject to long fits of apathy and extreme depression in the intervals between her short hours of abnormal activity. She knew that this was the result of the morphia she took in such quantities, and she resolved to make a great effort to cure herself of the fatal habit, if it were not already too late.

As has been said more than once, Adele Savelli had possessed a very determined will, and it had not yet been altogether destroyed. Having once made up her mind to free herself if she could, she made the attempt bravely and systematically. The result was that, in the course of several months, she had reduced the amount of her daily doses very considerably. The suffering was great, but the object to be gained was great also, and she steeled herself to endure all that a woman could. She was encouraged, also, by the fact that her mind began to act more regularly and seemed more reliable. Physically, she was growing very weak and was becoming almost emaciated. Francesco Savelli watched her narrowly, and it was his opinion that she could not last long. The Prince of Gerano was very anxious about her all through the spring which followed the events last described, and his wife, though she was far less fond of Adele than in former times, could not but feel a sorrowful regret as she saw the young life that had begun so brightly wearing itself away before her eyes. But the Princess had consolations in another direction. Laura Arden seemed to grow daily more lovely in her mature beauty, and Herbert was growing out of his babyhood into a sturdy little boy of phenomenal strength and of imperturbably good temper. Laura was headstrong where Ghisleri was concerned, but in all other respects she was herself still.

The first consequence of Adele's attempt to break the strong friendship which united Laura and Pietro, was to draw them still more closely together, and to make Laura, at least, more defiant of the world's opinion than ever. As for Ghisleri, he almost forgot to ask himself questions. The time to separate for the summer was drawing near, and he knew, when he thought of it, what a different parting this one would be from the one which had preceded it a year earlier. But he tried to think of the present and not of the weary months of solitude he looked forward to between June and November or December. He remembered, in spite of himself, how he had more than once enjoyed the lonely life, even refusing invitations to pleasant places rather than lose a single week of an existence so full of charm. But another interest had been growing, slowly, deep-sown, spreading its roots in silence, and fastening itself about his heart while he had not even suspected that it was there at all. Little by little, without visible manifestation, the strong thing had drawn more strength from his own life, mysteriously absorbing into itself the springs of thought and the sources of emotion, unifying them and assimilating them all into something which was a part, and was soon to be the chief part, of his being. And now, above the harrowed surface of that inner ground on which such fierce battles had been fought throughout his years of storm, a soft shoot raised its delicate head, not timidly, but quietly and unobtrusively, to meet the warm sunshine of the happier days to come. He saw it, and knew it, and held his peace, dreading it and yet loving it, for it was love itself;

but not knowing truly what the little blade would come to, whether it was to bloom all at once into a bright and poisonous flower of evil, bringing to him the death of all possible love for ever; or whether it would grow up slowly, calm and fair, from leaf to shrub, from shrub to sapling, from sapling at last to tree, straight, tall, and strong, able to face tempest and storm without bending its lofty head, rich to bear for him in the end the stately blossom and the heavenly fruit of passionate true love.

For before the day of parting came Pietro Ghisleri knew that he loved Laura Arden. Ever since that moment when she had quietly given him Adele's letter and had told him that she would believe no evil of him, he had begun to suspect that she was no longer what she had been to him once and what she had remained so long, a friend, kind, almost affectionate, for whom he would give all he had, but only a friend after all. It was different now. The thought of bidding Laura good-bye, even for a few months, sent a thrill of pain through his heart which he had not expected to feel — the small, sharp pain which tells a man the truth about a woman and himself as nothing else can. The prospect of the lonely summer was dreary.

Ghisleri was surprised, and almost startled. During nearly two years and a half he had honestly believed that he could never love again, and if a sincere wish, formulated in the shape he unconsciously chose, could be called a prayer, he earnestly prayed that so long as he lived he might not feel what he had felt very strongly twice, at least, since he had been a boy. But such a man could hardly expect that such a wish, or prayer, could be granted or heard, so long as he was spending many hours of each succeeding week in the company of Laura Arden. In the full strength of manhood, passionate, sensitive beneath a cold exterior, always attracted by women, and almost always repelled by men, Pietro Ghisleri could hardly expect that in one moment the capacity for loving should be wholly rooted out and destroyed by something

z

like an act of will, and as the consequence of his being disappointed and disgusted by his own fickleness. The new passion might turn out to be greater or less than the two which had hitherto disturbed his existence, but it could hardly be greater than the first. It would necessarily be different from either, in that it would be hopeless from the beginning, as he thought. For where he was very sincere, he was rarely very confident in himself, if the stake was woman's love, a fact more common with men who are at once sensitive and strong than is generally known.

But his first impulse was not to go away and escape from the temptation, as it would have been some time earlier. There was no reason for doing that, as he had reflected before, when he had considered the advisability of breaking off all intercourse with Laura for the sake of silencing the world's idle chatter. He was perfectly free to love her, and to tell her so, if he chose. No one could blame him for wishing to marry her; at most he might be thought foolish for desiring anything so very improbable as that she should accept him. But he was quite indifferent to what any one might think of him excepting Laura herself. One resolution only he made and did his best to keep, and it was a good one. He made up his mind that he would not make love to her, as he understood the meaning of the term. Possibly, as he told himself with a little scorn, this was no resolution at all, but only a way of expressing his conviction that he was quite unable to do what he so magnanimously refused to attempt. For his instinct told him that his love for Laura had already taken a shape which differed wholly from all former passions, one unfamiliar to him, one which would need a new expression if it continued to be sincere. But that he doubted. He was quite ready to admit that when Laura came back in the autumn, this early beginning of love would have disappeared again, and that the old strong friendship would be found in its place, solid, firmly based, and unchanged, a permanent happiness and a constant satisfaction. He was no longer a boy, to imagine that the first breath of love was the forerunner of an all-destroying storm in which he must perish, or of a clear, fair wind before which the ship of his life was to run her straight course to the haven of death's peace. He had seen too much fickleness in himself and in others to believe in any such thing; but if he had anticipated either it would have been the tempest. On the whole, he did the wisest thing he could. He changed nothing in his manner towards Laura and he waited as calmly as he was able, to see what the end would be. Once only before Laura went away the conversation turned upon love, and oddly enough it was Laura who brought up the subject.

She had been talking about little Herbert, as she often did, planning out his future according to her own wishes and making it happy in her own way, even to sketching the wife he was to win some five and twenty years hence.

"I should like her to be very fair," she said. "Herbert will be dark, as I am, and they say that contrasts attract each other most permanently. But of course, though she must be beautiful, she must have ever so many other good points besides. In the first place, she must be capable of loving him with all her heart and soul. I suppose that is really the hardest thing of all to find."

"The 'one-great-passion' sort of person, you mean, I fancy," observed Ghisleri, with a smile. "A rare bird — I agree with you."

"I doubt whether the individual exists," said Laura. "Except by accident, or when the course of true love runs so very smoothly that it would need superhuman ingenuity to fall off it."

"You are a constant revelation to me!" Ghisleri laughed, and looked at her.

"What is there surprising about what I said? You are not a believer in the universal stability of the human heart, are you?"

"Hardly that! But women very often are — at first.

And then, when they see that change is possible, they are apt to say that there is no such thing as true love at all, whereas we know that there is."

"In other words, you think that I take the sensible view. After all, what is the use of expecting humanity to be superhuman?"

"I always like the way in which you put things," said Ghisleri, thoughtfully. "That is exactly it. Homo sum. I am neither angel, nor ape, but man, and at present, I believe, no near relation of the seraph or the monkey."

"And as a man, changeable. So am I, as a woman, I have no doubt. Every one must be, and I do not think it is fair to respect people who do not change at all because they never have the chance."

"One cannot help it. Human nature instinctively places the man who has only loved once above the man who has shown that he can love often. It is connected with the idea of faith and loyalty."

"Often — that is too much. There comes the question of the limit. How often can a man love sincerely?"

"Three times — not more," answered Ghisleri, with conviction.

"Why not two, or four? How can you lay down the law in that way?"

"It is very simple. I think that no love is worth the name which does not influence a man strongly for at least ten years. Any really great passion will do that. But human life is short. Let a man fall in love at twenty, and three periods of ten years each will bring him to fifty. A man who falls in love after he is fifty is a rarity, and generally an object of ridicule. That seems to me a logical demonstration, and I do not see why it should not apply to a woman as well as to a man."

"Yes, I think there is truth in that," said Laura. "At all events, it looks true. Besides, there is something quite reasonable in the idea that a man naturally has three stages, when he is twenty years old, thirty, and forty. I should imagine that the middle stage, while he is still developing, might be the shortest."

It was impossible for Ghisleri to imagine that Laura was referring to his own life, but the remark was certainly very applicable to himself, so far. Would the third stage be permanent, if he really reached it? He was inclined to think that nothing about him had much stability, for within the last two years he had come to accept the fact as something which was part of his nature and from which there was no escape, despise the weakness and hate it as he would. It was a singular coincidence that since he had tormented himself less he had become really less changeable.

A month later he parted from Laura, to all outward appearances as quietly and calmly as in the previous year. If there were any difference, it was in her manner rather than in his. She said almost sadly that she was sorry the time had come, and that she looked forward to the meeting in the autumn as to one of the pleasantest things in the future. The words she spoke were almost commonplace, though even if taken literally they conveyed more than she had ever said before. But it was quite clear that she meant more than she said.

When she was gone Ghisleri felt more lonely than he had for years, and every interest seemed to have died out of his existence. He tried to laugh at himself for turning into a boy again, but even that diversion failed him. He could not even find the bitter words it had once amused him, in a grim way, to put together. Then he left Rome, weary of the sights and sounds of the streets, of the solitude of his rooms, of the effort to show some intelligence when he was obliged to talk with an acquaintance. He went to his own place in Tuscany and passed his time in trying to improve the condition of things. He knew something of practical architecture, and he rebuilt a staircase, and restored the vaulting in a part of the little castle to which he had never done anything before, and which had gone to ruin during the last hundred years or more, since it had last been inhabited. For he, his father, and his grandfather had been only sons, and his mother having died when he was a mere boy, his father had taken a dislike to Torre de' Ghisleri and had lived the remainder of his short life in Florence. Hence the general dilapidation of the old place which was not, however, without beauty. The occupation did him good, and the sight of the old familiar faces of his tenants and few retainers was pleasant, after facing the museum of society masks during seven months and more. But he felt that even here he could not stay any great length of time without a change, and as the summer advanced his restlessness became extreme.

He came down to Rome for a week in August. The first person he met in the street was Francesco Savelli, who stopped to speak with him. Ghisleri never voluntarily stopped any one.

"How is Donna Adele?" he asked, after they had exchanged the first greetings.

"Very nervous," answered Savelli, shaking his head with the air of concern he thought it proper to affect whenever he spoke of his wife's illness. "The nerves are something which no one can understand. I can tell you a story, for instance, about something which happened the other day — to be accurate, in June, when we were at Gerano. Do you remember the oubliette between the guard-room and the tower? Yes — my wife said she showed it to you. We were all staying together — all the children, her father, and the Princess and two or three friends. One morning she said she was quite sure that if we took up that slab of stone and lowered a man into the shaft, we should find a skeleton hanging there — Heaven knows what she imagined! The Prince said he had looked into the shaft scores of times when the trap-door still existed and there was a bar across the passage to prevent any one from going near; that he himself had ordered the stone to be put where it was and knew all about the place. The only skeleton ever found in the castle had been discovered walled up in the thickness of the north tower, with a little window just opposite the face, so that the individual must have died looking at the hills. Nobody knew anything about. it. But my wife insisted, and grew angry, and at last furious. It was of no use, of course. You know the old gentleman — he can be perfectly rigid. He answered that no one should touch the stone, that if she yielded to such ideas once, she would soon wish to pull Gerano to pieces to count the mice, and that if she could persuade my father to knock holes in the walls at Castel Savello, that was the affair of the Savelli, but that so long as he lived she should not make any experiments in excavation under his roof. If you will believe me, she had a fit of anger which brought on an attack of the nerves, and she never went out of her room for three days in consequence. Do you wonder that I am anxious?"

"Certainly not. It would be amazing if you were indifferent. The story gives one the idea that she is subject to delusions. I am very sorry she is no better. Pray remember me to her."

Thereupon Ghisleri passed on, inwardly wondering how long it would be before Adele became quite mad. Two days later he received a note from her. She had heard from her husband that he was in Rome, she said, and wrote to ask a great favour of him. He was doubtless aware of her father's passion for manuscripts, which was well known in Rome. It was reported that a certain dealer had bought Prince Montevarchi's library after the crash, and she very much wished to buy a very interesting manuscript of which she had often heard her father speak, and which contained an account of the famous, or infamous, Isabella Montevarchi's life, written with her own hand — a sort of confession, in fact. As she did not know the exact title of the document, if it had any, she would call it a confession, though, of course, in a strictly lay sense. Now, she inquired, would Ghisleri, for old friendship's sake, try to obtain it for her at a reasonable price? She knew, of course, that such an original would be expensive, but she was prepared to discuss the terms if not

wholly beyond her means. She sent her note by the car-
rier, as that was generally quicker than writing by the
post, she said. Would Ghisleri kindly answer by the
same means? The man would call again on the next day
but one. That would perhaps give time to make preliminary inquiries. With which observation, and with best
thanks in anticipation of the service he was about to
render, Adele called herself most sincerely his.

Ghisleri was not an extremely suspicious man, but he
would have given evidence of almost infantine simplicity
if he had not seen that there was something wrong about
Adele's note. It was certainly very well planned, and
if Laura had never shown him the letters Adele had sent
her, it might very possibly have succeeded. On ascer-
taining the price set by the dealer on the manuscript, he
would probably have written a few words, stating in a
business-like way the sum for which the so-called confession could be bought. In all likelihood, too, he would
have only dated his note by the day of the week, omitting
altogether the month and the year. He saw at a glance
how easily a communication of that kind might have
taken such a shape as to be very serviceable against him,
and how hard it might have been to show that he was
writing about a genuine transaction concerning a manuscript actually for sale. He determined to be very careful.

His first step was to find out the name of the dealer
who had bought the Montevarchi library. He next ascertained that what Adele wanted was still unsold, and that
he must therefore necessarily enter into correspondence
with her. After that he sought out a young lawyer whom
he had employed once or twice within the last few years
when he had needed legal advice in regard to some trifling
point, and laid the whole matter before him. This young
man, Ubaldini by name, had rapidly acquired a reputation as a criminal lawyer, and had successfully defended
some remarkable cases, but, as he justly observed,
acquitted prisoners of the classes in which crimes are
common, pay very little, and condemned criminals pay

nothing at all. He was therefore under the necessity of taking other kinds of business as a means of support. The last murderer who had escaped the law by Ubaldini's eloquence had sent him a bag of beans and a cream cheese, which was all the family could afford in the way of a fee, but upon which a barrister who had a taste for variety could not subsist any length of time.

Ghisleri explained at considerable length the whole story, as far as it has been told in these pages, and expressed the belief that Donna Adele Savelli was intent upon ruining him for what, after all, seemed very insufficient reasons.

"When a woman lives on morphia and the fear of discovery, instead of food and drink, I would not give much for the soundness of any of her reasons," said Ubaldini, with a laugh. "What shall we do with the Princess? Shall we convict her of homicide, or bring an action for defamation, which we are sure to win? I like this case. We shall amuse ourselves."

"I do not wish to bring any accusation nor any action against Donna Adele Savelli," answered Ghisleri. "All I wish to do is to protect myself. Of course I should be curious to know what became of that written confession of hers, if it ever existed. But at present I wish you to have certified copies made of all my letters to her, and to keep the originals of those she writes me. If she makes such another attack on me as the last one, I will ask you, perhaps, to take the matter up. In the mean time, I only desire to keep on the safe side."

"In a case like this," said the lawyer, "it is far safer to attack than to wait for the enemy. Be careful in what you write, at all events. It would be wiser to show me the letters before you send them. One never can tell at what point the error of omission or commission will be made, upon which everything will depend. As a bit of general advice, I should warn you always to date every sheet on which you write anything, always to mention the name of the dealer when you speak of him, and invariably to give in full the correct title by which the manuscript is known. If you do that, and take good care that the dealer knows you perfectly each time you see him, and remembers your visits, it will not be easy to manage. But Donna Adele Savelli is evidently a clever person, whether her reasons for hating you are good or bad. That little trick of sending her own letters to the other lady was masterly — absolutely diabolical. The reason she failed was that she struck too high. She over-reached herself. She accused you of too much. That shows that although her methods are clever her judgment is insufficient. The same is true of this last attempt. By the bye, have you ever mentioned me to her, so far as you can recollect?"

"No, I believe not."

"Then avoid doing so, if you please. It is always better to keep the opposite party in ignorance of one's lawyer's name until the last minute."

"Very well."

As soon as Ghisleri was gone Ubaldini wrote a draft of a letter to Adele, as follows:

"EXCELLENCY: — At the decease of a client of humble station a number of papers have come under my notice and are now in my hands. One of them, of some length, has evidently gone astray, for it is written by your Excellency and apparently addressed to a member of the clergy, besides containing, as one glance told me, matter of a private nature. It is my wish to restore it immediately, and I therefore write to inquire whether I may entrust it to the post-office, or whether I shall hand it sealed to your Excellency's legal representative. I need not add the assurance that so far as I am concerned the matter is a strict secret, nor that I desire to restore the document as a duty of honour, and could not consider for a moment the question of any remuneration.

"Deign, Excellency, to receive graciously the expression of profoundest respect with which I write myself,

"Your Excellency's most humble, obedient servant,

"RINALDO UBALDINI, *Advocate.*"

CHAPTER XXV.

As Ghisleri had anticipated, Adele kept up a lively correspondence with him for some time. All her letters were duly filed by Ubaldini, who took certified copies of Pietro's replies, but did not mention what he himself had done in the matter. Adele bargained sharply until Ghisleri wrote to her as plainly as he well could that the manuscript was not to be had for less than the sum he had repeatedly named, and that he could do nothing more for her. Thereupon she answered that she would consider the matter, and did not, write again. Pietro, after waiting several days, left Rome again, and returned to Torre de' Ghisleri, glad to be relieved at last from the irksome and dangerous task of writing concise and lawyer-like communications about a subject which did not interest him at all.

Meanwhile Adele had been through a series of emotions of which Pietro knew nothing, and which very nearly drove her to increasing her daily doses of morphia again. On receiving Ubaldini's very respectful and straightforward letter, she had felt that she was saved at last, though it definitely destroyed the illusion by which she had so long persuaded herself that the confession was still in the oubliette at Gerano. Without much hesitation she wrote to Ubaldini, and laid a bank-note for five hundred francs in the folded sheet. She begged him to send a special messenger with the sealed packet to Castel Savello, and requested him, in spite of his protest, to accept the enclosed sum to cover expenses.

During forty-eight hours she enjoyed to the full the anticipation of at last getting back the letter which had cost her such terrible anxiety at various times during the past two years and a half. Then came Ubaldini's answer, though when she opened it she had no idea that it was from him. He had made his clerk both write and sign

the fair copy of the first letter, which had been written
on paper not stamped with an address. He now wrote
with his own hand upon the paper he kept for business
correspondence upon which, of course, the address was
printed. There was consequently not the slightest resemblance between the two letters. But Adele was not prepared for the contents. The first thing she noticed was
her bank-note, carefully pinned inside the sheet. Even
the form of addressing her was not the same, and the one
now employed was the correct one, the Savelli being one
of the families in which the title of Prince and Princess
belongs indiscriminately to all the children, and consequently to the wives of all the sons. The letter was as
follows:

"Signora Principessa :— I have the honour to acknowledge
the receipt of a communication from your Excellency, in which
you request me to send a certain sealed packet to Castel Savello
by a special messenger, and enclosing a bank note for five hundred francs (Banca Romana S. $\frac{877}{5955}$) which I return herewith. I
take the occasion to say that I know nothing whatever of the
sealed packet referred to, and I beg to suggest that your Excellency
may have accidentally addressed the letter to me instead of to some
other person, perhaps in using a directory. If, however, it was
written in answer to one supposed to have been indited to you by
me, the letter must have been composed and sent by some design-
ing person in the hope of intercepting the reply and gaining possession of the money, which I am glad to be able to send back to
its original owner. Believe me, Signora Principessa,

"Your Excellency's most obedient,

"Rinaldo Ubaldini."

The shock was almost more than Adele could bear, and
the room reeled with her as she comprehended what had
happened, so far as she was able to understand it all.
The truth did not strike her, however. What she believed
was what the lawyer suggested, that some person had
played a trick on her, and had made use of Ubaldini's
name and address in the hope of getting the money he or
she naturally expected that she would send as compensa-

tion for such an important service. The hardest to
endure was the disappointment of finding that she was
not to have the confession after all. The point proved
was that, whether it were still in the oubliette or had been
found and carried off, there was in either case at least one
person at large who knew it existed, and who knew that
the contents would be greatly to her disadvantage if
known. And if one person knew it, she argued, all Rome
might be acquainted with the story, and probably was.
But the comforting conviction that the letter was still
safe at Gerano did not return. There was a tone about
the first communication disclaimed by Ubaldini, which
forced upon her the belief that the writer knew everything, and could ruin her at a moment's notice.

What Ubaldini gained was the certainty that the story
which Ghisleri described as current gossip was a fact,
and a very serious one. He had played detective instead
of lawyer, and he had been very successful. He knew
also, that, as he had acted altogether in the interests of
his client, Ghisleri, and had returned Adele's money, no
objection could, strictly speaking, be made to the stratagem, however it might be looked upon by gentlemen and
men of the world, like Ghisleri himself. But Ubaldini
was a lawyer, and it was not his business to consider
what the fine world would think of his doings. He filed
Adele's letter with the copies of his own.

In the course of a few days, Adele, who was all the
time carrying on her correspondence with Pietro, gathered
some hope from the latter's answers. She had a suspicion that he might keep all the notes he received from
her, and after the first she was as careful never to mention the manuscript except as "the confession," as he,
on his part, was always to write out its title in full. It
struck her, however, that a man playing such a part as
she wished to have it thought that he was playing,
would naturally use some such means for making his
letters seem commonplace if they should fall into the
wrong hands, and it would be easy to persuade her

friends that the autobiographic writings of Isabella Montevarchi meant Adele Savelli's confession, by common consent, though she herself had not taken the trouble to use such a long title more than once. The thought elated her, and comforted her in a measure for the disappointment she had suffered, and which had shaken her nerves severely.

She now spent much time in going over the correspondence, weighing each word in the attempt to establish its exact value if regarded from the point of view of a systematic attempt to extort money. With a relative coolness which would not have disgraced a strong man, and which showed how far she had recovered control of herself by diminishing the doses of morphia, she set to work to put her case together on the supposition that she meant to lay it before her husband, for instance, or any other intelligent person, with a request for advice. And the case, as she put it, was better than might have been expected, though it depended ultimately, for its solidity, on the supposition that the confession could never be found.

In the first place, she intended to admit that she had been jealous of Laura for years, and to own frankly that she had often said cruel and spiteful things of her, and of Arden, just as everybody she knew said spiteful things of somebody. She would even admit that she had first set afloat the rumour that Lord Herbert was intemperate, and that Laura had the evil eye. She could then point out that her conduct had suddenly changed in deference to her father's wishes, that there had been an open reconciliation, not very heartfelt on her part at first, but made sincere by the remorse she felt after Arden's death. For she meant to go even so far as to confess that Arden might have caught the scarlet fever in her house, seeing that her maid was only just recovering from it at the time. The woman's illness had been kept strictly secret, and she had been, from the first, taken to a distant part of the palace, so that Adele had not believed there could be any danger. Even her husband had not known what the maid's illness was, and poor Lucia had pleaded so hard not to be sent to the hospital that Adele had yielded. But to prove, she would say, how little fear of contagion she had, her own children had not been sent into the country. The Palazzo Savelli was big enough to have had a whole infirmary in one part of it, completely isolated from all the rest. Nevertheless, she had always felt that there was a possibility of Arden's last illness having been taken at that dinner-party, and her secret remorse had caused her the greatest suffering. Between that and a nervous disorder from which she had little hope of ever recovering, she had fallen very ill, and had gone to Gerano. While there, her conscience had so pricked her in the matter of her past unkindness to her step-sister and to Arden, that although she had been to confession at Easter, she wrote a long letter to her confessor in Rome, going again over the full details of the past winter. From that point she could tell the truth, without even sparing Lucia, until she came to the discovery that it was Ghisleri himself who had picked up the letter, or confession, under the shaft of the oubliette. And here she would lay great stress on Ghisleri's attachment to Laura, and consequent dislike of herself. The well-known fact that Pietro had fought a desperate duel merely because Campodonico said that Lady Herbert Arden might have the evil eye, sufficiently showed to what lengths he would go in her defence. Nothing more would really be needed. But there was plenty more. All Rome knew that he had broken with Maddalena dell' Armi for Laura's sake, and that he had exhibited the most untiring devotion ever afterwards. Never, since the death of the Princess Corleone, Adele would boldly assert, had he been faithful to any one woman for such a length of time. That was a strong point. The Princess of Gerano herself could testify to her own anxiety about Laura since Ghisleri had been so much with her. Laura herself had behaved in the most admirable manner ever since the reconciliation, but Ghisleri, in constituting himself her champion, had become, so to say, more royalist than the king, and more catholic than the pope. His dislike, if not his positive hatred, for Adele was apparent at every step in the story. He did not, it is true, speak of it to any one, but his reticence was a well-known peculiarity of his character. It was when he was alone in conversation with Adele that he showed what he felt. But his manner was always courteous and rather formal. It was by sarcastic hints that he conveyed his meaning. Nevertheless, Adele had maintained the outward forms of friendly acquaintance, and once, some six months after Arden's death, when matters had not been so bad as they now were, she had asked him to stay a few days at Gerano. Lucia could testify that he was there at the time when the confession disappeared, and Lucia, who had attempted to extort money for it, and would have succeeded if the document had been forthcoming, had naturally been as interested as any one to find it. Not until some time later had Adele suspected that it had been picked up by Ghisleri. The thing, of course, had not any very great value, but what woman, Adele would ask, could bear to think that the most private outpourings of her soul to her spiritual director were in the hands of a man who hated her, and who could, if he pleased, circulate them and make them the talk of the town? When Ghisleri, in the following winter, had begun to torment her systematically by quoting little phrases and expressions which she remembered to have written in the letter, she had at last boldly taxed him with having it in his possession, and he, with the unparalleled cynicism for which he was famous, had laughed at her and owned the truth. Every one would allow that this was very like him. She had threatened to complain to her husband, and he had expressed the utmost indifference. He was a known duelist and a dangerous adversary, and for her husband's sake she had held her tongue, while Ghisleri continued to make her life miserable with his witticisms. Then she had once asked him what he would consider an equivalent for the letter. He had laughed again, and had said that he would take a large sum of money in exchange for it, which, he added, he would devote to building a small hospital in the village of Torre de' Ghisleri, saying that it would be for the good of her soul to found a charity of that kind. She would not undertake to say whether he would have employed the money for that purpose or not, if she had given it to him. Possibly he would. But she had not been able to dispose of any such sum as he had then named. Under her marriage contract she controlled only her pin-money, and her father allowed her nothing out of the great fortune which would some day be hers. She and Ghisleri had corresponded about the matter in town, by notes sent backwards and forwards. She, on her part, had at that time thought she was doing wisely in burning his, but he had been less careful. He had, in fact, been so grossly negligent as to leave five of them at one time in the pocket of one of his coats. It was through his tailor to whom the coat had been sent for some alteration or repair that two of these notes had come back to Adele. A woman, apparently a seamstress, had come to her with them one day, and had offered them to her for sale, together with a card of Lady Herbert Arden's enclosed in an envelope addressed to "Maria B." at the general post-office. On the card were written the words : "For Maria B., with best thanks." The woman confessed that she was in great distress, that she had found the letters in a coat upon which she was working, had easily ascertained who Ghisleri was, and what his relations towards Lady Herbert were, and had appealed to the latter for help, offering the letters in exchange for any charity, and actually sending three of them when she had only received five francs. Lady Herbert had then sent her fifty francs more with the card in question, but the poor woman thought that very little. She bitterly repented not having brought them all at once to Donna Adele. Of

course they belonged to her, and Donna Adele had a
right to them all, without payment. But the woman
was very poor. Adele had unhesitatingly given her a
hundred francs and had kept the two notes and the card,
which proved at least that even at that time she had been
corresponding with Ghisleri and protesting her inability
to pay the sum he demanded, and that Laura Arden was
aware of the correspondence, and had been willing for
Ghisleri's sake to pay money to obtain it. For a long
time after this Adele had made no further attempt, but
had avoided finding herself alone in conversation with
Pietro, as many people had indeed noticed, because she
could not bear to be perpetually annoyed by his reference
to his power over her. Yet, out of fear lest some harm
should befall her husband, she had still held her peace.
Early in the preceding summer, shortly before leaving
for her annual visit to Gerano, Ghisleri had managed to
be alone with her, and had not lost the opportunity of
inflicting another wound, which had revived all her old
desire to obtain possession of the lost letter. He had,
indeed, almost admitted that unless she would reconsider
the matter he would send it to one of her friends to read.
The Montevarchi library was then about to be sold, and
many persons were talking of the famous confession of
Isabella Montevarchi. By way of safety, Adele, in
agreeing to think the whole thing over once more, had
told him that when writing she should speak of her own
letter as though it were this well-known manuscript.
She had already some experience of his carelessness in
regard to notes. Against his own statement, and against
her own secret positive conviction, yet to give him one
chance, as it were, she had made one desperate effort to
have the oubliette opened and searched. Her father
would remember how angry she had been, and, indeed,
she had lost her temper, being always ill and nervous.
He had positively refused. Then, in despair, she had
reopened negotiations with Ghisleri, whose demands,
though not so high as formerly, were still quite beyond

her means. As a matter of fact, the dealer had asked an exorbitant price for the manuscript, being well aware of its historical importance, which was little less than that attaching to the famous manuscript account of the Cenci trial. Adele was in despair. She had no means of raising such a sum as Ghisleri required, except by selling her jewels, which she could not possibly do without exciting her husband's suspicions. She was powerless. Had any woman ever been placed in such a situation? Ghisleri's last letter distinctly stated that he could do nothing more for her if she refused to buy the confession of Isabella Montevarchi at the price he had last named. Those were his very words. They meant that unless she paid, he would make use of the letter he had. He even added, that in that case the manuscript would probably before long be disposed of elsewhere, as though to make his meaning clearer.

Her position was very strong, Adele thought, as she reached the end of her statement as she first drew it up in her own mind. A clever lawyer could doubtless make it even stronger, for he would know how to take advantage of every point, and how to call attention to the strongest and pass smoothly over the weaker links in the chain. The real danger, and the only real danger, lay in the possibility that the confession itself might be found and might be produced, with all which she said it contained, and with the one central black statement of which she made no mention in working up the case. But who could produce it? If any one had it, that man was Ghisleri, who had more than once gone very near the truth in the hints he had thrown out. Say that he had it — suppose the hypothesis a fact. Its being in his possession would be the most ruining evidence of all. He would not dare to show it, for though it might ruin her, it would be far worse ruin to him, for it would of itself suffice to prove the truth of every word of her story, and he would not only incur the full penalty of the law for a most abominable attempt at levying blackmail, but his very memory would be blasted for ever as that of the most dastardly and cowardly villain ever sent to penal servitude. As for herself, she felt that she had not long to live, and if worse came to worst, a little over-dose of morphia would end it all. She would have had her triumph, and she would have seen Laura's face by that time.

It did not occur to her to ask herself any question about the origin of a hatred so implacable as to make the sacrifice of life itself seem easy in the accomplishment of its end. She was not able to trace the history of her jealousy backwards by a firm concentration of memory, as she was able by the force of vivid imagination to construct the vengeance she anticipated in the future. That the most dire revenge should be contemplated, pursued, and ultimately executed for the sake of a wrong wholly imaginary in the first instance is not altogether novel in the history of humanity. There are minds which under certain conditions cannot judge of the past as they can of events present and to come. Adele's hatred of Laura Arden amounted almost to a fixed idea. It had begun in very small things. Its origin lay, perhaps, in the simple fact that Laura was beautiful whereas Adele had been barely pretty at her best, and its first great development had been the consequence of Francesco Savelli's undisguised preference for the step-sister of his future wife. All the young girl's jealousy and vain nature had been roused and wounded by the slight, and as years had gone by and Savelli showed no signs of forgetting his early attachment to Laura, the wound had grown more sore and more angry until it had poisoned Adele's character and heart to the very core. The worst deed she ever did had not perhaps been the worst in intention. She had not been at all sure that Arden would take the fever, and she had assuredly not meant nor ever expected that he should die. Chance had put the information into her hands at a moment when, through Laura, as it seemed to her, she was suffering the most cruel humiliation she had ever

known. On that memorable evening when her father had
forced her to submit to his will, and when she was looking forward with bitter loathing to what was very like a
public reconciliation, she had been left alone. In attempting to control herself and to regain some outward calm,
she had taken up a review and had forced herself to read
the first article upon which she opened, and which happened to be a very dull one on the bacilli of various
diseases. But one passage had struck her forcibly — the
plain account of a case which had recently been observed,
in which few medical terms occurred, and which a child
could have understood. The extreme simplicity of the
facts had startled her, and she had suddenly resolved that
Laura and Arden should have cause to remember the reconciliation which would cost her vanity so dear. But she
had no intention of doing murder. In her heart she had
hardly believed that any result would follow, and remorse
had taken hold of her almost at once, simultaneously with
the horrible fear of discovery which has more than once
driven men and women mad. But remorse is by no means
repentance. With it comes often what has been called
the impossibility of pardoning the person one has injured,
and the insane desire to wreak vengeance upon that person for the acute sufferings endured in one's own conscience. Given the existence of this desire in a very
violent degree, and admitting the inevitable disturbance
of the faculties ensuing upon the long and vicious abuse
of such a poison as morphia, Adele's ultimate state
becomes comprehensible. She was, indeed, as Ghisleri
had said to Laura, hardly sane, and her incipient madness having originally resulted from jealousy, the latter
naturally remained the ruling influence in her unsettled
brain, and attained proportions hardly credible to those
who have not followed the steps by which the human
intelligence passes from sanity to madness.

And now that she had worked up her case against
Ghisleri, as a lawyer would express it, and had convinced
herself that she could tell a long and connected story in

which almost every detail should give colour to her principal assertion, she hesitated as to the course she should
pursue. It was not in her power to send for a lawyer
and to bring an action at law against Pietro, without her
husband's consent, and she knew how hard that would be
to obtain. Francesco Savelli was by no means a cowardly
man, and would, if necessary, have exposed his life in a
duel with Ghisleri, not for his wife's sake, but for the
sake of the family honour. But he had the true Roman's
abhorrence of publicity and scandal, and would make
great sacrifices to avoid anything of the kind. Her own
father might be willing to take the matter up, but it was
extremely hard to deceive him. She knew, however, that
if he were once persuaded of the justice of her cause, he
would go to any length in her defence and would prove an
implacable enemy to the man who, as he would suppose,
had injured her. The great difficulty lay in persuading
him at the outset. But for the unfortunate fact that he
had already once detected her in falsehood, the matter
would have been far easier. It was true that she meant
to admit all he had then forced her to own, and much
more besides, in order to show how high a value Ghisleri
set upon the confession which contained a concise account
of her doings. But he would, in any case, be prejudiced
against her from the first. One thing was in her favour,
she thought. The Princess of Gerano did not like Ghisleri, and would in all likelihood be ready to believe evil
of him, and to influence her husband, good and just
woman though she was. There was one other person to
whom Adele could apply — Prince Savelli himself. She
thought of him last and wondered why she had not remembered him first. He was a man of singular energy,
courage, and coolness, whose chief fault was a tendency
to overestimate beyond all limits the importance of his
family and the glory of his ancient name. She knew
that he was abnormally sensitive on these points and that
if she could rouse his ever ready pride, he would hesitate
at nothing in order to bring retribution upon any one rash

enough to insult or injure any member of his family. And he lived a life of his own and cared little for the world. His passion, strangely enough, was of a scientific kind. He was an astronomer, had built himself an observatory on the top of the massive old palace, and spent the greater part of his time there. Such existences, in the very heart of society, are not unknown in Rome. Prince Savelli had remained what he was by nature, a true student, and was perfectly happy in his own way, caring very little for the world and hardly ever showing himself in it. The Princess was a placid person, extremely devout, but also extremely selfish. It was from her that Francesco inherited his disposition and his yellow hair.

It struck Adele that if she could win her father-in-law's sympathy and rouse him to action in her behalf, it would be far easier to persuade her own father that she was in the right. Gerano had a boundless respect for the elder Savelli's opinion, though if he had known him better, he would have discovered that his judgment was far too easily influenced where his exaggerated family pride was concerned.

A long time passed before Adele finally made up her mind to the great attempt. Ghisleri had already returned to Rome and Laura Arden was expected in two or three weeks, according to news received by her mother.

An incident, trivial in itself, at last decided her to act at once. She and Francesco were dining with the Prince and Princess of Gerano as they did regularly once a week. As a rule nobody was invited to these family meetings, but on that particular evening Gianforte Campodonico and Donna Christina had been asked. It was convenient to have them when Laura was not there, and they were much liked in Casa Gerano where, as has been said, Ghisleri was not a favourite. There was, moreover, a distant relationship between the families of Braccio and Campodonico of which, as they liked one another, both were fond of speaking.

Adele looked very ill. By this time her complexion

was of a pale yellow, and she was thin to absolute emaciation. In spite of her determined efforts to break the habit that was killing her, or perhaps as a first consequence of them, she was liable to moments of nervousness in which she could hardly control herself and in which she did not seem to remember what had happened a few minutes earlier. Her sufferings at such times were painful to see. She could hardly keep her hands from moving about in a helpless fashion, and her face was often slightly contorted. Very rarely, on fine days when she had been driving, a little colour came into her ghastly cheeks. It was easy to see that only her strong will supported her continually, and that women more weakly organized would long ago have succumbed to the effects of the poison.

When she felt that she was liable to a crisis of the nerves she was careful to stay at home, but occasionally she was attacked unawares, more or less violently, when she had believed herself well enough to go out. When this happened she sat in silence while the suffering lasted, and did her best to keep her unruly hands clasped together. By a strong effort she sometimes succeeded in concealing from others what she felt, but the exertion of her will made her irritable to the last degree, if she was called upon to speak or forced to try and join in the conversation.

CHAPTER XXVI.

The dinner passed off quietly and pleasantly enough until towards the end, when the conversation turned upon the coming season, and all began to speculate as to whether it would be gay or dull, as people always do when they meet after the long separation in the summer.

"There will be all the usual pleasant things," observed Francesco Savelli, who loved society as much as his wife did. "Let me see. There will be the evenings in Casa

Frangipani, and they will give their two balls as usual at
the end. The Marchesa di San Giacinto will do as she
did last year — a dance and a ball alternately after the
fifteenth of January. Of course Casa Montevarchi does
not exist any more since the crash, but that is the only
one. Then there are your evenings," he continued, turning to the mistress of the house, "and there are ours,
of course, and I suppose Gouache and Donna Faustina
will give something at the studio. Have you seen her
this year, Adele?"

He looked across the table at his wife, and saw that
she was beginning to suffer from an unexpected attack.
He knew the symptoms well, and was aware that there
was nothing to be done but to leave her alone and take
no notice of her. She merely nodded in answer to his
question, and he went on speaking.

"Gouache always does something original," he said.
"Do you remember that supper on Shrove Tuesday years
ago? It was the most successful thing of that season.
By the bye, I saw Ghisleri yesterday. He has come back."

It was rather tactless of him to drag Ghisleri's name
into the conversation in the presence of Campodonico.
But the Princess of Gerano was even more tactless than
he.

"That wild Ghisleri!" she immediately exclaimed, as
she always did when Pietro was mentioned.

"Ghisleri is no worse than the rest of us, I am sure,"
said Campodonico, anxious to show that he was not in
the least annoyed. "He has as many good qualities as
most men, and perhaps a few more."

"It is generous of you to say that," observed Donna
Christina, looking at her husband with loving admiration.

"I do not see that there is much generosity about it,
my dear," he answered warmly. "It would be very
spiteful of me not to give him his due, that is all. He
is brave and honourable, and that is something to say
of any man. Besides, look at his friends — look at the

people who like him, beginning with most of you here. That is a very good test of what a man is."

He looked straight at Adele Savelli as he spoke, for no special reason except that he always looked straight at somebody when he was speaking. He was hot-tempered, passionate, generous, and truthful, and there was a great directness about everything he did and said. But at that moment Adele was in great pain and was doing her best to hide it. She fancied that Campodonico had noticed what was the matter.

" Why do you look at me in that way ? " she asked irritably, but with a nervous attempt at a laugh.

" I do not know," answered Gianforte. " I suppose I expected you to agree with me. I know Ghisleri is a friend of yours."

" How do you know that ? " Adele's irritation increased rapidly. " Have you any reason to suppose that I am particularly fond of him ? Have I ever done anything to show it ? "

" Why are you so much annoyed ? " asked Savelli, who generally felt uncomfortable when his wife was in such moods, and feared that she would say something to make herself and him ridiculous. " You always liked him."

Adele's hand twitched and moved on the table against her will, and she upset some salt. The little incident sufficed to make her lose her head completely.

"If people knew what Pietro Ghisleri really is, there is not a house in Rome where he would be received," she said angrily.

The dead silence which followed this categorical statement brought her to her senses too late. Campodonico was the first to speak.

" I should find it very hard to believe that Ghisleri ever committed a dishonourable action," he said gravely. " That is a very serious statement, Donna Adele."

" Yes, indeed," put in the Prince, turning to his daughter. " You should consider what you are saying, my dear, before going so far as that. I think you ought to explain yourself. We may not all like Ghisleri, and if we please we are at liberty to say so here, in the family; but it is quite another matter to say that he is not a fit person to associate with us. To say that, you must be quite sure that he has done something disgraceful, of which we are all in ignorance."

"I quite agree with you," said Francesco Savelli. "You only make yourself ridiculous by saying such things," he added, looking coldly at his wife, for he was anxious that none of the ridicule should reflect upon himself, especially in Campodonico's presence.

"I am sure, when I call Ghisleri wild," said the Princess, "I mean nothing more than that he is fast. But I am very sorry to have brought about such a discussion. Adele, my dear, what do you mean? Are you in earnest?"

"One does not say such things for nothing," answered Adele, angrily.

"Then I wonder that you receive him," said the Prince, coldly. "I hope you will explain to me by and by what you refer to."

"I will, some day," said Adele, in a low voice. She felt that she had cast the die, and she hardly saw how she could draw back.

"In that case, we will say no more about the matter at present," said the master of the house, in a tone of authority. "I had meant to ask you for news of your brother," he said, turning to Campodonico. "I was very sorry to hear that he had been ill. Is he better?"

Gianforte answered, and every one made an effort to restore the outward calm which had been so disturbed by Adele's speech. Soon after dinner she went home, and instead of going to his club as usual Francesco got into the carriage with her.

"I insist upon knowing what you meant by your accusation against Ghisleri," he said, as soon as they were driving away.

"I will not tell you," Adele answered firmly. "You will find it out in time — quite soon enough, I daresay."

"I have the right to know. In the world in which we live one makes oneself ridiculous by saying such things. Everybody will laugh at you, and then you will expect me to take your part."

"I shall not expect anything of the sort, for I am not so foolish. You never had the slightest affection for me, and you have lost such little decent regard for me as you once felt, because I am always ill and it gives you trouble to be considerate. You would not raise a finger to help me or protect me unless you were afraid of the world's opinion. I have known that a long time, and now that I am in trouble I will not come to you. Why should I? You are only waiting for me to die, in order to ask Laura to marry you. It would annoy you extremely if I lived long enough to give her time to marry Ghisleri."

"I think remarks of that sort are in the worst possible taste," answered Savelli, "besides being without the least foundation in truth. I will beg you not to make any more of them. As for what you say about Ghisleri, if you refuse to tell me what you know I shall ask advice of my father, as that is the only proper course I could follow under the circumstances."

"For once we agree!" exclaimed Adele, with a scornful laugh. "That is precisely what I mean to do myself, and I will go to him to-morrow morning and tell him the whole story. But I will not tell it to you. He may, if he pleases, and thinks it best."

"In that case I have nothing more to say," answered Francesco. "You could not select a more fit person than my father."

"I am perfectly well aware of the fact." Adele, womanlike, was determined to have the last word, no matter how insignificant.

Both were silent during the remainder of the drive home. At the foot of the grand staircase Francesco left his wife and got into the carriage to be driven to his club. He reflected on the truth of Adele's observation, when

she had said that she might live until Laura and Ghisleri were married, and he was by no means pleased as he
realised how probable that contingency was. Since she
had become a slave to morphia he had, of course, been
at some pains to ascertain the limits of the disease, and
the possible duration of it, and he was aware that some
persons lived for many years in spite of a constant and
increasing abuse of the poison.

Adele once more went over the whole story in her
mind, preparing the details of it and polishing all the
parts into a harmonious whole. In spite of what she had
suffered that evening she would not increase her dose,
though she knew that she must very probably spend a
sleepless night. She profited by the hours to review the
story she intended to tell her father-in-law. At eleven
o'clock on the following morning she sent up to inquire
whether he would see her, and he at once appeared in
person at the door of her boudoir, — a tall, bearded man
of fifty years or more, slightly stooping, not over-care-
fully dressed, wearing spectacles, and chiefly remarkable
for his very beautifully shaped hands, with which he
made energetic gestures at almost every minute, when
speaking.

Adele began in some trepidation to explain how, on
the previous evening, she had lost her temper and had
been betrayed into making a remark about Ghisleri of
which her husband had demanded an explanation. She
felt, she said, that the matter was so serious as to justify
her in referring it at once to the head of the family, who
might then act as he thought best with regard to keeping
it a secret or informing his son of what had happened.
She did not fail to add that one of her motives in refusing to tell what she knew to Francesco, was her anxiety
for his safety, since the affair concerned herself and he
would undoubtedly take it up as a personal matter and
quarrel with the dangerous man who had so long been
her enemy. The Prince approved this course with a
grave nod, and waited for more.

Then she told her story from beginning to end. She of course took advantage of the fact that her father-in-law was but slightly acquainted with Ghisleri to paint his character with the colours best suited to her purpose, while asserting nothing about him which could be in direct contradiction to the testimony of others. She spoke very lucidly and connectedly, for she knew the lesson well and she was conscious that her whole existence was at stake. One fault, one little error sufficient to cast suspicion on her veracity, might be enough to ruin her in the end. She concluded by a well-turned and pathetic allusion to her state of health, which indeed was pitiable enough. She knew that she was dying, but it would make death doubly painful to think that such an enemy as Ghisleri was left behind to blacken her memory and perhaps hereafter to poison the thought of her in her children's hearts. She also read extracts from Ghisleri's letters and showed Laura's card, before mentioned.

As she proceeded she watched the Prince's face, and she saw that she had produced the right impression from the first. The plausibility of the tale, as she told it, was undeniable, and might have shaken the belief in Ghisleri's integrity in the minds of men who knew him far better than the elder Savelli. As she had anticipated, the latter took up the question as one deeply affecting the honour of his name. He was very angry in his calm way, and his blue eyes flashed through his great gold-rimmed spectacles, while his slender, energetic white hand clenched itself and opened frequently upon his knee.

" You have done right in coming to me directly," he said, when she had finished and was wiping away the tears which, in her nervous state, she had found easy to bring to her eyes. "Francesco would not have known how to act. He would probably have done the villain the honour of fighting with him. But I will bring him to justice. The law provides very amply for crimes of this sort. I confess I am strongly tempted to go and speak to the man myself. Francesco could not resist the temp-

tation, but he is almost a boy. The cowardly scoundrel
of a Tuscan!"

He thrust back his long, greyish-brown hair from his
forehead with one hand, and shook the other in the air as
though at a real adversary. When he did that he was
always roused to real anger, as Adele knew. She feared
lest he should do something more or less rash which
would not ultimately be of any advantage to her.

"Would it not be wise to speak to my father?" she
asked. "He knows a great deal about the law, I believe."

"Yes, perhaps so. Gerano is a very sensible man. As
this affects you, besides Francesco and all of us, it might
be as well to consult him, or at all events to put him in
possession of all the facts. In the meanwhile, you know
I am a methodical man. I must have proper notes to go
upon from the first. If it does not pain you too much
to go over the main points once more, I will write down
what I need."

"And I will hand you these papers to keep," said
Adele, giving him the correspondence, which comprised
the greater number of Ghisleri's letters, the two of her
own which she had not sent to Laura, the two she had
received from the lawyer Ubaldini, and Laura Arden's
card in its envelope to "Maria B." With regard to
Ubaldini, she told exactly what had happened, and what
she had written, for that incident at least was still a
mystery to her, and she thought it unwise to conceal
what might subsequently come to light through other
persons.

"I have heard of this fellow," said the Prince, thoughtfully. "He is a very clever criminal lawyer. I should
not wonder if Ghisleri had already consulted him. One
may expect anything after what you have told me."

Adele recapitulated the story with extraordinary exactness, stopping and repeating those portions of it which
her father-in-law desired to note.

"I have never seen a more complete chain of evidence,"
exclaimed the latter, when he had finished and was fold-

ing up the sheets neatly to match the size of the letters Adele had given him. "There is no court of justice in the world that would not convict a man of extortion on such testimony, and if there is one, I hope it is not in Rome."

"I hope not," said Adele, who would have smiled had she been alone. "But you may find it harder to convince my father than a Roman jury. He is prejudiced in Ghisleri's favour — like most people who do not know him as I do."

"He shall change his prejudices before long," answered Savelli, in a tone of certainty. "I will send word to him to expect me after breakfast, and I will explain the whole matter to him and show him the letters. If he does not at once understand, it would be better that we should both come to you together. You would make it clearer than I could, perhaps. But it seems clear enough to me. What an infamous affair — and how you must have suffered!"

"It is killing me!" said Adele, in a low voice.

Savelli left her with many expressions of kindly sympathy. He was not a good judge of human nature, for he lived too much in his studies and in the world of mathematics to understand or appreciate the motives of men and women. But he was kind of heart and affectionate by disposition. So far as he knew, Adele had been a good wife to his eldest son, and was the mother of strong, well-grown children who bore the ancient name in which he took such pride. Moreover, Adele had the honour of lending still greater lustre to the race by means of the great Braccio inheritance, which was all to come to the Savelli through her. She was, therefore, a very important personage, as well as a dutiful daughter-in-law and a good mother, in the eyes of the head of the house, and it would no more have crossed his mind that the story she had just told him was a fabrication, from first to last, than that the Greenwich Almanack for the year could be a fraud and a malicious misstatement of the movements of the heavenly bodies. Moreover, the evidence was, on the whole, such as would have staggered the faith of most of Ghisleri's acquaintances. The Prince lost no time in going to see Gerano, prepared at all points and armed with the papers Adele had given him.

The interview lasted fully two hours, and when it was over, Adele's father was almost as thoroughly persuaded of Ghisleri's guilt as Savelli himself. His face was very grave and thoughtful as he leaned back in his easy-chair and looked into his old friend's clear blue eyes.

"The man should be tried, convicted, and sent to the galleys," said Gerano. "There can be no doubt of the justice of that, if all this can be established in court. Remember I do not doubt my daughter's word, and it would be monstrous to suppose that she has invented this story. Whatever the truth about it may be, it must be thoroughly investigated. But there may be a good deal of exaggeration about it, for I have known Adele to overstate a case. There is a great difference between shutting one's door on a man, or turning him out of his club, and bringing an accusation against him which, if proved, will entail a term of penal servitude. You see that, I am sure. Do you not think that we ought to go and see Ghisleri together, tell him what we have learned, and ask him to justify himself if he can?"

"I think it would be wiser to consult the lawyers first," answered Savelli. "If they are of opinion that he is a criminal, there is no reason why we should give him warning that he may defend himself, as though he were an honest man. If they believe that this is not a case for the law, there will always be time for us to go and see him, since no open steps will have been taken."

Gerano was obliged to admit that there was truth in this, though his instinct told him that Ghisleri should be heard before being accused. He was one of those men whose faith being once shaken is not easily re-established, and he could not forget that his daughter had once deceived him, a fact with which Savelli was now also

2 B

acquainted, since Adele had told him the whole truth about that part of the story, but to which he attached relatively little importance as compared with Ghisleri's villanous conduct in attempting to extort money from a member of the Savelli family.

The two agreed upon the lawyer whom they would consult, and on the next day the first meeting took place at the Palazzo Braccio. The man they employed was elderly, steady, and experienced, and rather inclined to be over-cautious. He refused to give any decisive opinion on the case until he had studied it in all its bearings, thoroughly examined the letters, and ascertained the authenticity of the card on which Lady Herbert had written her thanks in pencil. This, of course, was the only one of the documents in evidence of which he could doubt the genuineness, since it was the only one which had not come direct from the hand of the writer. Oddly enough, the lawyer attached very great weight to it, for he said that it proved conclusively that Lady Herbert Arden had considered the matter as serious and had really paid money — whether a small or a large amount mattered little — in order to get possession of some of the letters which proved Ghisleri's guilt. It would be very useful if the woman "Maria B." could be traced and called as a witness, but even if she could not be found, Lady Herbert could not refuse her evidence and would not, upon her oath, deny having sent the money or having received Adele's letters in return for it. Considering the terms of intimacy on which she stood with Ghisleri, the point was a very strong one against the latter's innocence. The two princes were of the same opinion. Gerano was for asking Laura directly if she knew of the affair, but was overruled by Savelli and the lawyer, who objected that she might give Ghisleri warning. Gerano could not move in the matter without the consent of the other two, and resigned himself, though he looked upon the card as very doubtful evidence, and suggested that it might have been found accidentally by the woman who had come to Donna

Adele, and used by her as an additional means of induc-
ing the latter to give her money. But neither Prince
Savelli nor the lawyer was inclined to believe in any accident which could weaken the chain of evidence they held.

There was no further meeting for several days, during
which time the lawyer was at work in examining every
point which he considered vulnerable. Being himself a
perfectly honest man and having received the information he was to make use of from the father and father-in-
law of the lady concerned, it would have been very strange
if he had entertained any doubts as to her veracity.
Adele had thought of this herself and was satisfied that
throughout all the preliminaries her position would be as
strong as she could wish it to be. The struggle would
begin when Ghisleri was warned of what was now being
prepared against him, and began to defend himself. Of
one thing she was persuaded. If he had the confession
in his hands, he would not produce it. Nothing could
prove her case so conclusively as his avowal that the letter was in his hands. If he could demonstrate that he
had never seen it and was wholly ignorant of its contents,
her own case would fall through. The action, however,
if brought, would be a criminal one, and he would not
be allowed to give his own evidence. It would be hard,
indeed, to find any one who could swear to what would be
necessary to clear him.

The lawyer came back to his clients at last, and informed them that it was his opinion that there was sufficient evidence for obtaining a warrant of arrest against
Pietro Ghisleri, and that in all probability the latter
would be convicted, on his trial, of an infamous attempt
to extort money from the Princess Adele Savelli, as he
called her in his written notes. He warned them, however, that Ghisleri would almost undoubtedly be admitted
to bail, that he was a man who had numerous and powerful
friends in all parties, that he would doubtless be granted
a first and second appeal, and that the publicity and scandal of the whole case would be enormous. On the whole,

he advised his clients to settle the matter privately. He would, if they desired it, accompany them to Signor Ghisleri's lodgings, and state to him the legal point of view with all the clearness he had at his command. It was not impossible, it was even probable, that Ghisleri would quietly give up the document in question, and sign a paper binding himself never to refer to its existence again and acknowledging that he had made use of it to frighten the Princess Adele Savelli. The said document could then be returned to her and the affair might be considered as safely concluded. The lawyer did not believe that Signor Ghisleri would expose himself to certain arrest and probable conviction, when he had the means of escaping from both in his hands. Socially the two gentlemen could afterwards do what they pleased, and could of course force him to leave Rome with ignominy, never to show himself there again.

Prince Savelli, on the whole, concurred in this view. The Prince of Gerano said that he had known Ghisleri long and well, and that the latter would probably surprise them by throwing quite a new light on the case, though he would not be able to clear himself altogether. He, Gerano, was therefore of the same opinion as the others, and he quietly reminded Savelli that he had been the first to propose visiting Ghisleri and demanding a personal explanation.

On the same evening Pietro received a note. Prince Savelli and the Prince of Gerano presented their compliments to Signor Ghisleri, and begged to ask whether it would be convenient to him to receive them and their legal adviser on the following morning at half-past ten o'clock, to confer upon a question of grave importance. Ghisleri answered that he should be much honoured by the visit proposed, and he at once sent word to Ubaldini to come to him at eight o'clock, two hours and a half before he expected the others. He at once suspected mischief, though he had hardly been prepared to see it arrive in such a very solemn and dignified shape. He asked Ubaldini's opinion at once, when the latter came as requested.

"It is impossible to say what that good lady has done," said the young lawyer after some moments of thoughtful consideration. "You may take it for granted, however, that both Prince Savelli and the Prince of Gerano believe that you are in possession of the lost letter, and that they will make an attempt to force you to give it up. You would do well not to speak of me, but you can say that you foresaw that Donna Adele intended to make use of your letters when she wrote the first one, asking you to purchase the manuscript for her, and that you have kept copies of your answers, as well as the originals of her communications. If we are quick about it, we can bring an action against her for defamation before she can do anything definite."

"I will never consent to that," answered Ghisleri, smiling at Ubaldini's ideas of social honour.

"Why not?" asked the lawyer, in some surprise. "You would very probably win it and cast her for heavy damages."

"I would certainly never do such a thing," replied Pietro. "I should not think it honourable to bring any such action against a lady."

Ubaldini shrugged his shoulders, being quite unable to comprehend his client's point of view.

"I cannot do anything to help you, until we know what these gentlemen have to say," he observed. "If you wish it, I will be present at the interview, but it is as well that they should not find out who your lawyer is, until something definite is to be done."

Ghisleri agreed, and Ubaldini went away, promising to hold himself at his client's disposal at a moment's notice. Pietro sat down to think over the situation. Danger of some sort was evidently imminent, but he could only form a very vague idea of its nature, and Ubaldini had certainly not helped him much, sharp-witted and keen as he was. Ghisleri, who, of course, could not see the case as Adele had stated it to her father-in-law, and as it was now to be stated to himself, could not conceive it possible that he could be indicted for extortion on such slender evidence as he supposed she had been able to fabricate. He imagined that she desired his social ruin, and above all, to make him for ever contemptible in the eyes of Laura Arden; and this he well knew, or thought that he knew, she could never accomplish.

Laura had not yet returned, and he was glad, on the whole, that she was away. Matters were evidently coming to a crisis, and he believed that whatever was to happen would have long been over by the time she was in Rome again. If she had already arrived he would have found it hard not to tell her of what occurred from day to day, and, indeed, he would have felt almost obliged to do so for the sake of her opinion of him, seeing how frankly and loyally she had acted in the case of the letters she had received from the supposititious "Maria B." On the other hand, he longed to see her for her own sake. The summer months had been desperately long and lonely. He did not remember that he had ever found the time weigh so heavily on his hands as this year, both at Torre de' Ghisleri and in Rome. He forgot his present danger and the interview before him in thinking of Laura Arden, when Bonifazio threw open the door and announced Prince Savelli, the Prince of Gerano, and the Advocato Geronimo Grondona.

CHAPTER XXVII.

GHISLERI rose to meet his visitors, who greeted him gravely and sat down opposite him so that they could all look at his face while speaking. Prince Savelli naturally spoke first.

"We have come to you," he said, "upon a very difficult and unpleasant affair. In the first place, I must beg you to listen to what I have to say as calmly as you can, remembering that we have not come here to quarrel with you, but to act on behalf of a lady. This being the case, we claim to be treated as ambassadors, to be heard and to be answered."

"You speak as though you were about to make a very disagreeable communication," answered Ghisleri. "The presence of Signor Grondona either shows that you intend to make use of what I may say, or that your business is of a legal nature. If the latter supposition is the true one, it would be much better that we should leave the whole matter to our respective lawyers rather than run the risk of useless discussion. But if your lawyer is here to watch me and make notes, I would point out that I have a right to resent such observation, and to request you to find some other means of informing me of your meaning. As you tell me that you are acting for a lady, however, and claim personal immunity, so to say, for yourselves, I am willing to listen to you and to consider what you say as proceeding from her and not from you. But in no case have you any claim to be answered. That is the most I can do towards helping you with your errand. Judge for yourselves whether you will execute it or not."

"I will certainly not go away without saying what I have come to say," replied Savelli, fixing his bright, spectacled eyes upon Ghisleri's face. "We are here to represent Donna Adele Savelli — let that be understood, if you please. She wishes you to hand over to us a certain letter, of the nature of a confession, which you found at Gerano about two years and a half ago, and which you still hold."

Ghisleri was less surprised than might have been expected. His face grew slowly pale as he listened, steadily returning the speaker's gaze.

"I promised you personal immunity from the consequences of what you were about to say," he answered slowly. "It was a rash promise, I find, but I will keep it. You may inform Donna Adele Savelli that although it is commonly said in the world that she has actually lost such a letter as you mention, I have never seen it, nor have I any knowledge of its contents. Further, I demand, as a right, to be told upon what imaginary evidence she ventures to bring such an outrageous accusation against me."

The Advocato Grondona smiled, but the two noblemen preserved an unmoved manner. Of the two, Gerano was the more surprised by Ghisleri's answer. He had believed that a letter really existed and was in the latter's hands, but that it would not prove to have the importance his daughter attached to it. Prince Savelli produced a bundle of papers from his pocket.

"I am quite prepared," he said. "I will state my daughter-in-law's case as accurately as I can, and as nearly as possible in her own words, a great part of which I have here, in the form of notes."

"It is understood that Donna Adele Savelli is speaking, gentlemen. On that understanding you have my permission to proceed. I will not interrupt you."

Savelli began to speak, and, as he had promised, he stated the case as he had heard it from Adele and, on the whole, very much as she had summed it up in her own mind before going to him. Ghisleri sat with folded arms and bent brows, listening to the wonderfully connected chain of false testimony she brought against him, with all the courage and calmness he could command.

"Have you done?" he inquired in a voice shaking with anger, when Savelli had finished.

"Yes," answered the latter coolly. "I believe that is all."

"Then I have to say that a more villanous calumny was never invented to ruin any man. Good morning, gentlemen." He rose, and the three others were obliged to rise also.

"And so you positively refuse to give up the letter?"

inquired Savelli; there was an angry light in his eyes, too.

"I have given you my answer already. Be good enough to convey it to Donna Adele Savelli."

"Are you aware, Signore," said the lawyer, stepping in front of his two clients, "that upon such evidence as we possess you are liable to be indicted for an attempt to extort money from the Princess Adele Savelli?"

"You are not privileged, like these gentlemen," said Ghisleri, white to the lips. "If you venture to speak again, my servant will silence you. I have already hinted that this interview is ended," he added to Savelli and Gerano.

The three went out in silence and left him alone. With characteristic coolness he sat down to recover from the violent shock he had sustained, and to reflect upon his future conduct, before sending for Ubaldini and consulting with him. He had almost expected the demand to restore a document he did not possess, but he was not prepared for the well-constructed story by which Savelli, Gerano, and their lawyer had been persuaded of his guilt. The lawyer's words had placed the whole affair in a light which showed how thoroughly convinced the three men were of the justice of their accusation, and Ghisleri understood well enough that Savelli intended to take legal steps. What those steps might be, Pietro had not the least idea. He rang for Bonifazio and sent him out to buy the Penal Code. It was probably the wisest thing he could do under the circumstances, as he did not even know whether, if he were arrested, he should be admitted to bail or not. He saw well enough that an order for his arrest might very possibly be issued. Grondona was far too grave and learned a lawyer to have uttered such a threat in vain, and was not the man to waste time or words when action was possible. If he had spoken as he had, he had done so for his clients' advantage, in the hope that Ghisleri might be frightened at the last minute into giving up the letter. In that way all publicity and scandal could have been avoided.

But it was clear that the die was cast, and that war was declared. More than ever, he was glad that Laura Arden was not in Rome. The thought that if she were present she would necessarily have to follow the course of events little by little, as he must himself, and the certainty that she knew the truth and would feel the keenest sympathy for him, made him rejoice at her absence. When she learned what had taken place, she would know all the circumstances at once, including Ghisleri's proof of his innocence, which, as he felt sure, would be triumphant. In the meantime, she should be kept in ignorance of what was occurring. Having decided this point, he began to think of choosing some person to whom, if he were actually arrested, he might apply for assistance in the matter of obtaining bail. There was no time to be lost, as he was well aware. Since Savelli really believed him guilty of the abominable crime with which he was charged, it was not likely that time would be given him to leave the country, as his adversaries would naturally expect that he would attempt to do. They had probably gone straight from his lodging to the office of the chief of police, — the questore, as he is called in Italy, — and if they succeeded, as in all likelihood they would, in getting a warrant for his arrest, he might expect the warrant to be executed at any moment during the day. It was extremely important that he should be prepared for the worst. ' He thought of all the men he knew, and after a little hesitation he decided that he would write to San Giacinto. The latter had always been friendly to him, and Pietro remembered how he had spoken at the club, years ago, when Pietrasanta was gossiping about Arden's supposed intemperance. San Giacinto's very great moral weight in the world, due in different degrees to his character, his superior judgment, and his enormous wealth, made him the most desirable of allies. While he was waiting for Bonifazio's return, Ghisleri occupied himself in writing a note advising San Giacinto of the circumstances, and inquiring whether he might ask him for help.

The servant returned as he finished, and handed his master the little yellow-covered volume with an expression of inquiry on his face. Ghisleri looked at him and hesitated, debating whether it would be wise to warn the man of what might take place at any moment. There was much friendliness in the. relations between the two. Bonifazio had been with Pietro many years and perhaps understood the latter's character better than any one. The servant was almost as unlike other people, in his own way, as Ghisleri himself, and was in two respects a remarkable contrast to him. He was imperturbably good-tempered in the first place, and, in the second, he was extremely devout. But there were resemblances also, and it was for these that Ghisleri liked him. He was honest to a fault. He had more than once proved himself to be coolly courageous in some of his master's dangerous expeditions. Finally, he was discretion itself, and reticent in the highest degree. That such an otherwise perfect creature should have defects was only to be expected. Bonifazio was as obstinate as flint when he had made up his mind as to how any particular thing was to be done. He was silently officious, in his anxiety to be always ready to fulfil his master's wishes, and often annoyed him in small ways by thrusting services upon him which he did not require. On rare occasions he would insist upon giving very useless and uncalled-for advice.

Faithful and devoted in every way, he wholly disapproved, on religious grounds, of Ghisleri's mode of life, even so far as he was acquainted with it. He considered that Pietro lived and had lived for many years in sevenfold deadly sin, and he daily offered up the most sincere prayers for Pietro's repentance and reformation. Twice a year, also, he privately presented the parish priest with a small charity out of his savings, requesting him to say a mass for Ghisleri's benefit. Obstinate in this as in everything else, he firmly believed that his master's soul might ultimately be saved by sheer prayer-power, so to say.

These last facts, of course, did not come within Ghisleri's knowledge, for Bonifazio made no outward show of pious interest in Pietro's spiritual welfare, well knowing that he could not keep his situation an hour, if he were so unwise as to risk anything of the kind. But his silent disapproval showed itself in his mournful expression when Pietro had done anything which struck him as more than usually wicked and wild. The question of informing him that the police might be expected at any moment was not in itself a serious one. He would assuredly disbelieve the whole story, and vigorously deny the accusation when acquainted with both. Ghisleri determined to say nothing and immediately sent him out again with the note for San Giacinto. He then took up the Penal Code, and found the article referring to the misdeed of which he was accused. It read as follows:

ART. 409. Whosoever, by in any way inspiring fear of severe injury to the person, the honour, or the property of another, or by falsely representing the order of an Authority, constrains that other to send, deposit, or place at the disposal of the delinquent money, objects, or documents having any legal import whatsoever, is punished with imprisonment for a term of from two to ten years.

The law was clear enough. With regard to bail, he discovered with some difficulty that in such cases it could be obtained immediately, either on depositing the sum of money considered requisite according to circumstances, or by the surety of one or more well-known persons.

San Giacinto answered the note by appearing in person. When he undertook anything, he generally proceeded to the scene of action at once to ascertain for himself the true state of the case. Ghisleri explained matters as succinctly as possible.

"You will hardly believe that such things can be done in our day," he said as he concluded.

"I have seen enough in my time, and amongst my own near connexions, to know that almost anything conceivable may happen," answered the giant. "Meanwhile I shall not leave you until the police come, or until we know definitely that they are not coming. My carriage is below and has orders to wait all day and all night."

"You do not mean to say you really intend to stay with me?" asked Ghisleri, who was not prepared for such a manifestation of friendship.

"That is my intention," replied the other, calmly lighting a long black cigar. "If it lasts long, I will sleep on your sofa. If, however, you prefer that I should go to Savelli and make him tell me what he intends to do, I am quite ready. I think I could make him tell me."

"I think you could," said Ghisleri, with a smile, as he looked at his friend.

The huge, giant strength of the man was imposing in itself, apart from the terribly determined look of the iron features and deep-set eyes. Few men would have cared to find themselves opposed to San Giacinto even when he was perfectly calm, hardly any, perhaps, if his anger was roused. The last time he had been angry had been when he dragged the forger, Arnoldo Meschini, from the library to the study in Palazzo Montevarchi more than twenty years earlier. His hair was turning grey now, but there were no outward signs of any diminution in his powers, physical or mental.

"In any case," he said, "some time must elapse. It will need the greater part of the day to get a warrant of arrest."

Ghisleri would have been glad to end his suspense by allowing his friend to go directly to Savelli, as he had proposed to do. But considering what he had already shown himself ready to do, Pietro did not wish to involve him in the affair any further than necessary.

"Is it of any use to send for my lawyer?" asked Ghisleri, well aware of San Giacinto's superior experience in all legal matters.

"There is not the least hurry," answered the latter. "If the affair is brought to trial, there will be time enough and to spare. But if it amuses you, let us have the man here and ask his opinion. It can do no harm."

Accordingly Ubaldini was sent for. He looked very grave when Ghisleri had repeated all that Savelli had told him.

"But the mere fact that I consulted you when I did," said Ghisleri, "and had copies of my answers made, ought to prove at once that I knew even then what Donna Adele wished to attempt." But Ubaldini only shrugged his shoulders.

"That will be against you," answered San Giacinto. "It will be said that you were well aware of what you were doing, and that you were taking precautions in case of exposure. Even if Lady Herbert were here to give evidence, it would not help you much. After all, Donna Adele's story about the seamstress is plausible, and Lady Herbert took your explanation on faith."

"Lady Herbert shall not be called as a witness, if I can help it," said Ghisleri. "It is bad enough that her name should appear at all."

"The difficulty," observed Ubaldini, "is that every point can be turned against you from first to last. I am afraid that even my little stratagem has done no good. I wished to find out whether the confession really existed, and I thought it best that you should be in ignorance of the steps I took and of the result I obtained, in case you should be called upon to swear to anything in a possible action brought by you for defamation. The less an innocent man knows of the facts of a case, when he is on his oath, the better it generally turns out for him. The first thing to be done is to find the dealer with whom you negotiated for the purchase of the manuscript. His evidence will be the strongest we can get. Of course, even to that they will answer that you would not be so foolish as to write what looked like an account of a genuine transaction without lending an air of truth to it, in case of necessity, by actually making inquiries about it. If it is found that the prices named in your letters agree with those asked by the dealer, they will say that you cleverly chose a very valuable work, and

determined to be guided by the value of it, in appraising
the letter you held. If the prices did not agree, they
would say that even if the transaction were genuine, you
had conducted it dishonestly; but then, as a matter of
fact, the discovery was a good proof that it was a mere
sham. Of course, too, you will have friends, like the Signor Marchese here present, who will swear to your previous character; but you must not forget that in a case like
this the great body of educated public and social opinion
is with the woman rather than the man."

"In other words," said Ghisleri, with a laugh, "I am
to stand my trial for extortion, and am very likely to be
convicted. You are not very encouraging, Signor Ubaldini, but I suppose you will find a word to say in my
defence before everything is over."

"I will do my best," answered the young lawyer,
thoughtfully. "I would like to know where this confession is. One thing is quite certain: if it had got into
the hands of a dishonest person, Donna Adele would
have heard of it before now, and would have tried to
buy it, as she did try to get it from the maid Lucia,
according to her own account, and from me. In the
meanwhile, I will go and examine the dealer. Will you
kindly give me his name and address."

Ghisleri wrote both on a card and Ubaldini went away.
Before Ghisleri and San Giacinto had been alone together half an hour, he came back, looking rather pale
and excited.

"It is most unfortunate," he exclaimed. "The devil
is certainly in this business. The man was buried yesterday. He died of apoplexy two days ago."

"Nothing surpasses the stupidity of that!" cried San
Giacinto, angrily. "Why could not the idiot have lived
a fortnight longer?"

Ghisleri said nothing, but he saw what importance both
his friend and the lawyer had attached to the dead man's
testimony. There was little hope that his clerk would
be able to say anything in Ghisleri's favour. He had of

course only spoken with the dealer himself, generally in a private room and without witnesses. He began to fear that his case was even worse than he had at first supposed.

"The best possible defence, in my opinion," said Ubaldini, "is to tell your own story and compare it, inch by inch, with theirs. I believe that, after all, yours will seem by far the more probable in the eyes of any court of justice. Then we will question Donna Adele's sanity, and bring a couple of celebrated authorities to prove that people who use morphia often go mad and have fixed ideas. Donna Adele's delusion is that you are the possessor of her confession. If we cannot prove that it has been all this time in the hands of some one else, we may at least be able to show that there is no particular reason why it should have been in yours, that you are certainly not in need of fifty thousand francs, and that, so far as any one knows, you are not the man to try and get it in this way if you were. We will do the best we can. I got a man off scot free the other day who had murdered his brother in the presence of three witnesses. I proved that one was half-witted, that the second was drunk, and that the third could not possibly have been present at all, because he ought to have been somewhere else. That was a much harder case than this. The jury shed tears of pity for my ill-used client."

"I will do without the tears," said Ghisleri, with a smile, "provided they will see the truth this time."

San Giacinto kept his word, and refused to leave Ghisleri's lodging that night, sending Bonifazio to his house for clothes and necessaries, and ordering fresh horses and another coachman and footman to replace those that had waited all day. He distinctly objected to cabs, he said, because they were always too small for him; and if Ghisleri was to be arrested, he intended to drive with him to the prison in order to give bail for him immediately. And so he did. On the following day Rome was surprised by a spectacle unique in the recollection of its inhabitants, high or low. The largest of the large open carriages belonging to Casa San Giacinto was seen rolling solemnly through the city, bearing Pietro Ghisleri, the Marchese di San Giacinto himself, and two policemen, who looked very uncomfortable as they sat, bolt upright, side by side, with their backs to the horses. A few hours later, the same carriage appeared again, Pietro and the giant being still in it, but without the officers of the law. San Giacinto insisted upon driving his friend six times round the Villa Borghese, six times round the Pincio, and four times the length of the Corso, before taking him back at last to his lodgings.

"It will produce a good effect," he said; "most people are fools or cowards, or both, and imitation as a rule needs neither courage nor wisdom. Come and dine with us to-morrow night, and I will have a party ready for you who do not belong to the majority. I shall go to the club now and give an account of the day's doings."

"Why not wait and let people find out for themselves what has happened?" asked Pietro. "Will it do any good to talk of it?"

"Since people must talk or die," answered San Giacinto, "I am of opinion that they had better tell the truth than invent lies."

When he was gone Ghisleri wondered what had impelled him to take so much trouble. It would have been quite enough if he had appeared at the right moment to give security for him, and that alone would have been a very valuable service. But San Giacinto had done much more, for his action had shown the world from the first that he intended to take Ghisleri's side. The latter, who was always surprised when any one showed anything approaching to friendship for him, was exceedingly grateful, and determined that he would not in future laugh at the idea of spontaneous human kindness without motive, as he had often laughed in the past.

Meanwhile San Giacinto went to his club. A score of men were lounging in the rooms, and most of them

2 c

had been talking of the new scandal, though in a rather guarded way, for no one wished to quarrel either with Ghisleri or his ally. On seeing the latter go to the smoking-room, almost every one in the club followed him, out of curiosity, in the hope that he would give some explanation of what had occurred. They were not disappointed. San Giacinto stood with his back to the fireplace, looking at each face that presented itself before him.

"Gentlemen," he began : " I see that you expect me to say something. I will. I do not wish to offend any one; but, with the exception of all of ourselves here assembled, most people tell lies, consciously or unconsciously, when they do not know the truth, and sometimes when they do, which is worse. So I mean to tell you the truth about my driving with Ghisleri and two policemen to-day, and the reason why I have been driving with him all the afternoon. After that you may believe what you like about the matter. The facts are these. Yesterday Ghisleri wrote me a note telling me that he expected shortly to be arrested on a charge of extortion and asking if I would be bail for him. That is what I have done. The accusation comes from Casa Savelli, and declares that for two years and a half Ghisleri has had possession of that letter belonging to Donna Adele which she wrote to her confessor, which was lost on the way, and of which we have all heard vague hints for some time. Casa Savelli says that Ghisleri has been trying to make her pay money for it, and has otherwise made her life unbearable to her by means of it. There are letters of Ghisleri's referring to the manuscript of Isabella Montevarchi's confession which was for sale this autumn, and Casa Savelli says that this manuscript was spoken of in order to disguise the real transaction contemplated. Ghisleri says it is a plot to ruin him, and that he has been aware of it ever since last spring. Meanwhile he has actually been arrested and I have given bail for him. That is the story. I drove about with him this afternoon to show that I, for my part, take his side, and believe him to be perfectly innocent. That is what I had to say. I am obliged to you for having listened so patiently."

As he turned to go away, not caring for any further discussion at the time, he was aware that a dark man of medium height, with very broad shoulders and fierce, black eyes, was standing beside him, facing the crowd.

"I am entirely of San Giacinto's opinion," said Gianforte Campodonico, in clear tones. "I believe Ghisleri utterly incapable of any such baseness. Donna Adele Savelli is a relation of mine, but I will stand by Ghisleri in this, come what may. I hope that no one will have the audacity to propose any action of the club in the case, such as requesting him to withdraw, until after the trial."

"But when a man is indicted for crime, and has been arrested —" began some one in the crowd.

"I said," repeated Gianforte, interrupting the speaker in a hard and menacing voice, "that I hoped no one would have the audacity to propose that the club should take any action in the case. I hope I have made myself clearly understood."

Such was the character and reputation of Campodonico that the man who had begun to speak did not attempt to proceed, not so much from timidity, perhaps, as because he felt that in the end two men like Gianforte and San Giacinto must carry public opinion with them. As they stood side by side before the fireplace, they were as strong and determined a pair of champions as any one could have wished to have.

"You are quite right," said San Giacinto, in an approving tone. "Of course I have neither the power nor the right to prevent discussion. Every one will talk about this case and the trial, and as it is a public affair every one has a right to do so, I suppose. I only wish it to be known that I believe Ghisleri innocent, and I am glad to see that Campodonico, who knows him very well, is of my opinion."

After this there was nothing more to be said, and the crowd dispersed, talking together in low tones. The two men who had undertaken Ghisleri's defence remained together. San Giacinto looked down at his young companion, and his stern face softened strangely. A certain kind of manly courage and generosity was the only thing that ever really touched him.

"I am glad to see that there are still men in the world," he said. "Will you have a game of billiards?"

The first result of this was that there was relatively very little talk about Ghisleri among the men when they were together. It is probable that both San Giacinto and Campodonico would have spoken precisely as they did, if all the assembled tribe of Savelli and Gerano had been present to hear them; and when the two families heard what had been said, they were very angry indeed. Unfortunately for them, nothing could be done. As San Giacinto had rightly put it, the trial was to be a public affair, and every one had a right to his own opinion. But there were not wanting those who sided with the Savelli, for though Ghisleri had few enemies, if any, besides Adele, yet there were many who were jealous of him for his social successes, and who disliked his calm air of superiority. The story became the constant topic of conversation in most of the Roman families, and many who had for years received Ghisleri immediately determined that they would be very cautious and cool until he should prove his innocence to the world.

He himself, during the days which followed, saw much of San Giacinto, who told him what Campodonico had said at the club.

CHAPTER XXVIII.

WHEN Laura Arden returned to Rome, she was met by her mother with a full account of what had taken place. Under any ordinary circumstances the Princess of Gerano would have been very merciful in her judgment and would assuredly not have hastened to give her daughter every detail of the last great scandal. But she had never liked Ghisleri, and she had feared that Laura was falling in love with him, and he with Laura. Moreover, neither her love for her own child nor Adele's shortcomings had destroyed all her affection for the latter, and under her husband's influence she had lately come to look upon Ghisleri as a monster of iniquity and on Adele as little less than a martyr. She spared Laura nothing as she told the story, and was unconsciously guilty of considerable exaggeration in explaining the view the world in general took of the case, though that was bad enough at best. Laura's dark eyes flashed with indignation as she listened.

"I do not believe a word of this story, mother," she said. "As for the part I am supposed to have played in it, you had better know the truth at once. When I got those letters, I sent for Signor Ghisleri, and gave them to him. We knew at once that they came from Adele herself."

She told her mother exactly what had occurred, and how she had believed in him then, and should believe in him still. The Princess sighed and shook her head.

"There is very little left to believe in, my dear," she said, "trustful though you are, to a fault. I hope you will at all events not receive him until after the trial. Indeed, it will be quite impossible — I am sure you would not think of it. If he has any sense of decency left, he will not call."

"I will not only receive him," answered Laura, without

hesitation : "whenever he chooses to come, but if he does not come of his own accord, I will make him. What is the use of friendship, if it will not bear any test?"

"I suppose it is of no use to discuss the matter," said the Princess, wearily. "You will do as you please. I do not recognise you any longer."

As soon as her mother was gone, Laura wrote a note to Pietro, telling him that she had heard all the story, that she believed in him as firmly as ever, and begging him to come and see her on the following day at the usual hour. The last words dropped from her pen naturally. It seemed but yesterday that they had spoken of meeting "at the usual hour" on the morrow of the day after that. Ghisleri's heart beat faster as he broke the seal, and when he came to the words he was conscious that its beating annoyed him. He knew, now, that he loved her well, as he had loved but once before in his life. But he determined that he would not go and see her. He blessed her for believing in his innocence, but there were many strong reasons against his going to her house, or even seeing her. Merely on general grounds he would have kept away, while under the accusation which hung over him, as even the Princess of Gerano had anticipated that he would, and feeling as he did that he loved her in good earnest, it would have seemed absolutely dishonourable to renew their former relations until he had cleared himself. He wrote her a short note.

"My Dear Friend: — I am deeply touched by your wishing to see me, and I am more than ever grateful for your friendship and for the faith you have in me. But I will not come to you at present. I am accused of a crime worse than most crimes, in my opinion, and the world is by no means altogether on my side. When I have cleared myself publicly, I will come and thank you — if I can find words for the thanks you deserve.

"Most gratefully and faithfully,

"Pietro Ghisleri."

He was not prepared for the answer which came within the hour in the shape of a second note, short, vigorous, and decisive. It seemed hard to realise that the sweet, dark woman with deep, holy eyes, as he had once described her, could be the writer of such determined words.

"MY DEAR SIGNOR GHISLERI: — I care for the world and its opinion much less than you do for my sake, or than you suppose I do for myself. I mean to see you, and to have it known that I see you, and I will. If you are not here to-morrow at precisely one o'clock I will go to your lodgings and wait for you if you are out. People may say what they please.

"Ever yours sincerely,

"LAURA ARDEN."

Ghisleri read the note over several times, to be quite sure that he had not misunderstood it, and then burned it, as he had always burned everything in the nature of writing until his last difficulties had begun. He saw that Laura had forced the situation, and he knew her well enough not to doubt that she would execute her threat to the letter, and wait for him, watch in hand, on the morrow. He hated himself for being glad, for he knew that the world she despised would give her little credit for her generous act. Yet, in spite of his self-contempt, he was happy. Five minutes before one o'clock on the next day he rang at her door. She had returned as usual to the small apartment she had occupied since leaving the Tempietto.

He found her dressed for walking, all in black, and looking at the clock. As he entered she turned and laughed happily. There was a faint colour in her cheeks too.

"I knew you would not let me ruin my reputation for the sake of your obstinacy," she said, as she came forward to meet him. "In four minutes I would have left the house." She grasped his hand warmly as she spoke.

"No," he said, "I could not have done that. What ways you have of forcing people to obey you! But you are very wrong; I still maintain that."

"Sit down," she said, "and let us talk of more interesting things. I must hear the whole story from your own lips, though I am sure my mother did her best to be quite truthful; but she does not understand you and never will, as I begin to think."

"Tell me first how you are, and about Herbert," said Ghisleri. "You will hear quite enough of this miserable affair. It will keep a day or two."

"It need not keep so long as that," answered Laura, "I can tell you the news in a few words. I am perfectly well. Herbert is perfectly well too, thank God, and has outgrown his clothes twice and his shoes four times since we have been away. Since I last wrote great things have happened. I have been in England again at last, and have stayed with the Lulworths. You see I am in mourning. Uncle Herbert died a month ago. I never saw the old gentleman but once, for he lived in the most extraordinary way, in complete isolation. You know that —well, he is dead, and he has left all the fortune to my Herbert, with a life interest in one-quarter of it for me, besides an enormous allowance for Herbert's education. That is all there is to tell."

"It is good news indeed," said Ghisleri. "I am so glad. It will make an immense difference to you, though of course you have known of it a long time."

"It will not make so much difference as you fancy. I shall go on living much as I do, for I have had almost all I wanted in these years. But I am glad for Herbert's sake, of course. And now begin, please, and do not stop until you have told me everything."

"Needs must, when you will anything," Ghisleri answered, with a faint smile.

So he told her the story, while she listened and watched him. She had developed in strength and decision during the last year, more rapidly than before, and he felt in speaking to her as though she had power to help him and would use it. He was grateful, and more than grateful. Within the last few weeks he had learned that the strongest and most determined men may sometimes need a friend. He had long had one in her, and he had found a new one in San Giacinto; but though the latter's imposing personality had more influence in the world than that of any man Ghisleri knew, there was that in Laura's sympathy which gave him a new strength of his own, and fresh courage to face the many troubles he expected to encounter before long. For man gets no such strength in life to do great deeds or to bear torments sudden and sharp or mean, little and harassing, as he gets from the woman he loves, even though he does not yet know that she loves him again.

"I hope I do not take my own side too much," he said, as he ended the long tale, "though I suppose that when a man is perfectly innocent he has a right to say hard things of people who accuse him. For my own part, I believe that Donna Adele is mad. There is the ingenuity of madness in everything she does in this affair. No sane person could invent such a story almost out of nothing, and make half the world believe it."

"She may be mad," Laura answered, "but she is bad, too. It will all come out at the trial, and she will get what she deserves."

"I hope so. But do you know what I really expect? Unless it can be proved that the confession has been all the time in the safe keeping of some person who has not even read it, I shall be convicted and imprisoned. I am quite prepared for that. I suppose that will come to me by way of expiation for my sins."

"Please do not talk like that," cried Laura. "It is absurd! There is no court in the world that would convict you—a perfectly innocent man. Besides I shall give my evidence about those letters. I shall insist upon it. That alone would be enough to clear you."

"I am afraid not. Even my lawyer thinks that your testimony would not help me much. After all, you know what happened. I told you that I was innocent, and you believed me. Or, if you please, you believed me innocent before I said I was. There is only your belief or my word to fall back upon, and neither would prove anything in court. Ubaldini says so. I really expect to be convicted, and I will bear it as well as I can. I will certainly not do anything to escape from it all." He had hesitated as he reached the last words, but he saw that Laura understood.

"You should not even think of such things," she said gravely. "You are far too brave a man to take your own life even if you were convicted, and you shall not be. I tell you that you shall not be!" she repeated, with sudden energy.

"No one can tell. But I am inclined to think that if you were angry you might terrify judge and jury into doing whatever you pleased." He laughed a little. "You have grown so strong of late that I hardly recognise you. What has made the change?"

"Something — I cannot explain it to you. Besides — was I ever a weak woman? Did I ever hesitate much?"

"No, that is true. Perhaps I did not use the right word. You seem more active, more alive, more determined to influence other people."

"Do I? It may be true. I fancy I am less saint-like in your opinion than I was. I am glad of it. You used to think me quite different from what I was. But I know that I have changed during this summer. I feel it now."

"So have I. The change began before you went away." Ghisleri glanced at her, and then looked at the wall.

A short silence followed. Both felt strangely conscious that their former relation had not been renewed exactly where it had been interrupted by their separation in the summer. But there was nothing awkward about the present break in the conversation.

"In what way have you changed?" asked Laura at last. She had evidently been thinking of his words during the pause.

"Indeed I should find it hard to tell you now," Ghisleri answered, with a smile at the thought uppermost in his mind. "I would rather not try."

"Is it for the worse, then?" Laura's eyes sought his.

"No. It is for the better. Perhaps, some day, if all this turns out less badly—" He stopped, angry with himself for having said even that much.

"Shall you have more confidence in me when the trial is over?" asked Laura, leaning back and looking down. "Have I shown that I believe in you, or not, to-day?" Had she known what was so near his lips to say, she might not have spoken.

"You have done what few women would have done. You know that I know it. If I will not say what I am thinking of, it is for that very reason." His fingers clasped each other and unclasped again with a sharp, nervous movement.

"I am sorry you do not trust me altogether," said Laura.

"Please do not say that. I do trust you altogether. But I respect you too. Will you forgive me if I go away rather suddenly?" He rose as he spoke and held out his hand.

"You are not ill, are you?" Laura stood up, looking anxiously into his face. Unconsciously she had taken his hand in both of her own.

"No—I am not ill. Good-bye!"

"Come to-morrow, please. I want to see you often. Promise to come to-morrow." Her tone was imperative, and he knew that she had the power to force him to compliance.

He yielded out of necessity, and left her. When he was in the street he stood still a few moments, leaning upon his stick as though he were exhausted. His face was white. Oddly enough, what he felt recalled an accident which had once happened to him. On a calm, hot day, several years earlier, he had been slowly sailing along a southern shore. The heat had been intense, and he had thrown himself into the water to get a little coolness, holding by a rope, and allowing himself to be towed along under the side of the boat. Then one of the men called to him loudly to come aboard as quickly as he could. As he reached the deck, the straight black fin of a big shark glided smoothly by. He could remember the shadow it cast on the bright blue water, and the sensation he experienced when he saw how near he had unconsciously been to a hideous death. Like many brave but very sensitive men, he had turned pale when the danger was quite past and had felt for one moment something like physical exhaustion. The same feeling overtook him now as he paused on the pavement before the house in which Laura Arden lived. An instant later he was walking rapidly homeward.

At the corner of a street he came suddenly upon Gianforte Campodonico. Both men raised their hats almost at the same moment, for their relations were necessarily maintained upon rather formal terms. Ghisleri owed his old adversary a debt of gratitude for his conduct at the club, but a rather exaggerated sense of delicacy hindered Pietro from stopping and speaking with him in the street. Campodonico, however, would not let him pass on and stood still as Ghisleri came up to him.

"I wish to thank you with all my heart for the generous way in which you have spoken of me," said Ghisleri, grasping the other's ready outstretched hand.

"You have nothing to thank me for," replied Gianforte. "Knowing you to be a perfectly honourable and honest man, I should have been a coward if I had held my tongue. You have a good friend in San Giacinto, and I suppose I cannot be of much use to you. But if I can, send for me. I shall never like you perhaps, but I will stand by you, because I respect you as much as any man living."

"I thank you sincerely," said Ghisleri, pressing his hand again. "You are very generous."

"No, but I try to be just."

They parted, and Ghisleri pursued his way, meditating on the contradictions of life, and wondering why at the most critical moment of his existence the one man who had come forward unasked and of his own free impulse to defend him publicly and to offer his help, should be his oldest and most implacable enemy. He was profoundly conscious of the man's generosity. The world, he said to himself, might not be such a bad place after all. But he did not guess how soon he was to need the assistance so freely proffered.

He went home at once. Bonifazio closed the door behind him and followed him respectfully into the sitting-room.

"I beg pardon, signore," he began, standing still as he waited for Ghisleri to turn and look at him.

"Do you need money?" asked the latter carelessly.

"No, signore. You have perhaps forgotten that you gave me money yesterday. It is something which I have had upon my conscience a long time, and now that you are falsely accused, signore, it is my duty to speak, if you permit me."

"Tell me what it is." Ghisleri sat down at his writing-table, and lit a cigarette.

"It is a very secret matter, signore. But if I keep it a secret any longer, I shall be doing wrong, though I also did wrong in coming by the information I have, though I did not know it. I have also been to a lawyer who understands these matters, and takes an interest in the case, and he has told me that unless some saint performs a miracle nothing can save you at the trial. So that I must give my evidence. But if I do, the Princess Adele will go to the galleys, and the house of Savelli will be quite ruined. For the Princess murdered Lord Herbert Arden, and tried to murder Donna Laura, as we call her. She invited them to dinner and gave them napkins which she with her own hand had poisoned with infection of the scarlet fever, her maid Lucia having had it at the time. And Lord Herbert died within three days, but

Donna Laura did not catch it. And I have read how she did this, and many other wicked things, in a letter written with her own hand. For it was I who found the confession they speak of, when I went alone to look at the old prisons at Gerano, while you and the signori were out driving. And now I do not know what to do, but I had to speak in order to save you, and you must judge of the rest, signore, and pardon me if I have done wrong."

Ghisleri knew the truth at last, and his lean, weather-beaten face expressed well enough the thirst for vengeance that burned him. He waited a few moments and then spoke calmly enough.

"Have you got the confession here?" he asked. "If it is found in my house it will ruin me, though it may ruin Donna Adele too."

"I understand, signore. Have no fear. I read it through, because I found it open and the leaves scattered as it must have fallen, though how it fell there I do not know. But it is still at Gerano. If you will allow me, I will explain what I did. When I had read it, I put it into my pocket, saying to myself that it was a difficult case for the conscience. And I thought about it for more than an hour while I walked about the castle. Then I went and got an envelope and I put the leaves into it thinking that perhaps it would be wrong to burn it. So I wrote on the outside: 'This was found in the prison of the castle of Gerano by Bonifazio di Rienzo,' and I also wrote the date in full. Then at the tobacconist's shop in the village I bought some wax, and took a seal I have, which is this one, signore. It has 'B. R.' on it. And I sealed the letter with much wax, so that the tobacconist laughed at me. But I did not let him see what was written on the envelope. Then I took it to the parish priest whose name is Don Tebaldo, and who seemed to me to be a very respectable and good man. I told him in confidence that I had found something which it was not possible for me to give to the rightful owner, but which I thought it would be wrong to destroy, because the rightful owner might some day make inquiry for it and wish to have it. He asked many questions, but I would not answer them all, and he did not know what the letter was about nor that it was a confession. So I begged him to put it into another envelope and to seal it again with his own seal, and I gave him what was left of the wax I had bought. Then he did as I asked him, and wrote on the back: 'This was brought to me to be kept, by one Bonifazio di Rienzo, until the owner claims it. But it is to be burned when I die.' And there it is to this day, for I have made inquiries and Don Tebaldo is alive and well, and God bless him! So I come to tell you all this, in order that you may act as you see fit, signore. For Don Tebaldo can swear that I gave him the letter on the day I found it and I can swear that you never knew anything of it."

Ghisleri looked at his faithful old servant, whose round brown eyes met his so steadily and quietly.

"I can never thank you enough, my dear Bonifazio," he said. "You have saved me. I will not forget it."

"As for that, signore, I will not accept any present, and I humbly beg you not to offer me any, for it would be the price of blood, such as Judas Iscariot received, seeing that the Princess Adele will go to the galleys."

"You need not be afraid of that, Bonifazio," answered Ghisleri. "Casa Savelli will easily prove that she was mad, as I believe she is, and she will end her life in a lunatic asylum. But you must not bring either Don Tebaldo or the letter here. Go at once to the Marchese di San Giacinto and tell him exactly what you have told me, and that I sent you. He will know what to do. Take money with you and execute his orders exactly without returning here, no matter what they are. I can do without you for a week if necessary, and I wish to know nothing of the matter until it is over."

"Yes, signore," answered Bonifazio, and without more words he left the room and went directly to San Giacinto's house.

The latter received him in his study, and listened to his story with calm attention. Then, without making any remark, he smoked nearly half a cigar, while Bonifazio stood motionless, respectfully watching him. Then he rang the bell, and gave the man who answered it instructions to order out a sort of mail-cart he used for driving himself, and the strongest horses in the stable.

"You must come with me," he said to Bonifazio. "We can be back before midnight." Then he began to write rapidly.

He wrote a note to his cousin, the Prince of Sant' Ilario, another to Gianforte Campodonico, and then a rather longer one to Savelli. In the last mentioned, he informed the Prince that he would appear on the morrow, with Campodonico and Sant' Ilario, and that he desired to be received by Savelli himself in the presence of Francesco and Adele, as he had a communication of the highest importance to make. In his usual hard way he managed to convey the impression that it would be decidedly the worse for the whole house of Savelli and for Adele in particular if his request were not complied with to the letter. By the time he had finished a servant announced that the carriage was waiting. San Giacinto thrust a handful of black cigars and a box of matches into his outer pocket.

"Come," he said to Bonifazio, "I am ready. It is a long drive to Gerano."

It was nearly three o'clock in the afternoon when they started, and the days were very short and the weather threatening. But the horses were splendid animals, and there were few roads between Rome and the Abbruzzi which San Giacinto did not know well. He was acting as he always did, swiftly, surely, and in person, trusting to no one, and making himself alone responsible for the result. Before one o'clock in the morning he was back, bringing with him a mild and timid old priest, muffled in a horse blanket against the bitter wind. But the sealed packet containing Adele Savelli's confession was in his own pocket.

On his table he found three notes, which satisfied him that everything would take place as he had hastily planned it before his departure. Campodonico expressed his readiness to serve Ghisleri in any way, Sant' Ilario said that he was ready to support San Giacinto in anything he undertook, though he had never been intimate with Ghisleri, who was much younger than he. Savelli answered coldly that he would receive the three men as requested, adding that he hoped the communication would prove to be of such importance as to justify putting his daughter-in-law to the inconvenience which any prolonged interview caused her in her present state of ill-health. San Giacinto smiled rather grimly. He did not think that his visit to Casa Savelli need be a very long one. Before he went to bed, he debated whether he should send word to Gerano to be present also, but he ultimately decided not to do so. It seemed useless to make Adele's father witness his daughter's humiliation, though he meant not to spare either Savelli or his son. Towards Adele he was absolutely pitiless. It was his nature. If she had been dying, he would have found means to make her listen to what he had to say. If she had been at the very last gasp he would have forced his way to her bedside to say it. He was by no means a man without faults.

Meanwhile Ghisleri was pacing his room in solitude, reflecting on the sudden change in all the prospects of the future, and wondering how matters would be managed, but feeling himself perfectly safe in San Giacinto's hands, and well understanding that he was not to be informed of what had happened until all was over. That San Giacinto would face all the assembled Savelli and force them then and there to withdraw all charges against Ghisleri, the latter was sure, and, on the whole, he was glad that he was not to witness their discomfiture. But it was not only of his being in one moment cleared of every accusation that he thought. The consequences to himself were enormous. He remembered the sickening horror he had felt that afternoon when he realised how nearly he had told Laura that he loved her. In four and twenty hours there would be nothing to hinder him from speaking out what filled his heart. If he chose to do so, he might even now write to her and tell her what he had struggled so hard to hide when they had been face to face. But he was not the man to write when there was a possibility of speaking, nor to trust to the black and white of ink and paper to say for him what he could say better for himself.

Then the old doubt came back, and he spent a night of strange self-questioning and much useless moral torment. Was this the last, the very last of his loves? He remembered how a little less than three years earlier he had bid good-bye to Maddalena dell' Armi, saying to himself that he could never again feel his heart beat at a woman's voice, nor his face turn pale with passion for a woman's kiss. And now he loved again, perhaps with little hope of seeing his love returned, but with the mad desire to stake his fate upon one cast, and win or lose all for ever. He had never felt that irresistible longing before, not even when he had first loved Bianca Corleone in his early days. Then, it was true, he had been very young, and Bianca had not been like Laura. She had been young herself as he was, and had loved him from the first, almost without hiding it. There had been little need for words on either side, for love told his own tale plainly. Yet it seemed to him now that if he had then thought Bianca as cold as he had reason to believe that Laura was, he might have resigned himself to his fate at the beginning — he might not have found the strength he now had to risk such a defeat as perhaps waited him, to run any danger, now that he was free, rather than live in suspense another day.

CHAPTER XXIX.

SANT' ILARIO and Gianforte Campodonico rang at San Giacinto's door half an hour before the time the latter had appointed for his descent upon Casa Savelli. He had not explained the situation in the hurried notes he had written them on the previous day, and they did not know what was to take place.

"It is very simple," said San Giacinto, coolly. "The whole story was a lie from beginning to end, as I always believed. The confession was found at Gerano and deposited with the parish priest under seal on the same day. I went to Gerano and brought the priest and the letter back. Here it is, if you wish to see the outside of it, and the priest is waiting in the next room. This is the document which Donna Adele will have signed an hour hence."

He produced a sheet of stamped paper from the drawer of his writing-table and read aloud what was written upon it, as follows:

"I, the undersigned, being in full possession of my faculties, and free of my will, hereby publicly withdraw each and every one of the accusations I have made, publicly or privately, either in my own person or through my father, the Prince of Gerano, or my father-in-law, Prince Savelli, my husband, Francesco, Prince Savelli, or through any other persons purporting to represent me, against Pietro Nobile Ghisleri; and I declare upon my oath before God that there is not and never was any truth whatsoever in any one of the said accusations upon which the said Pietro Nobile Ghisleri was unjustly arrested and accused of extortion under Article 409 of the Penal Code. And I further declare that the letters of his which I hold do and did refer directly to the purchase of the manuscript writings of Donna Isabella Montevarchi which were at that time for sale, and to no other manuscript or writing whatsoever; and further, I declare that no such person as ' Maria B.' was ever known to me, but that I wrote the letters received from ' Maria B.' by Lady Herbert Arden, and that I withdrew her answers myself from the general post-office. And if I have done anything else to strengthen the false accusation against the said Pietro Nobile

Ghisleri such as may hereafter come to light, this present retraction and denial shall be held to cover it by anticipation. And hereunto I set my hand and seal in the presence of Don Giovanni Saracinesca, Prince of Sant' Ilario, of Don Giovanni Saracinesca, Marchese di San Giacinto, and of Don Gianforte Campodonico di Norba, who in my presence and in the presence of each other are witnesses of this act."

San Giacinto ceased reading, and looked at his two companions. Campodonico was grave, but Sant' Ilario smiled.

"If you can make her sign that, you are stronger than I supposed, Giovanni," said the latter.

"So it seems to me," said Gianforte.

"I do not think she will offer much resistance," answered San Giacinto, quietly pocketing the confession and the document he had just read. "I suppose what I am going to do is unscrupulous, but I do not think that Donna Adele has shown any uncommon delicacy of feeling in this little affair. Let us go and see whether she has any objection to signing her name."

Don Tebaldo, the priest, and Bonifazio followed the three gentlemen in a cab to the Palazzo Savelli, and all five went up the grand staircase together. Neither Don Tebaldo nor the servant had received any instructions beyond being told that if they were called into the room when the reading took place, they were to answer truthfully any questions which might be put to them.

Prince Savelli met them all in an outer drawing-room, the same indeed in which poor Herbert Arden had talked with Francesco a few days before his death. He was coldly courteous to San Giacinto, but greeted the others somewhat more warmly.

"May I ask what the nature of your communication is?" he inquired of the former.

"I prefer to explain it in the presence of Donna Adele, as it concerns her directly," answered San Giacinto: "It is useless to tell a story twice."

The extremely high and mighty head of all the Savelli stared up at the giant through his big spectacles. He was not at all used to being treated with so little consideration. But the other was a match for him, and stood carelessly waiting for the master of the house to lead the way.

"Considering whom you represent," said the Prince, "your manner is somewhat imperative."

San Giacinto's heavy brows bent in an ominous frown, and Savelli found it impossible to meet the gaze of the hard, deep-set eyes for more than a few seconds.

"I represent an innocent man, whom you and yours are trying to ruin. As for my manners, they were learned in an inn and not in Casa Savelli. I shall be obliged if you will lead the way."

Sant' Ilario suppressed a smile. He had seen his strong cousin in more than one such encounter, but he had never seen any one resist him long. Savelli did not reply, but turned and went before them and opened the door. They passed through another drawing-room and through a third, and then found themselves in Adele's boudoir. She was seated in a deep chair near the fire, warming her transparent hands at the flame. Her face was exactly of the colour of the yellow ashes of certain kinds of wood. It seemed impossible that any human being could be so thin as she seemed, and live. But there was yet some strength left, and her strong will, aided by the silent but insane satisfaction she felt in Ghisleri's ruin, kept her still in a sort of animation which was sometimes almost like her old activity. She had, of course, been warned of the impending interview, but she thought that San Giacinto had come to propose some compromise to the advantage of Ghisleri, and her father-in-law and husband were inclined to share her opinion; she meant to refuse everything, and to say that she would abide the judgment of the courts. She did not rise when the party entered, but held out her hand to each in succession. Francesco Savelli stood beside her, and also shook hands with each, but made no remark.

"Sit down," said Prince Savelli, moving forward a chair.

"Thank you," answered San Giacinto, "but it is useless. We shall stay only long enough for Donna Adele to sign a paper I have brought with me. We do not wish to disturb you further than necessary. With your permission I will read the document."

And thereupon, standing before her, he read it slowly and distinctly. Prince Savelli gradually turned pale, for he knew the man, and guessed that he possessed some terribly sure means of enforcing his will. But Adele laughed scornfully and her husband followed her example.

"Is there any reason why I should sign that very singular and untrue declaration?" she asked, with contempt.

San Giacinto looked at her steadily for a moment, and without reasoning she began to feel afraid.

"I have a strong argument in my pocket," he said. "For I have your confession here, and the priest with whom it has been deposited since the day it was found is waiting in the hall, if you wish to see him."

Adele shook from head to foot, and her hands moved spasmodically. She made a great effort, however, and succeeded in speaking.

"The fact that it has been in a place where Ghisleri knew how to find it is the last proof of his guilt we required," she said, mechanically repeating the words she had heard her father-in-law use more than once.

"Ghisleri never saw it and never knew where it was until yesterday," answered San Giacinto. "If you will oblige me by signing this paper, I will not trouble you any further."

"I will not sign it, nor anything of such a nature," said Adele, desperately.

"You are perfectly free to do as you please," answered San Giacinto. "And so am I. Since you positively refuse, there is nothing left for me to do but to go away.

But I forgot to tell you that the humble person who found it was able to read, and read it, before taking it to the priest, and that he has informed me most minutely of the contents. I see you are annoyed at that, and I am not surprised, for in half an hour it will be in the hands of the attorney-general. Good morning, Princess."

In the dead silence that followed one might have heard a pin fall, or a feather. San Giacinto waited a few moments and then turned to go. Instantly Adele uttered a sharp cry and sprang to her feet. With a quickness of which no one present would have believed her capable, she was at his side, and holding him back by the arm. He turned again and looked calmly down at her.

"You do not mean to do what you threaten?" she cried, in abject terror.

"I mean to take this sealed document to the attorney-general without losing a moment," he answered. "You know very well what will happen if I do that."

Both Savelli and his son came forward while he was speaking.

"I will not allow you to hint in my house that anything in that confession could have any consequences to my daughter-in-law," said the Prince, in a loud voice. "You have no right to make any such assertions."

"If Donna Adele wishes it, I will break the seal and read her own account," answered San Giacinto. He put his hand into the breast pocket of his coat and drew out the packet.

Altogether losing control of herself, Adele tried to snatch it from his hand, but he held it high in air, and his vast figure towered above the rest of the group, still more colossal by the gesture of the upstretched arm.

"You see for yourselves what importance Donna Adele attaches to this trifle," he said, in deep tones. "You would do well to persuade her to sign that paper. That is the only exchange I will take for what I hold. She knows that every word written there is true — as true as every word she has written here," he added, glancing up at the sealed letter. "I will wait one minute more by that clock, and then I will go."

The two Savelli gazed at Adele in undisguised astonishment and horror. It was clear enough from her face and terrified manner that San Giacinto spoke the truth, and that the confession he held contained some awful secret of which they were wholly ignorant.

"What is the meaning of all this, Adele?" asked the Prince, sternly. "What does that confession contain?"

But she did not answer, as she sank into a chair before the table, and almost mechanically dipped a pen into the ink. San Giacinto laid the formal denial before her, holding the confession behind him, for he believed her capable of snatching it from him and tossing it into the fire at any moment. She signed painfully in large, sloping characters that decreased rapidly in size at the end of each of her two names. The pen fell from her hand as she finished, and San Giacinto quietly laid the sealed letter before her. If she had been on the point of fainting, the sight recalled her to herself. She seized it eagerly and broke the seals, one after the other. Then she went to the fire, assured herself that the sheets were all there, and were genuine, and thrust the whole into the flames, watching until the last shred was consumed.

Meanwhile San Giacinto silently handed the pen to Sant' Ilario, who signed and passed it to Gianforte. He in his turn gave it to San Giacinto, and the transaction was concluded. The two cousins, as though by common instinct, glanced at the page on which was written twice "Giovanni Saracinesca," and each thought of all the pain and anxiety the coincidence had caused in days long gone by. The last time they had signed a document together had been in the study of the Palazzo Montevarchi more than twenty years earlier, when they were still young men.

"You see for yourselves," said San Giacinto, turning to the two Savelli as he neatly folded the paper, "that

Donna Adele desires no further explanation, and wishes the contents of the letter she has burned to remain a secret. So far as I am concerned I pledge my word never to divulge it, nor to hint at it, and I have reason to believe that those who are acquainted with it will do the same. So far as one man can answer for another, I will be responsible for them. With regard to the finding of the letter and to the manner of its being kept so long, I leave Don Tebaldo, the parish priest of Gerano, to explain that. You can question him at your leisure. Our mission is accomplished, and Pietro Ghisleri's innocence is established for ever. That is all I wished. Good morning."

After burning the confession Adele had let herself fall into the deep chair in which she had been sitting when the three friends entered the room. Her head had fallen back, and her jaw dropped in a ghastly fashion. She looked as though she were dead; but her hands twitched convulsively, rising suddenly and falling again upon her knees. It was impossible to say whether she was conscious or not.

The two Savelli, father and son, stood on the other side of the fireplace and looked at her, still speechless at her conduct, which they could only half understand, but which could mean nothing but disgrace to her and dishonour to them. The elder man seemed to suffer the more, and he leaned heavily against the chimney-piece, supporting his head with his hand. Neither the one nor the other paid any attention to the three men as they silently left the room.

San Giacinto begged Don Tebaldo to wait a short time, and then to send a messenger inquiring whether the Prince wished to see him, and if not, to return at once to the palace in which San Giacinto lived. Then he took Bonifazio with him as well as Campodonico and Sant' Ilario, and went at once to Ghisleri's lodging. They found him breakfasting alone in a rather sketchy fashion, for Bonifazio had not been allowed by San Giacinto to return to his master until everything was accomplished. He showed some surprise when he opened the door himself, and found the three together on the landing.

"Is anything the matter?" he inquired, as he ushered them into the sitting-room, where he had been taking his meal.

"On the contrary," said San Giacinto, "we have come to tell you that nothing is the matter. This paper may amuse you; but it is worth keeping, as Campodonico and my cousin can testify, for their names appear in it as witnesses."

Ghisleri read the contents carefully, and they could see how his brow cleared at every word.

"You have been the best friend to me that any man ever had," he said, grasping San Giacinto's huge hand.

"You could have done it quite as well yourself, only I knew you would not do it at all," answered the latter. "I have no scruples in dealing with such people, nor do I see why any one should have any. But you would have gone delicately and presented Donna Adele with the confession, and then when she had burned it before your eyes, you would have told her that you trusted to her sense of justice to right you in the opinion of the world."

Ghisleri laughed. He was so happy that he would have laughed at anything. After giving him a short account of what had taken place, all three left him, going, as they said, to breakfast at the club, and inform the world of what had happened. And so they did. And before the clock struck eight that night, Bonifazio had received a hundred visiting cards, each with two words, "to congratulate," written upon it in pencil, and four invitations to dinner addressed to Pietro Ghisleri. For the world is unconsciously wise in its generation, and on the rare occasions when it has found out that it has made a mistake, its haste to do the civil thing is almost indecent. In eight and forty hours the whole Savelli family and the Prince and Princess of Gerano had left Rome, and Ghisleri found it hard to keep one evening a week free for himself.

But in the afternoon of that day on which San Giacinto had so suddenly turned the tables upon Pietro's adversaries, Pietro went to see Laura Arden. She, of course, was in ignorance of what had occurred, and was amazed by the change she saw in his face when he entered.

"Something good has happened, I am sure!" she exclaimed, as she came half-way across the room to meet him with outstretched hands.

"Yes," he said, "something very unexpected has happened. The confession has been found, Donna Adele has admitted that the whole story was a fabrication, and she has signed a formal denial of every accusation, past, present, and to come. I am altogether cleared."

"Thank God! Thank God!" Laura cried, wringing his two hands, and gazing into his eyes.

"You are glad," he said. "I suppose I knew you would be, but I could not realise that it would make so much difference to you."

"In one way it makes no difference," she said more quietly, as she sat down and pointed to his accustomed place. "I knew the truth from the beginning. But it is for you. I saw how unhappy you were yesterday. Now tell me all about it."

He told her all that had taken place since he had left her on the previous day, as it has been told in these pages, and his heart beat fast as he saw in her eyes the constant and great interest she felt.

"And so I am quite free of it all at last," he said, when he had finished.

"And you will be happy now," answered Laura, softly. "You have been through almost everything, it seems to me. Do you realise how much I know of all your life? It is strange, is it not? You are not fond of making confidences, and you never made but one to me, when you could not help yourself. Yes; it is very strange that I should know so much about you."

"And still be willing to call me your friend?" added Ghisleri. "I do not know how you can — and yet —" He stopped. "The reason is," he said suddenly, "that you have long been a part of my life — that is why you know me so well. I think that even long ago we were much more intimate than we knew or dreamed of. There were many reasons for that."

"Yes," Laura answered. "And then, after all, I have known you ever since I first went out as a young girl. I did not like you at first, I remember, though I could never tell why. But as for your saying that you cannot see why I should still be your friend, I do not understand how you mean it. It seems to me that you have done much to get my friendship and to strengthen it, and nothing to lose it. Besides, you yourself know that you are not what you were. You have changed. You were saying so only yesterday, and you said the change was for the better."

"Yes, I have changed," said Ghisleri. "It is of no use to deny it. I do not mean in everything, though I do not lead the life I did. Perhaps it all goes together after all."

"That is not very clear," observed Laura, with a low laugh.

Ghisleri was silent for a moment.

"I do not think of you as I did," he said. "That is the greatest change of all."

Laura did not answer. She leaned back in her seat, and looked across the room.

"I never thought it would come," he said. "For years I honourably believed I could be your friend. I know, now, that I cannot. I love you far too deeply — with far too little right."

Still Laura did not speak. But she turned her face from him, laying her cheek against the silken cushion behind her.

"Perhaps I am doing very wrong in telling you this," said Ghisleri, trying to steady his voice. "But I made up my mind that it was better, and more honest. I do not believe that you love me, that you ever can love me in the most distant future of our lives. I am prepared for that. I will not trouble you with my love. I will never speak of it again — for I can never hope to win you. But at least you know the truth."

Slowly Laura turned her face again and her eyes met his. There was a deep, warm light in them. She seemed to hesitate. Then the words came sharply, in a loud, clear voice, unlike her own, as though the great secret had burst every barrier and had broken out against her will by its own strength, sudden, startling, new to herself and to the man who heard it.

"I love you now!"

Ghisleri turned as deadly pale as when Gianforte's bullet had so nearly gone through his heart. The words rang out in the quiet room with an intensity and distinctness of tone not to be described. He had not even guessed that she might love him. For one moment they looked at one another, both white with passion, both trembling a little, the black eyes and the blue both gleaming darkly. Then Ghisleri took the two hands that were stretched out to meet his own, and each felt that the other's were very cold. As though by a common instinct they both rose, and stood a moment face to face. Then his arms went round her. He did not know until long afterwards that when he kissed her he lifted her from the ground.

It had all been sudden, strange, and unlike anything in his whole life, unexpected beyond anything that had ever happened to him. Perhaps it was so with her, too. They remembered little of what they said in those first moments, but by and by, as they sat side by side on the sofa, words came again.

"I knew it when you went away last summer," said Ghisleri. "And then I thought I should never tell you."

"And I found it out when I left you," answered Laura. "I found that I could not live without you and be happy.

Did you guess nothing when I made you come to me yesterday? Yesterday — only yesterday! It seems like last year. Did you think it was mere friendship?"

"Yes, I thought it was that and nothing more — but such friendship as I had never dreamed of."

"Nor any one else, perhaps," said Laura, with a happy smile. "For I would have come, you know, in spite of every one. What would you have done then, I wonder?"

"Then? Do not speak of yesterday. What could I have done? Could I have told you that I loved you with such an accusation hanging over me? No, you know that. It was only yesterday that I asked you to let me leave you rather suddenly — did you not guess the reason?"

"I thought you were ill — no — well, it crossed my mind that you might be a little, just a little, in love with me." She laughed.

"I felt ill afterwards. I was horrified when I thought how nearly I had spoken."

"And why should you not have spoken, if it was in your heart?" asked Laura, taking his hand again. "Why should you have thought, even for a moment, that I could care what people said. You are you, and I am I, whether the world is with us or against us. And I think, dear, that we shall need the world very little now. Perhaps it will change its mind and pretend it needs us."

"There is no doubt of that. It always happens so. Why should we care?" He paused a moment, then, as his eyes met hers, the great dominating passion broke out again: "Ah — darling — heart's heart — beloved! There are not words to tell you how I love you and bless you, and worship you with all my soul. What can I say, what can I do, to make you understand?"

"Love me, dear," she said, "and be faithful, as I will be." And their lips met again.

They loved well and-truly. Strange, some may say, that a love of that good kind should have begun in friendship on the one side, and indifference if not dislike on

the other. But neither had understood the other at all
in the beginning. The world-tired and world-weary man
had not guessed at the real woman who lived so humanly,
and could love so passionately, and whom nature had
clothed with such saint-like, holy beauty as to make her
seem a creature above all earthly feeling and all mortal
weakness. Her eyes had seemed fixed on far-distant,
heavenly sights, gazing upon the world only to wonder
at its vanity and to loathe its uncleanness. Her best and
her greatest thoughts had been, he fancied, of things
altogether divine and supernatural, of love celestial, of
beatific vision, of the waters of paradise, of goodness and
of God. And something of all this there was in her, but
there was room for more both in heart and soul, and more
was there — the deep, human sympathy, the simple
strength to love one man wholly, the singleness of
thought and judgment to see the good in him and love
it, and to understand and forgive the bad — and far down
in the strong, quiet nature was hidden the passion but
newly awakened whose irresistible force would have
broken every barrier and despised every convention, respecting only its own purity in taking what it loved and
desired, and would have at any cost, save the defilement
of the soul it moved. Small wonder that when it awoke
at last unresisted and meeting its like, it burst into sight
with a sudden violence that startled the woman herself,
and amazed the man who had not suspected its existence.

But she, on her side, had learned to know him more
slowly, not ever analysing him, nor trying to guess at
his motives, but merely seeing little by little how great
and wide was the discrepancy between the hard, sceptical, cynic thoughts he expressed so readily, and the constant, unchangingly brave effort of his heart to do in all
cases what was honourable, just, and brave according to
his light. She saw him ever striving, often failing, sometimes succeeding in the doing of good actions, and she
saw the strange love of truth and simplicity which per-

vaded and primarily moved the most complicated character she had ever known. He who at first had seemed to
her the most worldly of all worldly men, was in reality one
whose whole life was lived in his own heart for the one,
or two, or three beings who had known how to touch it.
To all else he was absolutely and coldly indifferent. She
had, indeed, as she said, guessed at last that he loved her
a little and more than a little, and she had known for
months before he spoke that he was really a part of her
life and of all her thoughts and actions. But she had
not asked herself what she would do or say when the
great moment came, any more than she had accused
herself of being unfaithful to the memory of the man
whose dying words had bidden her to be happy, if she
would have him rest in peace. And now that she loved
again, so differently, so passionately, so much more
humanly, she realised all the great unselfishness of him
who was gone and who had not been willing to leave in
her heart the least seed of future self-accusation or the
least ground for refusing anything good which life might
have in store for her. She saw that she could take what
was offered her, freely, without one regret, without one
prick of conscience, or one passing thought that Herbert
Arden would have suffered an instant's pain could he
have known what was passing in the existence of the
woman who had loved him so well.

Late on that afternoon, Ghisleri went to see Maddalena dell' Armi. There was a drop of bitterness in his
cup yet, and something hard for him to do, but he would
not let the woman who had sacrificed everything for him
in days gone by learn the news from a stranger.

"I have come to tell you that I am going to marry
Lady Herbert Arden," he said gently, as he took her
hand.

She looked up quickly, and for a moment he felt a
strange anxiety.

"I knew that you would, long ago," she answered.
"I am glad of it. No, do not think that is a phrase.

I do not love you any more. Are you glad to know it? I wish I did. But I am far too fond of you not to wish you to be happy if you can. You are my dearest and best friend. It is strange, is it not? Think of me kindly sometimes, in your new life. And — and do not speak my name before her, if you can help it. She knows what we were to each other once, and it might hurt her."

"How changed you are!" exclaimed Ghisleri. But he pressed the hand that lay near him.

"I am trying to be a good woman," she answered simply.

"If there were more like you, the world would be a better place," he said.

CHAPTER XXX.

"Just fancy, my dear," exclaimed Donna Maria Boccapaduli to the Marchesa di San Giacinto on the evening of the following day, "Pietro Ghisleri is going to marry Laura Arden, after all! That horrid, spiteful, wicked Adele will die of rage. And they say that the old uncle is dead and has left Laura one of those enormous English fortunes one reads about, and they are going to take the first floor of your brother's palace — your husband says he will buy it some day — I hope he will — and Laura is going to rebuild Ghisleri's queer little castle in Tuscany. What a delightful series of surprises! And two days ago every one believed he was on the point of being sent to prison for ever so many years. But I was always sure he was innocent, though of course one did not like to have him about while the thing was going on."

"Giovanni said from the first that it was all an abominable lie," answered the Marchesa. "And Giovanni is generally right. What a charming house it will be! Of course they will give balls."

2 E

"They say that in the confession there was a full account of the way in which she started the story of the evil eye — what nonsense it was! You have only to look into Laura Arden's eyes — do you think she is as beautiful as Corona Saracinesca ever could have been?"

"No, no," exclaimed the Marchesa, who had known the Princess of Sant' Ilario more than twenty years earlier. "No one was ever so beautiful as Corona. Laura is much shorter, too, and that makes a difference. Laura reminds one of a saint, and Corona looked an empress — or what empresses are supposed to be like. But Laura is a beautiful woman. There is no one to compare with her now but Christina Campodonico, and she is too thin. What a good looking couple Ghisleri and his wife will make. He has grown younger during the last two years."

"No wonder — when one thinks of the life he used to lead. Every time he quarrelled with Maddalena he used to get at least five pounds thinner. I wonder how she takes it."

"She is far too clever a woman to show what she thinks. But I know she has not cared for him for a long time. They have not quarrelled for two years at least, so of course there cannot be any love left on either side. They still sit in corners occasionally. I suppose they like each other. It is very odd. But I shall never understand those things."

The last remark was very true, for Flavia Saracinesca loved her giant husband with all her heart and always had, and she knew also that Maria Boccapaduli was the best of wives and mothers, if she was also the greatest of gossips.

What the two ladies said to each other represented very well the world's opinion, hastily formed, on the spur of the moment, to meet the exigencies of the altered situation, but immutable now. It shrugged its shoulders as it referred to its past errors of judgment, and said that it could not have been expected to know that Adele Savelli was raving mad when she was allowed to go everywhere just like a sane being, although her eyes had undeniably had a wild look for some time, and she might have been taken for a galvanised corpse. For of course it was now quite certain that she had been out of her mind from the very beginning, seeing that she had concocted her dreadful plot without the slightest reason. As for the old story that Laura Arden loved Francesco, that was downright nonsense! It was another of Adele's scandalous falsehoods—or insane delusions, if you chose to be so good-natured as to use that expression. If anything, it was Francesco who loved Laura, and he ought to be ashamed of himself, considering what a fortune his wife had brought him. But human nature was very ungrateful, especially when it bore the name of Savelli. They did not seem at all thankful for that dear Ghisleri's forbearance. He could have brought an action against them for any number of things—defamation, false imprisonment—almost anything. But he had acted with his usual generosity, and told every one that he had always believed Adele to be insane, and bore no one the least ill-will, since he had been put to no inconvenience whatever, thanks to San Giacinto's timely action. And, said the world, when a man consistently behaved as Pietro Ghisleri had done, he was certain to get his reward. What could any man desire more than to have that dear, beautiful, good Laura Arden for his wife, especially since she was so immensely rich? Doubt the justice of Heaven after that, if you could! As for the world, it meant to tell them both how sorry it was that it had misunderstood them. Of course it would be sinful not to hope that Adele might some day get well, but she had her deserts, and if she ever came back to society, people would not care to meet her. She might go mad again at any moment and try to ruin some one else, and might succeed the next time, too.

That was the way in which most people talked during

the season, and the world acted up to its words as it generally does when there are balls and dinners to be got by merely being consistent. It was much more agreeable, too, to live on terms of pleasant intercourse with Laura and her betrothed, and much easier, because it is always tiresome to keep up a prejudice against really charming people.

But Adele was not mad as people said, and as the two families gave out. There had undoubtedly been a strain of insanity through all her conduct, and that might, some day, develop into real madness. She was sane enough still, however, to suffer, and no such merciful termination to her sufferings as the loss of her reason would be seemed at all imminent. The strong will and acute intelligence had survived, for the poisonous drug she loved had attacked the body, which was the weaker portion of her being. Adele was hopelessly paralysed. The last great effort had been too much for the overstrung nerves. Her hands still moved convulsively, but she could not direct them at all. Her jaw had dropped, as it almost always does in advanced cases of morphiuism, and her lower limbs were useless. Day after day she sat or lay before the fire in her room at Castel Savello, as she might remain for years, tended by paid nurses, and helpless to do the slightest thing for herself — through the short days and the long nights of winter, hardly cheered by the sunshine when spring came at last, longing for the end. It was indeed a dreadful existence. Nothing to do, nothing to think of but the terrible black past, nothing to occupy her, save the monotonous tracing back of her present state to her first misdeeds, step by step, inch by inch, in the cold light of an inexorable logic. It was hard to believe what her confessor told her, that she should be grateful for having time and reason left to repent of what she had done, and to expiate, in a measure, the evil of her life. As yet, that was the only comfort she got from any one. She had disgraced the name of Savelli, she was told, and no suffering could atone for that. She felt that she was hated and despised, and that although everything which money could do was done to prolong her wretched being, her death was anticipated as a relief from her detested presence in the household upon which she had brought such shame. It would be hard to conceive a more fearful punishment than she was made to undergo, forcibly kept alive by the constant care and forethought of the most experienced persons, and allowed only just so much of the morphia as was positively necessary. She had no longer the power to grasp the little instrument. If she had been able to do that, she would have found rest for ever, as she told herself. And they cruelly diminished the dose, though they would not tell her by how much. She would live longer, they said, if the quantity could be greatly reduced. She begged, implored, entreated them not to torture her. But they could hardly understand what she said, for the paralysis had made her speech indistinct, and even if they could have distinguished the meaning of all her words they would have paid no attention to them. The orders were strict and were rigidly obeyed in every particular. She was to be made to live as long as possible, and life meant torment, unceasing, passing words to describe. How long it might last she had no idea. She could only hope against hope that it might end soon. The news of Laura's engagement and approaching marriage had been kept from her for some time, it being feared that it might agitate her, but she was told at last, and the knowledge of her step-sister's happiness was an added bitterness in what remained to her of life. Vividly she saw them before her, Laura in her fresh beauty, Ghisleri in his strength, little Herbert with his father's eyes — the eyes that haunted Adele Savelli by night and gazed upon her by day out of the shadowy corners of her room. The three were ever before her moving, as she fancied, through a garden of exquisite flowers, in a clear, bright light. That was doubtless the way in which her diseased brain represented their happiness, for she had loved flowers in the old days, and had associated everything that was pleasant with them in her thoughts. But she hated them now, as she hated everything, even to her own children, whom she refused to see because they reminded her of better times, and her step-mother, whom she was obliged to receive because the good lady would take no denial. The Princess was, indeed, one of her most regular and kindly visitors. A very constant and good woman, she would not and could not turn upon Adele as all the rest had done, even to her own father, who in the bitterness of his heart, had said that he would never see his daughter again, alive or dead. But Adele hated her none the less, and dreaded her long homilies and exhortations to be penitent, and the little printed prayers and books of devotion she generally brought with her. For the Princess was deeply concerned for the welfare of Adele's soul, and being very much in earnest in the matter of religion, she did what she could to save it according to her own views. Possibly her sermons might hereafter bear fruit, but for the present the wretched woman who was forced to listen to them found them almost unbearable. And so her unhappy days dragged on without prospect of relief or termination, no longer in any real meaning of the word a life at all, but only a consequence, the result of what she had made herself when she had been really alive.

The Princess of Gerano was the last person won over to a good opinion of Ghisleri, but before the wedding day she had formally avowed to Laura that she had been mistaken in him. She had been most of all impressed by his dignity during the very great difficulties in which he had been placed, and by his gentle forbearance when his innocence had been established and when no one would have blamed him if he had cursed the whole Savelli and Gerano tribe by every devil in Satan's calendar. Instead, he had uniformly said that he had believed Donna Adele to be mad, and that what had happened had therefore not come about by any one's fault. She told Laura that there must be more good than any one had dreamt of in a man who could act as Pietro did under the circumstances, and perhaps she was right. At all events, she was convinced and having once reached conviction she took him to her heart and found that he was a man much more to her taste, and much more worthy of Laura than she had supposed. For the rest, the match was an admirable one. Ghisleri was certainly very far from rich, but he was by no means a pauper, and what he possessed had been wisely administered. He was neither a prince, nor the son of a princely house, but there was many a prince of Europe, and more than one of the Holy Empire, too, whose forefathers had been trudging behind the plough long after the Nobili Ghisleri had built their tower and held their own in it for generations. Then, too, whatever the Princess might think of his past and of his reputation, he had rather a singular position in society, and was respected as many were not, who possessed ten times as many virtues as he. She admitted quite frankly that she had been wrong, and she made ample amends for her former cold treatment of him by the liking she now showed.

"I shall never be able to think of you as a serious married man, my dear friend," said Gouache one day when Ghisleri was lounging in the studio with a cigarette, after they had breakfasted together.

"I hope you will," was the laconic answer.

"No, I never shall. I have always had a sort of artistic satisfaction in your character — for there was much that was really artistic about you, especially as regards your taste in sin, which was perfect and perhaps is still. But marriage is not at all artistic, my dear Ghisleri, until it becomes unhappy, and the husband goes about with a revolver in every pocket, and the wife with a scent bottle full of morphia in hers, and they treat each other with distant civility in private, and with effusive affection when a third person is present, especially the third person who has contributed the most to producing the artistic effect in question. Then the matter becomes interesting."

"Like your own marriage," suggested Ghisleri, with a laugh. Gouache and Donna Faustina had not had an unkind thought for one another in nearly twenty years of cloudless happiness.

"Ah, my friend, you must not take my case as an instance. There is something almost comic in being as happy as I am. We should never make a subject for a play writer, my wife and I, nor for a novelist either. No man would risk his reputation for truthfulness by describing our life as it is. But then, is there anything artistic about me? Nothing, except that I am an artist. If I had any money I should be called an amateur. To be an artist it is essential to starve — at one time or another. The public never believe that a man who has not been dangerously hungry can paint a picture, or play the fiddle, or write a book. If I had money I would still paint — subjects like Michael Angelo's Last Judgment with the souls of Donna Tullia, Del Ferice, and Donna Adele Savelli frying prominently on the left, and portraits of my wife and myself in the foreground on the right with perfectly new crowns of glory and beatific smiles from ear to ear. If you go on as you have been living since the reformation set in, you will have to bore yourself on our side too, with a little variation in your crown to show what a sinner you have been."

"I am quite willing to be bored in your way," answered Ghisleri, laughing again.

The marriage took place late in February, to the immense delight of the world, and with the unanimous applause of all society. The newspapers gave minute accounts of all the gowns, and of all the people who wore them, and surprised Ghisleri by informing him that his ancestors had been Guelphs, whereas he had some reason to believe that they had been Ghibellines, and by creating him a commander of the order of Saint Maurice and Saint Lazarus, whereas he was an hereditary Knight of Malta.

The description of Laura was an extraordinary contribution to the literature of beauty, and left nothing to be desired except a positive or two to contrast with the endless string of superlatives.

Ghisleri and Laura left Rome with a little caravan of servants. Neither the faithful Donald nor the equally faithful Bonifazio could be left behind, and there was Laura's maid, and little Herbert's nurse, both indispensable. The boy was overjoyed by the arrangement which gave him the advantage of Pietro's society "for every day," as he expressed it, and especially at the prospect of living all the summer in a real castle. He was three years old and talked fluently, when he talked at all — a strong, brave-looking little fellow, with clear brown eyes and a well-shaped head, set on a sturdy frame that promised well for his coming manhood. Ghisleri delighted in him, though he was not generally amused by very small children. But they always came to him of their own accord, which some people say is a sign of a good disposition in a man, for children and animals are rarely mistaken in their likes and dislikes.

San Giacinto and Gianforte Campodonico went to the station to see them off after the wedding, and threw armfuls of roses and lilies of the valley into the carriage before the door was finally shut by the guard as the preliminary bell was sounded.

"Without you two, we two should not be here," said Ghisleri, as he shook hands with them both.

"No," added Laura happily. "But we should have been together, if it had been in prison. Good-bye, dear friends."

The train moved away, and the two men were left on the platform, waving their hats to the last.

"That is a good thing well done," said San Giacinto, lighting a cigar. "They will be happy together."

"Yes," said Gianforte, thoughtfully. "I think they will. Women love that man, and he knows how to love them."

San Giacinto looked down at him and said nothing. He knew something of Bianca Corleone's short, sad life, and of what had passed between her brother and Ghisleri. He liked them both more than almost any of the younger men he knew, and he honestly admired them for their behaviour towards each other. He guessed what thoughts were passing through Campodonico's mind as he looked after the train that was bearing away Pietro Ghisleri, a married man at last.

For Gianforte was saying to himself that though he could neither wholly forget nor freely forgive the past, he could have loved him had fate been different. If ten years ago Ghisleri could have married Bianca, and if Bianca could have lived, the two would have been happy, for even Gianforte admitted that both had loved truly and well until the end. But that was a dream and reality had raised the impassable barrier between men who might have been firm friends. Their hands might stretch across it, and grasp one another from time to time, and their eyes might read good faith and the will to be generous each in the other's soul, but nearer than that they could never be, for the sake of the beautiful dead woman who would not be forgotten by either.

One more picture and one word more, and the curtain must fall at last.

In the early summer Laura and her husband were at Torre de' Ghisleri in the Tuscan hills. The small castle was very habitable as compared with its former condition, and small as it was by comparison with such fortresses as Gerano, was by no means the mere ruined tower which many people supposed it to be. The square grey keep from which it took its name was flanked by a mass of smaller buildings, irregular and of different epochs, all more or less covered with ivy or with creepers now in bloom. The wide castle yard, in the midst of which stood the ancient well with its wonderfully wrought yoke of iron, its heavy chain, and its two buckets, had been converted into a garden long ago for the bride of some Ghisleri of those days, and the plants and trees had run almost wild for a hundred years, irregularly, as some had survived and others had perished in the winter storms. Here a cypress, there an oak, further on again three laurels, of the Laura Regia kind, side by side in a row, then two cypresses again, growing up straight and slim and dark out of a plot of close-cut grass. And there were roses everywhere, and stiff camelia trees and feathery azaleas and all manner of bright, growing things without order or symmetry, beautiful in their wildness. But in and out there were narrow paths, in which two might walk together, and these were now swept and cared for as they had never been in Pietro's bachelor days. Other things were changed too, but not much, and for the better. A woman's hand had touched, had waked a sweet new life in the old place.

The afternoon sun, still above the low surrounding hills, cast the shadow of the tower across the lawn and upon the flowers beyond. There were chairs before the arched doorway, and a garden table. Laura sat watching the swallows as they flew down from the keep to the garden and upwards again in their short, circling flight. A book she had not even thought of reading lay beside her. At her elbow sat Ghisleri in a white jacket, with a straw hat tilted over his eyes which little Herbert was trying to get at, as he rode on Pietro's knee. The man's face had changed wonderfully during the last six months. All the hardness was gone from it, and the contemptuous, discontented look that had once come so readily was never seen now.

"You never told me it was so beautiful," said Laura, still watching the swallows and gazing at the flowers. "When we first came, and I looked out of the window in the morning, I thought I had never seen any place so lovely. You used to talk of it in such a careless way."

"It is you who make it beautiful for me," answered Ghisleri. "A year ago it seemed dull and ugly enough, when I used to sit here and think of you."

"I was not the first woman you had thought of, on this very spot, I daresay," said Laura, with a happy laugh.

"No, dear, you were not." He smiled as he admitted the fact. "But you were the last, and unless you turn out to be as bad as you seem to be good, you will have no successor."

"What's successor mean?" lisped Herbert, desisting from his attempt to get at the hat and listening.

"Somebody who comes after another," answered Laura. "I will try to be good, dear," she said to Ghisleri, laughing again.

"So'll I," exclaimed Herbert promptly, doubtless supposing that it was expected of him.

"Yes," said Ghisleri, thoughtfully. "I have sat here many a time for hours, dreaming about you, and wishing for you, and trying to see you just as you are now, in a chair beside me. Yes, I have thought of other women here, but it is very long since I wished to see one there — if I ever did. I hardly ever came here when I was very young."

There was a pause. His voice had a little sadness in it as he spoke the last words — not the sadness of regret, but of reverence. He was thinking of Bianca Corleone. Then Laura laid her hand upon his arm, and her eyes met his, for he turned as he felt her touch.

"Dear, you would have been happy with her," she said very gravely. "But I will be all to you that woman can be to man, if I live to show you how I love you."

"No woman ever was what you are to me already," he answered. "No woman, living or dead. You have done everything for me since I first knew you well, and you did much more than you know before I knew what you really were. There can be nothing in the world beyond what you have given, and give me."

"I wish I were quite, quite sure of that," said Laura, still looking into his face.

"You must be — you shall be!" he said, with sudden

energy, and his glance lightened with passion. "You must. Words are not much, I know, nor oaths, nor anything of that sort. But I will tell you this — and by the light and goodness of God, it is true. If I could doubt for one moment that I love you beyond any love I have ever dreamed of, I would tear out my heart with my hands!"

"What's love?" asked little Herbert timidly, for he was afraid that it must be something very dreadful as he watched Ghisleri's pale face and blazing eyes.

But the lips that might have answered could not; they were sealing the truth they had spoken, upon others that had uttered a doubt for the last time.

THE END.

KATHARINE LAUDERDALE.

TWO VOLUMES. CLOTH. $2.00.

The first of a series of novels dealing with New York life.

PRESS COMMENTS.

"Mr. Crawford at his best is a great novelist, and in *Katharine Lauderdale* we have him at his best." — *Boston Daily Advertiser.*

"A most admirable novel, excellent in style, flashing with humor, and full of the ripest and wisest reflections upon men and women." — *The Westminster Gazette.*

"It is the first time, we think, in American fiction that any such breadth of view has shown itself in the study of our social framework." — *Life.*

"Admirable in its simple pathos, its enforced humor, and, above all, in its truths to human nature. . . . There is not a tedious page or paragraph in it." — *Punch.*

"It need scarcely be said that the story is skilfully and picturesquely written, portraying sharply individual characters in well-defined surroundings." — *New York Commercial Advertiser.*

"*Katharine Lauderdale* is a tale of New York, and is up to the highest level of his work. In some respects it will probably be regarded as his best. None of his works, with the exception of *Mr. Isaacs,* show so clearly his skill as a literary artist." — *San Francisco Evening Bulletin.*

"The book shows the inventive power, the ingenuity of plot, the subtle analysis of character, the skilfulness in presenting shifting scenes, the patient working-out of details, the aptitude of deduction, and vividness of description which characterize the Saracinesca romances." — *New York Home Journal.*

"Nowhere has the author shown more admirable understanding and command of the novel-writer's art. . . . Whoever wants an original and fascinating book can be commended to this one." — *Philadelphia Evening Telegraph.*

A Sequel to "KATHARINE LAUDERDALE,"

THE RALSTONS.

THE MACMILLAN COMPANY,
66 FIFTH AVENUE, NEW YORK.

THE SARACINESCA SERIES.

DON ORSINO.

A CONTINUATION OF "SARACINESCA" AND "SANT' ILARIO."

" The third in a rather remarkable series of novels dealing with three generations of the Saracinesca family, entitled respectively 'Saracinesca,' 'Sant' Ilario' and 'Don Orsino,' and these novels present an important study of Italian life, customs, and conditions during the present century. Each one of these novels is worthy of very careful reading and offers exceptional enjoyment in many ways, in the fascinating absorption of good fiction, in interest of faithful historic accuracy, and in charm of style. The 'new Italy' is strikingly revealed in 'Don Orsino.' "—*Boston Budget.*

" We are inclined to regard the book as the most ingenious of all Mr. Crawford's fictions. Certainly it is the best novel of the season." —*Evening Bulletin.*

SANT' ILARIO. A Sequel to "Saracinesca."

" The author shows steady and constant improvement in his art. 'Sant' Ilario' is a continuation of the chronicles of the Saracinesca family. . . . A singularly powerful and beautiful story. . . . Admirably developed, with a naturalness beyond praise. . . . It must rank with 'Greifenstein' as the best work the author has produced. It fulfils every requirement of artistic fiction. It brings out what is most impressive in human action, without owing any of its effectiveness to sensationalism or artifice. It is natural, fluent in evolution, accordant with experience, graphic in description, penetrating in analysis, and absorbing in interest."—*New York Tribune.*

SARACINESCA.

" His highest achievement, as yet, in the realms of fiction. The work has two distinct merits, either of which would serve to make it great,—that of telling a perfect story in a perfect way, and of giving a graphic picture of Roman society in the last days of the Pope's temporal power. . . . The story is exquisitely told."—*Boston Traveller.*

" One of the most engrossing novels we have ever read."—*Boston Times.*

The three volumes in a box, $3.00.
Half morocco, $8.00. Half calf, $7.50.

THE THREE FATES.

" The strength of the story lies in its portrayal of the aspirations, disciplinary efforts, trials and triumphs of the man who is a born writer, and who, by long and painful experiences, learns the good that is in him and the way in which to give it effectual expression. The analytical quality of the book is excellent, and the individuality of each one of the very dissimilar three fates is set forth in an entirely satisfactory manner. . . . Mr. Crawford has manifestly brought his best qualities as a student of human nature and his finest resources as a master of an original and picturesque style to bear upon this story. Taken for all in all it is one of the most pleasing of all his productions in fiction, and it affords a view of certain phases of American, or perhaps we should say of New York, life that have not hitherto been treated with anything like the same adequacy and felicity."—*Boston Beacon.*

THE WITCH OF PRAGUE.

A FANTASTIC TALE.

ILLUSTRATED BY W. J. HENNESSY.

" ' The Witch of Prague' is so remarkable a book as to be certain of as wide a popularity as any of its predecessors. The keenest interest for most readers will lie in its demonstration of the latest revelations of hypnotic science. . . . But ' The Witch of Prague ' is not merely a striking exposition of the far-reaching possibilities of a new science ; it is a romance of singular daring and power."—*London Academy.*

" Mr. Crawford has written in many keys, but never in so strange a one as that which dominates 'The Witch of Prague.' . . . The artistic skill with which this extraordinary story is constructed and carried out is admirable and delightful. . . . Mr. Crawford has scored a decided triumph, for the interest of the tale is sustained throughout. . . . A very remarkable, powerful, and interesting story."—*New York Tribune.*

" But Mr. Crawford has not lost his oft-proved skill in holding his readers' attention, and there are single scenes and passages in this book that rival in intensity anything he has ever written."—*Christian Union.*

A CIGARETTE-MAKER'S ROMANCE.

"It is a touching romance, filled with scenes of great dramatic power."—*Boston Commercial Bulletin.*

"It is full of life and movement, and is one of the best of Mr. Crawford's books."—*Boston Saturday Evening Gazette.*

"The interest is unflagging throughout. Never has Mr. Crawford done more brilliant realistic work than here. But his realism is only the case and cover for those intense feelings which, placed under no matter what humble conditions, produce the most dramatic and the most tragic situations. . . . This is a secret of genius, to take the most coarse and common material, the meanest surroundings, the most sordid material prospects, and out of the vehement passions which sometimes dominate all human beings to build up with these poor elements scenes and passages, the dramatic and emotional power of which at once enforce attention and awaken the profoundest interest."—*New York Tribune.*

"In the 'Cigarette-maker's Romance' Mr. Crawford may be said to have given new evidence of the novel-maker's art. . . . It is to be hoped that every one who reads Mr. Crawford's tale will heed of the rare finish of his literary work, a model in its kind."—*The Critic.*

GREIFENSTEIN.

"'Greifenstein' is a remarkable novel, and while it illustrates once more the author's unusual versatility, it also shows that he has not been tempted into careless writing by the vogue of his earlier books. . . . There is nothing weak or small or frivolous in the story. The author deals with tremendous passions working at the height of their energy. His characters are stern, rugged, determined men and women, governed by powerful prejudices and iron conventions, types of a military people, in whom the sense of duty has been cultivated until it dominates all other motives, and in whom the principle of 'noblesse oblige' is, so far as the aristocratic class is concerned, the fundamental rule of conduct. What such people may be capable of is startlingly shown."—*New York Tribune.*

". . . Another notable contribution to the literature of the day. It possesses originality in its conception and is a work of unusual ability. Its interest is sustained to the close, and it is an advance even on the previous work of this talented author Like all Mr. Crawford's work this novel is crisp, clear, and vigorous, and will be read with a great deal of interest."—*New York Evening Telegram.*

MR. ISAACS.

A TALE OF MODERN INDIA.

" The writer first shows the hero in relation with the people of the East and then skilfully brings into connection the Anglo-Saxon race. It is in this showing of the different effects which the two classes of minds have upon the central figure of the story that one of its chief merits lies. The characters are original and one does not recognize any of the hackneyed personages who are so apt to be considered indispensable to novelists, and which, dressed in one guise or another, are but the marionettes, which are all dominated by the same mind, moved by the same motive force. The men are all endowed with individualism and independent life and thought. . . . There is a strong tinge of mysticism about the book which is one of its greatest charms."—*Boston Transcript*.

" No story of human experience that we have met with since ' John Inglesant ' has such an effect of transporting the reader into regions differing from his own. ' Mr. Isaacs ' is the best novel that has ever laid its scenes in our Indian dominions."—*The Daily News, London*.

" This is a fine and noble story. It has freshness like a new and striking scene on which one has never looked before. It has character and individuality. It has meaning. It is lofty and uplifting, It is strongly, sweetly, tenderly written. It is in all respects an uncommon novel. . . . In fine, ' Mr. Isaacs ' is an acquaintance to be made."
—*The Literary World*.

DR. CLAUDIUS.

A TRUE STORY.

" There is a suggestion of strength, of a mastery of facts, of a fund of knowledge, that speaks well for future production. . . . To be thoroughly enjoyed, however, this book must be read, as no mere cursory notice can give an adequate idea of its many interesting points and excellences, for without a doubt ' Dr. Claudius ' is the most interesting book that has been published for many months, and richly deserves a high place in the public favor."—*St. Louis Spectator*.

" ' Dr. Claudius ' is surprisingly good, coming after a story of so much merit as ' Mr. Isaacs.' The hero is a magnificent specimen of humanity, and sympathetic readers will be fascinated by his chivalrous wooing of the beautiful American countess."—*Boston Traveller*.

" To our mind it by no means belies the promises of its predecessor. The story, an exceedingly improbable and romantic one, is told with much skill; the characters are strongly marked without any suspicion of caricature, and the author's ideas on social and political subjects are often brilliant and always striking. It is no exaggeration to say that there is not a dull page in the book, which is peculiarly adapted for the recreation of student or thinker."—*Living Church*.

WITH THE IMMORTALS.

"Altogether an admirable piece of art worked in the spirit of a thorough artist. Every reader of cultivated tastes will find it a book prolific in entertainment of the most refined description, and to all such we commend it heartily."—*Boston Saturday Evening Gazette.*

"The strange central idea of the story could have occurred only to a writer whose mind was very sensitive to the current of modern thought and progress, while its execution, the setting it forth in proper literary clothing, could be successfully attempted only by one whose active literary ability should be fully equalled by his power of assimilative knowledge both literary and scientific, and no less by his courage and capacity for hard work. The book will be found to have a fascination entirely new for the habitual reader of novels. Indeed Mr. Crawford has succeeded in taking his readers quite above the ordinary plane of novel interest."—*Boston Advertiser.*

MARZIO'S CRUCIFIX.

"We take the liberty of saying that this work belongs to the highest department of character-painting in words."—*Churchman.*

"'Marzio's Crucifix' is another of those tales of modern Rome which show the author so much at his ease. A subtle compound of artistic feeling, avarice, malice, and criminal frenzy is this carver of silver chalices and crucifixes."—*The Times.*

"We have repeatedly had occasion to say that Mr. Crawford possesses in an extraordinary degree the art of constructing a story. His sense of proportion is just, and his narrative flows along with ease and perspicuity. It is as if it could not have been written otherwise, so naturally does the story unfold itself, and so logical and consistent is the sequence of incident after incident. As a story 'Marzio's Crucifix' is perfectly constructed."—*New York Commercial Advertiser.*

KHALED.

A STORY OF ARABIA.

"Throughout the fascinating story runs the subtlest analysis, suggested rather than elaborately worked out, of human passion and motive, the building out and development of the character of the woman who becomes the hero's wife and whose love he finally wins being an especially acute and highly-finished example of the story-teller's art. . . . That it is beautifully written and holds the interest of the reader, fanciful as it all is, to the very end, none who know the depth and artistic finish of Mr. Crawford's work need be told.
— *The Chicago Times.*

"It abounds in stirring incidents and barbaric picturesqueness; and the love struggle of the unloved Khaled is manly in its simplicity and noble in its ending. Mr. Crawford has done nothing better than, if he has done anything as good as, 'Khaled.'"—*The Mail and Express.*

ZOROASTER.

"The novel opens with a magnificent description of the march of the Babylonian court to Belshazzar's feast, with the sudden and awful ending of the latter by the marvellous writing on the wall which Daniel is called to interpret. From that point the story moves on in a series of grand and dramatic scenes and incidents which will not fail to hold the reader fascinated and spell-bound to the end."—*Christian at Work.*

"The field of Mr. Crawford's imagination appears to be unbounded. . . . In 'Zoroaster' Mr. Crawford's winged fancy ventures a daring flight. . . . Yet 'Zoroaster' is a novel rather than a drama. It is a drama in the force of its situations and in the poetry and dignity of its language; but its men and women are not men and women of a play. By the naturalness of their conversation and behavior they seem to live and lay hold of our human sympathy more than the same characters on a stage could possibly do."—*The Times.*

"As a matter of literary art solely, we doubt if Mr. Crawford has ever before given us better work than the description of Belshazzar's feast with which the story begins, or the death-scene with which it closes."—*The Christian Union.*

A TALE OF A LONELY PARISH.

"It is a pleasure to have anything so perfect of its kind as this brief and vivid story. . . . It is doubly a success, being full of human sympathy, as well as thoroughly artistic in its nice balancing of the unusual with the commonplace, the clever juxtaposition of innocence and guilt, comedy and tragedy, simplicity and intrigue."—*Critic.*

"Of all the stories Mr. Crawford has written, it is the most dramatic, the most finished, the most compact. . . . The taste which is left in one's mind after the story is finished is exactly what the fine reader desires and the novelist intends. . . . It has no defects. It is neither trifling nor trivial. It is a work of art. It is perfect."
—*Boston Beacon.*

"The plot is unfolded and the character-drawing given with the well-known artistic skill of Mr. Crawford, and to those who have not before read it this story will furnish a rare literary treat."
—*Home Journal*